BLACK AUTUMN

A POST–APOCALYPTIC SAGA

READYMAN SERIES, BOOK ONE

JEFF KIRKHAM & JASON ROSS

DEFIANCE PRESS
& PUBLISHING

Black Autumn

ISBN-13: 978-1-948035-16-3 (Paperback)
ISBN-13: 978-1-948035-17-0 (Hardcover)
ISBN-13: 978-1-948035-18-7 (eBook)

Published by Defiance Press & Publishing, LLC
Printed in the United States of America
10 9 8 7 6 5 4 3 2 1

Bulk orders of this book may be obtained by contacting Defiance Press & Publishing, LLC at: www.defiancepress.com.

Public Relations Dept. – Defiance Press & Publishing, LLC
281-581-9300
pr@defiancepress.com

Defiance Press & Publishing, LLC
281-581-9300
info@defiancepress.com

BLACK
AUTUMN

PROLOGUE

[Two Weeks Ago]
Santa Catalina Island, California
Near Avalon Bay

AFTER FOUR MONTHS OF LIVING with a nuclear bomb in the hold of their sailboat, even the Koran's promise of seventy-two bare-breasted virgins wore a little thin. When they left the Sulu Archipelago of the Philippines, dying in an atomic flash sounded like a small price to pay for even one virgin, much less six dozen. Now, with the end near at hand, the unspoken truth between the two Filipino villagers was that neither of them felt particularly eager to die.

They decided to wait for a sign from Allah before completing the last twenty-six miles of the voyage to America. The two villagers, far from home, anchored on the east side of Catalina Island, just a handful of hours from the bustling coast of Los Angeles, California.

They had been loitering there for nearly two months and, amazingly, nobody had so much as spoken to them.

Njay and Miguel had settled into a daily routine. *Wake up. Defecate off the side of the boat. Make tea. Defecate off the side of the boat. Fish all morning. Nap. Fish all afternoon. Defecate. Eat fish. Sleep.*

The journey from the Philippines had gone exactly as planned, which amounted to a miracle in sailing. Nothing ever went exactly as planned. The well-provisioned sailboat had contributed to their successful journey. Neither of the men had ever sailed in a boat so well stocked. The boat even came with a desalination filter sufficient for a couple of months. With such a fine craft, they had been able to set a simple tack into the north-northeast trade winds directly at the coast of California. For fifty-eight days, they kept the boat pointed on a steady course, barely having to trim the sails. It had been the easiest sailing of Njay's life.

But time was running out. Both men felt sick. They suspected the desalination filter had worn out and was letting a small amount of salt into their drinking water. The other possibility was that the crate-sized nuclear bomb in their hold was leaking radiation.

Their village imam had given Miguel and Njay simple instructions, but Njay suspected the instructions had come from the light-haired, tall man who had been skulking around their village for months. Everyone seemed to know that gossiping about Tall Man would be a violation of obedience to the imam. Njay concluded that the man must be Middle Easterner or Russian, given the nature of their mission. No Pacific Rim nation would risk war with America.

In truth, Njay knew little of the world outside his island chain, but he'd been taught much about America, with its Special Forces murderers and its weapons of unimaginable power. The United States lorded over the Pacific, threatening to blow their enemies back to the Stone Age. Like a disease consuming the hearts of man, America plagued the world, and Islam would cure it. Such a plague could be stopped by the tiniest of medicines: one small boat and two small men could vaporize the Hollywood movie stars and shake the Wall Street skyscrapers. In Allah's wise path, giants were often felled by pebbles.

The two Filipinos talked about sailing into Avalon Bay for another desalination filter, but the risk of being discovered, especially considering their almost non-existent English, was too great.

Njay and Miguel spoke endlessly about God's will while crossing the ocean and then fishing off the coast of Catalina. Would Allah really want them to sacrifice their lives if it wasn't necessary?

Based on their time in Catalina, it didn't seem like Americans worried much about the coming and going of sailboats in their waters. Over four months, the two men received nothing more than hearty waves from other boaters. Perhaps they could sail into Long Beach Harbor, tie up their sailboat, set the bomb to explode, then walk into America. Surely there were other Filipino Muslims in America who would shelter them.

They even discussed how to build a time delay device for the bomb. They pulled the crate below decks apart, only to find that the bomb was a steel box with a single green button. The box had been welded shut, and the men hadn't brought any tools capable of cutting steel. The button protruded through the metal box and through the slats in the crate. Their instructions had been simple: sail into Long Beach Harbor and press the button.

They talked about a time delay device where a candle could burn through a rope and release a hammer to swing into the button. The contraption could give them a few minutes to get clear of the bomb. If they ran, they might make it.

They didn't know how big the explosion would be, nor did they know if a hammer strike would sufficiently depress the button without breaking it. Of course, it could not be tested in advance.

The men eventually set their time delay idea aside and put the decision in the hands of Allah. They listened to American radio as they fished, talking into the evening about how a sign from Allah might appear.

The sickness had them both concerned. Their daily defecations into the ocean were audible from everywhere on the boat, and they agreed the sickness was worsening, compelling them to relieve themselves more often.

Time grew short.

• • •

[Two Weeks Ago]
Mongratay Province, Afghanistan

Jeff Kirkham's adrenaline spiked before he even knew why, his subconscious recognizing the blue-white trail of a rocket-propelled grenade as it whistled into his column of trucks. The low growl of a PKM machine gun and a swarm of AK-47s joined the chorus as the battlefield roared to life.

This had been the wrong place to drop overwatch, and it had been Jeff's bad call. He rocked forward, squinting through the filthy windshield, hoping he wasn't seeing what he was seeing. Some of his best men were in the Corolla, still the lead vehicle, and they were hanging way out in the wind.

Jeff rode in the passenger seat of the command truck toward the back of the column with his shorty AK wedged between his butt and the door. Only the medical truck lagged behind them.

Endless hours of experience and training kicked in, and Jeff launched from his seat, slamming the passenger door forward, pinning it with his boot to keep it from bouncing back. He cleared his rifle and rolled out of the truck, scrambling for cover behind the rear axle. None of their vehicles offered much in the way of cover, and their best play was to fight through the ambush. Getting everyone turned around and moving back the way they had come wasn't an option.

As soon as Jeff reached the rear of the column, he ran into Wakiel, a tall, sinewy Afghan from the Panjshir Valley. They had worked together for years. In broken Dari, Jeff ordered Wakiel to gather his squad for a flanking maneuver. Wakiel chattered into his radio and, within a few moments, the assault squad piled up behind the medical truck, ready to roll.

Jeff didn't remember the Dari word for "flank," so he just stabbed a knife hand up and to the left. His Afghani assaulters knew what to do and they were hot to fight.

The twelve of them, including Jeff, sprinted up the closest ravine, working to gain altitude so they could drop down on the Taliban-infested ridge line. As he pounded up the hill, Jeff could see the

Corolla getting mauled in the middle of the bowl. One glance at the car told Jeff he would have men to mourn when the dust settled.

At forty-three years of age, it almost didn't matter how fit Jeff was. Running straight up a mountain in body armor at seven thousand feet made him feel like a lung was going to pop out of his mouth. He had been born with the furthest thing from a "runner's physique." Between his Irish genes and a thousand hours on the weight bench, Jeff could fight eyeball to eyeball with a silverback gorilla. He had no neck, a foot-thick chest, huge arms, and thighs the size of tree trunks. Like most of the Special Forces operators getting on in age, Jeff didn't mind a bit of a belly bulge sticking over his waistband. His enormous upper body mass and the belly bulge added up to dead weight, though, when running up a mountain in Afghanistan in the middle of a fire fight.

He wasn't about to let Wakiel and his guys get away from him, so Jeff drove harder up the sand and moon dust, his boots filling with gravel and debris, his throat burning like he was sucking on a blow torch. They had been pushing up a ravine and, as they crested the hill, Jeff could see they were now above the Taliban force.

"Shift fire. Shift fire." Jeff coughed into the radio as his assault team reached the top. Jeff knew his men would plow straight into the Taliban positions without considering that their truck column below, with more than a dozen crew-served machine guns, was pounding that area with everything they had.

"Shift fire, copy?" Jeff heaved for air, trying to gulp down oxygen and listen intently at the same time.

"Roger. Shifting fire up and right," one of the other Green Berets with the column replied, no doubt running up and down the string of trucks trying to get control of sixty adrenaline-crazed Afghani commandos and their belt-fed machine guns.

With his command job done, Jeff launched into the fight himself, hammering rounds from his AK and catching up to his men. They leapfrogged from one piece of cover to the next, driving down on the Taliban positions.

V

Jeff dove behind a huge boulder and flopped to one side, crabbing around the rock and catching a full view of the battlefield. By climbing high up the hillside, he and his assault team had side-doored the Taliban force and he could see lengthwise into several foxholes filled with enemy. Jeff pushed his AK around the edge of the boulder and dumped rounds into one open foxhole after another, dropping some men to the ground and forcing others to leap out of their trenches and flee into the open. When they did, the truck column in the valley below cut them to pieces.

There was no stopping the carnage now that the smell of blood was in the air. Jeff leapt from behind the boulder, ran forward and fell hard into a hole, stomping a dead man's open guts. The mushy footing caused Jeff to tip and slam into the wall of the ditch. The stench of the man's open bowel hit his face like a slap, making him grimace and turn his head.

The gunfire slowed. Jeff could see four or five surviving Taliban running away over the ridge. The hillside and ridge were littered with bodies. Jeff crawled out of his foxhole and maneuvered over to Wakiel.

"How are the men?" Jeff asked in Dari.

"Is good," Wakiel panted in broken English, coming down from the rush of the last murderous drive.

"*Katar.* Danger," Jeff reminded him. Wakiel nodded.

Jeff had been in hundreds of gunfights and he knew that winning the fight was only the beginning of the work. Policing up the bodies, and figuring out which of them were dead and which were waiting to blow the victors up with a hand grenade, would take hours. There was nothing glamorous about policing a battlefield.

It took three hours for Jeff and his guys to clear the field, and they lined up ten dead Taliban in a row, their AKs, PKMs and RPGs piled beside them. A couple of Jeff's indigenous *"Indij"* guys started taking pictures with their trashy cell phones, holding dead guys up by their hair. They needed the pictures to match against the "most wanted" list. Still, the grisly scene made Jeff turn away.

He looked back at his column of trucks. He could see three black body bags lying outside the lead Corolla—the car that had contained his Amniat scouts, some of his best friends and finest warriors. The medics were smoking cigarettes instead of working on his men, which meant Jeff had lost more friends.

Jeff's body felt drained, like a fist unclenching. He would complete this last mission, and then he would leave Afghanistan and warfighting behind forever.

He had been in command of the column of fifteen trucks for three days, and road dust coated his face and the inside of his nose, dragging on every breath. For hours on end over the last three days, his binoculars had come up and down searching for an ambush, like genuflecting to the gods of war.

Lift the binos. Scan the horizon. Scan big rocks. Scan all potential hiding places. Lower the binos. Check the position of his trucks. Repeat every ninety seconds, forty-five times an hour, five hundred times a day.

From the center of his head to the marrow of his bones, fatigue dogged him. A fighter could only stay hard for so long. For him, it had been twenty-eight years.

Driving for days had worn him down to a nub. The rocking motion of the truck and the chemical body odor from the men commingled with exhaust fumes, kicking his motion sickness into overdrive. Even so, seventy lives depended on him staying rock solid, and now men had died on his watch.

The distance to the Forward Operating Base wasn't the problem. They could have made the drive in ninety minutes going balls out, but the province crawled with Taliban and Jeff's column was anything but low profile: fifteen Toyota Tacomas, painted desert tan, each one of them with a Russian-made belt-fed machine gun bolted to the truck bed.

Jeff had ordered his Amniat scouts in the beat-up Corolla to range out every ten kilometers to reconnoiter the road ahead. Since the scout vehicle looked just like every other piece of junk in this desert, he had hoped the Taliban wouldn't waste bullets on it. Three of Jeff's best *Indij* fighters had been crammed into that little car.

For eight hours, the column had run with two overwatch trucks fanning out to the left and the right, up on the ridge tops, covering the column with their big fifty-caliber belt-fed machine guns. That meant a lot of stop-and-wait inaction as the overwatch trucks maneuvered into new positions. The column would drive a kilometer, wait fifteen minutes for overwatch to set up, then drive a kilometer more. The process yanked on the column like a ball and chain, but it had to be done. Without covering fire, they could find themselves on the death-eating side of an ambush.

War is work, Jeff had been telling himself, manual labor. It wasn't just physically exhausting. It was the waiting that ground the soul down—constant stress and usually nothing to show for it. He knew he was an excellent warfighter, a manual laborer of death and destruction with an iron will. He could control the chaos like few men on earth, and it was this unwavering faith in his own competency that powered Jeff through long, tedious missions like this one.

Now, with the ambush sprung, the battle finished and several of his men dead, Jeff was no longer feeling that same bullet-proof self-confidence.

Wakiel walked over to Jeff, smoking a cigarette.

"I guess that was a bad place to get ahead of our security element," Jeff said in English.

Wakiel knew Jeff well enough to understand and replied, "*Khalash*, Jeff." It was Dari for "finished," but today it meant "farewell."

After this mission, Jeff headed home forever, back to the other world—the world that didn't smell like the inside of an Afghani's lower intestines, the world where he could stay clean, sleep in on a Sunday with his wife, and take in the fresh smell of his sons' hair first thing in the morning.

The sweet-sour smell of shit wafted past his face, and Jeff searched for the offending stench, noticing a green, chunky glob on his boot. With nowhere to wipe it off, Jeff's aggravation peaked, his only solace that he was leaving this endless parade of rot and ruin.

Jeff vowed to never again smell the guts of a man, to never again face the buzz of angry bullets, and to never again watch friends die violent deaths. Back in the *real* world of America, Jeff would put a net around his family and tie it down tight. The demons of chaos and destruction would forever infest Afghanistan, but they would not follow him home. Whatever affection he had once had for the life of a soldier, it was over. Now he would make damned sure his family lived in peace.

"I am so sick of fighting death every day," Jeff said, looking at his Afghani friend for the last time.

The Afghani barely understood his English, which was the only reason Jeff allowed himself to put words to his fatigue.

Wakiel nodded and returned to smoking his cigarette.

• • •

Bandar Charak
Hormozgan Province, Iran
Present Day

In the end, Afshin Asadi would explode a dirty bomb over Saudi Arabian soil, not because of his religion or his politics, but because he couldn't stand to leave a project unfinished.

Somewhere in the back of his mind, the same place where he kept information on how to operate his microwave oven, Afshin knew he would go to paradise by sacrificing his life, if it came to that. He accepted the information without any particular interest.

Some might look at Afshin's story and draw the conclusion he had been imprisoned by a cruel government, a regime that would shackle a mentally challenged, but genius young man to an ignorant religion. In their rush to repudiate Islam, they would miss the point.

Truth was, Afshin already lived in paradise, and his government was doing him a favor by confining him to a workshop with a prototype nuclear device. Every morning he awoke with a burning desire to move the project one step closer to completion, and every night he lay down deeply satisfied by the work he had completed. On any given day, he might have tested a candidate polystyrene as a suspension material, or machined a new trial shield panel. Each small step toward completion scratched an itch deep in his soul, and he went to sleep happy as a man could be—in his case, as happy as an *autistic* man could be.

Five years previously, as Afshin studied at Amirkabir University of Technology in Tehran, one of his professors had asked him to visit during office hours. When Afshin arrived at the meeting in his professor's office—more a cubbyhole than an office—another man was wedged into a seat in the corner between piles of papers. The strange man wore a crumpled suit coat and a yellowing dress shirt. He was balding and peered over a pair of thick-framed glasses.

The stranger introduced himself, and Afshin failed to note his name, more interested in the big Western-made calculator poking out of the man's shirt pocket. Calculator Man peppered Afshin with engineering and physics questions, beginning simple and moving toward more complex. Afshin answered plainly, without wondering for a single second about the purpose of the meeting.

More than a month later, the same man interrupted a Thermal Engineering lecture. The teacher's aide pulled Afshin from class and Calculator Man showed him out the front door of the university to a waiting taxi. Afshin never saw the school, nor his family, again.

He might have enjoyed seeing his family, but he never requested it. Afshin feared interrupting the work, worried they might pull him off the intensely gratifying process of designing and building an entirely novel type of nuclear weapon. Nobody had ever exploded a dirty bomb before and the technical requirements for the explosive, and the radioactive shielding, ran deep into the speculative.

Afshin's father had served in the Iran-Iraq War, and his mother was a nomadic Iranian exposed to "yellow rain" during the war. His mother died of bone cancer, and his father was revered by their town as a war hero, though it only seemed to matter during patriotic holidays.

Afshin had no assistants and almost no supervision. His food and support were provided by government people who appeared occasionally to make sure his tools ran properly and that he was alive and well. When he needed a new end mill or, on the rare occasion when he wanted a pornographic magazine, he placed the order. Nobody bothered him about the pornography, even though it was technically illegal in Iran. The Lebanese porno magazines simply showed up in the bottom of the next box of tooling and raw materials. But the work was almost always more satisfying than the porn, and he took little time off to masturbate.

One day, after five years of laboring over the Russian surplus strontium-90 thermal generator he had been provided as a source for radioactive material, Afshin looked down at his stainless steel workbench and beheld a completed, highly sophisticated dirty bomb. It was no larger than the mini-refrigerator where he kept his sodas, and it weighed just under ninety kilos. The radiation pouring off the casing measured barely more than exposure to the sun in the upper atmosphere.

Two days after completing his bomb, Afshin heard the buzz of a small aircraft taxiing outside. The sounds of small aircraft were commonplace, since his workshop and living quarters were located in an airplane hangar. But this airplane approached his building, heralding the coming of his boss, Calculator Man.

By now, Afshin knew the professor's name: Ostãd Mumtãz Shahin Nazari. Professor Nazari had visited Afshin many times over the last years, receiving updates on progress and vetting Afshin's data and material requests. Afshin assumed the professor held some rank in the science or military ministry, though Iranian state government interested Afshin about as much as women's magazines which, was to say, not at all.

This visit was different from previous visits. For one thing, the bomb was complete. For another, Professor Nazari appeared to be dying. Afshin didn't ask, but he guessed that cancer was consuming his supervisor. For two reasons, Afshin's life was about to change, and that stressed him to distraction.

"*Salaam alaikum,*" the professor greeted him and took his hand. Afshin looked downward in a show of respect.

"*Salaam,* Professor. I am finished." Afshin continued to gaze at the concrete, uncomfortable with looking directly at other peoples' faces.

"Yes, my young friend, you are." The professor released Afshin's hand and shuffled to the work table. "It is beautiful. Allahu Akbar."

Afshin felt his face flush red with pleasure. Indeed, the device was beautiful and it was gratifying for the professor to say so. Afshin had nothing to say, so he remained silent.

"Are you prepared to test it?" the professor asked, caressing the aluminum casing.

"Yes, Jenaab." Afshin applied the honorific, pleased to have his work acknowledged.

"Afshin, I feel I must tell you, what we are about to do is more than a test. It is a victory for Islam. We shall detonate the device on the Wahhabis and their American pipeline. As we kill the pipeline, we kill the link between the Americans and the Saudis, and we force Persia to finally take a stand. Our government has lost the will to act and, like during the war with Iraq, they hold back, afraid of the West. The Saudis push their Wahhabist agenda across the globe, building schools and mosques in every corner of Islam: Afghanistan, Pakistan, Russia, and even America itself. They are the true enemy, but our government refuses to strike. With this bomb, we shall force the ayatollahs to take up the sword Allah has given them. Then the Persian Empire can resume its rightful place. Will you give your life to that cause?"

Afshin understood every word. He was a genius, after all. At the same time, he couldn't care less about religion or the Persian Empire. What he cared about, above all else, was seeing the device tested. He couldn't continue living without seeing the bomb detonate. If he died in the process, that concerned him very little.

"Yes, *Jenaab*," Afshin answered.

"Good, my son. I do consider you my son." The professor smiled. "I must also tell you this. The Guardian Council has not authorized this detonation. We will move forward without approval. My own time is at an end and I am afraid that, without me, our leaders will endlessly dither. We know the righteous path, you and I, and we must act for our country's future. Do you agree, *pesar*?"

"Yes, *Jenaab*," Afshin said for the third time.

"Very well. Please bring the device to my airplane."

Afshin lifted the bomb with a small electric winch hanging from the metal rafters and lowered it onto a pallet truck. He wheeled the bomb out the large door of the hangar, the dying man resting his hand on the younger man's shoulder. The bomb rolled across the tarmac into the sunlight, toward the waiting Cessna.

1

Ross Homestead
Oakwood, Utah

"WE NEED TO BURN DOWN the forest to open our fields of fire," Jeff Kirkham declared as he scanned the hills over Oakwood, a suburb of Salt Lake City, Utah.

Jason Ross smiled, but his brow furrowed. "Why is it always burning stuff down with you special ops guys? That's the same thing Chad said—burn the forest down to open up fields of fire. I brought you up here to tell us where to dig defenses, not to burn down my forest. Jesus, we do have neighbors. That's a town down there and I don't think they'd be happy with a forest fire."

Jeff stared out at the foothills of the Rocky Mountains, but his eyes hardened, as though searching the hills of Afghanistan and Northern Iraq. Those places had left their mark—Jeff's face had endured so much windburn and sunburn that he had developed a permanent squint—not to mention the deeper marks they had probably left.

"Well, then, Chad and I agree on one thing, at least," Jeff said, dropping the subject of burning the forest for the time being. "I don't like this location for an OP/LP," he stated flatly. Jeff was the kind of man who didn't flinch when it came to contradicting another person and upsetting his applecart.

Jason's voice jumped a bit, betraying his frustration. "What's an OP/LP?" He had already marked out locations for the defensive fortifications, based on his best guess while Jeff was overseas.

"Observation post/listening post," Jeff explained. "If we're going to build defensive positions, we need to start by setting up early detection. Then we can figure out fixed defensive positions, but right now we need to work on communication, roving patrols and a Quick Reaction Force."

Jason sighed, mentally abandoning the work he had already done and conceding to Jeff's knowledge and experience. "I only understood half of what you just said," Jason told Jeff. "Just tell me what we need to do next."

Jason Ross owned the Homestead, as well as the land around it, for hundreds of acres. Both men were on the Homestead steering committee, and Jeff had been invited to handle security and defense. So, while Jason actually owned everything the eye could see, he was reluctant to countermand Jeff. After all, Jeff had been asked to join the Homestead for his expertise in mountain warfare.

"What's on top of that ridge?" Jeff pointed east.

"It looks down into Tellers Canyon, and Tellers Canyon drops into Salt Lake City, but it doesn't matter, because that's all Forest Service land. I don't own it." Jason waved generally eastward.

"Who gives a crap what you own and don't own?" Jeff looked straight at Jason. "We'll own whatever we want to own if the stock market keeps dropping. Let's head up top. That's where we should place the OP/LP."

"Okay." Jason surrendered. Jeff might occasionally be wrong about this kind of thing but, if he was wrong, there were probably only a dozen men in the world with enough knowledge to credibly disagree with him.

After all, Jeff had seen the Apocalypse firsthand in a dozen countries. He had trained armies—small armies to be sure—but armies nonetheless. He had taken life with every weapon known to the modern battlefield. With the help of his Green Beret buddy, Evan, Jeff developed some of the most advanced gunfighting training in the era of the assault rifle.

To say Jeff was a twenty-eight-year Green Beret wouldn't come close to describing just how much warfighting he had survived. There were volumes about Jeff that Jason didn't know—much of Jeff's past was shrouded in the kind of secrecy that demanded *don't ask, don't tell*.

"Is this really going to happen?" Jason shouted over the engine of their off-highway vehicle (OHV) as they rattled and bounced to the top of the canyon.

"Is what going to happen?" Jeff shouted back. Half the time, Jeff Kirkham guessed at what other people were saying. He had been left nearly deaf in one ear from too many intimate encounters with Karl Gustav rifles and C4 plastic explosives.

"Is society really going to collapse?" Jason asked as they emerged from the oak forest. A 100,000-acre panorama opened up before them.

"It's happened throughout history," Jeff explained as they climbed out of the OHV and took in the view. "Just because we haven't seen civil disorder in the U.S. in a long time doesn't mean we're immune to it." He counted on his fingers. "The Revolutionary War. The Civil War. The Great Depression. We came very close to a nuclear holocaust during the Cuban Missile Crisis. We enjoy the *patina* of security here. It's an illusion, a trick of human psychology. Just because we don't see chaos in our daily lives doesn't mean it's not right below the surface. Plus, who says we're entitled to safety? The rest of the world doesn't have safety. Why should we?"

"That dirty bomb that went off last night in Saudi Arabia... You think the effects could reach us here?" Jason asked again.

"We'll see. Almost everything you can think of comes from oil. Plastic, roads, heat. Even your OHV vehicle is eighty percent oil in one form or another. The price of oil affects everything in our modern world. If Costco closes, we're fucked." Jeff finished his lecture, pulling out a small pair of binos to check something out on the horizon.

Jeff had two modes: stony silence and meticulous lecture—holding forth on historical and geopolitical nuances of one thing or another. For a quiet person, he had unusually big opinions.

"Costco? What's Costco got to do with anything?"

Jeff lowered the binos but kept gazing at a spot on the mountainside.

"We're too weak as a nation. If we were hardened, like Afghanis or Kurds—or even our grandparents who made it through the Great Depression—a failure of the stock market wouldn't be such a game changer. We would go back to growing food in our yards and raising goats in city parks. But we're the weakest society the world has ever seen. If the system fails, people will go ape shit. Any cop will tell you: there is a fine line between civility and savagery. When Costco closes in the middle of the day, that'll be our cue that the credit card machines aren't running and we're screwed."

"I hope you're wrong." Jason shook his head.

"I would love to be wrong, but I'm not." Jeff dialed in the binoculars again, scoping a distant target. "Who's that?" He passed the binos to Jason.

4

Jason picked out two figures standing beside four-wheelers higher on the mountain. "Oh, yeah. Those guys are the Beringers. They own cabin land a couple of canyons over."

"Are they friends of yours?"

"No, not friends. We've had a couple of nasty run-ins over the years."

"Run-ins?" Jeff reached for the binoculars again.

"Long story. They're locals. They've lived here in Oakwood for a few generations. They were offended when I bought this land. They used to think of it as their own private hunting preserve."

"Tell me about the run-ins," Jeff persisted.

"We used to keep a hunting tent at the top of the canyon. After we asked them to stop trespassing, one of their clan broke into our equipment locker and crapped all over the handles."

Jeff lowered the binos. "They literally shit on your equipment locker?"

Jason shrugged. "They're rednecks. Down on their land, they've built a ghetto survival retreat—they've got foxholes, buildings made out of pallets, tripwires. It's like a scene out of *Deliverance*."

"What did you do about them shitting on your locker?" Jeff drilled down.

"We let it go. Eventually they quit coming over the mountain to hunt." Jason's answer made him feel self-conscious, like he had compromised his "man card" by not making the Beringers face consequences for their disrespect.

By all accounts, Jason was a *man's man*. Tall and broad of shoulder, he had taken care of himself, working out daily, lifting weights and completing a handful of half-ironman triathlons over the years. He had been an Eagle Scout and, since boyhood, he had spent a large chunk of his life in the woods. But even a "man's man" felt self-conscious around Jeff Kirkham. No amount of civilized outdoorsmanship compared with two-and-a-half decades living in the muck as a Green Beret.

5

"Those Beringer people can't stay," Jeff concluded, not inviting discussion.

"I'd like them gone, too, but they own that land. I don't see how we can run them off their own land without inviting others to do the same to us."

"Where there's a will, there's a way." Jeff handed back the binoculars with a blank smile.

That smile made Jason uncomfortable. It implied gamesmanship. It hinted at a desire for a chess match, like something out of a Kipling novel, a penchant for cheating, a pleasure at defeating others through superior maneuvering. Nothing implied by that smile put Jason at ease with Jeff Kirkham.

Jason was well aware that American Special Forces operators cheated. They fought at night with night vision and air support. They used technological advantage to win with grotesque dominance over the enemy. Top-tier Green Berets were often loaned to the CIA, where the deeds ran dark and deep. Jeff had almost certainly triggered foreign insurgencies by employing carefully set layers of intrigue and connivance. He had spent a lifetime in the mind-bending juxtaposition where an operator's personal reputation and integrity among Americans was everything. That same operator would smile at a terrorist across the table, call him brother, use him like a dishrag, then radio in an air strike to kill him.

During the decades Jeff fought for his country using every trick in the book, Jason built wealth and honed his ability as a leader of enterprise. He made a career out of full disclosure and fair dealing. He had been taught early on that virtue won most battles on the fields of commerce and had made a great deal of money through cooperation, collaboration and respect.

Jason didn't know the half of Jeff's career, and he suspected Jeff had spent time within the shadowy elements of the United States government. Jason worried that the same subterfuge might someday be turned on *him*.

He looked at Jeff for a long moment. *What's good for the goose is good for the gander. What befell the Beringers could easily befall the Ross family,* Jason thought to himself.

"What?" Jeff's thin smile broke a little wider. He seemed to have an idea of what Jason was thinking.

"Hmm, nothing." What more could be said? Trust and ruthlessness danced a dangerous dance, especially now that the Ross Homestead might live or die based on Jeff's judgment. If the stock markets stayed closed, the world that Jason knew—the world of win-win contracts and business-casual lunches—was about to morph into something far more primitive. If that happened, it would be a world Jeff knew from the ground up, and a world Jason knew not at all.

Jeff headed back to the OHV and Jason followed. They drove down the hill toward the "Big House" but, halfway home, a lanky guy with long hair stepped to the edge of the OHV trail and waved them down. Teddy worked for Jason Ross, handling construction projects, landscape and heavy equipment work. Jason pulled over and Teddy propped his arms across the door of the vehicle.

"Morning, gentlemen," Teddy said, glancing from Jason to Jeff.

"Jeff, this is Teddy, our head of facilities. He runs all the grounds and construction projects. He'll be the guy digging your observation posts."

"Howdy do." Teddy shook Jeff's hand. "So, do you guys want to see the holding ponds? We're filling them with water right now for the first time."

Jason blinked. The water project wasn't something he wanted Jeff to see, but Teddy jumped the gun, more friendly than cautious. Jason and Teddy had agreed their water system would be top secret, but the cat was out of the bag now, so Jason went with it.

He popped open his door and Jeff followed suit, stepping out of the OHV and following Teddy down a narrow trail. The oak brush opened into a small clearing with several large excavations, lined with a black plastic sheet covered in river rock.

"Check out our secret reservoir, gentlemen," Teddy said. "The ponds will hold eighty thousand gallons of spring water and they'll be home to hundreds of trout and bluegill." Teddy had tucked the reservoir into a tiny meadow encircled by a tangle of oaks, hidden from view everywhere but inside the clearing. No doubt it would become a refuge for deer, elk and turkeys.

Once Teddy got going, he was hard to stop. He bragged about how he worked this project for the last two months so they could get the Homestead off municipal water. It would save a few thousand bucks a month and it would make the property self-sufficient, pulling water from a buried spring, stringing it across the mountainside beneath the maples, and dribbling it into this picture-perfect pond— much better than relying on the city for water.

"I borrowed the design for the spring from Eivin Kilcher in the TV show, *Alaska: the Last Frontier*." Teddy had watched the show several times, then dug a bigger version of Eivin's spring-fed well. "I planted six huge plastic pipes standing on end, punched small holes in them, surrounded the whole shebang with gravel, then re-buried it."

Sticking his chest out, Teddy kept talking. "Natural spring water will irrigate the whole property starting tomorrow."

While Jason shifted from foot to foot, Jeff stood like a statue. Teddy waxed philosophical about his water project.

"Most people don't think about water pressure. They only think about getting water to their mouths. But ground water isn't very helpful. A person can drink ground water with a purifier, but that's about all they're going to do. Gardening, washing clothes, showering—those tasks require water *pressure*. When a guy plans on carrying water to his garden by hand, he's not thinking about how many calories he'll burn carrying the water. He would have to eat every last plant, and then six times more, just to replace the calories spent hauling water."

"Thanks. Good work, Teddy." Jason turned to walk back to the OHV.

Teddy finally picked up on Jason's cues. "Oh, yeah. Thanks, guys." He reached over and shook hands with both men. "I just wanted you to see this. I thought you'd want to know we got it done, you know, especially with the problems going on in the stock market and all…"

"Absolutely," Jason said, "we'll sleep better knowing we have our water situation figured out. Thanks. Great work. Let your guys know I said 'thanks.'" Jason started back along the trail.

"Cool. I'm going to get back to it." Teddy awkwardly shook hands with Jeff again and returned to his Bobcat excavator.

"So you have spring water and a reservoir?" Jeff asked as they climbed into the OHV.

"Yeah. I haven't had time to catch you up on Homestead improvements since you got back from Afghanistan. I can brief you whenever you have a minute."

Jeff had only been invited as the newest member of the Homestead steering committee the week previous. Nobody on the committee knew Jeff particularly well, but there was no denying how useful he might be as a member of their preparedness community. Still, Jason had been careful not to tell any one person everything about the Homestead. Outside of family, trust only extended so far.

Prior to Jeff's last deployment to Afghanistan, Jason had given Jeff and Tara Kirkham a tour of the Homestead, launching into "The Conversation" with the couple. Many times before, and with many other couples, Jason had broached the conversation about survival and preparedness. He had even become pretty good at sneaking up on the big reveal—that they had spent hundreds of thousands of dollars creating a survival compound, barely concealed behind the fancy architecture and the wrought iron gates of the Homestead.

Ross knew from experience that "The Conversation" could take many interesting turns. Once, when talking to a young doctor and his wife, the couple had somehow gotten it in their heads that the awkward conversation was working its way toward an invitation to swing with Jason and his wife. When the truth finally emerged, the couple's relief had been palpable. Being asked to join a survivalist group was apparently much less awkward than being asked to wife swap.

With Jeff and Tara, "The Conversation" went a lot more smoothly. The couple had firsthand experience with the decrepitude of government, and Jeff had witnessed his share of post-apocalyptic suffering overseas. Considering their three children, Jeff and Tara didn't take long to warm to the idea of contributing to a hardened facility near their suburban home. Plus, the work that had already been completed on the Homestead would have impressed anyone.

The orchard covered dozens of acres and included over a hundred fruit trees, plus a small vineyard. Scattered around the property were seven greenhouses, all with LED grow lamps and solar back-up power. The greenhouses contained almost four thousand square feet of raised planter beds with year-round gardening capability.

The summer garden was a work of art, with another two thousand square feet of raised grow space neatly laid out in square-foot garden plots and giant Grecian urns. The tomato garden was more than eighty feet in diameter and sat on a beautifully stacked-stone retaining wall, towering over the gated entrance to the property.

Everywhere the Kirkhams looked, there were heavy groves of berries, fruit trees and vegetables. Wherever possible, Ross required the landscape to be fruit-bearing and edible.

Nestled behind the orchard, the property played host to a small herd of livestock. Ross bought into partnerships with four local farms scattered around the neighboring valleys. Every so often, a farmer would come by with a horse trailer and drop off a few more goats, sheep, chickens or ducks, just to top off the Homestead herd.

While they kept farm animals on the Ross property in small numbers, there was nothing small about their rabbit production. One of the finest buildings on the property was the rabbit warren. The entire building held dozens of stacked rabbit cages and feed systems.

The Ross clan and their friends hunted wild game on the Homestead. Elk, deer and turkeys wandered the property in great abundance, with wild deer and gobblers meandering through the orchards daily. They had hunting and butchery down to a science and the only meat served on the family table was killed on their property or grown on one of their farms.

Along the base of the woods that jutted from the east of the gardens, tens of thousands of bees browsed the gardens, turning out light, fragrant honey. As an avid gardener herself, Tara Kirkham had been openly impressed by the gardens and the bees.

The Kirkhams didn't seem to have a better plan at the moment, and the Homestead offered an alternative to "riding it out" solo if things went sideways. Jeff and Tara tentatively agreed to help with the Homestead, at least until everyone had a chance to feel out the new friendships.

That had been a few months back, and Jeff had spent most of those months overseas. He had barely returned home from his last deployment and, within weeks, a bomb went off in Saudi Arabia and the stock market started doing the herky-jerky.

Sooner than anyone would have preferred, the world took a precarious turn and, as Jason Ross drove the OHV down the hill, he looked straight ahead, uneasy with the formidable presence of Jeff Kirkham beside him. Like it or not, circumstances had forced them into relying upon one another—like two lions caught in the same enclosure, circling, never quite comfortable enough to lie down.

● ● ●

Federal Heights
Salt Lake City, Utah

Jimmy McGavin fingered the bump on his throat for the ten thousandth time and, for the ten thousandth time, he told himself that he needed to get it checked by a doctor. He had sliced it off

11

shaving more times than he could count, but it always came back, dark and ominous.

Looking at himself in the mirror, two conflicting emotions washed over him.

First, he liked the way he looked in a suit and tie. He was a commercial realtor, respected by his friends. He had done a masterful job of providing for his family. Living in Federal Heights was no small feat. Financially, he had achieved more than almost anyone else in his high school graduating class.

Second, even in the double-breasted suit, he made himself a little sick. There wasn't much of a man left behind those hanging jowls and pasty white skin. He rarely got outside and he almost never exercised, short of the once-quarterly trip to the gym. With work, church and mowing the yard on the weekends, he felt like a beast of burden. The edgy young man who once stole a neighbor's car for a joy ride was gone forever. He couldn't even remember the last time a woman looked at him with lust.

Other men treated him like he wasn't the slightest bit dangerous. By smiling at everyone and doing whatever it took to keep other people happy, he had allowed the *dangerous* in him to erode to a point where he no longer carried the scent of a real man.

In a Hail Mary attempt to restore some part of his virility, he insisted that his wife allow him to go deer hunting with his brothers each year. She always complained, citing the dozen things that needed to be done around the house. They never talked about it plainly, but anything that might vaguely threaten her dominance in their marriage, like owning guns, speeding on the freeway or deer hunting, she fought with a relentlessness that only a woman with an expanding waistline could understand.

Jimmy knew that, if it weren't for the four or five days hunting each year, he might actually kill himself, so deep was the silent despair of his life. So he made the hunting trip happen regardless of the crap his wife dished out.

Occasionally, he would go down to the basement, open his gun safe and hold his Savage 30-06 rifle, working the bolt a couple of times to enjoy the feel of it, stirring up the smell of Hoppe's No. 9 bore cleaner. He knew he wasn't much of a hunter, but those motions and smells restored something in him. It wasn't much, but it was enough to keep him moving, enough to keep him plodding forward.

Today there wasn't time for a trip down to the basement. He noticed a worrisome number of messages on his cell phone, even before 8:00 a.m. That meant his investor clients were calling, trying to figure out how to manage their money during the shift in the markets. Because he was a commercial real estate professional, folks turned to him when stocks became unstable. With the dirty bomb attack last night in the Middle East, the market would be doing backflips, and that meant one thing for him as a commercial realtor: opportunity.

On his drive into South Valley, Jimmy tuned to CNBC Radio, hoping to catch news of the stock market. Right away, it was obvious something big was going down, even bigger than the bomb.

The SEC had executed a market-wide trading halt, something Jimmy didn't remember ever happening. The Dow had dropped over twenty percent in two hours in response to the news of the nuclear attack on a major energy resource.

According to the radio, the dirty bomb exploded near the city of Abqaiq, Saudi Arabia, at the head of the East-West Pipeline, destroying the pumping station and raining radioactive fallout over a wide region, including the oil tanker pumping stations at Al Juaymah. The same pumping stations had been attacked with car bombs by Al Qaeda in 2006, but nobody could say for sure who was behind last night's attack. There was no evidence of a missile launch. Suspicions, of course, ran toward Iran, but the Iranians emphatically denied responsibility.

The actual damage to the world petroleum supply was unclear, especially since the Saudi royal family wasn't providing much information. Even so, enough was known to trigger a reaction from the markets: a bomb had hit the East-West Oil Pipeline, and an unknown number of oil fields and docking facilities had been destroyed or otherwise closed due to radiation.

The result was an overnight forty-three dollar increase in the price of a barrel of oil, more than three times the largest single-day jump ever recorded. Energy experts were screaming that such a price increase was unjustified—that new oil capacity in the United States and Canada would more than make up for the loss. But nobody was listening to the experts at this point.

Oil prices had previously reached historic lows and the global economy had been building a bubble on the back of cheap gas. With cheap energy becoming expensive energy overnight, nobody could predict how it would impact anything, from the price of feed corn to the value of Apple Computer stock. The confusion had only one direction to go—panic.

The SEC pulled the plug on all stock trades in the United States, and the other stock exchanges quickly followed suit. The markets went dark.

Jimmy knew enough about markets to know this was bad—really bad. He considered turning his car around and heading back home. He shook off the rumble in the pit of his gut and kept heading toward the office. His boss wanted him there to help put out fires. Jimmy was working a $4.2 million property deal that was supposed to close tomorrow. It was anyone's guess how the bank was going to respond to the market closures.

Things would be fine, Jimmy told himself. He stared out his car window as he drove south along the Interstate 215 belt route looking out over the Salt Lake Valley. It was a gorgeous day. The fall-dressed mountains towered over the freeway, fresh and pristine. The valley below bustled with activity, its inhabitants going about life like any other day.

It was hard to picture the number of people living in the Salt Lake metropolitan area. He knew the number—more than one million people—but he couldn't imagine what a million people actually *looked* like. From the freeway, high on the bench, he could see businesses, parks, homes, and office buildings stretching out all the way to the Oquirrh Mountains on the west side of the valley. A shallow bowl cradled Salt Lake City, rimmed by granite-capped mountains, ten miles wide by twenty-five miles long—and it held that multitude of people, all going about their business.

How unfathomable would it be if a single bomb eight thousand miles away could disrupt the lives of a million souls in Salt Lake City on this perfect day? The idea seemed ludicrous.

Something tickled the back of Jimmy's mind—a book he had read when he was in college. More accurately, it was a book he'd skimmed. Jimmy had taken an upper-level economics class and his professor recommended a book as extra credit—*The Coming Dark Age*, by an Italian economist, Roberto Vacca.

Jimmy needed the extra credit, so he'd bounced around the book barely well enough to sound knowledgeable. It had been an awful read, but the main idea suddenly reappeared, in the mystical calculus of memory, twenty-five years later.

The author had argued that the post-industrial world was actually more fragile than the pre-industrial world—that relatively small disturbances could push complex, modern society off the edge of a socio-economic cliff. The old economy, where people grew their own food and fixed their own cars, was capable of absorbing bigger hiccups, much like Third World countries do every day, but because each person in Western civilization only knew how to do his or her specialized job, and because they demanded an extraordinarily high standard of living, the author argued that people would freak out and burn society to the ground if a big enough "black swan event" shocked the system.

The example that came to Jimmy's mind was trucking. He had heard somewhere that stores held only three days of food on hand at any given moment. If an interruption occurred in finance, and a truck driver wasn't convinced that a paycheck awaited him at the end of his run, he wouldn't make the drive. He would go home instead. If a lot of truck drivers shared the same lack of confidence at the same moment, grocery stores would run short of food and people would panic, hoarding whatever they could find and leaving stores wiped out. Along with hoarding would come rioting and, with rioting, would come even greater fear. After a big enough surge of fear, *all* the systems of modern society would crash.

Jimmy looked over the valley and thought again about those million people. What would they look like jammed into a stadium? He tried to picture it.

He had heard statistics at a Rotary Club meeting last winter: the million people of Salt Lake City required about twenty million gallons of clean water each day. They consumed over two thousand megawatts of electricity. They each ate two thousand calories of food per day. Almost all of that food came from far away—a good portion from Mexico and Brazil, some five thousand miles over water and rails.

What if the threads of finance, food and electricity all broke at once? Could the spider web of modern society crash to the ground?

This idea defied Jimmy's imagination. Modern society had *always* made it possible for more and more people to live healthy, abundant lives. The old economist had written his doom-and-gloom book back in the seventies. But the prosperity of the United States since then had utterly disproved his warnings. Things had continued better than ever.

Still, in light of what he was hearing on the radio, Jimmy wondered. Could economic dominoes—energy, banking, transportation, communications, law and government—fall because of some weird event half-way around the globe?

It seemed impossible, especially on this fine day, in his fine car, wearing his fine suit.

• • •

Levan, Utah
Union Pacific Railroad Yard

By 11:00 a.m., there were already a hundred fifty semis piled up in the yard, waiting to offload coal from the biggest coal mine in Utah, the SUFCO mine in Sevier County. But there were no trains, which meant no coal could be offloaded.

Because of endless government dickering and countless environmental impact studies, the mine and the railroad had been struggling unsuccessfully for sixteen years to get a short-line railroad to connect the SUFCO mine with the town of Levan. Each day, six hundred semis drove from Sevier to Levan, an unnecessary trip of eighty-five miles.

Dante Morales, director of the yard where the coal transferred from the trucks to rail cars, had been yelling at everyone he could at Union Pacific headquarters in Omaha, Nebraska. Those hundred fifty trucks waited like ugly prom dates for a train to arrive. So far, nothing. Still no train.

In the previous months before the market crash, Union Pacific Railroad found itself in a precarious position, getting both lifted up and dragged down by energy markets, like a kite made out of hardwood.

Coal shipping was Union Pacific's bread and butter, but coal was out of favor with the politicos in Washington, as well as every other state and municipality. Little by little, cleaner fuels were choking out the market for coal and Wall Street traders knew it. At the same time, the price of diesel—the fuel used by trains—had dropped so low it made Union Pacific's profit-and-loss statement look almost rosy.

Most stock wasn't traded by a bunch of old ladies tinkering with their retirement accounts. Most stock trades in the modern age were executed by razor-sharp experts. Most of the Union Pacific Railroad trades were being done by men who knew the exact strengths and weaknesses of UPR, diesel costs, and the coal markets.

When oil prices skyrocketed in the morning hours of trading due to uncertainty in the Middle East, the stock experts bailed out of Union Pacific like fleas off a drowning dog, knowing the railroad's profit-and-loss statement would turn tits up.

Dante Morales knew nothing of stocks. He only knew that things had gone nuts in his coal yard. From his steel-cube office, he could see the yard was completely jam-packed with trucks full of coal, and they were lining up along the highway for a mile. The last time he lined up trucks on the highway, the Utah Highway Patrol and the state environmental protection douchebags had filed a formal complaint and he almost lost his job.

In a fit of exasperation, Dante called his counterpart at the SUFCO coal mine. "Turn those trucks around, Bill. We got no trains, and both our asses will be grass if we don't get those trucks off the highway."

"What do you mean, we got no trains?" Bill stammered. "You mean the train's late?"

"No, Bill, I mean there are no damned trains. Not today. If they haven't left Las Vegas by now, they're not coming. You can leave a hundred trucks here in the yard, but all the rest need to go back right now."

The guy at the mine couldn't get his mind around what he was hearing. "That can't be. Check again."

"I already checked all goddamned morning, and there isn't a single locomotive between here and Los Angeles. I don't know what's going on, but it has something to do with Union Pacific stock taking a dump and the West Coast diesel pricks screwing them on their contract."

"I don't think you understand," Bill explained. "That coal gets burned by the power plant down in Delta and eight other power plants in Utah. It's not like they keep a bunch of coal sitting around out in the weather. If we don't get that coal up north, right fucking now, lights are going to start flickering in California and all around Utah. Then our asses will *really* be in a sling."

"Of course I know what the coal is for, Bill. But I got no trains, so the power plants are just going to have to make do with what they got until the bean counters over at Union Pacific get their heads out of their asses. Please, pretty please, with sugar on top, get your goddamned trucks off the highway. Thank you!" Dante slammed the phone in its cradle and turned back to the window, praying the Utah Highway Patrol was tied up at a donut convention.

Dante had never placed a call to the Intermountain Power Plant in Delta, Utah before, but some industrious soul had written the phone number on a Post-it note and taped it to the side of his computer years ago. He had been looking at it, meaning to throw it away for as long as he could remember. It felt like destiny when he finally called the number.

"Hello."

"Hello, is this the power plant in Delta?" Dante asked.

"Yes. Who's this?" came the guarded reply.

"This is Dante Morales, director of the Levan rail yard for Union Pacific. Who am I talking to?"

"Ron Weber. What can I do you for?" Weber asked.

Dante didn't quite know how to say it. "I just wanted to make sure you knew there wasn't any coal coming today."

"What are you talking about?" the man asked.

"Union Pacific isn't running trains today. Some kind of headquarters SNAFU."

"Bullshit," Weber cursed, echoing Dante's own thoughts.

"Well, have you seen any trains today? Have you?" Dante asked him.

"I'm not sure. Can you hold on, Mr. Morales?"

Dante waited almost ten minutes before another person picked up.

"Hello. This is Senior Operations Director Dale Price. Who are you?"

"This is Dante Morales, director of the Levan rail yard," Dante repeated.

"Hello, Dante. Where's our coal?" the senior operations director wasn't in the mood for chit-chat.

"As I was telling your man, the coal is sitting here in trucks, but the trains aren't running today."

"That's not possible. We have a contract with Union Pacific that guarantees daily delivery," Price said firmly.

Dante knew he had pretty much reached the edge of his pay grade. "I let my license to practice law lapse some time back, so I'm not much help with your contract. I just thought you'd want to know that your coal is sitting right here outside my window instead of on its way to your plant."

"I understand," the senior engineer replied. "Thank you. I need to get off the phone and make some calls."

"Okay. Have a good day." Dante hung up. It occurred to him that "have a good day" was probably a stupid way to end that conversation.

• • •

California Governor's Office
Sacramento, California

Within three hours, the mayor of the City of Los Angeles was on a conference call with three power company commissioners and the California governor. The governor asked the obvious question: "Why don't the trucks just *drive* the coal to the power plant?"

The Intermountain Power Plant in Delta was actually owned by the Los Angeles Department of Water and Power, and seventy-five percent of the power produced poured directly into southern California via the HVDC Intermountain transmission line that carried twenty-four hundred megawatts at a blistering five hundred kilovolts from middle-of-nowhere Utah to the city of Adelanto, California.

How California had convinced Utah to host their dirty coal power plant was one of the seven wonders of American political chicanery.

In any case, when the senior operations director in Delta, Utah called his boss, he placed the call to the 213 area code: Los Angeles, California.

Since the Intermountain Power Plant supplied an enormous amount of power directly to the three-and-a-half million homes of Los Angeles, Anaheim, Riverside, Pasadena, Glendale and Burbank, the call was taken seriously.

Nobody on the conference call had an answer to the governor's question, so he repeated himself. "Why don't the trucks with the coal just *drive* to our power plant and drop it off?"

Sometimes the simplest answers can be the hardest to see, especially when hog-tied by bureaucracy and wrapped in decades of procedure. Sometimes the simplest answers can also lead straight down the road to hell.

2

IT WAS THE FIRST TIME in four months they had heard the music on the radio interrupted by an announcement. Both Filipino men, now very sick, looked up from their fishing lines and stared blankly at one another, trying to interpret the rapid-fire English of the radio announcer.

The little English they had been taught covered the basic conversation of a tourist in America: "Where is the bathroom?" "Nice to meet you." "My name is Mickey Mouse." In the tiny Muslim islands of the Philippines, nobody harbored any hope of going to America as a tourist but the teachers still taught the perfunctory phrases of all language teachers everywhere.

As fighting-age men, both Njay and Miguel had also picked up English words related to *jihad*: military terms, praises to God, expressions of faith and the particulars of weapons and explosives.

When the radio announcer mentioned that a nuclear dirty bomb had been detonated in Saudi Arabia, both men knew enough English to grab their attention. But the radio station returned to its top-forty music before either could make sense of the news. Njay scrambled up, his stomach reeling, and pattered over to the radio. He turned the dial until he found a proper news channel. The two men listened intently for the next forty-five minutes.

They eventually came to agreement about what had happened: a nuclear attack had struck Saudi Arabia—the heart of Islam. Neither man understood the differences between the sects of Islam and both men reached the logical but erroneous conclusion that America had struck the Holy Land of Islam with a nuclear missile.

In their nauseated haze, Njay and Miguel decided the attack was the sign from Allah they had been waiting for, though neither was eager to believe it. They talked and talked, stalling. In the end, they did not want to die, even as sick as they felt. A direct attack against the people of Allah in Saudi Arabia enraged the men but their desire to live dragged on their resolve.

Njay remembered the faces of his mother and siblings. Now stooped and aging, Njay's mother had beamed with pride as he left on this mission for the imam, certain she would see her son again in paradise.

Njay could not go home without completing the mission. He could not face his mother as a failure. He no longer had a home because there was nowhere he could return without dishonor. He didn't want to die, but to fail the mission and wander the earth without a home and without a mother would be worse than death.

Like sleepwalkers, Njay and Miguel wordlessly prepared the boat to sail for California. It felt somehow important that the boat be made immaculate to do God's work, even though they knew it would be vaporized. Almost like a ritual, they packed away their fishing tackle, cleaned the fish offal from the deck and mopped the fiberglass gangways of the sailboat. By the time the boat was ready, the sun had set on the horizon.

They agreed to approach the coast in daylight the next morning. They took turns defecating over the rail, then trundled below deck for a final sleep.

• • •

Within two hours of the brown-out in Orange County, four of the most powerful men in California joined a second conference call: the governor, the mayor of Los Angeles, the adjutant general of the California National Guard, and Robbie Fulton.

Robbie marshalled the influence of over three-hundred-fifty-thousand union workers in the State of California. If there was something big that needed to be done, politicians saw him as the go-to guy. It had been natural for the governor to dial him in on the conference call, even though Robbie wasn't an elected official.

"How the HELL is ONE power plant in Utah kicking our asses?" the governor nearly screamed into the phone.

The rant was directed at the L.A. mayor, since he controlled the L.A. Department of Water and Power, the agency that controlled the power plant in question.

"Mr. Governor, it is my understanding that we consume, at peak times, about seven thousand megawatts in our service area. Over the years, Intermountain has provided an ever-increasing percentage of that demand. Today it provides almost a third of our power during peak periods."

The governor waded right in with the question on everyone's mind. "And why are one-third of our goddamn eggs in one basket?"

"Sir, respectfully, your push for air quality and a lower carbon footprint in this state has had a variety of unintended consequences. One of those consequences is that we've had to drastically reduce our reliance on California-based coal and natural gas power generation. We've mothballed turbines in California, which has left us more dependent on Utah."

"You're telling me that our 'Leaps Toward Low Carbon' have been us pushing the carbon six hundred miles east? That's what you're telling me?"

"Essentially, sir, yes," the mayor admitted. "You wanted immediate action, so the folks in California EPA have been pressuring us to stop using power plants inside the state."

Watching one politician pass the buck back to another politician was such a regular part of Robbie's life that he hardly noticed. It was like people using their turn signals. After a while, it didn't even rise to the level of consciousness.

Robbie had to wonder how he had gone from being a master ironworker, perched on a steel I-beam three hundred feet above L.A., to listening to politicians grovel and peacock with one another. They called his career a meteoric rise in Capitol Weekly Magazine. Robbie called it drowning in bullshit.

"What happened to my plan where the trucks would drive the coal down to the power plant?" the governor followed up with his idea from the day before. He had been proud of that no-nonsense idea, so nobody on the call wanted to be the bearer of bad news.

After a long pause, the mayor replied like a man on his way to the executioner, "The mine owners wouldn't do it. They say it would take them three weeks to get those trucks re-tasked and re-routed."

"You've gotta be bullshitting me!" The governor was picking up steam on the Angry Train. Robbie kind of liked having another former actor as California governor. At least the political doublespeak and spin-doctoring was colorful.

The governor popped into solution mode again. "Okay, boys, here's what we're going to do: let's send a detachment of National Guard with a couple of hundred of our *own* trucks and let's move that coal *ourselves.*"

Goddamn, Robbie thought, this dude's not just an actor; he's a real son-of-a-bitching cowboy.

The L.A. mayor and adjutant general of the California National Guard both spoke at the same time. The mayor was happy to concede the line to the general.

"Governor, sir, are you suggesting we send troops into a neighboring state?"

"Don't make it sound like we're *invading* Utah. Let's just send a small detachment to make sure nothing stops us from getting that power plant back online. If these power outages hit Los Angeles, we'll see riots. Am I correct, Mr. Mayor?"

Someone, presumably the mayor, grunted agreement.

"I need someone in Utah who can follow goddamned orders. Can you provide that, General?"

"Of course, Governor, I can provide troops. But I need you to be absolutely clear with your orders: how many troops, how should they be armed, and what are their Rules of Engagement?"

"Can't we just DO something without a bureaucratic circle-jerk?" The governor was feigning exasperation. Everyone knew he was squirming because the blame, if anything went wrong, would land squarely in his lap.

"Of course, sir. Please issue orders and we will follow them to a 'T.'" The general was probably remembering the Los Angeles riots, twenty-five years back, and the Watts riots thirty years before that. California National Guard troops had been called in to keep the peace, but confusion regarding the Rules of Engagement had cost several Army officers their careers.

"Jesus, it won't take much. Just send thirty soldiers plus several hundred coal trucks. Your men don't even need to bring guns."

"I understand, sir," the general pressed. "I apologize, but I don't believe the Guard possesses that many trucks equipped to move coal, nor do we have the truck drivers."

Robbie spoke up for the first time on the call. "I can get the trucks and drivers. Where and when should they meet up with your men, General?"

"Oh-seven-hundred tomorrow morning in Barstow."

"Done," Robbie agreed.

"Now THAT'S what I'm talking about, gentlemen," the Cowboy Governor gushed. "THAT'S how shit gets done!"

3

Shortwave Radio 7150kHz 1:00am CST

"THIS IS JT TAYLOR. PIRATE of Info Porn, Alcoholic of the Apocalypse… Drinkin' Bro Extraordinaire… broadcasting from a stolen vehicle courtesy of the United States Army, Fort Bliss. Thank you, boys, for the sweet-ass ride and the huge pile of MREs.

"Yes, folks, I'm rolling in a vintage SINCGARS Humvee with a rock-hard 8 meter antenna, on a personal JIHAD against the US Guv and their bullshit propaganda. I'm collecting pirate news from Drinkin' Bro servicemen and babes all over the globe, receiving on the 49 meter band, 6000kHz right on the nose. If you're a Bro or Bro-ette, and you're in the shit, give me a jingle on the radio tonight and we'll tell the world what's REALLY going on.

"According to Drinkin' Bro Reggy Ingleson, specialist in the Marine Corps in the sandbox right now, that dirty bomb royally cocked-up the port and pumping station at Abqaiq. Is that even how you say that? Ub-Kack? Ab-cock? Whatever. It's just another greased Arab shithole now.

"For some reason that bomb gave the stock market whiskey dick, then the lights started flickering in southern California. What do these two things have in common? Who the fuck knows? Anything's possible at this point…

"A Navy commo babe, whose name I will only mention in the boudoir, called in last night from the fleet in the Persian Gulf and let it slip that they're steaming toward the Suez Canal. That should get exciting. Kind of makes you wonder about the Israelis and 300 million pissed-off Arabs and what they're going to do now that the Middle East has become an even bigger dumpster fire. Let it all burn, I say. Let that dumpster burn. But then again, I'm drunk as shit.

"I gotta go now and find a new hole to hide in. If you're a Drinkin' Bro in Fort Bliss, give me a call tonight at 6000kHz and let me know if they're missing their Humvee. Until they hit me with a Tomahawk cruise missile, I'll be on this freq, every night, dealing you into the truth they don't want you to hear. Until then, drink on, sweet princes. Fuck censorship and pass the bourbon."

Interstate 15
Barstow, California

Four hundred semi-trucks with coal trailers stretched from the megalithic roadside McDonalds in Barstow, California, almost five miles down the shoulder of the I-15 Freeway.

The general hedged his bet like a true career Army officer, sending only thirty guys, two M1117s—Armored Security Vehicles— and half a dozen Humvees. Even the M240s, the belt-fed machine guns, had been stripped from the M1117s for this "training mission," as the general had called it when he telephoned his counterpart in the Utah National Guard. Not a single live round was to be found anywhere on the men or the vehicles, despite the fact that they carried rifles and sidearms. The general wasn't willing to put his career in the hands of a bunch of weekend warriors running around the West with live ammunition.

Just to cover his *own* ass, the L.A. mayor sent a Chevy Suburban full of engineers from the L.A. Department of Water and Power to meet the convoy and accompany them to the power plant. The Suburban was black. As it turned out, that would matter more than anyone might have guessed.

At 7:30 a.m., the convoy headed toward Sevier, Utah.

As planned, when the convoy reached the junction of I-70 and I-15 in southern Utah, one of the M1117s and three of the Humvees peeled off with the semis to accompany them to the coal mine. The California governor had spoken with the CEO of SUFCO mine and received approval for his plan to ship the coal to the Delta power plant in the semi-trucks from California. The governor figured he would ask for forgiveness later from the Utah environmental people.

The remaining armored troop transport, the other three Humvees, and the Suburban full of engineers continued on the I-15 Freeway, heading to the Intermountain Power Plant in Delta, Utah.

• • •

Hubb Pizza Co.
Delta, Utah

According to the Southern Poverty Law Center—the consumer advocate group that prides itself on being "the premier U.S. group fighting hate groups"—the State of Utah has thirty-seven "anti-government patriot militias." Strangely, the SPLC publishes its own intelligence report on these groups and, buried forty-two pages into the report, the Delta Desert Patriots can be found, marking them with an asterisk as a "Right-wing Militia."

A person could easily forgive the Delta Desert Patriots, and anyone residing in Delta, Utah, for being pissed off. The three-hundred-fifty-mile-long Sevier River flows muddy and sulfurous almost from its beginning in the mountains of Central Utah. The tail end of this river, by the time it gets to Delta, Utah, runs like a stinking river of Maalox. With this lone water source, Delta residents grow a patchwork of thin alfalfa fields that serve as the only buffer between them and a massive, blighted desert.

Calling it a "desert" elicits images of cactus, mesquite groves and plodding tortoises. Instead, the land around Delta looks like Jesus himself salted the ground, killing every living thing.

The Delta Desert Patriots might never have made it onto anyone's watch list, given that Delta is a smudge on the map, known only for its coal power plant and that it once hosted a World War II Japanese internment camp.

But, on April 12, 2014, the world got an eyeful of the rising anger of the Delta Desert Patriots when federal BLM agents attempted to round up the cattle of Cliven Bundy. Bundy had been grazing his cattle on disputed land claimed by the federal government in nearby Nevada. When several hundred local protestors showed up in the middle of nowhere, armed to the teeth with assault rifles and six-guns, and proceeded to stare down U.S. federal agents, the world took notice. The folks at the Southern Poverty Law Center nearly made a mess in their pants with anti-redneck fervor.

Among those railing against the federal government was none other than David Harold Bundy, son of the then-famous Cliven Bundy. Almost two years after the face-off between the cattlemen and the BLM, federal law enforcement agents closed in on Bundy while he re-roofed his home on the edge of Delta, Utah. They arrested him for his part in the stand-off and quietly whisked him out of town.

While he wasn't an anointed leader of the Delta Desert Patriots, Bundy was certainly a native son—loved by some and respected by all in the town of Delta. With his arrest, and with the bubbling spread of anti-federal sentiment in the deserts and plains of America, the ranks of the Patriots swelled exponentially. At least in the town of Delta, the militia had gone mainstream.

The same morning that the Intermountain Power Plant began to fail in its job of keeping the lights on in sunny southern California, the leadership of the Delta Desert Patriots met at Hubb Pizza Company, just off the main drag in Delta.

On the agenda for their weekly meeting, the DDP would decide who to back as mayor of Delta in the upcoming elections. Strangely, this decision would largely dictate the winner of the mayoral race. The DDP now boasted over three-hundred-fifty members, which might not seem like much until one considered the size of the town—just thirty-two-hundred souls.

But before talking about local politics, everyone wanted to talk about the teetering stock market and the nuclear event in Saudi Arabia. In preparation for what they hoped might be the collapse of the United States government, the militiamen had spent the day loading and re-loading AR-15 magazines, cleaning their guns, packing and re-packing their "go bags," and laying out their military gear.

On top of current events, it wasn't hard to imagine the Feds hitting Delta for reasons limited only by the imagination. After all, within recent memory, federal agents had slipped into town and absconded with David Bundy.

The door to the pizza parlor banged open, like in a Western movie. The men around the table looked up in unison at a wheezing boy standing in the doorway, trying to catch his breath.

"The Feds is here," the boy shouted as he heaved. "They're at the Delta Freeze!"

It didn't make a lick of sense to anyone, but the emotion in the room brooked no hesitation. The men leapt from the bench seats, struggling to get out from under the table. They ambled to their trucks, working to get the blood flowing back into their middle-aged legs.

The militia communications officer jumped into the back of another man's Ford F-350 and did his job with precision—triggering his preset message tree that would alert all three-hundred-fifty militiamen that an attack on the town was imminent.

Before the main body of the militia could muster, the leadership corps of the Patriots descended on the Delta Freeze in their pickup trucks. To their stunned eyes appeared the exact specter they had long feared and even dreamed about.

Three military Humvees and an M-1117 armored personnel carrier sat neatly parked in the Delta Freeze parking lot. Military men in camo wandered about, eating burgers and sucking on milk shakes with M4 rifles slung over their shoulders. It did not come as a shock to the militiamen that a black Chevy Suburban was parked right beside the military vehicles. An invasion of "black SUVs" and dark-souled federal agents had long been prophesied by anti-government pundits.

Clearly, the men in suits sitting at a picnic bench were "the Feds." And, seemingly, they were there to suppress Delta, Utah at the behest of the federal government of the United States of America.

Without hesitation, the militiamen jumped out of their vehicles, bringing their rifles and handguns to bear. Within about two seconds, the California engineers and National Guardsmen went from eating a greasy lunch to staring down the barrels of a dozen guns. One of the Guardsmen dropped his root beer float. It hit the pavement and exploded, splattering a tan slurry over his spit-shined boots.

"Drop your weapons!" the leader of the Delta Desert Patriots shouted, just like he had heard on TV.

The National Guardsmen were only too willing to comply, given that their rifles were empty anyway.

"You at the picnic table, in the suits, drop your weapons." The militiaman pointed his AR-15 at the engineers.

The engineers stared blankly. One of them had the presence of mind to put his double cheese burger down on the picnic bench and raise his hands in the air. The others followed suit.

"Drop your weapons!!" the militia boss roared again.

The engineer who had put his hands up replied, "Um, we don't have weapons."

The leader of the DDP turned to the man next to him and ordered, "Frisk them... Frisk them all."

Without firing a shot, the Delta Desert Patriot militia had re-taken their hometown. Now, in addition to twenty-one prisoners, they possessed an armored vehicle, three Humvees, and a stack of M4 rifles, strangely devoid of bullets.

Within the hour, the only way into town and the power plant, Highway 6, was barricaded, armed and dangerous.

Despite exasperated explanations from the California Guardsmen and the electrical engineers, there was no chance the already suspicious militiamen would consider any story other than the one they had first imagined—that military vehicles and government men in suits had rolled into their town uninvited, intent on oppressing the Sovereign Republic of Delta.

There was no chance whatsoever that four hundred trucks, loaded with coal, would be getting to the power plant anytime soon.

• • •

Alameda, California
Three Miles Outside of Alameda Harbor

The helicopter circled the two Muslim villagers and their sailboat once again, and it became obvious that the sailboat was the subject of the helicopter's interest. The gut-thumping throb of the rotor blades threw the Filipino sailors into a panic—Njay steered the boat while Miguel rushed to complete his ablutions to Allah in preparation for his death at the hands of the helicopter.

Njay shaded his eyes, searching for weapons. He knew little about military aircraft, but the helicopter was painted blue and white and it carried bulbous pods above the landing skids. Unless the pods were bombs, Njay could see no obvious threat. Still, the helicopter circled.

Even louder than the howling rotors, a loudspeaker blared from the aircraft. "Sailing craft, cut your engines immediately. We detect radiation aboard your vessel. Cut your engines immediately and wait to be boarded."

Miguel paused in his ritual cleansing and shouted something to Njay that he couldn't hear over the roar of the helicopter. Neither man understood the words from the loudspeaker, but the intent was clear. They were being intercepted. They would not reach Los Angeles. Njay ducked low behind the steering wheel and motored directly toward Alameda Harbor.

Miguel shouted again and pointed off their bow. In the distance, a large boat with a blaring siren and blue lights raced to block their course.

Njay's loose bowels tightened like an angry snake. He began muttering prayers to Allah, rushed down the narrow stairs and, as the prayer reached its crescendo, pressed the green button.

• • •

Ross Homestead
Oakwood, Utah

Jason hung up and walked out on his deck. He had been on the phone all evening, trying to bring children, family and loved ones to the safety of the Homestead.

It was after 1:00 a.m. and the valley below sulked in a strange pool of darkness, speckled only by a few headlights weaving along the Interstate. The electricity had gone out in Salt Lake City that evening, and what had once been a beautiful view of twinkling lights had become a black crater. He could sense the hundreds of thousands of souls below tossing and turning in their sleep, praying the lights would come back on.

Jason had spoken with Jenna's brothers. Both Tommy and Cameron were on the road, making a mad dash toward Salt Lake City and the Homestead. Jason had high hopes for Tommy—the run from Phoenix to Salt Lake would take him through four hundred miles of mountains and small towns without any foreseeable obstacles once they cleared the Phoenix metropolis.

Cameron and Anna were a different story. There was no telling if they had left L.A. soon enough, and there were still a number of population centers they would have to traverse, each one a formidable threat. The nuke off the coast was a wild card nobody had anticipated, and Jason couldn't count the number of factors that might stop Cameron's family from reaching Utah: civil disorder, traffic, government road blocks, gas shortages, medical quarantines…

Jason previously imagined that the Saudi attack and the stock market halts were worst-case scenarios. Now, with a nuclear detonation off the coast of California, he would have to completely redefine his definition of "worst-case scenario." There were so many variables it made him dizzy.

Jason inventoried the cities between Los Angeles and Salt Lake City: San Bernardino, Las Vegas, Saint George, Cedar City and Provo/Orem. Six hundred miles, four big population centers and a passel of small towns, any one of whom could block the road. The Virgin River Canyon, between Mesquite and Saint George, would be the ideal place to stop the tide of fleeing Californians entering Utah by closing off the gorge. For about ten miles, the Virgin River ran with a cliff on the left and a cliff on the right and a hundred foot-wide interstate running down the middle. If the good people of Saint George panicked, they would barricade the gorge just as sure as the Pope wears a funny hat. Two eighteen-wheelers could plug up the interstate in ten minutes.

Jason prayed for Cameron and Anna, frustrated he couldn't do more.

With the power out, it would be hard to call the members of the Homestead—his group of a couple of hundred preparedness-minded friends. There had been two warning emails to their group, one after the dirty bomb hit Saudi Arabia and another when the stock market first halted, but sending emails was probably unnecessary. With the California nuke, Jason expected to see them all by the next afternoon.

They had always joked about being "the Zombie Apocalypse Club," even throwing a huge "Zombie Apocalypse" Halloween party a couple of years back at the Homestead, complete with army tents, a bio-hazard banner, fire barrels, zombie costumes and military transport to and from the door. But the average member of the Homestead, including Jason and his wife Jenna, didn't actually believe that American civilization would collapse. They prepared anyway, more as an insurance policy than anything else. Plus, they were all friends, and any excuse to hang out was good enough for them. Shooting guns, baking bread and growing a community garden had always seemed like great fun.

Still, the group had been chosen with care. It took years of nominations and discussion to finally reach the ideal size of two hundred souls. Along the way, folks were encouraged to take professional firearms training, going together in big groups to Front Sight Firearms Training outside of Las Vegas.

Members of the Homestead got into hobbies like beekeeping, ham radio, gardening, canning, and shooting. With all the work they had put into it over the years, it wasn't hard to attract doctors, nurses and Special Forces veterans like Jeff Kirkham, Chad Wade and Evan Hafer.

Even this late at night, it was going to be difficult for Jason to get to sleep, but he knew tomorrow would be a ball-buster of a day. He took a final look off the balcony, contemplating the dark void where the Salt Lake Valley slept, wondering if he would ever see it sparkle again.

• • •

Kirkham Residence
Salt Lake City, Utah

"Jeff. I think we should go to my parents' cabin." Tara Kirkham planted her feet.

37

Jeff looked at her long and hard before speaking, thinking through the tactical situation, both on the ground and in his marriage.

"The cabin won't hold us all and I can't control the threat angles."

"*Threat angles?*" she asked, cocking her head.

"Never mind. I'm saying that I don't feel like I can do my job at your folks' cabin."

"We *can* all fit in the cabin. It's small but we'll make it work. It's in the woods and that's better than being near the city. We can pack up our emergency supplies and ride this out with my mom, dad and brothers," Tara argued.

Jeff shook his head slowly, struggling to find a way around his wife's reaction to the chaos they had been watching on TV. The power had gone off in the middle of a newscast, suddenly blacking out the television. The outage punctuated the bad news they had just been watching, almost like God alerting them to the chaos that knocked at their door.

"Sweetheart, I would love to protect your family, but that's a luxury we can't afford."

"What are you talking about, Jeff Kirkham? You can't seriously be thinking about leaving my parents in the woods alone?"

"The tactical situation at your parents' cabin couldn't be worse. Plus, the command structure almost guarantees we will not survive an attack."

Tara looked at him and shook her head. "Sometimes, I just don't know who you are. My family's life is on the line and you're talking about tactical *whatever* and *command structures?* I'm talking about my parents and brothers being in danger, Jeff."

Jeff broke her gaze and looked at the wall. A picture of their three boys stared back at him.

"Tara," he tried again, "there's only one thing in this world that will keep me from protecting your family."

Tara followed his gaze and her eyes softened.

"Jeff, you can protect them all," she argued, her voice reaching out.

He shook his head, still looking at the photo of the boys. ~~had been playing in the leaves that day, burying their little broth~~ Jeff took a wallet-sized version of that picture with him to Afghanistan, Haiti and Iraq, always stowing it in the radio pocket of his plate carrier vest. If he were mortally wounded in combat, he figured it would be even odds that he could get to the photo and look at his boys one last time before dying.

"I wish I had time to explain to you how that cabin could turn into a deathtrap. You're going to have to trust me on this, Tara. I know how command works and I know it'll be days, if not weeks, before your dad and brothers start trusting that I know what the fuck I'm doing. I've never been your dad's favorite person and your brothers feel about the same. They're not going to take orders from me until things get really, really bad. By then, I might already have lost one of you…" Jeff choked on the words and he mashed down his emotion.

Tara took a step toward him and Jeff looked down.

"Tara, I don't think this will end well. I think you should call your parents right now and tell them to go to the Ross place. Your parents' cabin won't fit my team and I'm pretty sure it's going to take a team to survive this—a team of commandos and a lot of food and water. That's impossible in your parents' three-bedroom cabin."

Tara reached out and put her hand on Jeff's shoulder. "What team, Jeff?"

"Evan and the guys. We need them and they need us."

"Okay, but we hardly even know Ross. Why would we trust them over my family?"

Jeff put his hand on Tara's. "We don't know Ross, but it won't matter once my team gets to his place. Ross won't be an issue. I'm not going to let anyone do anything to jeopardize my family. You should call your parents right now. I'm not sure how much longer cell phones are going to work."

4

Shortwave Radio 7150kHz 2:30am

"WELCOME TO THE APOCALYPSE, GOOD people of Planet Shortwave. This is JT Taylor, Alcoholic of the Apocalypse, fellow Drinkin' Bro at your service, broadcasting from a SINCGARS Humvee that I borrowed from Fort Bliss. A hearty shout-out to the Army Electronic Warfare team trying to cruise-missile my ass.

"We're hearing from Drinkin' Bros in the military all over the globe, violating the shit out of the chain of command, bouncing little signals off the ionosphere down to my earholes all night long. Thank you for the news not fit to broadcast. And here it is, friends, the real deal from the horse's mouth:

"So...a nuke went off in Los Angeles Harbor. You heard it here first, folks. I am the first broadcaster to admit the obvious: Martians are attacking America. It really is Independence Day and we really are being attacked by Martians. Will Smith is in the air, in his F-18, right now... Give 'em hell, Will. The trick is to fly right up their main weapon butthole when they're about to shoot it.

"All the xanaxed-out Hollywood types in Los Angeles have gone batshit crazy because of a teensy bit of nuclear fallout and they're burning down all the Neiman Marcus and Prada stores as we speak. The Los Angeles inferno is lighting up the night sky all the way out to Barstow..."

Federal Heights
Salt Lake City, Utah

Jimmy McGavin woke up in a fugue state.

"What?" He sat bolt upright, profoundly disturbed by something. Maybe a nightmare?

He could hear his neighbors talking outside his bedroom window. It sounded like a normal conversation, but it alarmed him on several levels.

First, his alarm clock hadn't gone off and, as he glared at it accusingly, he could see it wasn't lit.

Second, his neighbors never talked like this. Sure, they would talk at church, and Federal Heights was as friendly a neighborhood as one could find in America. The friendliness had a lot to do with the fact that ninety percent of the residents belonged to the same Mormon "ward."

The LDS Church, or Mormon Church, permeated every aspect of Utah culture and, arguably, had resulted in Utah remaining a promised land, at least for believers. Living in Utah, especially in Federal Heights, was like living in the 1950s set of *Leave It To Beaver*. The wholesomeness didn't only benefit Mormons. Everyone living in Utah enjoyed the friendliness and safety the Mormon Church brought. In most parts of Salt Lake City, kids still trick or treated door to door on Halloween. Few metropolitan areas in the U.S. could say the same.

Even so, neighbors didn't stand around chatting on their lawns, especially not at 7:00 a.m. on a weekday—or whatever time it was. They should have been heading to work.

Then he remembered. Things in the world weren't right. Someone had exploded a nuke off the coast of California. Another bomb had been detonated two days earlier in Saudi Arabia—the first nuclear weapons to be fired in anger since World War II. The stock market had been halted by the SEC, and Los Angeles had descended into a war zone with mass evacuation and raging civil disorder.

For the life of him, Jimmy couldn't figure out how the attacks were connected. He could not see the connection between the Saudi bomb, the stock market halt and the California bomb. Why would two nuclear attacks take place within two days of one another half a world away? It made absolutely no sense.

News out of California yesterday had been a horror show. For policy reasons, the state and federal government were being slow with information, but every post hitting Facebook had been worse than the last.

The afternoon before, an internet blogger had captured video of a dead baby strapped in her car seat, sitting in the bushes alongside Interstate 15 while cars passed by at a crawl. While nobody knew why the baby had died, the Facebooker implied that the child had perished from radiation poisoning. Mainstream media ran jaded reports claiming that the story about the radiation-dead child might be Russian-sponsored fake news, but the TV stories only succeeded in driving more people to watch the footage of the dead baby. True or not, each view and share cartwheeled southern California into greater chaos.

According to CNN, the Los Angeles Police Department had detected a radiation signature off Alameda Harbor ten minutes before detonation. Thankfully, the bomb had gone off three miles out to sea, and less than a hundred people had been killed by the nuke itself. The dead had been boaters, the police helicopter crew, a Coast Guard patrol boat crew, and several dozen Los Angelinos who had crashed their cars because of the blinding flash. Direct damage to Los Angeles wasn't catastrophic; it was more typical of a large earthquake than a nuclear weapon. Thousands of windows had been shattered and hundreds of people had minor injuries from flying glass.

None of that explained why the southern half of California had come completely unhinged. Nobody could say for sure how much radiation risk Los Angeles faced. Millions of tons of mud and water, possibly radioactive, had been torn from the bottom of the ocean and misted over greater Los Angeles, most of the moisture wafting along in the atmosphere.

Despite the minor damage, the coastal region from Santa Barbara down to San Diego had become the sixth circle of hell. Millions of people were trying to claw their way out of California just to get *anywhere* else.

Waking up to an avocado pit of fear in his stomach felt like the morning after Jimmy's dad died three years ago. The next day, Jimmy awakened in pretty good spirits, only to remember that his life would never be the same. His dad had died. A dark cloud had overtaken him. He had been forced, secretly, to see a therapist, but he had quit going after a couple of sessions. Digging into his feelings was making it hard for him at work, and there had been an unspoken possibility that he might actually choose to leave his wife if he kept doing the therapy.

Nothing, not even his life, was worth losing his family. He was definitely a true believer in the Mormon faith and, as a Mormon, one's personal well-being took a back seat to one's family. So Jimmy swallowed it all down and eventually worked his way out of the funk through prayer and scripture study.

Jimmy couldn't tell what the neighbors were saying outside his bedroom window, but he could hear the occasional laugh, incongruous considering what had happened in the world.

Jimmy got out of bed, careful not to disturb his wife, and approached his closet. He might still go into work, but for now he grabbed his track suit. He and the track suit shared a love/hate relationship. He knew it made him look fat. Every time he put it on, he felt a dose of self-loathing, hating his body and hating his inability to control his weight. But the track suit was definitely comfortable, and he relished not feeling a leather belt cutting into his gut.

Jimmy pulled on his running shoes and slipped out the front door, careful not to slam it behind him. The neighborhood guys stood in his next-door neighbor's side yard, surrounding a small red generator.

"Ah, darn. Did we wake you, Jim?" Ron Marsdon asked.

"Nope. I was already up," Jimmy lied as he walked over to join the group.

"We were just wondering what time was too early to fire up the genny. Power's out at your place, too, right?"

Jimmy stabbed his hands into his track suit pockets and joined the circle. "Sure is. Has anyone heard what caused the power outage?"

"Tom called the power company on his cell phone, and the recording said there were 'widespread brown-outs in the Salt Lake Valley.'"

"Tom's cell phone worked?"

"Yeah, so there must be some power somewhere. They'll get it going again. If not, I'll bet the Church lights some fires under some butts!"

Federal Heights was only about ten blocks from the headquarters of the Mormon Church, and Church headquarters probably wasn't getting power from the grid, either.

Another neighbor, who Jimmy only knew as Brother Buchanan, chimed in. "The Brethren will get it handled. Or… maybe it's the Second Coming."

The guys all chuckled, finding it only partly humorous. For more than a hundred and seventy years, the Mormon Church had been predicting the end of the world. In the seventies and eighties, the leaders of the Church, "the Brethren," had counseled members to store a year's supply of food, to set aside drinking water and to grow a garden. "The end was near," the Brethren had said.

But, after decades of the world *not ending*, the prophetic warning tapered off. These days, the Mormon Church made a concerted effort to sound more mainstream, and talking about the end of the world from the pulpit was definitely *not* mainstream.

Still, when a prophet speaks in the Mormon faith, his words are immutable and eternal. Even though Church leaders weren't talking doom and gloom as much anymore, the old prophecies about the fall of the United States were definitely on the minds of the four men standing around the generator.

Jimmy's next-door neighbor Thad said, "Well, at least we all have our gardens and food storage." The guys laughed to be polite. Thad worked as some kind of lawyer, and he regularly made off-color comments in Gospel Doctrine class on Sunday. He was one of those guys who didn't seem to know when he was saying something that rubbed people wrong.

Disobedience was nothing to joke about. Even ignoring "stale" commandments, like the commandment to have a year's supply of food and to plant a garden, wouldn't be taken lightly by a faithful Mormon. Every man in the circle knew that none of them had gardens, and they could also guess that nobody had a proper year's supply of food, either.

Last year, on the deer hunt, Jimmy's brother talked a lot about the Church and food storage. He had been asked to volunteer as the Ward Emergency Preparedness Coordinator, and part of that job was to inventory the food storage of ward members. At the end of his survey, he had discovered that less than ten percent of ward members had a year's supply of food, and less than twenty-five percent had a three-month's supply.

The Church, as an institution, had been backing away from preparedness, too, Jimmy's brother confided. Most of their food storage centers east of the Mississippi were being shuttered, and the amount of food at the Bishop's Storehouse had been dialed way back. The big grain silos, owned by the Church in Salt Lake and Ogden, sat largely empty.

If his brother was correct about the Church dialing back, it gave Jimmy some peace. If the Brethren had backed away from emergency preparedness, then it probably meant the Apocalypse and the Second Coming were still a long way off. The leaders of the Church were prophets, after all.

Jimmy thought about his own woefully insufficient food storage. They had only what his wife had set aside in canned food and Jimmy suspected it was precious little. He looked at his watch and did a quick calculation.

The Costco in Salt Lake City had already opened, since it typically opened at 7:00 a.m.. The only reason Jimmy knew this was because he had volunteered to buy a birthday cake a couple of times at the office and he had hit the Costco on his way to work.

Right then and there, Jimmy decided to skip work and head to Costco. This would be the day he would buy his year's supply. He tried running the numbers on what it would cost compared to the limit on his American Express card, and he kept coming up against numbers that he simply did not know.

How many cans of food would his family eat in a year? What did a can of food even cost? How much toilet paper did his family use?

He would have to ask his wife. The thought of asking his wife stopped him in his tracks. She would reply with a million questions, challenge his decision, and then try to get him to do something that *she* wanted done. To heck with that.

Jimmy looked at his watch again. "Sorry, boys, I've got some stuff to do."

"No work today?" Thad asked.

"Don't think so. Without the computers running, I don't see how I can get anything done." Jimmy thought briefly of the real estate closing, knowing it would be postponed. "See you later, fellas."

With Jimmy heading toward his wife's big SUV, the guys returned to staring at the generator.

When Jimmy pulled onto Hartwell Avenue, the last turn to Costco, he uttered a rare expletive.

"What the freak!?"

Cars were parked up one side of the street and down the other. People were even parking on 300 West and walking two blocks to get to the store.

Jimmy parked on the little road behind Home Depot and made his way to the Costco parking lot on foot.

He had never seen anything like it. There were probably three thousand people, all standing in front of the store. The tide of people wasn't moving. Someone at the front was shouting and the crowd began shushing one another, trying to hear what was being said.

An invisible person at the front of the massive crowd, presumably a store manager, shouted at the top of his lungs, "I'm sorry, folks. We're closed…"

The crowd's reaction sounded like a combination of a wave hitting the beach and a bear growling. The shushing began again and the noise dropped.

"We can't run our credit card machines and we don't have lights." The emotion of the crowd again rose up, drowning out the manager. The shushing, mingled with the buzz of angry voices, restored silence.

"Please come back a little later today…" Then the angry roar overwhelmed all meaningful communication.

As Jimmy made his way back to his wife's SUV, the faces around him triggered a primal sense of foreboding in his gut. He had never seen people this freaked out. He actually feared a little for his own safety, even in broad daylight. He hurried back to the Suburban but got distracted by his cell phone buzzing.

It was a text from his wife. "Where is my car? I have to take Taylor to school and her backpack is in the SUV. Why'd you take my car without asking?"

The bile in Jimmy's stomach turned. He said a silent prayer and climbed into the driver's seat.

• • •

Fulton Residence

Sacramento, California

Robbie Fulton had been enjoying a rare interlude at home in Sacramento when California imploded.

As a union representative and political mover and shaker, Robbie traveled more than two hundred days a year working politicians, the unions and other special interest groups. If he had been out of town when things went crazy, his wife would have been lost without him.

The governor had been right about Los Angeles rioting if the power went out. But the Cowboy Governor, as Robbie had begun to call him in his head, had no way to predict a nuclear attack on his state, and they had *all* failed to foresee the racially-fueled meltdown of every major metropolitan area in California big enough to have low-income housing.

That morning, Robbie called in via satellite connection to participate in a Governor's Working Group. There had been more than thirty California political functionaries on the conference call. Robbie just listened.

Each new tidbit of information on the call was more terrifying than the last. The state representative from FEMA knew the most about conditions across the nation. While the initial power failure and nuke attack had struck the West Coast, the East Coast had a growing catastrophe of its own.

Without any obvious cause, rolling blackouts ravaged the Eastern seaboard from Ontario to South Carolina. Harried authorities at FEMA and Homeland Security could only speculate that the Russians had jumped at the chance to unleash the same malware virus they used against Ukrainian power companies in 2016. Government agencies stopped short of accusing Russia for the nuclear attack because there was no evidence, but it seemed increasingly likely that the Russians were using hackers to shut down power plants in the East, ensuring a full-blown national meltdown.

The NASDAQ and the NYSE stock exchanges were barely running; they would come alive only to have their automated emergency algorithms shut them back down, triggered by massive sell-offs of stock.

Of the top twenty property and casualty insurance companies insuring California, only two hadn't gone into free fall in the brief moments when the stock exchanges were operating. Several of the massive reinsurance companies that backed those insurance companies had tanked in the international stock markets. An unimaginable quantity of capital had gone to "money heaven" overnight because of the Los Angeles nuclear attack. The markets were anticipating trillions of dollars of loss due to the fires and civil disorder appearing on Facebook, Instagram, and YouTube. Most property insurance didn't cover a nuclear attack, but almost all property and casualty insurance covered rioting and fire. The markets were betting that insurance companies wouldn't get out of Los Angeles alive.

Nobody could guess the actual damage, but the sheer magnitude of the civil unrest and firestorm in Los Angeles made one wonder if L.A. wasn't a total loss. Could the national economy suffer the complete loss of Los Angeles? In 2007, the loss of a *single* insurance company almost triggered the collapse of the world economy. What might happen if twenty insurance companies and several reinsurance companies went bankrupt all at the same time?

The answer to that question seemed to be playing out across America. All banks had closed due to massive runs on accounts. Nobody could get their cash out, not through the banks and not through ATMs.

The stock market holds and the bank closures sent everyone rushing to stores to get whatever they could with their cash. Within hours, every shelf on the East and West coasts was empty. Then rioting began in earnest.

The president had authorized the military to step into the inner cities nationwide. Like California, the National Guard units would need some time to spin up. In that gap, whole city centers were being looted and burned to the ground.

If people had stayed in their homes, the National Guard might have been able to help. In fact, the government had broadcast pleas for citizens to stay in their homes for the last twenty-four hours. Nobody listened. The roads were choked with refugees leaving the big cities to escape the violence and chaos of the inner cities. Every road coming out of a city was utterly packed with vehicles fleeing civil disorder. Most National Guard units turned back to their bases within a few miles, unable to get past thousands of angry and desperate refugees.

No one in the Governor's Working Group had solutions. California was even worse than the East Coast, since Los Angeles had already been imploding for forty-eight hours. The call ended with flimsy ideas and even flimsier orders from the governor. Robbie had little hope that anyone could turn back the chaos. Like a brushfire running wild, this crisis would have to burn itself out.

Robbie's view of Sacramento from the front yard of his uptown home belied the truth. Civil unrest consumed the guts out of the state capitol. He heard the firecracker pop of distant gunfire and smoke curled into the air from dozens of fires.

Electric power still ran in Sacramento, at least for the time being. All infrastructure—transportation, internet, water, natural gas—continued to run. Yet downtown burned, undoubtedly as a result of rioting and looting.

If utilities and services were running, they wouldn't be for long. As morning dawned, every police officer, prison guard, military person, and civic leader would be looking at themselves in the mirror, asking the same question: "Do I do my job or do I protect my family?"

This morning, Robbie could only pray that the California National Guard would be worth a damn, but the cynical side of him suspected that the Army had become as fragile as the rest of the government.

He heard a loud roar and glanced up to see an unmuffled, late-model pickup truck race down the street perpendicular to his own. It blew past and he saw at least two men in the pickup bed. The roar of the engine faded in the distance.

Robbie shook off his malaise and went back inside. He headed to his gun safe at the back of his office and spun the tumblers, struggling to remember the code. Finally, the safe opened and he pulled out his Remington 870 Express shotgun. He broke into a new box of double-ought buck shells and loaded the magazine and the shell holder on the stock. As he loaded, Robbie reminded himself that one mistake with a firearm, no matter how slight, would end his career in the State of California. This was not the state to play fast and loose with firearms.

Many years back, when Robbie was still a union representative for the iron workers, he had taken a shooting class. Even then, he kept his guns secret. He hadn't practiced much because it would be too easy for someone to recognize him at a shooting range and make political hay out of it. But he knew how to use the shotgun, and it gave him some comfort. Politico or not, Robbie was willing to kill someone to protect his wife and property. More so than at any other moment in his sixty years, he thought it might come to that.

Robbie placed the loaded shotgun next to the front door and went upstairs to check on his wife. She would ask some tough questions. He wished he had better answers.

Sometime during the long, tear-punctuated conversation between Robbie and his wife, the dog began barking like mad.

Robbie had originally hated that dog—a Shinu-imu or some such breed. He counted it as another useless trapping of the showcase life they lived.

The more he watched the dog, the more he thought of it as a fox. The thing displayed almost-inconceivable athleticism, able to hop around on its hind legs and make incredible jumps from a dead stop.

A fox, Robbie could respect. He came to love that dog, and it was clear the dog preferred him over the lady of the house, despite Robbie's God-awful travel schedule.

He could hear the dog going berserk at the back sliding glass door. Robbie detoured by the front door and grabbed his 870 Express. He slid into the kitchen and looked around the edge of the glass door, using the wall as cover.

He couldn't see anyone in the backyard. Even with Robbie standing beside him, the dog wouldn't take his eyes off the back lawn and wouldn't stop barking. Somebody was definitely out there.

Robbie found himself in a quandary. He knew the gun laws of California and, worse yet, he knew the judicial record of the state dealing with armed homeowners who shot intruders. In a nutshell, if you shot someone on your property, you would be lucky to keep your freedom or your home. You might lawyer your way out of trouble if you shot someone *inside* your house, but shooting someone in your yard was inexcusable in the eyes of California law. It would definitely land you in deep shit.

Robbie leaned the 870 Express just inside the glass door, let it go, reached over to the door lock and flipped it up.

He considered calling the police, but he knew they had their hands full and they wouldn't respond in under an hour, if ever. Robbie took a few steps into the backyard and looked around. The dog hesitated at his leg then flew past him, running around the corner of the house.

The dog flew backward into the yard, yelping, obviously kicked. Two men came around the corner fast and moved straight for Robbie. Both carried revolvers and both revolvers were aimed at his chest.

"Hey, old man," said one of the men. He shot Robbie twice in the chest before Robbie could take a single step toward his shotgun.

• • •

Highway 6 Roadblock
Delta, Utah

Dale Trenton, commander of the Delta Desert Patriots militia, looked out at the endless column of semi-trucks stretching beyond the horizon on Highway 6.

Dale had spent his morning talking with his prisoner, the commander of the small detachment of what he now understood were California National Guardsmen. Looking at the semis, he actually believed the commander's story. The men he had captured were California engineers coming to get the power plant back online.

But Dale didn't think the new information changed things. He realized the power plant was offline and that it was causing outages in California. Half the guys in his militia worked at that plant.

He also knew that the world was going straight to hell. The Delta Desert Patriots ran their own ham radio repeater, and reports were coming to him outside the control of the Feds and the American oligarchy.

Los Angeles burned, as well as all the rest of the big cities in California. As of this morning, racial tensions had also erupted in the big, rotted-out cities of dying America: Detroit, Chicago, New York City, and Washington D.C. Most of Utah had gone dark, probably because the railroads weren't moving enough coal to cover Utah power plants. With only natural gas power, Utah couldn't feed the million air conditioners that flipped on the instant power resumed.

Like an old truck with a bad carburetor, the stock market kept firing up, then getting shut down by the bureaucrats as soon as the Wall Street corporate thieves started selling everything they could. In the last three days, the stock market had spent a grand total of twenty-three minutes up and running.

God only knew what was happening with that bomb over in the sandbox. Short-wave information came through a lot thinner about stuff happening worldwide. The few tidbits they had picked up made it sound like World War III was heating up; Russians, Turks, Iranians, Egyptians, and probably Americans were squaring off, and Dale couldn't even begin to understand who were the good guys and who were the bad guys. Considering the nuke that had hit Los Angeles,

Dale figured the whole shebang was just another false flag operation launched by the Soros/Clinton oligarchs trying to gain control of the world.

It all boiled down to this: the world was going to hell, and the only thing that really mattered was home and family.

If Dale let those trucks into Delta, it wasn't going to change a damned thing. His boys from the plant told him the Intermountain plant wasn't going to fire back up again, even if they refilled the coal field to overflowing. There were bigger problems in the world than one broken power plant.

More than half of the plant's staff hadn't shown up that morning. There were strict policies handed down from the muckety-mucks in California that dictated when the plant could run and when it couldn't.

The list of "Turbine Spin-up Critical Personnel" included a bunch of engineers, as well as safety monitors, environmental oversight folks and even union monitors. Every single one of those positions had to be staffed before the turbines could turn. All of those positions had back-ups and redundancies, but with half the staff unable to get to work because of road blockages or because they were scared, there was no way in hell that list of critical personnel was getting filled.

Even if Dale let the coal pass, it wasn't going to matter. He would be allowing strangers into Delta at the worst possible time. He couldn't save California even if he wanted to, but he *could* save Delta.

• • •

Reynolds Residence
Oakwood, Utah

Tom and Jacquelyn Reynolds had always been true-blue preppers. Being a prepper didn't mark a person as a freak in Utah, like in many areas of the United States. Thanks to rural living and the Mormon

Church, Utah had been chock-full of preppers since Brigham Young fought off the United States Army in the 1850s.

Neither Jacquelyn nor Tom considered themselves Mormon, but both their names appeared on the rolls of the Mormon Church because they had been baptized by their parents when they were eight years old. Jack-Mormons though they were, both inadvertently carried on the pioneer and anti-government sensibilities of Brigham Young, the second Mormon prophet. Pretty much the entire state, outside the urbane neighborhood surrounding the University of Utah, felt the same way.

In 1857, Brigham Young had received word that the United States Army was coming to kick his ass. The Mormons had been practicing polygamy in Utah for decades, much to the chagrin of the rest of America. Also, the threat of rebellion within the U.S. had become a hot topic for President Buchanan, with the southern states teetering on the brink of pre-Civil War secession. Smacking down the Mormons would provide an inexpensive object lesson in the realities of rebelling against the United States government. So Buchanan sent troops to Utah to bring Brigham Young to heel.

But no one on either side relished the thought of a shooting war. Over the next two years, the clever Mormons leveraged their courage and craftiness to harry the approaching troops—running off the Army mules, starving their pack animals, and eventually wearing them down without ever firing a shot. The Mormons won the conflict by stalling and by letting the harsh Rocky Mountain winter erode the Army's resolve.

The distrust of government had lingered in Utah, even as the memory of the "Utah War" faded. Tom and Jacquelyn hewed to the conventional prepper rhetoric: constitutionalism, local governance, and individualism should stand iron-clad. They would have made Brigham Young proud.

But the couple wanted nothing to do with either Mormonism nor the Christian faith that inspired many preppers. The "prepper movement," post-Y2K, had split into two factions: those who saw the Apocalypse as an act of divine retribution and those who saw the Apocalypse as a result of bad government. Both sides of prepperdom were companionable enough. They simply arrived at their belief in the Apocalypse from two different angles.

Now that the Apocalypse was upon them, Tom and Jacquelyn didn't waste time arguing why. Instead, they executed on their plan. They set to work packing the old Chevy truck Tom had restored and got ready to head up to the Ross Homestead.

As Tom cleared out his gun safe, Jacquelyn sat down beside him at his reloading bench. She wanted to talk. Tom wanted to keep working. After twelve years of marriage, they had figured out this dance. She started by perching herself on his bench, wooing him with her short-cut hair and almond eyes. Tom stopped what he was doing.

"I'm worried about my clients," Jacquelyn began. She worked as an "LMHC," or Licensed Mental Health Counselor. She had finished her advanced degree two years back when their youngest child went into first grade. She now managed a small client load of twenty people in need of talk therapy, mostly adult women.

Tom knew better than to wade in with solutions this early in the conversation. "How so?"

"How can I just dump them and head to Jason and Jenna's compound? My clients are going to need me now more than ever."

Tom made a "hmmm" sound and waited.

"And what about our families? Laura's in Galveston and they're not prepared for this." They both knew that Tom couldn't do anything about his own family. They had parted ways many years back. But Jacquelyn and her sister were close.

"Jacquelyn," Tom said. She hated it when people called her "Jackie." As was often his role, Tom spoke the hard truths they both were thinking. "We knew it would come to this someday and we did everything we could to educate our friends and family. With all we've done to support the Homestead over the years, we can request that Laura and Paul be allowed into the community. But they'll never make it to Salt Lake in time. They probably wouldn't even agree to come. They're pretty stubborn about how much they trust the government. Right?"

Jacquelyn sighed heavily, knowing he was right.

"And about your clients… There is not one damned thing you can do. It would have been unprofessional if you'd tried to get them to prepare."

"I know." She slumped. "Of course, you're right. But I'm worried for them."

"Sure. That's who you are, but our kids are top priority now."

She sighed again, getting up off the stool. Tom continued, "That means getting out of here before things get too dangerous in the valley."

"All right. I'm on it. Thanks for listening." She grabbed the list the Homestead had sent them. They needed to pack their food storage, guns, medicine, clothing and a hundred little things easily forgotten. The list went on for three tightly packed pages, but the task wasn't overwhelming. Tom and Jacquelyn had gone over the list half-a-dozen times during their marriage and a lot of the stuff on the list was pre-packed and ready in black plastic totes.

It took them half the day to get the truck and camper loaded. Jacquelyn hoped the list had been complete. Looking at her home, she couldn't shake the feeling that she would never see it again. Tom came trudging out of the house in full military kit: gun belt, chest rig, bump helmet, magazines, handgun, and an AR-15 rifle in his hands. He scanned for threats as he crossed the front yard.

Jacquelyn almost laughed, thinking that it was a little early for her neighborhood to be considered a "threat zone."

"Look who's a badass now," she joked. Tom was a member of the Homestead Quick Reaction Force, or QRF, and that meant he had done hundreds of hours of firearms training. Guns were a big part of Tom's life, but Jacquelyn had never seen him in full kit. The part of her brain that clung to the world of parent-teacher conferences and talk therapy recoiled at his ultra-macho outfit. The other part of her brain, the one that had prepared for a disaster, and learned how to make cheese and to bottle apricots, pushed back, reminding her the stock market had crashed, two nukes had exploded, and big cities around the country had dissolved into chaos.

Seeing Tom like this brought up all kinds of feelings. She knew her husband to be a competent man, repairing things around the house, fixing cars, building parts for his guns in his garage machine shop. She also knew him to be a dork. He rarely remembered to take out the trash on Wednesdays. He sang badly to the radio, usually screwing up the lyrics, and his personal hygiene left something to be desired. Unless she insisted, he neglected to cut his toenails, pluck his ear hairs and wear deodorant. In some ways, she thought of him as another one of her children.

Soon, this man might be the only thing standing between her children and starvation. The thought sent a shiver down her spine. It wasn't that Tom couldn't protect them; she had it on good authority he was an excellent shooter. What terrified her was the slim margin between life and death that real calamity might bring. All her money was on Tom. He was Plan A, B *and* C. Never before had she been forced to so completely rely on her husband.

Over the years, she had earned more than her fair share of the income. Tom treated her well. She couldn't complain. But she felt like she was the smart one in the marriage. Most of the time, she felt like Tom had no idea what she even did during the day.

Marrying him had been the right decision. Looking back, she loved the life they had cobbled together. But that was then, when the world made sense. Back then, when a kid was sick, the medical insurance would kick in. Back then, if they saw someone lurking in the neighborhood, they called the cops. Back then, if she and Tom weren't getting along, she could go stay with her mother for a few days. Now all they had was each other.

Tom walked around the truck, doing a last-minute mechanical check. When he reached the passenger door, he opened it.

"You drive, please." Jacquelyn slid across the bench seat and got behind the wheel. Before pulling the door closed, Tom laid his rifle across his lap, minding the muzzle and checking the kids in the back seat.

Maybe in this new world, Tom was the ultimate breadwinner after all—a skilled protector and a man who understood how things worked. In any case, he was her man and she knew she could do a hell of a lot worse.

She fired up the old truck and they rolled away from their family home of ten years. Tom had her go across town on side streets, and soon they began moving up the hill toward the Ross Homestead. They saw nothing more threatening in town than a few broken stop lights.

• • •

Ross Homestead
Oakwood, Utah

Jeff and Tara Kirkham arrived at the Homestead in their minivan, pulling a trailer stacked with supplies.

As soon as he planted his family in the Homestead barracks, Jeff switched into full non-commissioned officer—"NCO" mode. He wasn't going to wait around for a committee to decide the fate of his family. He would go to work and make it happen. At that moment, it meant burning up the phone lines.

"Hey, Alec. What's up, dude?"

"Hey, Jeff. You ready for the end of the world?" Alec Hammer had spent the previous ten years as an Army Ranger and a CIA contractor.

"Roger that," Jeff replied. "I'm just waiting for you to get over here so we can spool up and get this party started."

"You at your place?"

"Negative. I've got us set up in a hard point with a bunch of indigenous folks who we'll need to run through their paces. Are you ready to get to work?"

Alec took it in. "Are you serious? Do you really have a plan for this?"

"Affirmative," Jeff replied. "Why are we still talking about it? Grab your wife and your gear and get over here. I'll text the address. Write it down in case comms go south."

Alec continued, "Yeah, I was just kitting up. I thought I'd call a few guys and maybe get together… figure out a nice little farm somewhere we could vacation for a few weeks."

"I got something like that going on up here in Oakwood. It's a bunkered-up community of survival types with a shit-ton of food, water and solar. They're welcoming Special Operations Forces guys with open arms. You bring the gun; they bring the grub sort of thing. Operators and their families. You in?"

"Hell, yeah, I'm in. Let me call a few guys and I'll put together some more dudes. You good with that?"

"Yep. We'll take all Tier One and Two operators plus anyone with legit combat experience. Combat-experienced Marines too. SEALs. Air Force Para-rescue. TACPs. Of course, Rangers and Green Berets. I'll take as many shooters as you can muster."

"I'm on it. Text me the address and I'll start sending you resumes."

"Don't bother waiting for my say so. If you think they're good, I'll take them."

"Okay. I'll come up with my wife tomorrow morning, hopefully with a bunch of other guys. I'll see you tomorrow, Master Sergeant."

"See you then." Jeff hung up.

After a half-dozen calls like that, Jeff was satisfied that he could bring in at least a dozen SOF veterans. That would make up the core of what he wanted: a two-hundred-man army. Training the civilians would take some time and he would have to pull men from somewhere other than just the Homestead. The Homestead had some good enough shooters—they had been training for years—but they only had around a hundred people who were gun-capable and

Jeff admitted to himself that a good chunk of them weren't going to be worth a damn in combat, at least not at first.

He anticipated that a lot of the Homestead men would crumple at the sudden change of lifestyle. Going from cushy modern society to living in the dirt and eating weird food would flip the "depression switch" on a lot of folks. For some, it would be permanent. Other guys would fold under combat stress, and the vast majority would struggle at the moment of pulling the trigger, if it came to that. But all that was *de rigueur* for a Green Beret. He had trained indigenous fighters all around the world and the same factors applied to men everywhere.

Jeff recalled his earliest training as a Green Beret—learning that all animals have a strong aversion to killing their own kind. Even rattlesnakes and piranha elect to posture when fighting rather than killing members of their own species. Likewise, all men have a deep-seated resistance to aiming their rifles at one another and pulling the trigger. In his book, *On Killing*, the author collected data from wars throughout history and less than fifteen percent of soldiers would fire their weapons at the enemy in the heat of battle. That resistance to killing could be trained out of men, but it would take time and ammo. At the end of the day, Jeff figured he would be lucky if he could get thirty actual shooters out of the hundred or so citizen gun owners of the Homestead.

With ten or fifteen SOF guys, he would multiply his ability to train men. Green Berets would be ideal, since they had been trained to train local fighters—but he would take any military operator. At the very least, the operators could lead platoons.

Jeff watched a fat guy in a stretched-tight polo shirt make a beeline for him across the Homestead lawn. It wasn't anyone Jeff had met before. The guy walked up, his hand thrust out.

"Hello. I'm Doctor Frank Hodges."

"Hey, I'm Jeff Kirkham."

"Good to meetcha. I take it you're part of the club thing they've got going here, right? What do you do for a living?"

Doctor Hodges was working hard on making conversation. Jeff wasn't up for "making friends and influencing people" right then, but he didn't want to be rude, either. "I used to shoot people for a living. Now I just think about it a lot." Okay, maybe he was willing to be a little rude.

"Really?" The doctor laughed nervously. "Were you in the military?"

"Yeah, I'm a former Green Beret."

The doctor laughed, coughing like a sputtering two-stroke engine. "Well, I'm a physician. More of a plastic surgeon, to be honest. I actually spend more time selling creams and ointments than I do slicing people up. But a doctor's a doctor, I guess, and they invited us here. I live right down the street. Heck, maybe you can teach me to shoot sometime."

Jeff noted the man's loose skin and his willowy arms before answering. "Yeah, we'll see what comes up when we have some time to work on shooting. Won't you be needed in the infirmary?"

"Yeah, I guess so." The doctor deflated a little. "I've always meant to learn to shoot. I have a couple of Sig Sauer handguns, but I haven't had a chance to shoot them yet. I'm guessing now, without work, we'll have a lot of time for stuff like that."

Jeff thought the exact opposite. He thought they would be working harder than ever before, scraping for every minute of sleep they could scrounge. This doctor guy must figure the collapse would be like an extended camping trip, roasting marshmallows over a campfire singing *Boom Chicka Boom* and other Boy Scout favorites. If this was the kind of guy he'd be making into a fighter, he'd rather work with Iraqi teenagers. At least they knew enough to be scared.

"Well, Doc, I got to get going. The Apocalypse isn't going to un-fuck itself."

The doctor cut loose with the two-stroke-engine laugh again. "Okay, Mister-Sergeant Kirkham," he shot Jeff a mock salute, "we'll be seeing you around the compound."

"Yeah." Jeff turned and walked toward the office wing of the big house. Doctor Hodges glanced about, looking to find someone else to glad-hand.

• • •

Ross Homestead Ham Shack
Oakwood, Utah

Jason Ross stopped by the Ham Shack, tucked into the forest by the new ponds. A simplex ham radio call was scheduled with his brother-in-law Tommy, and Jason was dying to put some worries to rest.

Built inside a pimped-out shipping container, the Ham Shack barely fit a pair of desks, two guys and the rack of radio equipment. Zach, the head radio operator for the Homestead, was listening to a pirate radio news show that had sprung up on the shortwave bands. Never before had either of them heard anyone "hack" shortwave radio with a pirate broadcast. Fear of the Federal Communications Commission always halted such mischief, but things were slipping all across the gamut of government.

"What the heck is this?" Jason cocked his head as the pirate radio announcer cussed up a storm over the airwaves.

"Oh, hey, Jason." Zach turned the radio volume down a notch. "This guy apparently stole an Army Humvee radio rig from Fort Bliss in El Paso and he's running around the Southwest broadcasting the truth about the collapse. He says he's gathering info from military personnel that are part of an online community called 'Drinkin' Bros'."

"Okay, let's keep track of this guy. Are you set for the simplex call with my brother-in-law?"

"Sure. I've got it all set up right here." Zach turned off the shortwave receiver and fired up his ham set.

With any luck, tonight they would confirm Tommy's location—hopefully somewhere far away from Phoenix where Tommy and his family lived. Jason's last phone call with him painted a bleak picture of Phoenix, as though three million people had awakened that morning in a panic and realized *there wasn't any water.*

The shelves of the Ham Shack were loaded up like gizmo heaven. Black boxes, digital read-outs, big knobs and red LEDs all bounced a weird glow off Zach. With cell networks now teetering on the brink of oblivion, these ancient ham technologies would be the only threads holding the modern world together.

Reaching out to Jason's brother-in-law was job one today. The cell phone networks had already begun to collapse in rural pockets and now they were showing signs of strain, even in suburban Salt Lake City. Jason could still make a cell connection in the Valley, but his son traveling through Washington and his brother-in-law in northern Arizona had both fallen off the cell network.

Over years of preparation, ham radio had taken over Homestead communications. Security teams operating for the Homestead needed a bullet-proof way to communicate. Consumer radios weren't reliable in the mountains, so Jason had prepared a more powerful option: ham radio handsets.

The Homestead sat within walking distance of over a million people, most of whom would grow hungry, then angry, in a collapse. Locating a bug-out location in the suburbs penciled out to a tremendous risk and it worried Jason sick. But the advantages of staying close to the city had been considerable: a distant bug-out location might have been impossible to reach in a crisis. The freeway coursing across the Salt Lake Valley already looked like a serpentine parking lot with cars barely moving. How would people with ranches in the mountains reach them without roads?

In the collapse of Argentina in 1998, the remote farms and ranches had seen the worst criminal atrocities anywhere. Marauders had known they could subjugate isolated homesteads at their leisure and that's exactly what they had done, with rape and atrocities becoming commonplace in the Argentine countryside.

In many ways, bugging in instead of bugging out made sense near a city the size of Salt Lake. The Homestead had amassed a couple of hundred members, including the warfighters, doctors, solar experts, gardeners, beekeepers and mechanics. Being close to town had its advantages and the easy-to-reach location made it possible to build a well-staffed hard target. Still, Jason had to wonder: would the gamble pay off?

Jason listened while Zach called to Tommy on the ham. "KF7UCL is monitoring and listening for a call."

Immediately, Tommy responded on the first pre-arranged frequency for that day. "KF7UCL, this is W2ADL mobile near Gray Mountain, north of Flagstaff returning. This is Tommy. Back to you, KF7UCL."

They had made contact via UHF, even though Tommy's automotive ham radio was relatively small. At the Ross Homestead, they were pounding out two thousand watts on a multi-band beam antenna. Even so, the ionosphere had to be just right to make the simplex connection, especially on the first try.

Earlier, Jason tried a cell call to both Tommy and Cameron and got no love. That came as no surprise because Tommy was driving the "back way" into central Utah across the east side of the Wasatch Mountain Range. There were more dead spots there than the dark side of the Moon, even in the best of times.

"W2ADL, this is Zach, Oakwood, Utah. Reading you four by nine. Location received. Cameron's location is Cajon Pass, California. Relay travel conditions. Back to you."

"KF7UCL, you are five nine. Copy that: Cameron location Cajon Pass. Travel conditions very heavy but steady. Proceeding on Highway 89 to your location. Give my love to Jenna. Over."

There was no need to extend the conversation, especially since the ham frequencies had been bursting with traffic over the last day.

The traffic would definitely slow down as repeaters went offline and batteries began to die, but that might take weeks or even months.

"Thank you and safe travels, W2ADL. KF7UCL over and QRT." Zach finished the transmission with Jason standing over his shoulder.

Jason patted Zach on the shoulder and headed back into the sunshine. At least one worry could be crossed off his list.

• • •

It had taken Jeff Kirkham about an hour to find the Beringer camp. In the end, it was the sound of human voices that pegged their location. Just as Jason described, the Beringers had set up a wilderness camp that looked like a junkyard—tents surrounded by ramshackle structures made out of pallets covered with rotting tarps.

Glassing through the trees with his binoculars, it was hard to tell how many people inhabited the camp. Jeff figured eight families had holed up in the canyon bottom. The place crawled with women and children.

With that many dependents, he needed to rethink his strategy. Without a doubt, the Beringers couldn't be allowed to remain this close to the Homestead. Conflict would be unavoidable, especially after the Homestead solidified its defensive perimeter. These yokels would be chasing game all over the mountain, leading to his guys shooting at them, and then all-out war. If war was inevitable, Jeff wanted to strike first.

Before he had gone to Laos with the Green Berets, Jeff attended a school taught by the CIA on "Asymmetrical Warfare," which he discovered was a military euphemism for "fighting dirty."

One of the things he had been taught was how to weaken an enemy encampment through the use of necrotic matter, either human or animal. Surprisingly, decomposing corpses aren't particularly lethal, since the natural process of decomposition generates few pathogens. A rotting intestine, however, carries pathogens that can manifest similar to the stomach flu, especially in young people.

Jeff ran his binos along the Beringers' apparent water supply. A small creek ran within spitting distance of the encampment. Likely, they were filtering their water to some degree, but that wouldn't be enough to stop a steady exposure to coliform bacteria.

Ross and the rest of the civilians would never approve of using a pathogen to remove a rival group, especially considering these people were camping on their own land. But Jeff wouldn't tolerate a threat this close to his family.

He had seen a dead porcupine on his way to recon the Beringer camp. Thirty minutes later, Jeff returned and dumped the corpse of the porcupine in the creek about a half-mile above the Beringers. He carefully cut the bloated stomach cavity, making a small slit in the lowest section of the intestine. The contents of the gut would dribble out for days. He carefully covered the dead animal with rocks and branches, hiding it from all but the most careful search.

After Jeff felt satisfied that his "biological weapon" was well-concealed and faithfully leaking pathogens into the creek, he policed up the tarp he had used to carry the stinking animal, wadded it into a ball and stuffed it into his kit.

As he climbed out of the canyon, returning silently to Homestead land, Jeff smiled at his subterfuge. The dead animal wasn't the perfect weapon—careful water purification would defeat even the nastiest bacteria. But his observation of the camp convinced Jeff these folks weren't the tight-and-tidy types. If their water purification was anything like their sloppy camp craft, a lot of E.coli would make it into their food and water supply. With a little luck, an onslaught of mysterious diarrhea would convince the group to relocate their camp elsewhere.

Jeff liked winning a fight "the easy way" and he smiled all the way back to the Homestead.

• • •

Highway 275
Norfolk, Nebraska

Chad Wade, former Navy SEAL, was nine-hundred-twenty miles from his home in Salt Lake City when the power went out. He had been traveling the Midwest, visiting ReadyMan members and checking on his little girl in Omaha.

A restless soul, Chad enjoyed wandering the Earth in his Jeep doing good deeds. He was like David Carradine in the show *Kung Fu*. The endless cornfields of the American middle country gave him time to think and rest his frenetic mind.

At five feet, six inches, he thought of himself as "perfectly sized for the modern world." Since the advent of the firearm, Chad argued that anything over five-and-a-half feet tall for a warrior was redundant and likely to get shot off. This served as the basis for endless verbal sparring between Chad and Jason Ross, who stood six feet, two inches tall. Jason routinely lampooned Chad for having "twelve-year-old girl feet" and Chad fired back with soliloquies about Jason moving like "a half-stoned Sasquatch."

Chad met Jason Ross as Chad finished an instructor slot at BUD/S, Naval Special Warfare in Coronado, California, where Navy SEALs are selected and trained. In a chance encounter, Jason and Chad met while working out at the gym. Chad later snuck Jason onto the Navy SEAL base and they borrowed a couple of instructor kayaks and went for a paddle around Coronado.

Jason had no background in the military, and he had only been vacationing in Coronado to appease his wife. But, before long, Jason and Chad's conversation found common ground; they both loved garden composting. Chad was probably the first Navy SEAL in history to take classes on composting and organic gardening while instructing at BUD/S. There had been a hippie commune out by Imperial Beach, just to the south of Naval Special Warfare. Chad jumped into classes put on by local tree huggers on organic composting whenever he could. Taking hippie classes wasn't unusual for Chad; his rivals called him a "crazy" and his friends called him "iconoclastic." Chad secretly enjoyed both monikers.

Chad generally ignored pop culture, movies and anything written within the last hundred years. At the same time, he accumulated— and occasionally abandoned—huge libraries of classical non-fiction. He was fond of saying, "If it wasn't written more than a hundred years ago, it probably hasn't been proven yet." He loved his books, but he rarely read more than thirty percent of the words, scanning stacks of books like an endless succession of magazine articles.

While Chad was the weirdest person any of his friends knew, he also loved spiritual pursuits and he had toyed repeatedly with the idea of enrolling in theological seminary. In reality, no church on Earth would want Chad as a pastor. He was too odd, entirely unable to enter the paddock with the other sheep and enjoy the grass. Still, Chad loved people and he gravitated toward spirituality at every turn. Essentially a restless soul, Chad drifted like a leaf on the wind.

The SEALs hadn't done him any favors. He never talked about it, but he had served a hard-hitting tour in Iraq that would set him up, probably for life, with an unsolvable internal struggle. High passion, high sensitivity and six months of non-stop brutality don't mix in a man's psychology. Then again, the United States government didn't worry too much about the nuances of psychology when they sent Special Operations Forces to do their dirty work.

Chad's cell phone rang and he picked up, hands-free.

"Hello."

"Good morning. Where are you in the world today?" Jason Ross always started the conversation like this because, even though they were close friends, he never knew where Chad was at the moment.

"I'm in Nebraska heading toward Salt Lake."

"I don't suppose you've been following the news?" Jason asked, already knowing the answer.

"No. What's up?"

"Just the end of the world."

Chad assumed he was joking. "Is this about the Saudi Arabia thing?"

"Yeah, and a nuke going off in California. And about six other things that are taking the country down. The flag's going up and you're the last one to find out."

"Seriously?" Chad had no idea.

"Yeah. Is the power still on where you are?"

"Now that you mention it, the stop lights were out in the last town I drove through." Chad still didn't think the two things were necessarily connected, but he was intrigued.

"Will you listen if I give you some advice?" Jason asked. Chad was silent, which was as close to a "yes" as Jason was going to get. "Drive straight out to your little girl, pick her up and drive directly to Salt Lake. Or, dump your Jeep and get on an airplane if you can."

"Seriously?" Chad asked again, about two octaves higher.

"Yes. Get to Salt Lake City as quickly as possible. You're probably up shit creek as it is. I'm surprised this call even went through. There are a bunch of people I can't reach anymore by cell. I assume we'll lose comms after this call. Do you have a gun?"

"I have my 1911 and a box of shells. I'll be good. I also have my go bag." Chad pulled over to the side of the road and did a little mental math, thinking about the route back to his daughter in Omaha.

"What the hell am I going to do about Audrey?" Chad wondered aloud. Chad and Audrey had been divorced for several months and she was still as angry as a wasp in a dude's jockstrap.

"I think she needs to come to Utah for her own good. Your daughter will never forgive you if you leave her mom behind. Audrey absolutely must get in your car. There's no time to explain, and with her, explaining might take weeks."

"Damn…" Chad thought through how he was going to pull that off. Getting Audrey into his Jeep, under any pretext, would take some serious bullshitting. An airplane? No chance. But could he really tolerate being stuck in a car with that howling bobcat for nine hundred miles?

70

Jason was right and Chad knew it. Little Samantha would never forgive him if he left her mom behind. All bad feelings needed to be set aside right now if what Jason was saying was true. It sounded like warrior time, and all he really cared about in this world was that little girl. That meant Audrey came as part of the package.

"I hope you're right about how bad things are because, if I drag her into the car and I take off toward Salt Lake City, and then everything goes back to normal, the lawyers are going to have a good time with that one."

Jason wrapped up the call. "By the time you get back to Audrey and Sam in Omaha, you'll have no doubt the world is crashing. Dude, I'm looking out my balcony and I can see fires burning out of control in Ogden. No kidding. Get here fast."

"Okay," Chad agreed.

"Oh," Jason had one more thing to add, "you've always argued that the super-secret American oligarchs would never let a collapse happen. So, this goes on the LONG list of things when I was right and you were wrong."

"Screw you. I'll believe it when I see it." Chad laughed. "I'll see you in a few days. Keep everyone safe. Love you, brother."

"Godspeed." Jason hung up.

5

[Collapse Plus Four - Saturday, Sept. 23rd]

Shortwave Radio 7150kHz 2:30am

"YOUR SERVANT, JT TAYLOR HERE again, for another episode of As the World Burns.

"Saudis are flying bombing runs over Iran this fine evening in retaliation for Iran NUKING THEM. Lots of bang-bang over Tehran tonight. Couldn't happen to a nicer bunch of homophobic racists...

"The Russians are making a beer run into Ukraine in their T-90 main battle tanks, overrunning the entire country. It's like dad's out of town and the kids are breaking into the liquor cabinet and the stack of Playboys under the bed. No adult supervision in the world tonight, folks...

"Oh, and I have a bit of top secret news from a Drinkin' Bro in the 5th Fleet in the Med: Israel has rolled into the Sinai hammering the Egyptians once and for all. And our very own big boats are backing Israel's play.

"On a personal note, I'm running low on booze and I'm heading toward Arizona unless they blow me up first. I need a rendezvous with a certain Drinkin' Bro-ette who is holding a case of Leadslingers Whiskey for me, hopefully along with a badly-needed game of hide-the-sausage. I'll be the one rolling up in the Humvee bristling with antennas..."

Federal Heights
Salt Lake City, Utah

The view from the back of the kitchen had been the deal-clincher when Jimmy had bought his luxury home seven years ago.

At the end of the Avenues neighborhood, Federal Heights ran up against the University of Utah campus and the Jewish Community Center. Why anyone had built a Jewish Community Center in an almost completely Mormon town was a mystery to Jimmy. There must have been an underground Jewish crowd in Salt Lake because the Jewish Community Center looked fancier than anything except the Mormon Temple and the Mormon Tabernacle itself.

As the name implied, Federal Heights perched up on the high bench, with panoramic views of the Salt Lake Valley. They couldn't claim to be the richest neighborhood in Salt Lake, because the Heights had been built over a hundred years ago. Still, folks knew you had been blessed if you owned a home in Federal Heights.

Jimmy stood there mesmerized, his hands in his pockets, trying to decide if he was seeing fire or not. Almost ten miles across the valley, in what looked like West Jordan or Magna, he saw what looked like a plume of smoke, lazily reaching up to form a layer of haze, like a three-mile-wide mushroom. Six or seven miles to the north, mostly blocked out by his big cottonwood tree, Jimmy could see more smoke, maybe drifting south from Rose Park.

Jimmy knew his intelligence ran far above average. He had earned a scholarship to BYU, and that was no small feat. Even so, his mind struggled to accept the obvious truth—a reality that could be seen as plain as day through his bay window: Salt Lake had begun to burn.

He couldn't hear sirens from this distance and the evidence was hard to refute. Something gurgled and he felt that hard place in the pit of his stomach that had re-appeared two days ago. Every time he considered the danger brooding within that smoke a picture flashed to mind: his six-year-old daughter on Christmas morning in her Disney Princess pajamas.

Little Olivia was as smart as a whip and as sweet as a little girl could be. For Jimmy, she embodied purity and grace. He adored all his children, but his love wrapped around Olivia like a never-ending blanket.

What he saw out the bay window hinted at a malignancy beyond anything he'd ever faced. Jimmy was darn near certain he wasn't man enough to protect Olivia or his family from the maelstrom that smoke implied.

"Jim," a voice penetrated his foreboding like a slow knife. "JIM! I'm talking to you."

"Huh…" Jimmy turned, and his wife stood in front of him, a bit too close.

"What's wrong with you?" she asked rhetorically. "We need you to find all the flashlights in case the power doesn't come back on before night. We need flashlights and the Coleman stove so we can cook in here."

"Um." Jimmy came back to reality. "You don't need the Coleman. You can't run it inside anyway, I think, because of carbon monoxide. The stove works fine. Just light it with a match."

"We don't have matches, Jimmy. It's not like I'm a closet smoker."

Jimmy knew they were both on edge, so he let her snarky comment pass.

"We have matches in my backpack in the camping supplies. There's a whole box."

"Okay. Would you please get all the flashlights rounded up?"

"Sure, hon." Jimmy turned to the kitchen and began rummaging through the drawers looking for flashlights and "D" batteries.

• • •

Ross Homestead
Oakwood, Utah

I bet that's some kind of anti-tank gate, Alena thought to herself as they rolled up to the Homestead. "Wow. Somebody takes themselves seriously," she carped to her husband as she glanced at the two men bracketing the gate, armed with rifles.

She knew she wasn't angry with the Homestead people or with Jason and Jenna Ross. The events of the last two days had frazzled her, and she realized she was being irritable—pissed off that things weren't going her way, to say the least. Having her world out of control scared her. When Alena got scared, she got angry.

As a registered nurse, Alena had been invited to join the Homestead by one of the Ross brothers she knew back when she used to swing dance in college. She figured she had been invited because of her nursing background, but she never felt comfortable around the Homestead people.

Alena hated guns and, even though her husband served as a CBRN (Chemical, Biological, Radiological and Nuclear) specialist in the Utah National Guard, she would not allow firearms in her house.

Beyond the gate, the Homestead looked like a massive camp-out. Campers, trailers and a couple of RVs were jammed wherever they would fit. Military-style tents were going up on a big lawn, and people mulled about everywhere. Outside the gate, cars were parked tight on both sides of the street leading up to the entrance, all packed to the rafters with mattresses, chairs, coolers and camping equipment.

Her husband, Robert, pulled the car through the gate, and a big hairy guy she didn't know walked up to his open car window. Looking more Hell's Angel than helpful, the guy had long silver hair and a gun strapped to his belt. "Can I get your names, please?"

Robert answered, "Robert and Alena James."

"Great. I'm Ron. Do you want to sleep in the detached garage, or would you rather put up a tent on the Great Lawn?"

"Um, I think we'll need beds inside. We didn't bring a tent." Robert looked sheepish.

"That's great. We're running out of tent space anyway. Pull up the driveway, unload the stuff on this list, and then park back on the street. Leave everything not on the list in your car." Ron gave them a piece of paper. "Jordan will answer questions about the list when you get to the garage."

Robert thanked the big man and drove along the driveway to what must have been the "detached garage." A young man with a baseball cap approached them. He wore a handgun on his belt, too.

"Hey, I'm Jordan. Here's what you're gonna do… Did Ron give you a list?"

Robert nodded.

"Okay, you get two of these totes," the young man said, pointing to a tall stack of black plastic totes beside him. "It looks like you have kiddos back there. Okay, that'll be *three* totes for you guys. Everything you take with you into the detached garage *must* fit into these three totes. *Everything.* Otherwise, the garage will look like a tornado had sex with a garage sale. You follow me so far?"

Robert and Alena nodded.

"Anything you have on this list," Jordan pulled out another list, "we will inventory and store for you." Alena took the list from Robert and saw things like "extra prescription medicine" and "ammunition."

"Why are you keeping this stuff?" Alena asked, trying not to sound too aggressive. "Why wouldn't we keep it for ourselves?"

"Good question. That's the stuff we're pooling for everyone. We'll keep track of who gave it to us, but we'll probably all use it until it's gone."

Alena read the list while he was talking, and she stopped at "toilet paper."

She barked, "I'm supposed to give you our *toilet paper?*"

Jordan held up his hands in mock surrender. "Hey, I'm just telling you what everyone else has been contributing to the group. If you want to keep your toilet paper, that's your business. But everyone else is sharing this stuff. Oh, and if you have prescription medicine you're taking, keep it and report it to the head nurse."

"Who's the head nurse?" Alena asked, an edge to her voice.

Jordan searched around and came up with a clipboard that had been inside the top black tote. "The head nurse is Alena James."

"That's me," Alena replied.

"Awesome. You should probably go see the lady of the house. Jenna's right over there." Jordan pointed to an attractive woman in her early fifties, sitting behind a table talking to a gaggle of people. "She'll be stoked you made it."

As Alena and Robert loaded their personal belongings into the totes, she could see that their stuff wouldn't fit. She went back to the list she'd been handed at the gate.

The list made sense. It had everything they needed for daily life, such as rugged clothing, toothbrushes, towels, and such. It would be tight, and she didn't see how the kids' toys were going to fit. Down the list, she saw "kids' favorite toys." The Homestead people had thought of everything.

After she crammed the totes full and unloaded the car, she sent Robert to park on the street. Alena trundled down the stairs of the massive garage carrying a tote. As soon as she descended the stairs and looked around, the list and the totes made a lot more sense.

The basement of the garage reminded her of Costco, only it was people that were stacked on shelves instead of merchandise. She was pretty sure that the "bunks" were *actual* Costco shelving—with orange beams and steel mesh flooring.

Many of the people had already settled into their bed areas, with mattresses on each level of shelving and black totes stacked at the foot of each mattress. Layered like this on racking, she could see how the garage could house dozens of families.

Jesus help us if someone gets the flu.

Outside the big rolling door on the back of the garage was a large cook shed. Inside were three gigantic wood-burning stoves and, by the smell of it, someone had baked bread already. Inside the shed was an area large enough for five or six people to wash dishes or clothes around six huge industrial sinks. At that moment, someone was cutting up fresh vegetables, presumably for stew.

Alena had left the kids upstairs, so she headed back and found them playing. "Let's go, guys." She rounded up the little ones and made her way over to Jenna Ross, who was coordinating the mayhem from an eight-foot plastic table.

• • •

"Ron needs you at the gate." Jordan poked his head into Jason's office and interrupted him for the twentieth time that day.

"All right." Jason looked up from his list. He didn't bother asking Jordan what Ron needed. He could guess, and his gut filled with dread.

He walked down the driveway like a man heading to his execution. At the gate, he could see Ron talking to a family. As Jason recognized them, his heart sank even further.

This next week will be filled with this. Get used to it.

"Hi, Terry. Hi, Mark." Jason knew the family from church. As he approached the confrontation, he remembered how many times he had told Mark he loved him over the years. Maybe a dozen times?

Mark and Jason had grown close amidst the homeless of Salt Lake City's "Rio Grande" ghetto. They had spent countless hours sitting on the filthy concrete, listening to heroin addicts and schizophrenics mutter about their lives and their rocky relationships with God. He and Mark had seen God's apparent hand at work, over and over, as they listened to homeless men and women. Now, they stood on new ground, outside the black metal gates of the Homestead.

"We didn't know where to go," Mark launched into the inevitable explanation. "We're freaked out by the trouble we're seeing in the

78

city. We just had a van full of gang people drive down the street shooting at houses. We knew you had lots of guns, and we thought we could ride this out for a couple of days at your place until the authorities get things back to normal."

Mark looked across the drive at the multitude setting up tents and preparing to "ride this out" at the Homestead. "I guess we're not the only ones with that idea, right?" Mark said hopefully.

Jason had played this conversation in his mind a dozen times since first hearing about the nukes and the stock market. He knew it would come to this. As he had done many times before in business and in life, Jason reached down inside, envisioned a knob on his heart and turned the knob way down.

Jason had worked hard to grow his heart over the last few decades, expanding his humanity far beyond the sum of the traits that had been given him at birth. He suspected his personality resided somewhere along the slope of the Asperger's spectrum. He hated crowds. He liked being alone. He enjoyed project work more than being around people. Despite that, like a monk wearing a hair shirt, Jason forced himself into heavy human contact every day. However, when it was necessary, he could put steel in his back.

Jason knew he played a dangerous game when he turned that knob on his heart down; it was a game of chicken between the ties of humanness and the Devil himself. He also knew God stared directly into that tension, that He somehow occupied it. Under the eyes of God, Jason sensed that it was neither selfish nor inhuman to face suffering and refuse to blink.

"Mark, first of all, this almost certainly isn't a passing thing. This situation will get far worse and it'll stay bad for a long time. I want you to know this, and I beg you to believe me because the chance that your family will survive depends on you taking this seriously."

"What?" Mark looked confused. "Are you saying all these people can stay here and we can't?"

"Please, Mark, hear me out before you speak, okay?"

"Fine. But that's pretty hard to swallow." Mark physically choked back his desperation while anger played across his face. Then a primal urge to ingratiate himself—to somehow finagle a way past the black gate – took over and Mark's eyes shifted back and forth, searching for an argument.

Jason held out his hands, palms up. "All these people behind me have spent the last five years preparing for this day, and they built up this place for their families."

"You never asked us to join in all this. We would've helped!" Mark blurted out.

"True, but it wasn't my decision to make alone. For whatever reason, I never put you forward to be a part of this group. I have to live with that. But, Mark, you're fighting me when you should be listening to me. You need to get out of Salt Lake City and get someplace rural. Maybe somewhere you have family. You need to do it right now."

Mark's eyes narrowed. "So that's it. That's where your fellowship ends?"

"I suppose that's one way to say it. I'm sure you won't understand, but I'm praying for you and your family." Jason could feel his grip on that knob to his heart weaken.

"Let's go, guys." Mark gathered his family and walked back down the street to their car. His wife looked back, angry and bewildered.

Jason turned to Ron. "One down. Two hundred to go."

"Fuck me," Ron replied, "I don't know how you can do that."

"Me neither." They both laughed, trying to shake the tension. Jason suddenly wrapped his arms around Ron, hugging the massive, hairy man like he was hanging onto a barrel in the ocean.

The knob trembled but Jason held. He let Ron go and turned away. As he walked back up the drive, he took a deep breath.

"Motherfucker," Jason whispered to himself, speaking his tension into the fall afternoon.

Two hours later, Jason pulled out of the Homestead gates in his Ford F-350. Driving around town in a Tesla or a Range Rover would draw attention and could get him robbed or killed. He hadn't been off the property in a few days and this might be the last time he would take a drive around town.

He glanced up at the sky, exceptionally grateful for the chance to take this drive. He had four children still "out there" and one of those four, hopefully, would be landing at the Salt Lake airport any minute.

One of Jason's daughters was married to an Air Force medic stationed in northern California. His oldest boy served in the United States Marine Corps, deployed in Iraq. His seventeen-year-old son had been visiting Jenna's grandparents on the Olympic Peninsula in Washington and, hopefully, was on his way home by car. His daughter Emily had caught, quite possibly, the last flight departing Baltimore, Maryland, where she attended medical school at Johns Hopkins.

He had begged her to get on a plane for a couple of days, but the flights had been booked solid. Jason used every bit of pull he had with his American Express Black Card and a huge block of SkyMiles to finagle her ticket. He had no idea how the plane would be landing without electricity at the airport. He decided they must have back-up generators.

Four hours earlier, Emily called him from the plane. She had boarded and the doors were closing. Jason had literally done everything he could to avoid having a daughter stuck in the midst of twelve million confused, hungry East coasters.

When Jason and Emily visited Johns Hopkins years ago, he had huge misgivings. While it might have been the preeminent med school in the country, there was nothing posh about the neighborhood surrounding Johns Hopkins. Tucked up against Baltimore, the level of obvious crime scared him, even though he had grown up near the gangs of southern California himself.

When Emily had been accepted at Johns Hopkins, Jason put together a multi-tiered escape plan in case the world ever went through a collapse. It had been the weirdest thing Jason had ever done with his money, so he kept the plan secret from everyone he could.

Option Number One, thankfully the option that had ultimately panned out, had been for Emily to board a plane immediately when things got funky. This option led to a couple of instances where Emily had missed class due to "false alarm" trips back to Utah: once, when there had been a bad flu virus and another when the stock market took a big, but recoverable, downturn. Jason felt sheepish, like a tinfoil-hatted survivalist, when things returned to normal both times. Emily wisely lied to her friends about the true reason for her unscheduled trips home.

Option Number Two had been the "Escape Pod," as Emily called it. Over the course of two trips to Maryland, and countless hours of research, Jason engineered a plan for Emily to drive from the East Coast to Utah. This prepper escapade cost him about twenty-five-thousand dollars, a price he had been happy to pay to buy his daughter some hope of making it out of the East if society's bubble burst. All the equipment he bought now sat moldering in a "Storage Suite" in the Hampden EZ Storage close to the Johns Hopkins campus.

He thought about the Escape Pod as he drove toward the airport. Somebody was going to be a happy camper when they looted that place. The plan was for Emily to back her SUV into the storage unit, connect the trailer to the hitch, toss everything into the cargo compartment and drive like hell westward. The trailer carried a pair of ultra-light motorcycles that had been purchased based on two qualifications: could they go a long way on little gas, and could they support large panniers?

By Jason's calculations, the gas in the SUV, the gas on the trailer and the gas in the motorcycles would get Emily and a companion from Maryland to Utah. Accomplishing that feat would be harder than one might think, and it required bending the Hampden EZ Storage rules a fair bit when it came to the storage of fuels and ammunition.

Among other violations of the rules, the Escape Pod contained a hundred fifty gallons of unleaded gas and two thousand rounds of ammunition, along with two handguns, two AK-47 assault rifles, sixteen high capacity magazines, four cases of MREs (Meals Ready to Eat,) a half-dozen maps, a ham radio base station, two ham handsets, twenty-five-hundred dollars in gold and silver, and two thousand dollars in cold, hard cash. Costing as much as everything else combined, Jason bit the bullet and included two pairs of white phosphor night vision goggles (NVGs).

All of that premium survival gear… all gone to waste.

It had taken a few tries, but eventually Jason had enlisted a Baltimore-area Army Ranger on Craigslist to go shooting with Emily and teach her to ride the motorcycles. It hadn't hurt his proposition to the Army Ranger that Emily was exceedingly easy on the eyes.

Option One had prevailed and his daughter Emily had made her plane ride home. Jason would never get to meet the Ranger kid in person. While he wove his way through stalled cars and broken traffic patterns heading toward the airport, he texted a message to the Ranger kid, hoping the text would go through on his end.

I left a bunch of gear you're going to want in storage unit A5 at the Hampden EZ Storage. Bring a pair of bolt cutters. Thank you for taking care of Emily. Merry Christmas. Enjoy the NVGs.

Jason pulled into Salt Lake International Airport. People flooded the terminal with strange baggage—heirloom furniture, old-fashioned trunks and family picture albums; everyone was trying to get somewhere, anywhere else.

When he saw Emily at the curb, Jason's heart leapt, intensely grateful to have her home. She jumped into his arms as soon as he pulled in and stepped out the driver's side door.

"Oh, my God, Daddy, that was the weirdest flight ever. People were freaking out."

"I'm so glad you made it," he said as he smelled her hair, feeling like he could breathe a little better.

• • •

Fisker Residence
Omaha, Nebraska

Chad knew that the longer he sat outside in his Jeep, the more likely it would be that Audrey's dad would see him and come hassle him.

Audrey's parents had never been fans of Chad Wade. From Chad's point of view, her mom was a huge bitch, and her dad had surrendered his balls a long time back. When Audrey left Chad and headed home to her parents with their daughter Samantha, there must have been a mighty rag-fest in the Fisker home that day.

Since then, it had only gotten worse. Visiting Samantha was an exercise in intense humiliation, orchestrated by Chad's ex-wife and her mother. Every minute, they would hover over Chad, like self-appointed social workers for his "supervised visits."

There wasn't a damned thing in their divorce decree about supervised visits—Chad had full rights to visitation—but Audrey and her mom enjoyed making him squirm.

On the drive into Omaha, Chad got a front row seat to the collapse of America. Jason had been right; this was indeed the Apocalypse. At one point that morning, Chad had been forced to gun the Jeep and go rip-tearing through the grass around a roadblock that was being set up on a small town highway. There was no way he was going to stop and leave himself and his gear at the mercy of small town law enforcement.

As he made the sweeping turn into Omaha, onto the high-bridged belt route, Chad could see fires burning in the dense parts of town. On the opposite side of the freeway, the one leading out of town, cars were stacked bumper to bumper, barely moving.

Now he sat in his Jeep in front of Audrey's childhood home, not looking forward to the coming confrontation. And, yep, as predicted, Audrey's dad trudged out the front door with a rifle in his hands. He walked around to the driver's side window.

"G'morning, Chad." Robert mumbled. "I guess it's afternoon." He chuckled uncomfortably.

"Good morning, Robert." Chad stayed in his Jeep, talking through the open window.

"I'm not an idiot," Robert began unsteadily. "I know what I am, I know what my daughter is, and I sure as hell know what my wife is."

Chad wasn't following. He had serious doubts Robert actually did know who all those people were. *When in doubt, say nothing.* That was another one of Chad's life mottoes.

Robert shuffled. "I need you to take Audrey and the baby and go. Leave here. Go back to your Navy SEAL buddies or wherever you need to go to protect them. That okay with you?"

Flummoxed, Chad didn't know what to say. He nodded.

"Here's what I'm going to do," Robert continued. "I'm going to grab you a bunch of supplies from the house and the garage. I want you to load it all up in your rig. How about you just stay outside the house for now? That okay?"

"All right, Robert. Then what?"

"Then," Robert thought for a second, "I'm going to go inside and bring Audrey and Samantha out and I want you to leave with them."

"Um, are you sure you can pull that off?" Chad had serious doubts about Robert getting anyone or anything past his wife.

"Chad, this isn't going to end well." Robert waved the rifle barrel around, gesturing at the city. "I'm pretty sure you love our granddaughter, and that you stand a fair chance of keeping them both alive. Will you promise me to keep them both alive?"

"Robert, I will."

"Okay, then. Come get the stuff." Chad jumped down from the Jeep and followed Robert into his messy garage. They picked through piles of gear looking for useful supplies. Gas cans. Water jugs. A pair of binoculars. A compound bow with a quiver of arrows. Sleeping bags and a bunch of camping gear. Robert poked around until he found things that might be useful and handed them to his former son-in-law. Chad carried it all to the Jeep.

The front screen door banged open and Chad's ex-mother-in-law stormed onto the front lawn.

"What in the name of Jesus are you doing, Robert?"

"Reyna, go back in the house. I'm doing what I can for our daughter and our granddaughter."

Reyna stood with her hands on her hips. "You're not doing any such thing, especially not with *this person.*" She spat the last two words.

Robert handed his rifle to Chad, sighed, and walked over to his wife. He took her by the arm and Chad could see his aging muscles tighten as he steered her toward the front stoop.

"Now is not the time for your... *nonsense*, Reyna. Please get back in the house, and I will come talk to you shortly."

Reyna huffed and sputtered, not accustomed to Robert talking to her like that. Muttering, she went back inside.

Robert returned to the garage and to Chad. "That gear's about all I've got. I'll have Audrey bring out some food, too. Why don't you wait out here for a bit?"

"Okay, Robert." Chad's confidence in Robert had gone up six hundred percent in the last two minutes. In any case, what else could Chad do? Robert was his huckleberry, either way.

As soon as the screen door clacked shut, Chad heard shouting erupt from the house—Robert's booming bass, which Chad had never heard before, and Reyna's shrill soprano, which Chad had heard plenty of times. Then Audrey's pleading tenor joined the fray. Back and forth, inaudible except for tone, until a long and hardy stretch of bass ended the debate.

"That sounded promising," Chad said out loud to nobody.

About twenty minutes later, an angry, weeping Audrey blew through the front door, her mother close behind carrying little Samantha, dragging a car seat. Audrey carried a huge box of canned food, and she refused to look at Chad.

Chad stepped back, saying nothing, while the women loaded the cargo into the Jeep.

"I'll get that." Chad took the car seat from Reyna and went to work securing it in the backseat.

While the ladies buckled Samantha into her car seat, with tearful kisses and hugs from her grandma, Robert stepped up to Chad.

"I want you to take this." Robert placed the scoped bolt-action rifle in Chad's hands. Then he reached into his pocket and pulled out a box. "Here's 30-06 ammo for it." Robert slowly placed the box of shells in Chad's other hand.

"Son," he looked Chad in the eyes, "we've had our differences. But, man to man, I'm trusting you with my two most precious things."

"I understand, Robert. I'll protect them. Are you sure you'll be okay without the rifle?"

"Well," Robert drawled, "whatever happens to us, it'll be okay so long as you keep those two safe."

"You have my word." Chad climbed into the driver's seat.

"Reyna, say your goodbyes, please. They need to leave now," Robert ordered his wife.

As the divorced couple and their daughter drove down the street away from Audrey's home, Chad felt certain he should say something to his ex-wife. She was coming undone before his very eyes.

The moment he made the slightest exhale, as if to say something, she pounced. "Don't say a single word, Chad Wade! Not a single damn word."

Well, Chad thought, I guess I should count my blessings.

6

"THIS IS JT TAYLOR, COMING to you from an undisclosed location, thoroughly pickled in fine liquor, bringing you the news that makes the FCC, NSA, FBI and CIA piss themselves.

"First of all, nice try, Army Electronic Warfare team. I enjoyed the fireball when you hit my $129 repeater with your $1.5 million missile. Better luck next time. I'm still here, drunk dialing the world with your dirty secrets.

"Word on the street has it that the commander of Fort Bliss has seized control of the town of El Paso. I always knew that guy was a tyrant. Enjoy martial law, boys and girls. It's coming to a town near you.

"And… in the Middle Eastern dumpster fire: Iran GLASSED a chunk of Saudi Arabia yesterday, according to Drinkin' Bros in-theater. I guess Iran had nukes after all. How's it feel to get PLAYED, Mr. Obama?

"Closer to home, Marines at Camp LaJeune report that their base is closed up tighter than a Baptist girl's nethers. The Marines are going au natural without civilian contractors or outside support. Hey, if a cockroach can survive it, so can a Marine, I guess..."

Ross Homestead
Oakwood, Utah

As much as he would love to strangle Jeff Kirkham sometimes—which was likely impossible because Jeff didn't appear to have a neck—Jason felt like he might share some of his stress with the Green Beret. In Jason's mind, Jeff had slid into the role of second in command. Plus, Jason liked talking to Jeff. Jeff never failed to deliver perspective.

Jason walked down the drive with purpose, avoiding all eyes and sending out the vibe that he was on important business, which wasn't really true. Jeff was giving a property patrol last-minute instructions.

"Hey, Jeff, you got a second?"

"Sure." Jeff wrapped up and sent the armed men off, marching into the hills around the Homestead.

Jason dove right in. "I've sent probably fifteen families away today at the gate, and it makes me want to put a bullet in my head."

"No, it doesn't," Jeff snapped, rejecting Jason's hyperbole.

"Right, but you get what I mean. This is screwed up. If the collapse gets any worse, those people I sent away will die. There's no way I can reel those families back if we decide we can help them later. Those families are gone forever. Am I doing the right thing?" Jason laid it out, exasperated, hoping Jeff would bear some of the weight.

Jeff responded with certainty. "First off, it's not your decision. You're executing the decisions we made together when we set up this hard point. We have enough food for our people, plus seventy of their extended families based on our projected harvest from the greenhouses. We've already handed out the extra family slots, so that's a done deal. It's not your call. Send someone else to handle the gate if it's bothering you, because who stays and who goes isn't your call anymore."

Jason's eyebrows went heavy. "These are my friends I'm sending them away to starve. The least I can do is face them."

"Okay. Do whatever you need to do, but don't talk to anyone else like you're talking to me."

Jason cocked his head, a question in his eyes.

"You're making this personal," Jeff explained, "as though this whole collapse and Homestead thing is all about you and your feelings. Yes, you did set this all up originally, but that was then and this is now. This ain't no vanity project anymore. Hobby time is over. My family's life is on the line and you're talking as though this is some kind of popularity contest. Focus up."

Jason rubbed his face. "So, tell me then, how am I supposed to feel about dealing out death at those gates every day?"

"Consider this." Jeff turned and walked away a bit, finding an old stump on the edge of the forest to sit on. Jason followed him and remained standing. "Consider a convenience store with twenty people inside when a volcano erupts and buries the store in a hundred feet of ash. Among those twenty people are a nutritionist and a meteorologist."

Jason raised an eyebrow. "Is this a joke? Like when a German, an Irishman, and a Mexican walk into a bar?"

"Of course not. It's a hypothetical scenario from one of my instructors in SERE school. So picture that convenience store right after the volcano eruption. The meteorologist knows for certain that it'll take exactly ninety days for rescuers to dig them out. The nutritionist does an inventory of the store and calculates that, at near-starvation levels, only eight of the twenty people can possibly survive, and that's assuming the remaining twelve are killed immediately."

"Apparently, the model excludes cannibalism," Jason quipped.

"Affirmative. My first question, what's likely to happen?"

Jason thought about it for a second. "Based on my experience of most people, I'm guessing they won't make a decision at all. They'll do nothing."

Jeff nodded. "Right. Then everyone dies. In ninety days, when rescuers get there, the place will be wall-to-wall corpses because the food and water would've run out."

"So what's the *best* way?" Jason could think of a number of alternatives. "Women and children first" came immediately to mind.

"People often think that it could be handled with a lottery or some sort of voting system. But, in reality, for that to happen, a strong man would have to arise to enforce the lottery or whatever selection method they chose."

Jason was skeptical. With Jeff, things often came down to the need for a strong man.

"I'd like to think that people could come up with a benevolent solution," Jason argued.

"People might do that, but when it came time to murder twelve people, no matter how they were selected, it'd take a real asshole to make that happen."

Jeff was making sense, but Jason objected out of habit. "If there was a real asshole in the group, wouldn't he just choose himself, his family and the women he wanted to screw?"

"That's a strong possibility but, even in that case, the survivability of the group would be maximized. Think about it. Eight people would survive. In the alternative, all would die."

Jason objected again. "Yeah, but those who survive might not be the best people."

Jeff and his instructor had already thought of that. "For the 'best people' to survive, not only would the strong man enforce the elimination of some, but *he* would have to survive, too."

"Hold on," Jason argued, "if the strong guy is benevolent, he'd never let someone die in his place."

"He'd have to," Jeff disagreed. "Without the strong man, discipline would break down, someone would take more than their share, then everyone would take more than their share and they'd all die. In order to ensure the survival of the other seven, he would have to be one of the eight who survive, even if that means a child or pregnant woman dies in his stead. The group would insist on it if they had any sense."

"That's harsh, but probably true." Jason could see the parallels to their current situation. "If the 'convenience store' scenario were to go down, the benevolent strong man system would rarely happen. It'd take the perfect strong man—a guy with noble intentions *and* a guy who would vote for himself to live."

"Right. And you're describing a benevolent warlord. That's why my instructor and I had the conversation in the first place. We were in the business of setting up warlords."

"Does that make me the warlord?" Jason said, not comfortable with the idea.

"No. You're getting carried away. This is not about *you*. This Homestead. *We* are the warlord. Our group decides who lives and who dies. No matter how it feels, we have to execute on our plan. Otherwise, we'll end up being a convenience store full of corpses before this is over."

Jason sighed heavily. "Okay. Thanks, I suppose."

Jeff sat silently and Jason thought about Jeff and Tara for a second. Many of the Kirkhams' own family members were still out there on their own—most of Jeff's brothers and sisters hadn't taken his invitation to come seek shelter at the Homestead. Tara's parents and her brothers had refused to come to the Homestead, too, preferring their family cabin in the woods.

"That helps. Thanks." Jeff stood and they shook hands. Intellectually, Jason walked away with new perspective. Emotionally, nothing had changed.

• • •

On her third day at the Homestead, Jacquelyn approached Jenna, the lady of the house.

"Hey, Jenna, how's it going?"

Jacqueline gawked at Jenna's simple beauty, perhaps the most elegant fifty-year-old woman she'd ever seen.

Jenna blew a lock of auburn hair out of her eyes. "It's a regular three-ring circus around here. I answer questions all day and, truth is, I'm making it up as I go. I never was the Survival Lady. I spent more time on yoga and Pilates than on canning."

"Well," Jacquelyn said, "I can probably help you there. As you can tell from my thoroughly average figure, I didn't put much time into yoga and Pilates. As fate would have it, I do know a thing or two about canning. You want help?"

"Oh, boy, do I ever."

Two hours later, Jacquelyn sat working alone in a concrete box— a root cellar that held the Homestead's bucketed food. She hauled buckets outside, organizing them into piles of sugar, dried milk, beans, pasta and dried veggies.

The Homestead had a couple of thousand pounds of freeze-dried entrees, but the bulk of their food was hardy, inexpensive dried food. Jacquelyn had been there, five years ago, setting it all up. They had figured out how to get an entire year's supply, at two thousand calories a day, for only five hundred bucks per adult. It had required finding the cheapest bulk source, then sealing everything in surplus plastic food grade buckets.

The buried root cellar kept the dried food cool without air conditioning, but it made for cold and clammy work. Jacquelyn borrowed someone else's gloves, since God only knew where her gloves had ended up.

She could have asked others to help, but she needed time to herself. Jacquelyn fought to keep it together, imagining her loved ones and how scared they must be in Texas—her sister, her niece and nephews, and her mother. Cell service had dropped between Salt Lake and Texas the day before, so her imagination ran wild.

She kept imagining her family glued to their radio, yearning for some good bit of news that might allay their fears. No doubt, they remembered she and Tom's warnings over the years about a collapse. Back then, her family had either ignored them or joked about their paranoia. She had thought Tom a little over the top at moments, too, but she had conceded to him about preparing, for the kids' safety, if nothing else.

Driving home from Texas, she and Tom had often criticized her sister and brother-in-law for their blind faith in the government. While the kids slept in the back seat of their truck, they took pleasure in running Jacquelyn's family down, repeating back stupid things they had said and chiding them for their "sheep-like" trust in America. Back then, she and Tom enjoyed feeling "right"—being smart enough to see the inherent risks in modern civilization.

Years later, sitting on a plastic bucket in a concrete bunker with civilization crumbling by the day, Jacquelyn now knew the truth. *She* had been the fool. *She* had been the one on a power trip. Yes, she and Tom had seen through the thin optimism of American prosperity. So, what had they done with that foresight? They had used it to feel superior. Now her sister and her family would probably die horrific deaths.

All that rightness was gone, replaced by foreboding and shame. Any sense of victory vanished and it left behind only deep regret. She would trade all the rightness in the world to put just one of these goddamn buckets of food in the middle of her sister's living room in Galveston.

If she had been a little less self-righteous about preparing, maybe her sister and brother-in-law would have come around, at least enough to store a little bit. Or, maybe she could have given them some of her own food storage when they went down to visit. The Homestead had already set aside enough food for Jacquelyn and Tom. Why did they need their own food storage, too? They could have taken at least some of that extra food to Texas over Christmas last year. They'd had enough space in back of the truck for it. She had been so caught up feeling disdainful of her sister's reliance on the government that she didn't stop to think about simply giving her food storage. It was extra, for Christ's sake!

Jacquelyn slumped on the bucket outside the root cellar and cried. Her hands in someone else's gloves, she cried for her sister and for her family. She cried for shame in her own pride. She cried for what they were all losing and what might never return.

Why couldn't that beautiful world have kept going? Why couldn't they have lived forever in a society where a pasteurized gallon of milk waited just five minutes away on a chilled market shelf? Why couldn't food keep crossing the oceans, landing on their doorsteps as if by magic? Why did things have to go to hell and leave her sister, nieces and nephews terrified and probably starving?

A hand touched her shoulder and Jacquelyn jumped. It was Jenna Ross. Jacquelyn pulled herself together, wiping her nose on the sleeve of her jacket.

"Hey, girl, you need a hug?" Jenna helped her up from the bucket.

Jacquelyn threw her arms around Jenna and began crying again.

"I'm so worried about my family…" she muttered between the sobs. "My sister's in Galveston and I'm pretty sure they don't have any food or water at all."

"I'm so sorry," Jenna consoled her. "We need to hope and pray for our families. We need to pray for them to be clever and strong. There's a chance they can figure this out and pull through. There's a chance, Jacquelyn. We need to hope and pray they'll make it."

Jacquelyn and Jenna stood there for a long time holding one another, two women crying in a stumpy forest of white buckets amidst the death throes of America.

• • •

Road 199A
Outside Lewellen, Nebraska

His former father-in-law's binoculars were the crappiest binos he'd ever used, but Chad was glad to have them. He had been watching the bridge over the North Platte River for half an hour. He had already reconnoitered and rejected three other bridges—all of them being used as choke points for local towns to control ingress into their areas.

Chad knew if he went through enough roadblocks, someone would steal his supplies. He figured it would be best to avoid human interaction at all costs, and roadblocks were the worst kind of human interaction.

He hoped that the bridge on Road 199A had been overlooked by the town of Lewellen. He had already rejected the bigger bridge to the east, since the town had placed a roadblock of concrete barricades and a couple of trashed-out recreational vehicles.

This bridge looked like it had been built by drunken teenagers compared to that bridge, and Chad hoped against hope it was open, as unlikely as that might be. He glanced at his watch and decided to observe the bridge for forty-five minutes and then take a shot at crossing.

A few minutes later, he had run out of patience and hopped back in his Jeep.

"Keep down across this bridge."

Chad and Audrey communicated for survival and nothing more. Audrey shifted in her seat, slouching down.

Chad gunned the Jeep and careened onto the road, making a hard run at the bridge. Before committing, he slammed on the brakes, hoping to sucker someone out into the open.

Sure enough, an old pickup truck jumped the gun and popped out onto the road trying to catch him in the open on the bridge.

"Dumbass rednecks," Chad said aloud.

He yearned to pull out Robert's 30-06 and kill the man in that truck. Chad felt no compunction about opening a dude's melon if that dude meant to ambush his family, as this asshole clearly meant to do. But Chad had overcome the unchecked compulsion to attack long ago. This situation was no "close ambush" where he had no choice but to fight. He could back out now and live to fight another day.

In the SEAL teams, the mantra went something like this: "Any time you find yourself in a gunfight that you didn't plan, *you* are being ambushed. Never fight the other guy's ambush unless you have no other choice."

This time, Chad had a choice. He threw the Jeep into reverse and boogied backward onto Road 44.

Just five days after two nukes and the stock market destabilizing, the Midwest turned feudal. Every town had walled itself up to prevent enemy ingress. After today, Chad would travel only by night.

In two days, he had covered only two hundred twenty miles, a third of the way to Salt Lake City. But that wasn't his biggest problem. They had slowed down. With all the barricades and probable ambushes, Chad couldn't run in his favorite mode—speed over security. They barely crept along, making time-consuming detours to avoid the interstate and population centers.

The shit had undeniably hit the fan. Even tiny towns had hardened their chokepoints and were pointing guns at the highways and byways.

Chad couldn't imagine how difficult it would be to move on foot with his pissed-off ex-wife and their three-year-old daughter. Moving overland on foot four hundred miles with two dependents penciled out to certain death, if not from evildoers, then certainly from the elements. No matter what, they needed a vehicle in order to make it to Salt Lake City.

His second biggest problem was fuel. Even with the extra gas cans Audrey's dad had given him, they would be lucky to make it half-way to Utah. Chad would be forced to steal gas, and gas theft could get him killed faster than trying to outdrink an Irishman.

With that said, he had squirreled away two secret weapons in the back of his Jeep: NVGs and a GasTapper.

The world thought of American operators like gods of the battlefield. Chad wondered how much of that perception depended on the shit they pulled off thanks to NVGs. Always operating at night, teams of SEALs, Rangers and other cheating bastards of the USA could catch the suckers sleeping. Rolling up the bad guys wasn't nearly as difficult when they were sawing logs, dreaming about their seventy-two virgins.

Chad expected the same applied to Midwesterners, except they would be dreaming about Budweiser, and Chad Wade would be the guy stealing their gas.

The GasTapper completed his plan. While internet survival experts droned on about siphoning gas or spiking gas tanks and draining fuel in the Apocalypse, neither of these approaches worked for a good goddamn. Chad had tried both those methods on a video he shot for ReadyMan and they had been forced to scrap the video. Auto makers made it nearly impossible. Fuel tank necks had become engineering works of art, with an endless number of ways to keep folks from stealing gas. Siphoning a tank was easier said than done.

Even though most gas tanks were composed of plastic, it was always *heavy* plastic and close to the lowest point on a vehicle. Working under a low-slung car with a screwdriver and a catch basin required skills worthy of a Chinese contortionist. Then, after wedging your cranium, hammer and spike between the tank and the ground, you would have to bang away at the tank for a dangerously long time to pierce it just to see if the damned thing had any gas.

But all was not lost. The GasTapper hacked the anti-siphon system of almost every modern vehicle. With a series of tubes and a twelve-volt pump, Chad's field tests convinced him this was the ticket for stealing gas during a Zombie Apocalypse.

He never imagined it would really happen—he thought all that talk of a collapse was akin to fantasy football for outdoors guys—and the GasTapper was only in his Jeep because he forgot to give it back to Jason after running product tests. The catastrophic mess in the back of his Jeep made such an oversight entirely plausible.

The same couldn't be said for the NVGs. Those he had straight up stolen from Jason's vault. Considering the situation, he felt confident Jason wouldn't mind.

Better to ask forgiveness instead of permission, another informal mantra of the SEALs.

• • •

Federal Heights
Salt Lake City, Utah

The meeting crammed the chapel and the cultural hall, filling every seat and along the walls.

Jimmy McGavin noticed that half these people didn't show up for church on Sunday. Otherwise, Sunday services would be full to the gills. Now, with their rear ends in the proverbial sling, everyone in the neighborhood was suddenly a Mormon.

Attending Sunday services wasn't the *only* commandment. Storing a year's supply of food was also the holy word of the prophets and he had ignored it, just like most of the people in this chapel. Thinking again of the shrinking supply of food in his home, his throat constricted. They had enough canned goods for about three days and a bucketed "two-weeks' supply" that Jimmy bought from the Boy Scouts three years ago. The contents of the bucket read like something out of the Great Depression: five pounds of wheat, some dried milk, dried pinto beans and a bit of dried macaroni. He didn't own a wheat grinder or yeast, so the two-week supply added up to just a few days of food for his wife and four children.

Jimmy's whole hope, shamefully, rested on the verdict of his ward leader, the bishop, now speaking at the front of the chapel. The question of food weighed on everyone. So far, water still flowed through the pipes in Federal Heights, though the bishop asked them to use it only for drinking, as the concrete reservoir above their neighborhood would soon run dry.

Jimmy wished the bishop would quit dancing around the topic and just tell them: would the Church provide food?

"I've been instructed by the stake president to let you know that the Church doesn't have enough food in Salt Lake City to help all the wards. We must rely upon our own food storage to get us through these troubled times until help arrives."

The chapel erupted in angry chatter, which would normally never happen. Of course, many of those in attendance weren't regular churchgoers.

Someone shouted, "What if my family doesn't have food?" While Jimmy never spoke out of turn in the chapel, it had been the question on his mind, too.

The bishop shifted his weight on his feet before speaking. "We can figure that out between neighbors," he answered.

The bishop must have his own year's supply handled, Jimmy concluded.

The same guy from before shouted again. "But what if my neighbors won't share? Will Mormons be sharing only with other Mormons?" Jimmy figured the guy talking must be a non-member. This meeting wouldn't take long to get ugly, he realized. When the bishop didn't answer, the non-member guy continued. "You could *make* the Mormons share their food with the whole neighborhood."

The room exploded with angry conversation, and a member of Jimmy's ward, Bert Johanssen, shouted, "Those of us who followed the commandment to store food shouldn't be forced to do anything. It's *our family's* food."

People began shouting over one another, drowning out the bishop.

"Bishop! You can't ask us to put our families in jeopardy to feed the whole ward—even the non-members…"

"You FUCKING Mormons with your high and mighty bullshit…"

"How dare you come into this chapel only when it serves your interests and use language like that…"

100

"How dare YOU think your children are the only ones worthy to eat your precious food…"

The bishop tried to restore order, but he had nothing new to add. The crowd continued in its fear and rage until a scuffle broke out, probably for the first time ever in the history of the Federal Heights chapel. Jimmy couldn't see who was fighting nor did he really want to know. The whole scene made him sick to his stomach.

"Please leave," the bishop shouted from the pulpit. "Please go home and work this out between neighbors."

The fight broke up and people streamed out of the chapel, grumbling.

Jimmy walked home alone. He felt the crushing weight of a man failing his family.

Jimmy knew obedience was an all-or-nothing equation. He couldn't count himself among the faithful if he obeyed *most* of the commandments. While he had always known this, today he knew it on a new level. His stomach twisted precariously. For a moment, he felt like he might vomit on Sister Nelson's lawn. He had failed his family by sloughing off a commandment of the Lord, by ignoring the prophets.

He walked through his front door and came face to face with his wife, who had stayed home with the children, her hands slowly curling around each other. Luckily, the kids were someplace else.

"What did the bishop say?" she demanded.

"The Church doesn't have food right now." He softened the bad news. "They can't help just yet. We need to make our food storage stretch."

She looked in his eyes. "James, we do not have *food storage*. That little Boy Scout bucket doesn't count as food storage. We can't eat dried beans and wheat kernels."

"We're going to have to make do, at least until help arrives." Jimmy studied the floorboards.

7

"GOOD MORNING, AMERICA. BY THE way, you're on fire.

"Baltimore, New York, Boston, D.C., Detroit... I'm hearing chatter all night long about cities lighting up the sky like bonfires. A National Guard Bro-ette in Maryland just called in to say that they went to retake D.C. from the criminal element but they couldn't get out the gates of the base because of gridlock.

"I got a bounce off the ionosphere from our boys in Afghanistan and they tell me that the U.S. is flying sorties in support of the Saudis against Iran. Stick a fork in them. Iran is done. BUT, not before they scored chemical weapons hits against Mecca and Tabuk.

"For all of you fleeing out of the shit-show of southern California, don't head south. Camp Pendleton's closed the freeway. And why would you want to go to Mexico anyway? Pretty sure the cartels control northern Mexico by now..."

• • •

Ross Homestead
Oakwood, Utah

"Did I hear correctly? Did one of our men shoot at a hiker?" Nurse Alena was like a brushfire, whipping through the Homestead, igniting anything that would burn.

Jeff looked straight at her. "Yes. Only it wasn't a hiker."

"Were they on Ross property?"

"They were within our zone of control," Jeff replied stonily.

Alena's eyes widened with disbelief. "And what the hell is a 'zone of control,' if I may ask?"

"It's the buffer zone we patrol to turn people around before they disappear into our AO… our Area of Operation. If we don't stop them there, then we have to shoot them on our doorstep, here." Jeff pointed down at the ground.

"Why," Alena paused for effect, "is it necessary to shoot *anyone?*"

"Because, if we don't hold our boundaries, we'll be overrun and we'll all die."

"So let me get this straight," Alena said, "you've instructed your men to shoot at people passing by on *public land* just so there's no chance that we're overrun by the hordes that we haven't actually seen yet. Is that right?"

"Affirmative," Jeff said. "I don't expect you to understand."

"Don't talk down to me," Alena fumed. "I've been saving lives as long as you've been taking them, so don't act like I'm a child who doesn't understand how things work. You're going to start killing the neighbors here in a few days and I'm going to be complicit in *murder* because I'm part of this group. I'm telling you right now, I won't let that happen."

Alena had more experience than just saving lives, but she wasn't going to mention her experience with violent, controlling men in this conversation with Jeff Kirkham. She had been raised by what people

103

called a "mean drunk." Her father never laid a hand on her, but he had beaten her brothers senseless on numerous occasions. A few times, he had sent their mother to the emergency room for stitches.

When Alena was sixteen, she called the police while her father delivered a savage beating to her younger brother for leaving a screwdriver to rust in the yard. The police arrived and things got complicated. Her father served as a policeman himself in a neighboring town and the local cops caught him red-handed, beating the boy.

The consequences had been severe, with her father demoted and narrowly avoiding losing his career. Her mother had sent Alena off to live with her aunt for fear of reprisals. Alena never returned home to live, and she and her father gave one another a wide berth to this very day.

If she could face down a violent, overbearing alcoholic, she could face down the likes of Jeff Kirkham.

Jeff summed up his position. "I'm telling you that I'm going to protect this hard point, whatever it takes. If you don't like it, you can leave."

Alena spat back, "Or YOU can leave."

"I'm not leaving," Jeff stated flatly.

"Mark my words: you cannot control this situation." Alena took in the valley with her hand. "And you won't be able to force and *murder* your way out of danger here. If you try, innocent people will die and their blood will be on your hands."

"I'm prepared to pay that price if it means my family survives," Jeff replied.

"You think so, but you will not be prepared. Men like you say you will pay the price, but people like me end up doing the bloody work… and we end up doing all the grieving, too."

Alena turned and stormed back toward the infirmary.

• • •

"What happened out there?" Jason asked Jeff later that afternoon.

Jeff and Jason walked toward the office and suspended the conversation until they could get behind closed doors.

"Jeremy was on duty at the upper valley observation post, and a small group of trespassers crossed our *No Trespassing* line. Jeremy called to the overwatch guy—it was Tom—and Tom fired a warning shot. He didn't hit anyone."

Jason looked concerned. "It's starting already? We're shooting at people? Do we have barbed wire and signs up?"

"Yes. We strung the barbed wire and hung "No Trespassing" signs along the boundary. These guys crossed over the barbed wire."

"Were they armed?"

"Two of them had rifles."

"Jesus. Can we afford to be firing warning shots? Could that get one of our own guys killed?"

Jeff thought about it. "For now, we can get away with warning shots. Soon there'll be too many wanderers up there, and firing off rounds will draw attention and could get one of our guys shot. If nothing else, hungry people might think it means someone shot a deer and they'll come running. Keep in mind, most of the guns coming at us are scoped rifles in big calibers. They're no joke. Hunting rifles can tear a man's arm off."

"There's no way to keep it secret from our people when our guys shoot at trespassers. I've got people complaining about it already." Jason returned to the issue.

"That's *your* problem. I keep this location safe; you get to handle the politics back at the ranch," Jeff argued.

Jason deflated. "My dream job... Please call me on the radio when something goes down so I have a little notice before people start chewing my butt."

"Will do. We have another bunch of five or six SOF guys joining up. They're friends of mine and Evan's."

Jason nodded. "Yeah, okay. Send Jenna a list of the operators and their families, please. She will get them settled in." Jason did the mental math and concluded that addition put them at fifteen Special Forces guys, including Chad. They were bumping over their two-hundred-eighty mark, on paper. He didn't expect most peoples' extended families—the ones they had lately given permission to join—to make it to the Homestead, not with the civil disorder gripping the city with ever-greater intensity.

Years ago, the Homestead committee asked, "What about our extended families?" Many of the members had folks in town. If the world collapsed, what would happen to the extended families who weren't part of the group?

Survival math for a group the size of the Homestead wasn't easy. If a collapse occurred in the spring, the food-growing potential of the Homestead and its affiliated farms would factor in, solidly expanding their carrying capacity. But, if a collapse occurred right before winter, they would have only the greenhouses to grow food. Even with five thousand square feet of greenhouse space, the Homestead could only grow about ten percent of their nutritional needs. Growing calories was a lot harder than most people thought. Growing in winter was borderline impossible.

Every dystopian book, movie and TV show vastly underestimated the difficulty of growing food after a collapse. Under ideal circumstances, a person could grow enough food to support one adult with one acre of ground, and that required an up-and-running fruit, vegetable, compost and livestock program with perfect edibles, perfect timing and no devastating bacteria, mold or insects.

According to most survival fantasies, a couple of rows of thrown-together veggies can feed the whole family. In truth, that much garden would be hard-pressed to feed a toddler—and then only during the peak of the growing season.

In one TV show, a group of thirty survivors flourish on an acre of walled compound, working half-a-dozen grow beds. They even have food to give the local warlord half their produce in exchange for protection. In the cold hard math of small farming, that much garden space couldn't feed three rabbits, much less thirty humans.

Growing food was a tough business, and it had required generations of expertise and local experience for early settlers and natives to live off the land. If the Homestead counted on any amount of fresh food in their survival math, they would be taking a risk.

The committee took a leap of faith and decided to factor in their grown food and livestock in drawing up support estimates. The alternative was to let the extended families of Homestead members starve only to find out later that they had grown excess food. The collapse had come at the worst time of the year—fall—so the committee settled on a number of people whom the Homestead could support. The magic number had been two-hundred-eighty souls, including children. With two-hundred-four members already inside the gates, that left seventy-six extended family who could join the Homestead. On top of that, every possible accommodation had to be made to add experienced soldiers to the group.

The resources shepherded by the Homestead were a poorly kept secret in the community. Prior to the nuclear attacks, service personnel, friends and sundry locals had come through the gates of the Homestead on the order of a few per day. It didn't take much to notice that the place was like the Playboy Mansion of preparedness. The massive gardens, milling livestock and gleaming solar panels fairly screamed *prepper*.

With so much to lose, and little secrecy to protect them, Jason focused all available resources on defense. He figured the Homestead must appear as vicious as a wolverine and have the fangs to back it up.

"I'd like to put the SOF guys to work right away," Jeff said.

"What's that mean?" Jason asked, feeling a little hesitant. Jeff was pushing the envelope with the Homestead, recently inviting more veterans to join. Jason liked the idea, but didn't like that Jeff made the offer without consulting him.

"My guy Alec had an idea… the town of Oakwood is not going to hold together much longer. We were informed this morning that the hospital's still intact. I'd like to form a three-squad element to take down the hospital, the pharmacy and one of the refineries in North Salt Lake. We'll start with the hospital, leave a squad there, then hit the refinery with two squads. That'll leave one squad to take the pharmacy."

Jason sat back hard in his chair. "I see the logic in what you're suggesting, but the timing's got to be perfect. Otherwise, we're just thieves stealing a refinery and a hospital. If things go back to normal in the world, you and I go to jail."

"Who knows?" Jeff said. "Whoever's in charge of the hospital might welcome us with open arms."

"Do we know what the Oakwood police department is doing? Are they covering the hospital?"

"We'll need to do some recon on the hospital, the police station and the refinery. Either way, we should put our SOF operators to work. Otherwise, they'll start making trouble, screwing the housewives and all. They'll be champing at the bit to do something useful. Taking and holding a hospital and a refinery will keep them busy. Obviously, those big assets could speed up recovery later. We should keep them from burning to the ground. We can always give them back later if we feel like it."

Jason sighed. "I hope you're right. Otherwise, we'll go to prison for this little caper of yours."

"Three capers," Jeff corrected.

"I assume you'll be going with them on the assaults?"

"Of course." Jeff smiled.

This mission did nothing to assuage Jason's concerns about Jeff. He could see the logic in preserving local assets but, again, Jeff was proposing unlawful seizure of private property, plain and simple.

"Can you do your best to be diplomatic when you approach the people at those targets?" Jason pleaded. "Can you be more Bill Clinton than Joseph Stalin, please?"

"I'll be nothing but sugar," Jeff told him, "but I don't think you can expect me to be Bill Clinton."

"Yeah, probably not." Jason and Jeff stood up and shook hands. "Good luck. Please don't get us arrested."

· · ·

Federal Heights
Salt Lake City, Utah

It had been five days since his family had been able to shop for food, and already things felt desperate. Jimmy swallowed his pride and went door to door asking his neighbors for handouts. Some of them didn't answer the door, even though Jimmy knew they were home. Others answered but claimed to already have given their extra food away. Once again, Jimmy felt caught behind the curve— unwilling to take care of business until it was too late. He shuffled home with two cans of sauerkraut and half a box of children's cereal.

The day before, he and his wife had laid all their food out on the counter. At first, it looked like a lot. After just a day, Jimmy was startled at how quickly they had burned through it. As things stood, they were down to a day and a half of food, and most of it was virtually inedible. They would end up with a bunch of hard red winter wheat, but no way to grind it or bake it.

That morning, Jimmy's wife made an uncharacteristic suggestion. "It might be time for you to take that rifle of yours and shoot a deer."

She had always turned up her nose at game meat. In fact, she had wanted nothing to do with hunting since it had become a sore subject in their marriage—with Jimmy disobeying her wishes every time he hunted with his brother.

"You could do something useful with all that hunting knowledge you've been learning all these years." She couldn't help but take the poke.

She must have imagined that hunting one weekend a year made Jimmy an outdoorsman. He had only killed two deer in the last ten years, both of them small bucks. He had never risen above greenhorn status. The guys who knew what they were doing hunted many times a year, both in Utah and out of state. By comparison to them, Jimmy barely considered himself a novice.

"Hunting season doesn't open for another month," Jimmy argued out of reflex. Even as he said it, he asked himself if he really wanted to get caught behind the curve once again.

"I think you should risk it," she said, suggesting he break the law for the first time since he had known her.

Jimmy thought of his commercial real estate license. Hunting out of season was probably a felony, and he knew that a felony would disqualify him for a real estate license when renewals came up next year.

What if he just wandered the mountains a little with his rifle? He could make the decision to shoot or not if he actually saw a buck.

Jimmy kicked those questions aside for a moment. He went downstairs to his vault and pulled out his rifle and a half-dozen shells. He dug around in his hunting bin and found camo pants, shirt and his hunting boots.

A shock went down his spine as he considered hunting in broad daylight. What if his neighbors saw him hunting out of season, even without shooting anything? Jimmy lived at the foot of the mountain, and he had seen plenty of deer over the years, pawing around their neighborhood. The safest thing for him to do, considering the risk of a hunting violation, was to walk up the mountain and hopefully drag a deer straight home. Best-case scenario, the neighbors wouldn't call the wildlife people to report him—the phones weren't working, and the wildlife police probably weren't working, either.

But committing a crime in full view of the ward froze Jimmy in his tracks. How could the bishop give him a calling of responsibility if he was a known poacher? Jimmy didn't aspire to be bishop or anything high up, but he could imagine being relegated to minor callings for years, like membership clerk or elders' quorum secretary, until the stink of his poaching wore off.

Jimmy stuffed his boots and cammies to the bottom of his pack and then added a water bottle and the rifle shells on top. He walked out the back door, looked around, then made his way around out to the street with the rifle tucked along his leg, hoping a casual observer wouldn't notice.

He walked across the street and slipped between two neighbors' homes up onto the steep mountainside. He pushed hard up the hill, gasping for air, imagining the eyes of the neighbors on his back. When he couldn't stand any more exertion, he headed across the slope toward a small fold in the hill.

Jimmy plunked down on a rock, undressed and traded out his street clothes for his hunting clothes. The south-facing slopes of the Wasatch Range were almost completely devoid of plant life. Geologically, Jimmy knew this had been an ancient beach when Lake Bonneville filled the northern third of Utah. About fifteen thousand years ago, the huge lake busted through the Snake River Valley in Idaho and dumped all but a fraction of its water into the Pacific Ocean.

What had been left behind on the foothills of Salt Lake City looked like the bottom of a lake—stony and devoid of topsoil. Over fifteen thousand years, only the shady sections sprouted enough brush to cultivate topsoil. The south-facing sides burned to a crisp every July when the sun blazed, leaving them as fertile as Mars.

Jimmy's hillside definitely had more in common with Mars than he would have liked. Where deer hid in this terrain was anyone's guess. Now dressed to hunt, Jimmy marched upward again, hoping to get some elevation so he could look up-canyon for deer.

He reached a high outcropping overlooking the bottom section of Tellers Canyon. His breath caught in his throat. Every direction he looked, he saw other hunters. While his gut sank, he did his best to take it all in. Across the entire canyon, he guessed he could see more than three hundred hunters milling about, even though hunting season was almost a month away.

Mule deer, Jimmy remembered vaguely, required about one square mile per deer. So that meant he was looking at probably ten hunters per deer—assuming the deer hadn't headed for higher elevation at the first sign of a hundred stumbling foragers.

Once again, he found himself behind the curve.

Desperate to bring something home, Jimmy scoured the land for anything edible. Rabbits. Squirrels. Turkeys. Though his rifle was wrong for hunting small game, he would be happy with anything. His desperate hunter's vibe went out before him, like a dark wave of warning to animals. He didn't see so much as an ant.

Jimmy had no clue what kinds of wild plants might be edible. He knew that stinging nettle and cattails were edible, and the early Mormon pioneers had survived winters by eating sego lily bulbs. But either the plants weren't there in Tellers Canyon, or Jimmy didn't recognize them. He walked for three hours and found nothing.

Jimmy always imagined he could provide for his family, if absolutely necessary, by heading into the hills. When he bought his rifle at the sporting goods store twenty years ago, that had been part of his economic justification: the rifle was the back-up plan in case "times got tough."

Here he was, times were definitely tough, and there wasn't a bit of the romantic, man-against-nature struggle he had dreamed of when he bought the rifle. Jimmy knew failure was all but inevitable, the deck supremely stacked against him. Not only was he failing to bring home meat, but he was failing to perform as a man and a father.

Contemplating his failure as he stumbled down the rocky hillside, Jimmy admitted that he had been lulled to sleep by fantasies: the fantasy that his successful career made him a man. The fantasy that giving in to his wife made life easier. The fantasy that he could live in the starch-and-plastic world of civilization, touching the wilds every so often, and Mother Earth would welcome him in his hour of need.

His hopelessness splashed over onto his faith. Even with his failures to follow the old commandment of food storage, how could God allow his family to suffer, even risk starvation, given his lifelong faithfulness? Had he not done almost everything he was commanded to do? He had served an honorable mission. He had married in the temple. He had served faithfully in the ward and always paid his tithe. How could this be the outcome of his hard work?

Jimmy's thoughts were wrapped about him so tightly that he didn't worry about what his neighbors might see as he crossed the street, dejected and confused. Dusk had come while he had wrestled with his soul.

He caught the smallest motion out of the corner of his eye and turned. Lo and behold, there stood a mule deer doe, eating his neighbor's boxwood hedge. All the day's frustration and self-doubt drew down to this single moment in time.

Without thinking, Jimmy threw his rifle to his shoulder and fired. The unexpected recoil jerked the scope up and away from the animal and, when Jimmy returned to look at where the deer had stood, it was gone. The shot rang up and down the street. A couple at a time, the neighbors peeked out their doors, then stepped out onto their lawns.

Jimmy had no idea what to do, so he went with his first instinct; he checked his kill. Sure enough, the doe lay dead in Brother Thompson's bushes, blood spattered on his air conditioning unit and onto the stucco siding of his house.

Jimmy grabbed the back legs of the doe and dragged her toward his garage, leaving an accusing red streak behind the carcass. The neighbors stood awestruck, as though he was a sideshow freak, or maybe a hero.

Half-a-dozen worries hit Jimmy all at once: had he checked his back-stop before firing? What would Brother Thompson say about Jimmy killing a deer in his yard? What would the neighbors say to the bishop about the poached deer?

But the worries came through muted, diminished as he looked down and smelled the coppery blood bubbling out of the doe's mouth.

He had killed a deer and he would feed his family, at least tonight. What the neighbors thought and what his bishop might think? Those worries suddenly seemed less significant in the shadow of death and providence. As he pulled the doe across the street, Jimmy straightened his back and slowed his rush.

Like manna in the desert, God had provided.

• • •

Road 216
Outside Albin, Wyoming

According to Chad, he was *badass* at everything.

In less arrogant moments, he would admit that he almost washed out of the SEALs because he sucked at land navigation.

In the Teams, new SEALs are put through a map-and-compass challenge where they're given twenty-five waypoints and challenged to cover twenty miles in two days in a single-man overland scramble.

There were two ways to do the challenge: using brains or using brawn. Guys with brains marked the waypoints on their map, read the terrain and plotted the easiest route. Guys with brawn plotted a direct path from one point to another, then bulldozed their way through whatever terrain stood in their way.

While Chad undoubtedly scored in the genius range on IQ tests, he had chosen the "bulldozer path" because he knew he would otherwise fail the land navigation. Badass or not, he had to admit he couldn't find his butt with both hands when it came to land nav. He was the guy constantly getting lost. He was the kind of person who could live in the same place for a year and still take the long way home every time. A map and compass might as well have been a duck and blowtorch to him.

In the end, he'd made it through the SEAL navigation course with just twenty minutes to spare—out of forty-eight hours. He almost dropped from hypothermia in the process.

Chad sometimes wondered if God gave everyone talents from a fixed budget—everyone with the same *amount* of talent, just in a different distribution. Some guys raged on the guitar, but they couldn't do a single pull-up. Other guys benched three hundred, but they had zero game with the ladies. A Navy SEAL like Chad was supposedly "badass at everything," except he couldn't navigate his way out of a paper bag. And he couldn't win for losing when it came to women.

Chad previously believed a woman couldn't stay angry for more than a couple of hours. He'd been with Audrey for two days, and she'd been furious for forty-eight hours straight—even sleeping furiously. Chad looked over at his ex in the passenger seat, eyes closed, her head against a pillow against the window, and her face still appeared pissed off.

Tonight would be their first night of traveling "blacked out." Chad wasn't looking forward to the migraine that would come from driving with his NVGs.

Everything needed several names and at least two acronyms in the military. Apparently, there were half-a-dozen officers working 'round the clock in the Office of Redundancy Office coming up with better, more technical names for everything. His NVGs, or NODs, were also known as PVS-7s. Three acronyms for the same damned piece of kit.

Chad eventually figured out that the high-tech acronyms were just there to fuck with people who weren't in "The Mil." On a philosophical level, he was cool with that.

Tonight, there had been good news and bad news when it came to crossing the North Platte River. The bad news was that he couldn't find a way to cross that wasn't also roadblocked or a likely ambush. He had checked more than a dozen possible crossings.

The good news was that he might not have to cross the river at all. The closer he got to Wyoming, the more the North Platte River veered north, taking him away from the I-80 Interstate. He had been trying to parallel the I-80, staying alongside it but coming no closer than ten miles. Big roads, he figured, violated his First Rule of Post-Apocalypse Travel: no interaction with human beings.

The other good news was that Nebraska and eastern Wyoming had more dirt roads than people. The endless flats were interrupted only by the countless dirt roads, which made it ideal for overland travel during Zombie times.

In the back of Chad's mind, he worried that all those dirt roads would eventually funnel down to just a couple of roads as Wyoming became more mountainous and less agricultural. For now, he had dozens of east-west dirt roads to choose from, and no town could barricade more than a couple of them.

First on the agenda tonight would be gasoline. While he wasn't out of fuel, he was the kind of guy who pulled over immediately when the "low gas" light came on. He didn't like to run low on fuel. It was the single area in life where Chad was meticulous.

As he cruised steadily west, he reacquainted himself with his NVGs and picked up speed. At the same time, he searched for a farmhouse to rob.

Part of him hated it—that he would take something that wasn't his. The other part of him relished the breakdown of the Rule of Law. When overseas on deployment, he had gotten hooked on living outside the law, like an addict to heroin. Once he saw behind the curtain and realized he could break with civilized norms at will, assuming he was sufficiently badass, it was hard to go back.

Taking gas from a farmer, though disturbing to Chad's sense of honor, pumped him up. He had already decided that he would leave the farmer a couple of hundred bucks. That tipped the scales decidedly in favor of taking a walk on the wild side. Luckily, Audrey was asleep, or she'd definitely have an opinion about his plan. Not surprisingly, she had big opinions about Chad's personal morality.

Chad quietly kitted up with his AR-15, plate carrier and ceramic plates—they had "disappeared" with him when he left the SEALs—a few mags, his Sig Sauer 9mm, two five-gallon gas cans and the GasTapper. He wore his NVGs on his bump helmet.

It was just after midnight.

116

Chad parked a quarter mile from a likely looking farmhouse and went in on foot. As he approached, moving behind one grain silo at a time, he closed on the house. Two late model trucks were parked in front, along with an old tractor.

Chad wasn't sure if the tractor ran on diesel or unleaded, so he worked his way toward the trucks. Between the grain silos and the trucks was a forty-yard gap of gravel and he covered it in a sprint.

A dog started barking. Chad power-slid behind the first truck, juggling options in his mind. Technically, he should disengage. On any other assault, the dog would probably be a deal killer. He'd lost surprise and he needed at least ten or fifteen minutes to siphon the tank. That felt like a lot of time with a dog barking its fool head off. Someone was bound to come investigate.

But who would come? There wasn't another farmhouse for several miles, so he would be dealing with some old farmer and maybe his dog. Chad didn't want to shoot the dog or anyone, but he was pretty sure it wouldn't come to that. He figured he could probably talk the farmer through the transaction and disengage if necessary.

On cue, the screen door creaked open. Chad didn't like the sound of things because the farmer didn't yell at the dog. That meant the farmer knew something was up—maybe the tone of the hound dog's barking, which sounded a lot like a crow being beaten with a whiffle bat. Chad had to assume the farmer knew there was a real threat in his yard.

Oh, well, Chad thought, I suppose my ninja skills might be a *little* rusty.

"Hello," Chad called out. The screen door creaked again, presumably the farmer ducking back inside behind cover.

"Who's there?" the farmer bellowed.

Yep, Chad thought, old guy. "I'm just driving through and I'd like to buy some gas."

"This look like a service station to you, son? Why don't you head on down the road toward Albin? There's a service station there. Opens in the mornin'."

117

"They selling gas?" Chad asked, already knowing the answer, but hoping to talk the farmer into sharing some of his.

"Nope."

"Then why would I go there?"

"Why would you come here?" the farmer countered.

Chad felt a chill. The farmer was stalling. That could mean only one thing.

Chad jumped up and made a dash for the silos, deciding to break contact and end the mission. About half-way across the gravel driveway, something hit him in the chest like a two-pound ball peen hammer. He went flat on his back mid-run and hit the ground, gasping for air. As soon as he hit, he flipped over and crab-crawled to the first grain silo, still sucking air like a Shop-Vac through a pixie stick.

"You best start talking, asshole." A new voice came from very close, and it wasn't lost on Chad that the round had hit him in the front plate instead of the back plate. That old codger had sent someone out to flank him. Chad knew the gunfight was three-quarters lost, but he hadn't made it through BUD/S by being a quitter.

Fighting his way out of this pickle would leave at least one Nebraska farmer dead, assuming he survived himself. Better to talk.

"I'm just looking for gas. I got money to pay."

"Just stay exactly where you are, buddy. My old man will waste you with that 30-30 of his just as easy as I'll waste you with my own blaster. You maneuver at all and this conversation's over."

What the fuck? Chad thought. The dude talks like an operator. How the hell could that be?

"Hey, bro. Just a wild guess here, but that little love tap you gave me felt like an AR."

"Yeah," the voice from the dark replied, "and you must be wearing plates if you're still breathing."

"You SOF?" Chad asked.

"75th Rangers. What about you, trespassing asshole?"

"I'm from the Teams. West Coast."

"That explains why you think you can come in here and take what you want, I guess."

The old farmer yelled from the porch. "That boy say he's U.S. military, son?"

"Yeah, Pops. But he's a SEAL. Fuck him." He'd said it with a slight lilt in his voice, so Chad eased down to Defcon Two.

"Good thing I'm not a knuckle-dragging redneck asshole, or you'd probably want to make babies with me. Am I right?" Chad fired back.

The Ranger cut loose with a rumbling chuckle. "So, Navy princess, how we gonna back down from this little stand-off? I did shoot you, after all."

"I wouldn't get a big head over it. They're probably not going to put you up for a medal or anything."

"Yeah, but in a fair world, they would," the Ranger laughed.

The old guy interrupted. "What are you dumb sons a bitches going on about? We going to shoot this guy or bring him in for a drink?" The farmer didn't find the jabber as entertaining as the military vets.

"What about it, Navy? You going to put down your gun or are we gonna get to slinging hot rocks at each other?"

Every cell in Chad's body grated at backing down, but his oversized ego wasn't worth killing a farmer or a Ranger. Better to swallow a little pride than kill an American on some Nebraska driveway.

"All right, Army, I'm coming out with my rifle hanging." Without giving him a chance to insist on more, Chad walked out. He flipped his rifle around to his back on his two-point sling and put his hands on his hips. He might be giving in a little, but he wasn't putting his fucking hands up in the air.

"Put your hands up," the Ranger commanded as he came around the silo, rifle pointed at Chad's chest.

"Fuck you," Chad answered.

The Ranger let it slide. He dropped his AR to the low ready. "Why do you need gas so bad you'd die for it?"

Chad wasn't about to tell anyone that he had family nearby. He was trained to be more untrusting than that.

"I'm making my way across Hicksville, getting back to friends and family in Nevada," he lied just to feel like a professional.

The Ranger's dad came out of the house, shushed the dog, and walked over to the boys.

"Whatcha doing prowling around my spread, son? You look geared up to shoot Bin Laden."

"I apologize, sir. Frankly, I was planning on borrowing some of your gas and leaving you a couple hundred bucks."

"Hmpf," the farmer snorted, "if I had to guess, I'd say you got family somewhere out in the night waiting for you in a car." He looked Chad in the eyes and Chad did his best to betray nothing.

"Well," the old man continued, "come up on the porch for a quick snort and I'll give you some gas. No charge. We got plenty of gas."

Two hours later, the three men still sat on the front porch, drinking Jameson whiskey and telling lies. The men were bellowing loudly in a heated contest as to who could tell the dirtiest joke when Audrey appeared out of the darkness.

"What in God's Holy Name are you doing, Chad Wade?" She stood with one hand around a drowsy baby and another hand on her hip.

"Uh-oh. Navy's in trouble," the Ranger mumbled into his tumbler of whiskey.

"Sorry, ma'am, we didn't know our friend here had a missus waiting in the car. Please come sit down." The old farmer was never too drunk for manners. He stood up and offered his lawn chair.

Chad looked at her from the corner of his eye. "Ex-wife, fellas, ex-wife."

"Good evening, ma'am," the Ranger half-stood and reached out with his huge hand. "I'm Reggie Tasker and this is my father, Curtis Tasker."

"Hello, gentlemen. I'm not sure if it's evening or morning. But how is it Chad found two friends this far out in… in such a remote area?" Audrey asked.

Ranger led out. "We only just became friends. Earlier I shot him and it didn't take. So now we're talking a little story."

"Pardon me. Did you say you *shot him*?" she asked, incredulous.

Chad gave Ranger a sideways glance and Ranger squirmed a bit in his chair. "Well, it was more of a love tap, to be quite honest. And that's before we got to know one another."

Curtis, with more years of diplomacy under his belt, intervened. "Ma'am, we'll take care of your traveling companion here and get him all fixed up with gas and grub. Would you like to bring the baby back to the guest room and get some proper sleep?"

Audrey's face lit up as though she had been offered a first class upgrade.

"Could we please? A little sleep would do us both so much good."

"Of course. Come on in, ma'am." Curtis got up and showed Audrey and Samantha inside.

8

"THIS IS JT TAYLOR, ALCOHOLIC of the Apocalypse, coming at you with another night of fun and frolic at the end of the world. On a personal note, to the over-achieving Army bastards chasing me around the western United States, this is a pre-recorded show playing at random times. No need to blow up another repeater. Go home, boys. It's Miller Time. I'm sorry for stealing your shit. Get a hobby.

"Beginning with the bad news first, since California is almost entirely on fire, it looks like the next release of Marvel Comic movies will be delayed by twenty years. On our list of burning cities, we add Seattle, Saint Louis, Atlanta, Des Moines, Las Vegas... I'm not sure why you had to go and burn Vegas, you fascists. What kind of person burns Las Vegas?

"The Saudis, Iranians and Egyptians have shot everything they have so things have quieted down a lot over there due to the fact that they've returned to caveman times. But then again, so have we.

"I'm in need of some female companionship and maybe some diesel fuel. If you're a Drinkin' Bro in the general area of the four corners region, and you have a hot sister, ring me up on 30 megahertz on the VHF band and I'll drop by over the next couple of days..."

Ross Homestead
Oakwood, Utah

"You have a guest coming up the driveway," Jason Ross' radio squawked. Jason walked out on the colonnade and saw Bishop Decker coming up the drive.

"Good morning, Bishop," Jason called out. Both Jason and Jenna had left the Mormon Church over ten years earlier, but once a Mormon always a Mormon. Unless a person made it explicitly clear they were leaving the Mormon Church—writing letters and submitting themselves to interviews—the Mormon Church considered them a member for life. For Jason and Jenna, that had been fine. They attended another Christian church but, if the neighbors wanted to count them among their number, Jason and Jenna saw no reason to disagree. Being part of a neighborhood and part of a ward in Utah were pretty much the same thing. With the world falling apart, the Mormon Church might be the closest thing to civilization that still had a pulse. Jason hoped the bishop would organize the surrounding streets, maybe even the surrounding communities. Neighborhood organization, in these times, might be the difference between life and death.

"Morning, Brother Ross." The bishop smiled. Apparently, he knew using the "brother" moniker was pushing the Mormon thing a bit.

Jason laughed. "It's good to see you. How's the neighborhood holding up? Come inside."

"Well, we know we're living on borrowed time when it comes to water. We checked the cistern up on Elkwood Street, and we're down

123

to the last five feet. We expect the faucets to go dry tonight or tomorrow."

Jason scratched his stubble. "We have our spring up and running. We can't do anything to provide water pressure to the homes—we only have about fifty gallons a minute—but we can provide drinking water from a spigot. I can have a line extended down to Meadowlark Drive if that'll help."

"That would be fantastic," the bishop said, his face brightening. "You have no idea what a load off my mind that is. What can we do to return the favor?"

Jason hesitated, wondering how to approach the topic. He decided to go step by step. "There are lots of ways we can help one another. First, tell me: how're you doing with food?"

The bishop looked up and to the left. Jason noticed the glance and assumed the bishop would exaggerate the positive. "We're pretty good. Most of our member families have at least three months of food storage."

"What about the families without food?" Jason was thinking of the non-member families, wondering how this ward would handle people starving in their midst.

"We're thinking about pooling our food… but there're some members of the ward who aren't in agreement. They have their year's supply and they're not happy with the idea of giving it away."

"Hmm." Jason wanted to know who the holdouts were. They might be trouble. They were definitely assets. In truth, Jason wasn't about to pool Homestead resources with anyone, either. Ward holdouts, on the other hand, were people who had taken preparedness seriously. Every Mormon ward was bound to have a number of such folks—people with food and probably guns.

"Bishop, let's see how things go. I might be able to scrape together a few hundred pounds of wheat to contribute to the cause, and we might have a couple of extra hand grinders, too, if it comes to that."

The Homestead had set aside almost ten thousand pounds of wheat for neighborhood relief, but talking about it only seven days after the stock market crash seemed premature.

"Some of the men would like to talk to you about hunting up on the mountain. How's that sound?"

"Bishop, you probably aren't aware, but we're being pushed hard by hunters and trespassers from Tellers Canyon behind the ridge. We have full-time guards and roving patrols every moment of every day and night. If the neighborhood men hike up there, we'll have no way to prevent an accidental conflict. My security guys won't know who's who. That's just not going to work. Plus, our patrols have probably pushed all the deer out of here by now"

"What do you mean, 'accidental conflict?'" The bishop looked confused.

"First of all, I'm not counting on this situation getting better." Jason motioned toward the valley. "In fact, I'm betting on it getting worse. Our patrols have already had to fire warning shots to turn people around."

Bishop Decker's eyes widened, and he settled into a chair in Jason's conference room. "Maybe you better tell me what you think is going to happen here."

"If we do nothing to stop it, the neighborhood and this property will be overrun by hungry people who will loot our homes, take everything we have, and leave our families to die. I believe that will happen in a matter of days, not weeks."

"You've got to be joking," the bishop said, his mouth agape. "You're not planning on shooting people, right?"

Jason preferred to get bad news out front. This approach had served him well in business and it had become his knee-jerk reaction during tough conversations.

"If we haven't shot and killed someone by the end of the week, I'll be surprised."

The bishop sat back with an audible huff. He rubbed his eyes. "It can't be coming to this…"

"Bishop, we have a powerful shortwave radio. You've seen the antennas. Do you know what our ham guys are telling us about the world? They're telling us that tens of thousands are dying in the big cities. Salt Lake is better off than most, but I don't think the Church planned for this. They don't have silos of grain waiting for a catastrophe on this scale. We're better off here because of the Church, yes, but we're not safe. We're not safe at all. What're you hearing from Church headquarters?"

Bishop Decker looked like someone had gut-punched him. He thought about the question for a moment. "The Brethren are communicating with us through ham radios on the stake level. You remember: a stake is made up of five to ten wards. Each ward is about three hundred members. A stake is about fifteen hundred to three thousand members. The stake president has been talking to Salt Lake City—Church headquarters—every day."

Jason knew what stakes and wards were. He had spent the first half of his life in the Mormon Church, but he got the bishop's point. The Mormon Church was at least communicating to some degree.

"Our stake emergency communications coordinator talks with church headquarters, and church headquarters talks to FEMA."

Jason sat forward. He was particularly interested to know what FEMA was doing. There had long been rumors in the hard-core prepper community that FEMA, the Federal Emergency Management Agency, would be a tool of oppression, used in a crisis to dismantle the Constitution and enslave Americans. Jason didn't personally buy into that fear of government, but he had been wrong before. If FEMA was becoming a threat, he would like to know.

Bishop Decker continued, "The Church is telling our stake president that FEMA can't give a definite timeline for when assistance will arrive. Headquarters tells us the same thing each day: "rely on your own food storage, take care of each other, avoid panic." I wish I had more to tell you, but that's all we're getting."

It was about what Jason expected. Salt Lake City might be the last place FEMA would focus. For one thing, Utah had been a bastion of conservative electoral votes. Few people in the bureaucratic agencies of the federal government cared much for Utah.

More important, perhaps, was that Utah stood a good chance of helping themselves. The state had agriculture, a fairly competent state government, and it had the Mormon Church. The chance of Utah feeding its own was certainly better than Chicago, Baltimore or Atlanta.

If there was some nefarious federal scheme to turn the U.S. into a globalized, Socialist enclave, the odds of Utah submitting to federal authority, given that the state had more guns than pine trees, were long odds indeed. Jason continued, "So nothing new from Church headquarters? Could you please let me know if you hear anything?"

The bishop nodded, obviously wishing the Church would give him more to work with.

Jason turned back to the issue of defense. "My guys can maintain defense up on the ridge behind our neighborhood. Soon, those fifty or so people mulling around in front of the barricade down on Vista View Boulevard are going to become a thousand people, then maybe ten thousand. When that number gets big enough and hungry enough, they're going to march through us like cockroaches on their way through a cafeteria and they're going to clean us out."

"I can't believe the police would let that happen," the bishop argued.

"When's the last time you saw a police officer?"

Decker looked at Jason and nodded, conceding the point. "I need to go talk to my bishopric counselors. I'll try to reach the stake president and see what he thinks we should do next."

"Bishop, a couple more things to think about. I can arm and train about a hundred and fifty men if you provide the men. They would answer to the command of our Special Forces leader, Jeff Kirkham. You and I could save a lot of lives if we gathered the entire stake, and maybe the stake down on Parrish Street. If we got the stakes involved, and gathered a hundred more men, we could move our barricade down another half mile and get a lot more neighbors protected behind our security perimeter."

Jason could tell Bishop Decker was overwhelmed and that too much had been dropped on him too soon. But he needed the Mormon leaders to take security seriously; their help would radically increase everyone's survivability. Jason wanted to push the line of defense farther down the hill, farther away from the Homestead.

"Bishop, how about you and I meet every morning around this time? Maybe we should include your counselors."

The bishop nodded, got up and drifted toward the door. "Thank you for the water spigot," he said over his shoulder as he walked out of the conference room. He pivoted, like he was forgetting something, shook Jason's hand, and wandered back down the drive.

• • •

Alena was facing a situation she had never considered. On the gurney before her was a grown man who could possibly die in a matter of days just because he had slipped with a knife. Without antibiotics, did people actually die from bad cuts? She knew it to be true, but she had never seen anything like it in her career as a nurse.

"We've got to get this man to a hospital," she said to Doctor Larsen. "He needs to be stitched up and put on a course of Cipro."

The doctor shook his head, "I hear you, Alena. That's what we would've done last week, but I think the drive down to the hospital in town would be riskier than the infection. I took a look this morning, and there were half-a-dozen fires between here and the hospital."

"So what're we going to do about antibiotics? Do we have any here? And what about anesthesia?"

"You're going to laugh," Larsen said. "We do have antibiotics here, but they're all fish antibiotics."

"You've got to be kidding," she said.

"Nope, I checked them out myself before Ross started buying them in bulk. They work just like the pharmaceutical-grade stuff. Maybe there's a bit of fish food in there, too," Larsen joked, but Alena wasn't in a joking mood.

"And the anesthesia? You guys didn't buy fish-grade anesthesia, too, right?"

"Sorry, no," Larsen answered, put in his place by the nurse. "But let's not use anesthesia, anyway. Not for sutures, not anymore. Old boy over there," he motioned to the cobbled-together exam table with the unhappy gentleman holding his bloody hand, "can get his stitches the old-fashioned way, a shot of whiskey and a leather bite-strop."

"You're joking again, right?"

"Not a joke." Larsen smiled. "Whiskey's right over there on the shelf."

"Seriously, Doctor Larsen, we're not giving a patient *whiskey*," Alena said flatly. "It's a diuretic."

"Why don't we let him decide? You need me to do the stitches?"

"I can do them just fine, thank you, Doctor Larsen." Alena turned to the shelf, looking for sutures. She found them, a plastic tub full of assorted sutures, all of them expired. What kind of person stocked up on sutures?

• • •

"Mr. Ross," Alena said, stepping through the door in the Homestead office, interrupting Jason while he studied paperwork of some kind.

"Mrs. James, I'm so glad you came by. I saw you stitching up Rodney. How's he doing?"

"He didn't like getting fifteen stitches without anesthetic, I can tell you that."

"Did you offer him some booze, at least, before stitching him up?"

"I did not," Alena replied.

Jason shrugged. "I'll bet he thinks twice before he whittles toward himself again. We're going to have to tear the corner off his Totin' Chip."

"Excuse me? Tear up his what?"

"Totin' Chip. It's a Boy Scout thing. What can I help you with? How's our little infirmary?"

"We're doing fine. I wish we had anesthesia and about a hundred other things, but I'm frankly amazed at what you stockpiled in the first place."

Jason looked pleased. Stockpiling odd survival stuff had been his passion for years. The slimmest silver lining to this whole, dark mess was that his friends and family were enjoying the fruits of his obsession with stockpiling. A dozen times a day, someone approached Jason with a problem, and most of the time he had the perfect thing, squirreled away for just that moment.

"Narcotics of any kind were much harder to come by, especially if one fancied staying out of jail." Jason glanced at the paper he had been working on and caught himself. People before things, he reminded himself as he looked up and pulled the folder closed.

Alena didn't wait for an invitation to get to her point. "I'm sure you're aware that your guards are shooting at people who're doing nothing more than passing by, hiking in the mountains."

"Yes, I'm aware." Jason heard her out.

"I'd like to strenuously object to the military nature of this compound." Alena warmed to her protest. "I believe we have a moral obligation to use force only if and when necessary. And I don't think it'll become necessary unless *we* start a war against the world around us. Your men are inclined to start a war."

Jason didn't respond right away. In his experience, listening was generally cheap while making pronouncements was generally expensive. Especially, with Nurse Alena, he would err on the side of listening.

To his surprise, Alena waited *him* out, forcing him to speak first. Jason proceeded cautiously. "Who would you think would be the best person here to make the decision when to employ force and when not to employ force?"

He kicked the hot potato back to Alena, trying to keep her talking. One of Jason's business habits had been to let his leaders control their "ten acres" without meddling. Jason and the committee could dictate desired outcomes, but then they would step back and allow the leaders on the ground to do their jobs. Micro-managing was like herding goldfish with a chopstick—a fool's errand. Using influence instead of control might *seem* weaker to the neophyte, but influence always trumped control in the end, in Jason's experience. Influence ended the moment a leader used control.

At this point, Jason doubted he could control the military boys, even if he wanted to. Jeff Kirkham had a clear idea of how to run security and, as long as Jason got behind them, they would be friends. Jason had long ago decided that the only thing more stupid than trying to control people was trying to control a bunch of control freaks. Jason listened to Alena, but he had no intention of meddling with Jeff Kirkham and his men, no matter what they were doing. For one thing, Jason was scared shitless by the security threat probably coming their way—*one million hungry, angry residents of Salt Lake City, Utah*. He would not be screwing with Jeff Kirkham, no matter who complained.

"I suggest that lethal force decisions be made by a committee that represents *all* the members, not just the military-minded." Alena had thought this through. She wasn't leaving him any room to dance around the issue.

Jason steeled himself, forfeiting diplomacy for the moment. "You know this is how it's done in the military, right? Officers give the orders and men follow them. Any obstruction of that process risks the entire Homestead. We don't have a lot of soldiers to sacrifice before we get overrun. We can't afford delays and we can't afford mistakes."

Alena hit back ferociously, intelligently. "I know how it works. My husband is in the Army. Soldiers have rules of engagement. Maybe our country has rules of engagement because soldiers can't be trusted to act without civilian oversight. Civilian oversight sounds like 'best practice' to me. Why wouldn't we do the same?"

She had made a strong point, but it didn't matter. Jason's fear of seeing his children dead or starving trumped anything she could throw at him. He saw no alternative but to level with her.

"Alena, I need to admit something to you, something I hope you'll keep between the two of us."

She nodded.

"I believe we're facing a fifty-fifty chance that both of us and our children will be dead this time next month."

Alena's eyes widened; it was clearly not what she expected to hear.

"I pray that I'm wrong," Jason continued, "but look around you. I wasn't wrong about society collapsing. I prepared for something horrible, and I'm willing to bet you and Robert had conversations about what a *whacko* I was for setting this up and dedicating so much money to preparing for the Apocalypse." Her face gave away nothing. "You don't have to admit it. My next guess, Alena, is that we're going to see thousands of starving people pounding at our gates and it's going to be soon. It'll begin as a trickle, then it'll become a flood. Word will spread that we have electricity. Someone will see lights up on the hill. Rumors will fly that we have plenty of food and water. People with nowhere to go will come to our gates." Jason paused for effect. "They'll be angry, and that anger will be directed at us—you and me and our children."

"How does that impact my suggestion that we set up reasonable rules of engagement?" Alena was no fool. She knew genuine emotion and conviction when she saw it. But she would never give up a point without a fight.

"I'm telling you all this because I want you to know that I take your feelings on the matter seriously," Jason said. "I truly do. But I also want you to know that I'm not going to interfere with the men responsible for our security. In fact, I'm going to give them all the support I can. I will not second-guess their judgment."

The blood rose in Alena's face. Jason felt the need to follow up with some emotional salve. "When it comes to the infirmary, I likewise respect your judgment."

Alena had no interest in being appeased. "Thank you for taking the time. I think you are wrong. Dead wrong. And, before this is over, you will have carelessly wasted human life. God save us all from men and their guns." She did an about-face and plowed out of the office, leaving behind her a wake of fury.

• • •

Twenty-year-old Emily Ross did an inventory of her life as she gazed at the muzzle end of her Glock handgun. She tried to think of another moment when she had felt such crippling malaise.

Perhaps she'd been this bored long distance swimming or training to do a half-Ironman with her dad. Counting a thousand strokes in the pool with nothing more to look at than pool tile… that had been pretty boring.

Would anyone ever make music on iTunes again?

She would kill for some *Mumford and Sons* right now. Like so many things in the Apocalypse, music was forbidden on guard duty. She would get in serious trouble if she didn't pay absolute attention to the absolute *nothing* that was going on cross-canyon from her lookout post.

They'd assigned her to watch the mountainside on the upper-north boundary of the Homestead. Every few minutes, she scanned the mountainside with her binoculars, looking for trespassers. She couldn't put her tunes on because she had been ordered to listen for anyone sneaking up behind her, as though that was ever going to happen. She hadn't seen a soul trespassing after many hours on duty.

The edges of the Homestead were pocked with dank, little spider hole look-outs like the one she sat in now. At the onset of the collapse, before Emily made it home from med school, someone had dug these hidey-holes where two people could sit, spying for trespassers. She was assigned to "Position Eight North." Someone had nailed a little sign on the lip of the six-by-six redwood shelf below the observation slit. The sign must have been there in case a guard forgot where he was. Since all the positions looked exactly the same, and since the guards were in the process of slowly going bonkers with boredom, such a precaution seemed sensible to Emily.

Would anyone ever make a French macaroon again? Emily loved Paris. She had visited many times with her parents, basking in the precious neighborhoods of Montmartre and Saint-Germain-des-Prés.

Emily shared Position Eight North with Don something-or-another. She didn't know who decided it was a good idea to stick her in a dirt box with a guy as old as her dad. They couldn't talk; that was also part of the rules, so the old man became a piece of background furniture to her, like the binoculars on the tripod or the shelf full of Meals Ready to Eat stacked in the corner.

Right now, Don something-or-another snoozed in a camp chair against the dirt wall of the spider hole, his mouth gaping open. They alternated resting and scanning every thirty minutes for six endless hours until their shift change showed up. Their replacements would silently creep in the trenched backdoor of the hole, buried into the forest. The idea was to make it difficult for anyone to spot their location or observe the change of guard.

Emily holstered her handgun, worried that Don Sleepyhead would crack an eye and see her looking down her gun barrel. It might freak him out.

Amidst the boredom, Emily's mind wandered to her friends. By her reckoning, every one of her friends right now must be living in terror. Either back east at Johns Hopkins or in Salt Lake City, every person she cared about outside her family must be facing a gut-wrenching doom. Most of her friends probably wouldn't have begun to starve yet, but some would likely be hungry. More frightening, perhaps, would be the growing knowledge that their dreams for the future had, with the drop of a couple of bombs and the flip of a stock market, turned to ash.

Why go on living in a world without a future?

Emily didn't consider herself the typical millennial. She'd listened to her dad carp on millennials for years—the same carping old men had done about young adults for eons of time. She begrudgingly admitted, though, that she and her peers had a problem with entitlement. They had grown up in a world that granted their every wish. They had felt loved and supported, winning shelves of participation trophies, and rarely experiencing the sting of their own failures.

The new future, the one that loomed, demanded more work, more effort, and certainly more risk of failure than the world before. To say that this world demanded "more" effort was a gross understatement. If this Apocalypse stuck, millennials would be living in an alien environment, a world where they would die if they didn't take care of their own needs.

Like stock markets and housing markets had for centuries, the self-esteem market would also experience a correction. Emily could feel it happening at the Homestead itself; people were judged and esteemed based on the value they created. Nothing more; nothing less.

Something about this new world scared Emily to death. And it excited her. She knew that she had always been an obsessive-compulsive value creator—a high achiever. After all, she had clawed her way into a top ten college for her undergrad degree and she had clawed her way into a top ten med school. Among entitled millennials, she stood out.

None of her friends had been prepared for a world gone mad. They hadn't run marathons like Emily, hardening their bodies and their minds. They hadn't shadowed dozens of surgeries to prepare for med school. They hadn't backpacked miles and miles in the backcountry, living out of their packs and summiting mountains. And they hadn't gone to combat shooting schools to learn the oily charms of the AR-15 rifle.

Emily had hung around Zach and the Ham Shack enough to know that the last couple of days had been brutal on the eastern seaboard. Even if her friends made it back to their hometowns, spread across the east and the south of the U.S., those populations were turning on themselves, going savage within mere days of the stock market crash.

The big cities had reverted to barbarism with rampant murder, rape and looting. Emily felt certain that her friends from the big cities—Atlanta, D.C., New York and Philly—had made it out to their summer homes and family farms in the countryside. But the shortwave radio told of masses of desperate people flooding into rural areas, devouring everything in their path.

Emily's mind recalled pictures from the space station, where the city lights of the U.S. looked so beautiful, so festive from two-hundred-fifty miles in the sky. She remembered how the lights in the western U.S. spread apart, like a gauzy spider web. Back east, though, the lights crammed together, clumping into a solid blot of population, brighter and denser around the big cities and filling in almost every millimeter except for the Appalachian Mountains and a small spot over Maine. From the Mississippi River to the shores of the Atlantic, Americans lived tightly packed.

Emily feared, if things kept devolving from order to chaos, Americans would die tightly packed as well. They were probably dying already. She wondered if any of her friends had died yet, and the thought sent a chill down her spine. She imagined Dotty, her vivacious roommate at Johns Hopkins, dead on the lawn of her parents' summer home outside Baton Rouge. The terrifying thought made her reach for the reassuring heft of her Glock, as though the gun could put distance between herself and horror.

The news from Europe, when it skipped across the ionosphere and fluttered down upon the huge antennas of the Homestead, could not be imagined. The horrors were too great. Europe had imploded into a charnel house. With the stutter-step of world markets, and the twin blasts of nuclear bombs, hard-core Muslims had gone berserk, overtaking helpless populations of city dwellers. All major cities in Western Europe were being overrun. Reports from Europe claimed that people were eating people. ISIS rose as the only surviving organization once government power vanished. Religious organizations in Europe had dissipated over the last twenty years, all except for Islam. Now that a social gap appeared where any organized group had tremendous leverage, Islam became a powerhouse. ISIS was the organizational arm of Islam, and ISIS had been sitting on a plan for this moment for decades.

Emily couldn't accept the injustice. Europe had been so accommodating, so kind to Islamic refugees. Without exception, she and her friends considered Europe the front line of compassion, social welfare and forward thinking. But Europe had been the *first* to be consumed by savagery. How could that be?

Emily shuddered and pushed the thoughts away. She pulled up her binoculars and began her scan of the dips and rises of the mountainside facing Position Eight North.

Scan left to right. Bump down five degrees. Scan right to left. Bump down five degrees. Scan left to right.

She settled into a rhythm. Thoughts of death and horror receded into her subconscious, gathering into a dark cloud that had no intention of abating.

• • •

The Avenues Cemetery
Federal Heights, Salt Lake City, Utah

"Woompf!" the Remington 30-06 thundered for the fourth time that morning.

Four shots and three deer down. Jimmy couldn't be more pleased with the results, even as he knew it couldn't go on forever.

After killing the doe in his neighborhood the night before, he had remembered the small deer herd living in the cemetery a few blocks up the street. With help from a couple of buddies from his ward elder's quorum, Jimmy mounted an expedition to harvest as many deer as possible before the cemetery herd was killed off or headed for high ground. The herd of deer had probably lived in the local cemetery their whole lives, but Jimmy felt certain being hunted daily would send them to higher altitudes.

He and his buddies returned home with three deer, enough to feed the neighborhood fresh meat at least for a couple of days. His previous concerns about the ward judging him for poaching had dissipated as other men jumped on board. Hunting made sense, and all thoughts of game laws and poaching disappeared like tales of old. In the eyes of the neighborhood, Jimmy rose to the level of a mythical figure. There would be another street barbecue this evening, and he would receive dozens of back slaps and high fives.

Not bad for a novice.

Later that evening, Jimmy gnawed on a mule deer rib, his belly full. He found himself eating every last bit of meat, even the connective tissue. Heck, he had never even thought to eat the sinewy ribs of a deer. They'd barely seemed worth the effort. Now he couldn't conceive of wasting meat of any kind.

When he finished the rib, he looked at the bone, sure there was still nutrition there, but unsure of how to get it. The bone would go bad in a day, so he tossed it to a dog.

Jimmy stood and joined a group of neighborhood men. He noticed his status had shifted. The real men stood with him now. The rest of the neighborhood guys, the ones still wearing loafers without socks or spotless tennis shoes, drifted among the women or pooled together in loose conversations of their own.

Those other guys, drifting about, were like "satellite bulls" in an elk herd. Jimmy had hunted high country elk with his brother once and he learned a lot more than he had anticipated about breeding behavior. The satellite bulls were the males who couldn't hold a herd of females because they were too young, unskilled or too unhealthy to fight off other males. Of course, the neighborhood hadn't resorted to collecting harems of females, and that wasn't going to happen for a hundred reasons. Besides, not even the horniest male would want more mouths to feed right now.

Even so, Jimmy was beginning to see why the Lord might have commanded the Law of Plural Marriage back in the early days of the Latter-Day Saints. Strong men, like those he stood with, could support more women. They guaranteed survival in a harsh world. Not only could they support more women, but they would be driven— even entitled—to breed with them. After just two days of hunting and providing, that drive didn't strike Jimmy as so alien anymore.

Of course, he would never take another wife, not unless the Lord commanded it through His anointed leaders. Jimmy's sex drive didn't run toward womanizing. However, he had noticed a couple of the sisters from the ward looking at him differently.

He had worn his camo and leather hunting boots all day. The rough clothes made more sense, since all he'd done that day was hunt and butcher. Plus, he had to admit, he liked the way the camo felt, pegging him as a provider. He earned the distinction.

Standing with the "herd bulls," Jimmy could feel the eyes of his wife. Something had turned inside her, too, altered with that first deer kill. She hadn't henpecked him once today. If he didn't know better, he'd think she was looking at him with some primal respect, like she was fortunate to be with him. It had been a long time since he'd felt that sensation in his marriage.

What a difference a day makes…

Brother Campbell, standing next to him, gestured out to the valley. "Where's all the gosh-darn food? What about the storehouses and distribution centers?"

"You know," Carl Redmund, a non-member, jumped on the question with his customary preamble. Carl had played football for the University of Utah twenty years back. "The stores these days practice just-in-time inventory. That means there aren't any big warehouses full of food anymore. Everything's controlled by computers. Every can of food you buy is replaced with one can of the exact same food, quick as a whistle, coming in on a semi from the distribution center down in southern Utah. Almost every bit of food in Salt Lake was already sitting on shelves when the market went to crap. Grocery stores don't have stockrooms anymore."

"Yeah, but where'd all that food go?" Art Campbell followed up. "It couldn't have just disappeared."

Jimmy jumped in. "I was at Costco the morning after the market halts began—the Costco over on Three Hundred West and Seventeen Hundred South. There were thousands of people in the parking lot. They were ready to storm the place. I'm sure they've stormed it by now."

"If all the food was evenly divided between every family in Salt Lake City, we would have had three, maybe four days' worth of food for everyone." Redmund was obviously pulling from something he'd read or heard. "Three days' worth of food—that's all any city really has on its shelves. But that food didn't get divided evenly. It got hoarded."

Redmund paused for effect. "That food got hoarded by the sons of bitches who hit those markets first. They bought up everything they could. Probably stole it, in fact. Didn't pay on their way out. Then they piled it in their minivans and to hell with the rest of us. That's where the food is—hoarded by selfish sons of bitches. Forty-nine out of fifty families got nothing, and one out of fifty families is living high on the hog. That's why folks are hungry just a week after the market goes to hell."

It was a lot of swearing for this crowd, and Jimmy could see the Mormon guys glancing about uncomfortably. Jimmy jumped in to smooth things over.

"I'm guessing you're right, Carl. In any case, I'm positive Costco is as empty as the tomb of Jesus on Easter morning. Right now, our best bet is to stick together and follow the Brethren."

Carl snorted, not offering a comeback. It had been a long time since he had given a darn about what the Brethren had to say. "Well, gents, I gotta go figure out how to get some water outta my kids' swimming pool. It's already turning green, and I've gotta find a way to clean it. Otherwise, we'll all have the trots around the Redmund house. Thanks for the barbecue." The former football player turned away from the group. Jimmy could feel the tension melt as Redmund left.

Jimmy turned to Brandon Lister, his backyard neighbor. "So, Brother Lister, are we going hunting this evening?"

"Sure thing. Where you want to try?"

"Let's hit the cemetery again. See if our luck holds."

"You got it, Jim. See you at three-thirty at the gates?"

"Sounds good." At that, the small knot of herd bulls broke up and headed back to their families.

• • •

Utah State Prison
Bluffdale, Utah

Ole man trouble, leave me lonely.
Go find you someone else to pick on.
Without thinking about it, Tom Comstock had been humming the Otis Redding tune all day. In fact, he'd been humming it all week—a habit he'd picked up from his old man. His dad had also been in law enforcement. He would have been proud to see how far Tom had risen.

Prison warden.

Yes, his dad would have been proud, had the cancer not taken him first.

The back-up generators still ran, thank God. Even so, a hundred other gargantuan issues drove his prison down a path to oblivion.

Ole man trouble. He had come to Tom's world and made himself at home.

The 3,653 incarcerated men and women had nothing to eat, and they were dipping their drinking water out of buckets, just like in the fifties. Tom suspected the water wasn't even sanitary anymore. His men had pulled it from open cisterns meant for watering the greenhouses where minimum security inmates did work release.

Out of three-hundred-seventy-five corrections officers, at last count, only eighty-two of them showed up for work this morning.

As one might expect, without stringent cleanliness procedures, diarrhea and flu skipped its way through the prison like a three-year-old on amphetamines.

At this point, Tom had almost no medical staff. Almost no cleaning staff. Exactly zero cooks. He didn't have a single pharmacist to issue the drugs that prevented his inmates from going berserk. God himself knew when resupply would arrive.

The situation was almost beyond resupply already, Tom admitted to himself. Even if resupply showed up, he didn't think he could placate the inmates before they rioted. There were too many exceptions to the rules right now, and the rules were the only thing keeping the animals in their cages. A prison guard started making exceptions, and it was one hundred percent guaranteed that he would get his hand bitten off.

Tom Comstock guessed he ranked as the highest prison authority in the state, given that the Division of Utah Correctional Industries had stopped answering its main phone number. Calling any of his bosses by cell phone proved equally pointless.

Amazingly, cell service seemed to be working, with terrible reception and a lot of busy signals, but the cell phone system itself appeared to be up and running between him and downtown. Tom vaguely remembered that most of the cell towers had about a week of back-up power.

All the corrections division directors were briefed on emergency communications as part of the big disaster response field day the division held every three years. He had been bored to tears by the egghead communications guy droning on and on about the cell system and how the network would be reliable in case of disaster.

Yeah, right.

Anyone who worked around technical types knew that all those tech systems were supposedly bulletproof right up until they broke, which happened about every three days. The tech guy would then swoop in and show everyone just how easy it was to fix things. Of course, nobody but the tech guy could ever fix it. Everyone got used to the reality that all systems broke, pretty much constantly, and that the tech guy was a permanent addition to any team.

The cell phone communications dork at the field day had gone on and on with his PowerPoint presentation. Tom tried for about five minutes to figure out what the guy's diagram meant before he gave up and went back to daydreaming.

He remembered that most cell towers had back-up power and generators that would run for less than a week. Every cell tower had to send signal back to the central computer at the cell phone company. There were these long lines of fiber optic cable that had to be amplified every mile or two. He remembered thinking that each one of those amplifiers also required power, and not all of them had back-up power. So the chain would be as strong as its weakest link and who knew which link it was? Tom guessed it depended on the coverage area and the network.

As far as Tom could tell, cell phones were still working seven days after the collapse. But hardly anyone was answering. Apparently the "weakest link" was the cell phone owner himself. Without power to electrical sockets, charging a cell phone became a big hassle. Tom had to run out to his truck and plug in his phone just to get a little juice.

As fate would have it, that's when one of his bosses called him back—while his phone sat charging on the seat of his truck.

Tom stewed in his juices inside his concrete office on the prison complex. He was about ten miles from the state capital. That's where his superiors should be right now—at the Office of Corrections, working out his problems.

That ten miles had become a thousand miles in the last three days. He'd sent three of his corrections officers to the capital in person. Only one had returned, and that guy reported that the state correctional offices were vacant, the doors flapping in the breeze.

The funny thing, Tom realized, was that this was one of the most common questions regular citizens asked him when they found out he was a prison warden.

What would you do if the power went out?

Such a dumb question… The anti-government types sat around dreaming about ways the system might crash and how convicts might run loose in the streets. The thought used to make him laugh. Policies and procedures for prison systems were excruciatingly well thought out. Every possible scenario had been documented and there was a step-by-step plan to handle each and every possible event. The prison industry employed an army of people whose only job was to think of what could go wrong and plan for it.

So when someone asked him what he would do if the power went out, he would laugh. "I wouldn't notice if the power went out because the back-up generators would kick on before the lights even flickered."

They would follow up with, "Yeah. But what if the power went out and then you ran out of gas?"

He would shake his head and think of the two-week fuel supply in bunkers under the Olympus wing of the prison, as well as the back-up fuel resupply that came by tanker truck to top them off every three days.

If that failed, he was to load up his prisoners and shuttle them to the Central Utah Prison in Gunnison, Utah. They drilled the prisoner transfer routine every four years. It would take him two days of shuttling to move all the prisoners to Gunnison Penitentiary.

Policies and procedures—two false gods of the Modern Age.

Ole man trouble, leave me lonely.

Tom tried to picture executing on the contingency plan to move prisoners to Gunnison. First off, if he so much as cracked those jail cells, there would be a riot, and he would lose control of the prison.

Inmates were like dogs. They could smell fear. They knew something was wrong and they were the kind of animals who thrived on stuff going wrong. He could see Interstate 15 from his office and it looked like a damned used car lot. His big white prison buses wouldn't make it to Provo, much less Gunnison.

Power wasn't the problem. They had plenty of fuel for the generator. What they didn't have was guards, cooks, pharmacists and *water*. They had spent so much time worrying about the back-up generators that they forgot the hundred other things required to keep human beasts locked in cages.

That brought Tom full circle in his thinking, right back to where he had started.

Ole man trouble.

He would be forced to make up some new policies and procedures right here, right now. Tom imagined firing up his computer and banging out a memo.

Prison Policy for a Complete Fuck-stick Mess

I. Should everything go completely tits-up in the world, Warden and Corrections staff shall execute the following procedures:

a. Leave the maximum security inmates in Uinta Building to die like the mutts they are. Shut down the mag-locks and do whatever you can to permanently disable the manual override. Sorry, folks. Thirst and starvation is what you get—you rapists, pedophiles and murdering shit bags.

b. Throw open all the cages in the other buildings beside Uinta and instruct the corrections officers to run like hell.

It ain't pretty, thought Tom, but it'll do.

He grabbed his bull horn and headed out of his office to call the last staff meeting he would ever call.

• • •

By the sound of the uproar, Francisco could tell his boys were taking over the prison. Even the roaring noise sounded Latino.

He wondered why that was. Why did white people and black people sound different from brown people when it was just a roar of a crowd?

Francisco loved everything about being Latino. He had grown up in Los Angeles—so close to Mexico you could almost smell the tortillerias. All Latino pride aside, though, he thought Mexico sucked ass. For whatever reason, the people there lived like sheep. They had nothing in common with great Mexicans like his namesake: Francisco "Pancho" Villa.

Francisco harbored a personal belief that most Mexicans with cojones had emigrated to the U.S. over the last twenty years, leaving Mexico alone with the spineless cowards. The cartels stood out as the last shining hope against American imperialism. He and his gang family, Los Latigos al Norteños, did whatever they could to help the cartels and the cartels paid them well for their loyalty.

Pancho, short for "Francisco," had dedicated his life to La Revolución, and crime had paved his way. During several sabbaticals in prison, he had studied the life of Pancho Villa, particularly the way Villa set up his own estate. Bucking the trend in Mexico, Villa eschewed the hacienda system of lords and laborers and made his own lands into idyllic social experiments, the common soldier elevated, children educated, and respect given to all.

Francisco's own vision borrowed from Villa's, bringing it into modern times. He dreamed of being an aristocrat who labored alongside his soldiers, educating their children and respecting them as men. Noble Mexicans, enjoying their birthright of self-respect and self-determination.

Other than his stops in prison, Francisco lived the dream. He had risen through the ranks of the Norteños gang, achieving lieutenant rank at only twenty-five and now captain at thirty-six. He was the top-ranked Mexican Mafioso in the State of Utah.

With each act of crime, he struck at the heart of the American system, feeding the gringos their drugs and taking advantage of their moral decrepitude. He didn't know what had gone wrong with the prison over the last week, though he knew it was serious. In his revolutionary heart, he dreamed that the concrete world of the whites had cracked open. He would flow into that crack, hard and strong, breaking the whites' hold on this prison and even this state.

He didn't bother getting off his bunk to look out his cell through the grating. His men would come get him when they defeated the mag locks. If he stood at the bars, he would look weak. Pancho Villa never looked weak.

Francisco laid back on his bunk, confident he would see freedom soon enough.

• • •

Ross Homestead
Oakwood, Utah

Jacquelyn roamed around the Homestead with a shirt full of potatoes. It seemed like she spent a lot of time doing this—walking around looking for a particular person. She had even started developing a route.

Start at the kitchen, head toward the clotheslines, loop over to the showers, then walk to the big greenhouses, then the small greenhouses. Head up the drive to the big house. Check the office. Go by the infirmary. Finish at the bunkhouse. If that failed, start over again at the kitchen.

The simple truth was, as much as everyone bitched about cell phones, life sucked without them. She ached to send a simple text and locate Amanda, the gardener. She spent half her day looking for

147

people, even though the Homestead proper only occupied about five acres and fifteen buildings.

Finally, Jacquelyn saw Amanda off in the distance, carrying trays of vegetable starts.

"Hold up…" Jacquelyn trotted over to Amanda, awkwardly cradling the potatoes in her shirt and trying not to let her ample boobs peek out the bottom.

"Hey, Jackie." Amanda stopped. She didn't know Jacquelyn well enough to realize she hated being called "Jackie."

"Hey, sister. We were about to throw the last of the potatoes from the cold storage into today's stew, and it dawned on me that we might need them for potato starts. I wanted to make sure before we boiled them."

"Oh, crap." Amanda covered her mouth with one free hand. "I was supposed to pull some seed potatoes out a couple of days back and it slipped my mind." She giggled. "That would've been some kind of screw-up, right?"

"No harm, no foul. I grabbed these," Jacquelyn told her. "Do you need more?"

Amanda looked over the spuds in Jacquelyn's shirt. "Yeah. We need three times that many for seed potatoes. Are they already in the stew pot?" Amanda gritted her teeth.

"They're chopped up, but I asked the girls to hold off putting them in the stew."

"Oh, good. It doesn't matter that they're cut up, but we'll have to put them in water right away for them to sprout. I'll meet you over at the kitchen."

"Disaster averted," Jacquelyn laughed. "See you at the kitchen in a minute."

In truth, cooking the seed potatoes would've been a catastrophe. At this point in the collapse, potatoes would be rare, bordering on non-existent. Every potato in or around cities would have been gobbled up by now. The potatoes in her shirt might be the last raw potatoes for a hundred miles. If they ever did find anyone with potatoes, they would cost a fortune in trade.

Jacquelyn and Amanda would have to drop everything right away to get these potatoes cut into "eyes" and sprouting in water. Each whole potato would make six to ten sprouts. Then, each sprout would grow six to ten whole potatoes when planted. Luckily, Jacquelyn had been the one to get the potatoes out of cold storage. Otherwise, the Homestead would have eaten the last of their potatoes without a second thought.

Damn close call. How many of these close calls are we screwing up? she wondered.

She laughed out loud as she remembered her and her husband's fantasies about *When the Shit Hits the Fan*. Admittedly, she had romanticized the Apocalypse. She and Tom had read at least a dozen books about the post-Apocalyptic world, and she had woven together an idea that it would be like *Swiss Family Robinson* meets *Little House on the Prairie*, but with guns. She had imagined the joys of "rough living"—the pace of life slowing down and enjoying little things like playing with the kids, the dew on the grass and long sunsets.

In reality, she had never been so busy in all her life. There was nowhere near enough time for making the rough-hewn improvements to daily life, like learning to whittle, then carving a butter churn out of old wood. What a joke! There wasn't even time to plant the greenhouses. Just cooking, cleaning, sanitation, and getting living arrangements set up consumed every minute of every day. They all worked by lantern into the night.

She had daydreamed about just spending time with good people after modern society collapsed. The people around her were certainly good people, but half the time they wanted to strangle one another. Almost every person in the Homestead was in some stage of losing his or her mind, and culture shock took a devastating toll. Under this level of stress, even moderate personality disorders, largely dormant before the collapse, were going ballistic. She was the only therapist in the group, a major oversight by Jason Ross. She fielded the entire responsibility of helping three dozen destabilized people pull their minds back together, as though talk therapy was some one-stop solution.

Before the collapse, she and Tom had, admittedly, glamorized the guns. Back when the world was sane, owning guns felt like some stand for individuality and self-sufficiency. Now, with the shit actually hitting the proverbial fan, the guns felt dangerous to her. Sooner or later, someone would die from a bullet wound, either by accident or from a gunfight.

At what point was a person a murderer when killing people stealing their supplies? Was it okay to kill someone for plucking a wild plant from your land? And, even when justified, how hard was it to sleep at night after killing someone?

Every time she holstered her gun in the morning, she wondered if today would be the day she killed someone. The romance and cool factor of firearms had entirely evaporated. Her gun had become a battered tool and she resented what the gun implied.

Once Tom had given her a funny, over-sized tee shirt for Christmas that said, "Prepared, not Scared" with a picture of a bullet between "Prepared" and "not Scared." It had become one of her sexy, funny nighties. Every time she thought of that tee shirt—she'd left it at the house—she shook her head and smiled at how asinine she had been.

She and Tom had been fairly well prepared. Even so, like the potato fiasco, they now spent every minute painfully aware of all the things they had forgotten. This whole Homestead group had been *maybe* fifty percent prepared. That put them ahead of the curve of ninety-nine percent of humanity. But it did not mean they would survive. They weren't competing against that ninety-nine percent of humanity. They were competing against Mother Nature *plus* the rest of humanity. Just one mistake like eating the last of their potatoes could mean starvation.

A hundred terrifying deaths awaited them and their children—marauders, rogue government forces, disease, crop failure, animal sickness. Every day, new threats emerged, and those threats weren't like the threats from the old, modern world. They no longer faced fears of tax audits or rumors getting back to their boss about spending a sick day on the lake. The new fears carried the ultimate consequence—death. For the first time in her life, Jacquelyn felt like it was very possible she would die at a young age. Worse yet, her children might never see adulthood.

Prepared or not, the odds of a life free from crippling grief were not good.

• • •

Peña Residence
Rose Park, Salt Lake City, Utah

The smell of wood smoke. What could be better? For Gabriel Peña, wood smoke evoked memories of sitting around a campfire with his father, enjoying tacos de carne asada. If only life could have remained that elemental, that simple.

Laced with the smell of plastic and oil, the wood smoke today foretold menace. It hung over Rose Park like the coming of death. This smoke scared the hell out of Gabriel.

The last thing his brother Francisco told him before the court sentenced him to prison was, "Take care of Mama and Abuelita. You're the man of the house now."

Nothing mattered more to Gabriel than the respect of his brother, and he would do anything to carry his brother's burden. But the smoke troubled him to the point of distraction. Drifting into every corner of every room of the house, every piece of clothing, every bite of food, the smoke threatened terrors that Gabriel could not fight with fist or gun. The smoke brought death—dark, silent, and ephemeral as a curse.

Gabriel could fight; his brother had taught him. Gabe kept a fully-loaded *Cuerno de Chivo*, or AK-47, behind his bed, unbeknown to his mama. He owned two knives and several handguns as well. Still, Francisco forbade him from joining the gang and, as captain of Los Norteños del Utah, Francisco's word was law.

Gabriel put on a good show of resenting his brother's mandate, just to protect his scrim of machismo. But, secretly, he knew the life of a gang soldier wasn't for him. He liked his brother's vision of laboring beside the common man, sacrificing privilege in the name of equality, but Gabriel and Francisco both knew they were fundamentally different people from the gang soldiers who followed Francisco's every word. The Peña brothers were more intelligent and capable of greater things than the other gangbangers.

Francisco used his intelligence as a leader in the Mexican underworld, planning operations and calling shots. The path of a criminal revolutionary required total commitment to brutality, and Francisco built his street reputation with the flair of a Hollywood image consultant. Behind his back, the soldiers called him "El Barbero"—"The Barber"—because Francisco employed an old-fashioned straight razor in moments requiring a dash of vicious showmanship. He lashed out at anyone using the nickname "El Barbero," but it was a calculated response meant to inspire trepidation.

"Just Francisco," he would insist, "like Francisco 'Pancho' Villa." Even so, Francisco had intentionally inspired the nickname "El Barbero" and he wanted his men to think of him as a vicious killer. He certainly was a vicious killer, and a criminal genius.

Gabriel was just as smart, but he lacked the darkness of his brother. Francisco understood the difference and he permitted Gabe no opportunity to join the criminal world of Salt Lake City. Like a good mother's son, Gabriel worked at a small Latino grocery around the corner from his home.

"Gabriel, *no vas afuera.*" Don't go outside, his grandma insisted, her eyes darting around the living room, glancing out the front window. A group of teens howled as they passed by on the sidewalk dragging a shopping cart full of electronics. Gabe's grandma seemed to shrink with the racket.

He led his *abuelita* back to her room, helping her into her favorite chair. Gabriel dashed into his room and came right back with his iPod and Beats headphones. He scrolled through his music list and found Pedro Vargas, his grandmother's favorite crooner. Gabe gently popped the headphones over her ears.

She quieted and he took it as his cue to check on his mama and sister. The ladies had been going through the pantry, getting ready to boil beans for tomorrow's meals. As a single Hispanic mother who knew food was never guaranteed, his mama was a bit of a hoarder. Ever since Francisco had risen in the world of crime, showering the family with gifts and money, their mama kept a massive amount of food in the cupboard, perhaps a silent nod to the impermanent nature of their good fortune. Beans, rice, cooking oil, flour and sugar were stacked in bags and huge gallon jugs. His sister sometimes criticized her mother's obsession with stockpiling. Nobody criticized her now. The store had been closed for a week and the Peña family still had enough food for a month or more.

Despite the revelry and violence outside, no one so much as stepped a toe on their front yard. Everyone in the neighborhood knew the home was protected by Los Latigos, and Gabriel had noticed Latigos soldiers passing by, checking in on the family.

While he watched his mama and sister work in the kitchen, Gabriel heard something thud to the floor in his *abuelita's* room.

He jogged down the hall and peeked inside. His *abuelita* dozed in her chair, still enjoying *The Songs of the Golden Age of Mexican Cinema*. Half inside the room through the window, a white man stared back at Gabriel. The man was filthy, with matted hair, and flecks of food caught up in the tangle of his wild beard. The two men paused for a millisecond staring at one another, then both men sprang into action. The intruder, clearly a homeless man looking for drugs or food, scrambled inside the room, struggling to climb across a bookshelf while holding a kitchen knife.

Gabriel bolted for his bedroom. He dove across his bed and grabbed the AK-47, working the bolt as he launched himself back toward the intruder. As he burst back into the room, the homeless man stood behind his *abuelita*. Seeing the gun, the man shielded himself behind her small body in the chair and put the kitchen knife to her throat.

His *abuelita* awoke to find her grandson pointing a rifle at her and somebody behind her, grabbing her around the shoulders. She flew into a frenzy, bucking and shrieking like a dog caught in a net. The homeless man tried to restrain her, but she flopped so violently that she flew up and out of the chair and dropped to the floor, holding her throat.

While the men stood facing each other, dazed, blood began to pulse between his *abuelita's* fingers in a great flood. Her shrieking tightened into a high-pitched gurgle.

Gabriel snapped back into the horrible reality, took three steps forward and thrust the muzzle of the assault rifle against the homeless man's chest. The small room roared with gunfire, temporarily deafening everyone. The homeless man absorbed six rounds in and around his heart. He slumped to his knees behind the chair, wavered for a moment, then collapsed sideways.

Gabriel's *abuelita* tried to stand, turning toward the chair, still holding her gushing throat with one hand. Gabriel dropped the rifle and held her. He grabbed the crocheted doily on her chair and worked it under her hand onto her neck, adding pressure to the gushing wound.

His mother and sister came running through the door and began screaming.

"Get me a towel," Gabriel shouted over them. "Now!"

His sister disappeared from the doorway and ran back with a bath towel.

By then, his *abuelita* was fading fast, having poured much of her blood onto the carpet. Gabriel clamped the towel around her neck and pulled her onto his lap, cradling her head, tearlessly weeping. His mama and sister joined him on the floor and they held the old woman as she slipped silently from this world to the next.

• • •

Around eleven p.m., Francisco returned home to Rose Park from prison, along with a hundred and twenty of his men. They set up camp in the neighbors' homes, the neighbors allowing the gang members to stay, like a quartering army of old. It wasn't as though they had much choice. Without police anywhere to be found, any law was good law.

Abuelita lay out on the couch in her favorite dress, bloodless and dead. Their sister had placed a dusty bouquet of artificial flowers in her hands over her chest. Francisco's mama and sister had cleaned the blood away and Gabriel had dragged the homeless man's body outside and laid it carefully on the picnic bench in their backyard.

Francisco stood in the backyard, staring at the dead homeless man. Part of him was angry with Gabriel. His brother had promised to protect the family while Francisco was away. Another part of him knew that expecting an eighteen-year-old boy to stop a chance encounter with the Fates was absurd. He promised himself that he would not let Gabriel see his disappointment or anger.

"*Hermano*, I failed you. I'm sorry." Gabriel stepped quietly out of the dark and stood beside Francisco. Francisco pretended not to hear the tears just beneath Gabriel's words. Francisco looked back at the body, noticing how Gabriel had cared for this homeless dirt bag, laying him out with respect. The thought almost brought tears to Francisco's eyes. His little brother had a beautiful heart. If it had been Francisco, he would have tossed the body of the man over by the garbage cans.

"Gabriel, sometimes things just happen and they cannot be stopped."

"But I should have been watching the house more carefully, *hermano*," Gabriel said with conviction, his self-judgment ramping. "I should have caught him before he came in. The window wasn't even locked." Gabriel cried openly now.

"No, *hermanito*. You're wrong. You couldn't have stopped him. Not in a million years and not with a million tries."

You have no idea how cruel this world is, *hermanito*, Francisco thought to himself. I have protected you from the truth. Now you are starting to see. You and everyone else. I've lost my *abuelita* and worse, my brother has lost the untainted life I wanted for him. That can't be changed now.

But now, no man is better suited to rule this place than I am. In this season, cruelty will reign and it will erase the fucking whites. Nobody is ready for this new world—a world of violence. Nobody but me.

• • •

Wyoming Road 713G
Outside Laramie, Wyoming

As Chad Wade approached the mountains of central Wyoming in the dark of autumn night, the back roads had gone from an orderly grid to spaghetti. For a terrible navigator like Chad, it was hell on earth.

But I'm badass at everything else, Chad assured himself.

He juggled back and forth between watching the road through his NVGs and reading the map. The goggles could only focus on one thing at a time—close or far—and they had to be manually re-focused to switch back and forth, a maddening process.

Chad, Audrey and their little girl occasionally drove by camps alongside the dirt roads. People were moving from one point to another during the day and flopping their stuff down at night. Some people headed east, others headed west, and still others headed south. Chad had no clue where they were going nor what they hoped to find.

While he drove, Chad periodically flipped through the radio bands—FM, then AM. He rarely found anyone broadcasting, which wasn't surprising since they were in the middle of nowhere. Once in a while, he found a channel broadcasting from a great distance, always on the AM band.

The U.S. government ran a series of informational broadcasts on the public stations, but the information seemed contrived and contradictory. The federal government encouraged everyone to sit tight, that the power would come back on shortly. He caught a speech by the president, urging calm and condemning the rioters and looters in the major cities.

Some few radio shows told the truth: there had been a mass exodus out of the cities into the mountains and countryside with untold numbers of people starving alongside the roads. Police, fire and military had almost disappeared, presumably returning home to their families. So far, there were no reports of the federal government showing up with FEMA feeding stations. Those organizations, while certainly real, seemed to have vanished with the corporations and other governmental agencies. At this point in time, almost anything requiring organization any bigger than a local church or small town had ceased to exist.

Chad laughed at this last part. His prepper buddies were totally convinced the Feds would come racing in after the Apocalypse, eager to gobble up everyone's constitutional rights. But Chad had experienced the government firsthand. In fact, as a SEAL, he had his PhD in how effective the government really was. In short, they could barely keep their shit squared away on a good day, with power humming, air conditioners running, and supply chains working. Like a hooker without hands, the United States government had trouble just getting undressed, not to mention the finer arts of seduction. In the midst of chaos, Chad guessed, just about everyone drawing a paycheck from "the Gov" would steal their staplers and head home.

The evil Feds might have *intended* to implement draconian FEMA camps, trampling on people's constitutional rights. Who knows? But almost all the folks working for the government, on just about every level, were too inept or too lazy to make anything that nefarious happen, especially under unpredictable circumstances. Without the certainty of a paycheck, why would FEMA "stormtroopers" even show up for work, much less carry out an agenda of questionable oppression? What would be in it for them?

The United States military suffered from the same disease. The rank and file of the branches of the military, while good folks, were professionals. They weren't fanatics, especially the POGs—People Other Than Grunts—the supply and support soldiers and sailors that made up the bulk of the U.S. forces. The POGs often enlisted in the military for free college tuition and a solid paycheck. If all the upsides of being in the military got sketchy, both the POGs and the grunts would start drifting away. Apparently, that's exactly what had happened; the military had largely vanished like a hard-drinking party at clean-up time.

Chad was lost in thought, scanning through the AM band and driving like a bat out of hell, when he rounded a bend outside Laramie, Wyoming. As the corner opened up, something in the middle of the road flashed onto his NVGs. Chad slammed on the brakes and skidded to the outside of the curve, ass-first. He felt the Jeep clip the obstacle and then slide off the road, bouncing over the brush until the vehicle lurched to a stop.

He jumped out of the Jeep with his 1911 at the ready and scrambled up the embankment. In the middle of the gravel road, a boy lay curled up and moaning. Chad didn't immediately move to assist, running down the road first, then crossing far below the injured boy. Once he was confident he hadn't fallen into a trap, Chad approached, still ready for a surprise gunfight.

The boy looked fuzzy in the NVGs since Chad hadn't focused them down yet. He had to stay ready, so he was caught in a pickle between checking the boy for weapons and readying himself for an ambush from the shadows. After a second, he turned the knob, caught a quick visual of the boy and returned the NVGs to an infinite focus. The boy had nothing on him resembling a gun and there was no obvious trauma.

"You okay, kid?" Chad scanned the horizon for threats.

"Yes. I think maybe," the boy said with a Hispanic accent.

"What're you doing in the middle of the road?"

"I walk to Evanston where my family lives."

"The hell you are," Chad replied with a laugh. "That's three hundred miles from here."

"I go to Evanston."

"Okay," Chad relented. "Come with me to my Jeep. I don't want to check you in the middle of the road. Can you walk?"

"I think I can walk." Chad helped the boy up and they hobbled over to his Jeep.

The boy wasn't screaming in pain. He probably wouldn't need medical attention, as though there was such a thing as "medical attention" anymore.

"What's happening out there?" Audrey asked as they approached.

"I sort of hit someone on the road."

Chad had pulled all the fuses from the dome lights, so Audrey had to wait in the dark. "You either hit someone or you didn't. Are they okay?"

"I think so. What's your name?"

"My name is Pacheco."

Chad focused down his NVG and fired up the IR illuminator, like an invisible flashlight on his NVGs. "Where are you hurt?"

"My leg is hurt." Pacheco unbuckled his pants and stepped around to the front fender where the lady couldn't see him. Chad followed. Pacheco pulled his pants down. There was a scrape and one hell of a bruise forming, but there didn't seem to be any major damage.

"Anywhere else?" Chad asked.

"No, just my leg hurt." Pacheco touched his leg and winced.

"Well, stop poking it." Chad laughed, shaking off the anxiety. "You want a ride to Evanston?"

"A ride? Yes." Pacheco nodded. Now that he could see him better, Chad figured the boy was older than he'd initially figured, more like a young man.

"How old are you?" Chad asked out of curiosity.

"I'm eighteen years old."

"And what are you doing way out here, walking in the night?"

Pacheco gave him a quizzical look.

"I mean, why are you so far from your family?"

"I work as cowboy… *vaquero*. I work on the cows."

"Right on, Pacheco. Hop in the back." Chad tilted his seat forward and motioned for Pacheco to get in.

Chad stole a glance at Audrey in the passenger seat. If she had an opinion about their new travel companion, she wasn't saying.

"Amigo," Chad leaned in toward the boy, "can I look through your bag?" He pantomimed taking Pacheco's pack and pawing through it.

"Okay." Pacheco handed him the backpack.

Chad found a little water, a small pocketknife, some food wrapped in tinfoil and personal papers: a birth certificate from Honduras, a state-issued ID card from Wyoming, some pay stubs and some letters. Chad palmed the pocketknife and slipped it into his own pocket.

"No guns?" Chad asked, making the universal symbol for gun with his thumb and finger.

"No. No guns." Pacheco shook his head.

"Okay, then. Good. Let's hit the road." Chad hopped in and steered the Jeep in and around a clump of bushes and bounded back up onto the highway.

They drove for a while, maintaining almost forty miles an hour blacked out. Chad made a few educated guesses with the map, which turned into major mistakes. By the time Chad admitted to himself he had taken them down the wrong road, they had gone twenty-five miles in the opposite direction.

"Damnit!" Chad cursed as he sat alongside the road, trying to bend the map into giving him a different answer. Apparently, he had headed north almost to the town of Lookout, which put him a long-ass way from where he wanted to be.

Getting lost is a lot more frustrating when gas is scarce, Chad realized.

"Screw it." Chad did a messy U-turn and headed back. From here on out, he was going to stay on the interstate. Maybe it wouldn't be so damned confusing.

• • •

"Son of a bitch!" Chad swore for the twentieth time that night. Dawn approached and he had propped his NVGs up and out of the way on his Team Wendy helmet. Instead, he peered through his father-in-law's binoculars. A mile ahead, a roadblock crossed both sides of the interstate.

Apparently, the enterprising men of Elk Mountain, Wyoming were stopping cars and collecting tolls. Elk Mountain sat a good mile off the interstate, so this roadblock wasn't designed to protect the town. This was post-Apocalypse capitalism in action.

The roadblock spanned both sides of the bridge over the Medicine Bow River. It had been strategically located so nobody could drive around it. The map showed no side roads circumventing the blockade, which made sense since the Medicine Bow River was seventy yards wide and necessitated a serious bridge.

The problem with toll booths these days, Chad reminded himself, is you don't know if they'll collect a dollar or collect your life.

Chad drove a couple of miles away from the roadblock, backtracking on the interstate, looking for a place to bed down for the morning. They got off the blacktop and ran dirt roads along the river until they found a remote hidey-hole where Chad could sleep.

Too exhausted to think about the roadblock, he closed his eyes and his head lolled against the cold of the driver's side window. His sleep-addled mind pecked at the problem of the roadblock. What he needed was another SEAL. With two operators, he could have some fun with that roadblock. The delirium of sleep began to carry him away and his mind broke free.

Maybe I could *make* another SEAL, he confabulated as he slipped away, slumped over in his seat.

• • •

"*Buenos dias.*" Pacheco's face peered in through the driver's side window.

Audrey and Sam were already outside, playing by the river.

Chad opened the door and rolled out of the Jeep, his legs stiff. "*Buenos dias, amigo.*"

Chad was one of those guys who thought every idea that crossed his mind popped into his head God-dappled and inspired. He returned to his nighttime bout of inspiration like a retriever going for his tennis ball.

"Pacheco, you want to become a Navy SEAL?" Chad didn't talk much but, when he did, he liked to amuse himself.

Pacheco raised his eyebrows, understanding the words but not the meaning.

"You want to become an American operator? Shoot bad guys? Be very good soldier?"

"Ahh." Pacheco lit up. "Navy SEAL. Best soldier. Charlie Sheen."

Chad tossed his head back and laughed. "Yeah, Charlie Sheen… I make you like Charlie Sheen today. Okay?" He could see this made no sense to the boy, but the kid looked game for anything.

"I'm a Navy SEAL," Chad said, louder than necessary.

Pacheco's expression morphed into disbelief. "You are no Navy SEAL. *¿De veres?* For real?"

Chad laughed again. "I *am* a Navy SEAL." He flexed his biceps. "See. Badass."

162

Pacheco chuckled and pretended to believe him. "Okay. You are Navy SEAL. Maybe."

Chad went through a mental inventory of everything he used to teach in BUD/S—the Navy SEAL selection course. But BUD/S wasn't really training. It had been selection. Selection found guys with the "right stuff" to be SEALs, not to train them *per se*. He supposed he had already completed the selection process by running this kid over in the first place.

Now that he thought about it, what he really needed right now was a sniper. Maybe he would train Pacheco on that first.

Chad dug out the 30-06 and set aside some shells.

"You learn to shoot with these." Chad held up the shells. "You shoot rifle before?"

Pacheco shook his head.

"I teach you."

They shot most of the shells in the box, leaving only six rounds. Pacheco took to shooting like a woman, and Chad had taught many women. Women had no ego tied up in the process, unlike men. They listened to every bit of instruction and applied that instruction relentlessly.

Ninety-nine percent of accuracy, especially with a long rifle, boiled down to trigger squeeze. If the shooter achieved a surprise break—where the pressure increased incrementally on the trigger until the gun fired—then the shot would be good. If the shooter "mashed" the trigger, like snapping his fingers, the shot would go wide of the target every time.

Pacheco picked up right away on shooting dead calm. He was a natural at controlling the aggression response that often proceeded trigger mash. The boy performed so well Chad kept moving the target farther and farther, picking out distant rocks for Pacheco to bust. Before they knew it, they had blown through most of their ammo.

The last watermelon-sized boulder "killed" by Pacheco was almost five hundred yards away. Secretly, Chad had doubts he could make the shot himself.

163

Chad clapped with exuberance. "Muy bueno, amigo! You are a sniper."

Pacheco's grin looked like it might break his face.

"I think you like to shoot, huh?"

"Yes. Shooting is good."

"You ready for a fight? With the rifle?"

"I help you fight. With this." Pacheco held up the 30-06.

We'll see, Chad thought. Busting rocks is a lot different than busting men. Anyone can kill a rock.

• • •

Around 2:00 a.m., Chad and Pacheco parked alongside the road, and jogged the last mile to the bridge with the roadblock. They had taken plenty of time to discuss the plan beforehand, not moving out until Chad was convinced Pacheco understood exactly what he was supposed to do.

They could see the floodlight illuminating the barricade and could hear the generator humming. Without any further instruction, Pacheco broke right and slid down the embankment, wading into the deep grass. He set a course toward the Medicine Bow River several hundred yards downstream from the bridge.

Chad carefully picked apart the roadblock with his NVGs. Nothing had changed from the night before. A jumble of beat-up trucks, parked ass to nose, blocked all four lanes of the freeway in two rows, creating a gap in between. In the gap, the country boys had lined up a row of plastic camping chairs, each with its own cooler. Three of the chairs were occupied by the graveyard shift, young lads who had no doubt drawn the short straws of dark and cold night duty.

Good. Chad hoped they were comfy in those chairs.

Behind the chairs and coolers, they had parked a Chevy Blazer off the side of the road. The vehicle must have been used to shuttle back and forth between town and the roadblock. All three men sat in the lawn chairs, talking smack and telling tales, probably trying to stay awake.

Their operational procedure, apparently, was to wait until a car came into view, then step up to the barricade. Until such time, they defaulted to country-time lawn chair routine: sitting around with guns slung across their laps, downing Pabst Blue Ribbon.

The bridge made a perfect chokepoint. Nobody could drive around the roadblock. The Medicine Bow River presented an absolute barrier to vehicles.

However, as Chad thought about it from the perspective of an assaulter, the bridge made the guards sitting ducks. The guards couldn't counter-flank. In a fight, the local yokels would have to win a head-on gunfight against an approaching enemy. While the guards could hide behind the old pickup trucks, those approaching could hide behind their own cars, too, evening the odds. The guards had only one direction to retreat, and that would leave them running down the middle of an open road, tucking tail back to the Chevy Blazer.

The most lethal disadvantage of their roadblock was the same for any roadblock: it inspired false confidence. Anyone willing to swim the Medicine Bow River could come up behind the guards and slit their throats. They were betting their lives on human nature, that an opponent would take the lazy path.

Little did the local boys know they would be squaring off with one-and-a-half Navy SEALs. Navy SEALs didn't mind getting wet, so long as they got to kill or screw someone afterward.

Liking what he saw at the barricade, Chad committed to the assault, breaking to the left and sliding down the embankment. Before slipping into the river, Chad pulled a pair of Ziploc bags out of his pocket and sealed up his Rob Leatham 1911 handgun and five magazines. He felt confident the water wouldn't screw up the ammo and he knew it wouldn't hurt the gun, but a gunfight was the wrong time to find out your ammo sucked.

He wore his bump helmet, and he had clipped his NVGs to it. He had swum a cumulative total of about fifty miles in his life doing the Navy SEAL sidestroke, and there was zero chance Chad would get his helmet and NVGs wet while crossing.

The Medicine Bow ran smooth, brown and calm, and Chad made short work of paddling across. He swam directly under the trestles of the bridge, completely hidden from sight.

On the other side of the interstate, Pacheco crossed the same river, but Chad wasn't worried. He had made the boy test-swim the river a couple of times that day, just to make sure he wouldn't drown. Pacheco did fine. He had given the boy double garbage bags to seal up his rifle and the ammo, mostly worried about the optic getting wet.

Chad climbed onto a boulder, unwrapped his handgun, and returned the mags to his now-soaked chest rig. Not wanting to jinx the mission by littering, Chad folded up the Ziplocs and tucked them into an empty mag pouch.

The embankment under the bridge was all sharp boulders, and he quietly climbed up, waiting just below the guardrail. The plan was for Chad to spring into action as soon as Pacheco gave the signal.

Several minutes later, right on cue, the floodlight exploded in a shower of glass. The light winked out. A half-second later, the 30-06 boomed.

Chad sprinted for the Chevy Blazer.

The local boys sprang to their feet with the explosion. They jumped behind the old trucks, pointing their guns up the interstate, the opposite direction from Chad.

Chad reached the Blazer and crouched behind the front wheel, unnoticed by the local boys. He smiled big, getting that rush when he "back-doored" someone and they didn't know it yet. The boys had their backs to him. His only concern was that Pacheco might shoot him accidentally—or the even less likely possibility that the shitkickers had some kind of overwatch guy with a long rifle covering the roadblock from a distance.

166

Chad figured the country boys were in Pacheco's scope, their denim-clad asses filling his reticle. By swimming the river, both Chad and the boy had these guys dead to rights on the wrong side of their roadblock. The only thing left was the crying.

Chad stood up behind the engine block of the Chevy Blazer and took his time formulating what he would say. He didn't like to rush a sweet coup de grâce.

"If you turn around, I'm going to shoot you another asshole, right through your Wranglers."

Of course, the dumbest one of the bunch turned around, startled.

Boom!

Chad's 1911 punched a hole in the guy's shoulder, deliberately hitting him off-center.

"Stay put, dumb ass!" Chad yelled. The guy he'd shot whimpered loudly.

"Shut up, numb nuts. Put your guns down on the asphalt and show me your hands over your heads."

The boys complied.

As soon as they were disarmed, Chad glanced over his shoulder, checking his six. About seventy yards down the road, he saw a shadow scamper across the pavement—Pacheco, moving to cover the road from town in case someone heard the shots and came to investigate.

Navy SEAL material, Chad smiled. The boy had just needed a bad-ass instructor.

"Step away from the roadblock backward and stand in front of your lawn chairs." The cowboys shuffled back toward the chairs. "Keep your hands straight up, shitkickers. Look straight forward. Don't look at me."

Chad walked behind and checked them one at a time for other weapons, finding a handgun and a knife on all but the guy he'd shot.

"Now sit your asses down." The guy who'd been shot squealed as he flopped into the chair.

"Where are the other guards?" Chad yelled at them.

"There ain't no one but us."

"Well, if anyone else shows up, I'll be ventilating your fool heads. So speak up now or you'll get some brain juice in your lap."

"Honest. It's just us."

Chad slipped off his go-bag and pulled out a roll of duct tape, still soggy. He stepped to the side of the biggest cowboy, a sloppy-gutted giant of a boy, and dropped the duct tape into his lap.

"Okay, Lennie Small, you're going to tape these two other shitkickers real tight to their chairs and you're going to do it without looking at me. I'll save you the trouble. I'm a Special Forces operator and I have a huge hand cannon and night vision goggles. You're about as fucked as it gets, so your best play here is to go with *my* program. If you don't believe me, it's all good. I've got plenty of night-night pills in this hand cannon."

Even though Chad was positive the hicks wouldn't catch his Steinbeck reference to Lennie Small, it amused *him* and he had to take his pleasure where he could get it.

As soon as the big cowboy finished, Chad ordered him back to his chair and taped him up, too.

Chad refocused his NVGs and walked around to the guns the boys had left on the ground.

"Hot damn," he said and whistled. Two AR-15s and another long rifle with a scope. "Now that wouldn't happen to be a 30-06, would it?" Chad looked at his prisoners and one of them nodded.

"Sweet." Chad scooped the guns up and ran them over to the Blazer, popping the back door and awkwardly tossing them inside. Next, he ran back and grabbed the handguns and knives, dumping them in the Blazer, too.

Chad whistled and Pacheco came running.

"I'd love to stay and drink with you, boys, but we gotta git. At some point, I imagine your mamas will come looking for you for breakfast, and I wouldn't want any of them to be tempted by my sweet loving and maybe bail on your papas."

Pacheco jumped in the Blazer, moving to the "getaway" phase of the plan. He fired up the SUV and flashed the headlights four times, Audrey's signal to drive the Jeep forward.

Chad hopped in one of the beater trucks and backed it out of blocking position. Audrey rolled though the gap and Chad climbed out. Before he shut off the ignition, he paused.

It was a stupid idea, but he couldn't help himself. He ran over to the big cowboy and pulled off one of his boots. Chad ran back to the old pickup, still idling.

He jammed the boot on top of the gas pedal, making the engine scream like a chimp on fire. Chad shut the door, reached in the window and threw the gear selector in reverse.

The truck launched into gear and just about ripped Chad's arm off. It caromed into the other truck, crossed the lanes and punched through the guardrail, falling eighty feet into the Medicine Bow River.

Chad couldn't hold back his shit-eating grin, even though his arm hurt like hell.

Audrey gave him the look of death. "Asshole," she said.

He ran around to the driver's side of the Jeep, switching places with his ex, and sped off into the night, westbound, with Pacheco following behind him in the Blazer.

• • •

Ten miles down the road, Chad turned onto a dirt road, and Pacheco followed him. They pulled over and Chad came round to the passenger side of the Blazer. He yanked the door open and the dome light came on.

"Lookey here." Chad could see that the backseat and the rear cargo compartment were full of supplies. Ammo, food, booze, and the guns Chad had taken from the men. Apparently, the Blazer was where the cowboys stored the "road tolls" for the day.

Pacheco hopped out and opened the tailgate. Chad joined him.

"We're in business. High five, *amigo*." Chad held up his hand. Pacheco smiled big, looking like he was twelve years old. He gave Chad a big high five.

"Good swim?" Chad joked. "Was it like when you swam into *los Estados Unidos?*"

Pacheco had no problem understanding the insinuation and he glared at Chad.

"I crossed the border in a minivan."

9

"THIS IS YOUR HOST AND humble servant, JT Taylor, getting the evening started with a brown bottle and a bunch of news—none of it good.

"Two days ago, Turkey decided to roll into Iraq with their main fighting force, blowing past the Kurds and working their way toward the oil fields. Not sure there's much of a market for oil right now, boys, but old dreams die hard, I suppose.

"Here's where I read the list of cities that're now burning: San Fran, Sacramento, San Diego, San Antonio—shitty night for 'S' cities, apparently. Phoenix is burning. There's a 'P' city for you. So, that's pretty much all of them. All of the cities are burning, so please stop calling me and asking which cities are burning. You're harshing my mellow.

"Oh, and Europe. I got a questionable call from one of our Army bases in Germany saying that ISIS is taking down civilian targets. How the hell did ISIS get to Germany? Weren't they in Syria?..."

Peña Residence
Rose Park, Salt Lake City, Utah

Life was serving Francisco a fleeting opportunity, like a beautiful woman across a room—once she walked away, the threads of fate would whither to dust and there would be nothing but regret. He needed to act now and act with boldness.

The American ways were quickly dying. The blood of white Americans had grown thinner each decade with greed, wealth and too much power. They turned their backs on their poor. They cast their elderly aside. They slaved away in corporations to buy one week per year on a beach in Mexico, sipping drinks and tanning their lily-white skin in the sunshine.

His people, *los Mexicanos*, always had sunshine. They always had one another. They honored their elders. They never turned their backs on family. Their food remained wholesome and fresh. Their claims on the land stayed pure.

The white Americans didn't know who they were. They only knew selfishness. The gringos had no compass, no culture of their own. They straddled the lands of others and fed themselves on dreams of money.

Like Pancho Villa, Francisco would begin his attack with the haciendas. Poor people usually destroyed their own neighborhoods when they rioted, but Francisco would riot with intelligence. His violence would have meaning. His violence would carry the seeds of revolution.

Francisco and his men would sweep the haciendas clean, and then turn the palaces of white greed over to his soldiers and their mothers. And the white people would die with their diseased culture on their breath.

172

On the ten-mile walk from prison to his home in Rose Park, Francisco's gang had moved through the white people like a snake through water. The gringos couldn't function outside their controlled civilization; they thought rules still applied and that the police would come. They were not prepared for the violent decisiveness of Francisco and his men. They were unprepared for men who didn't hesitate.

Soon the white people would understand the true way of the world, but for now they were like children, wandering and unsure. Francisco and his people would take back as much as possible, as quickly as possible. It would be easy at first, but it would grow more difficult as time passed.

He knew he must attack today, even though he lacked information. His instincts told him that he and his men could take the entire wealthy area above the capital—the Avenues—within a day or two. Hundreds of homes and many tons of supplies would be theirs. And he had always dreamed of moving his mama into a big home in the Avenues.

With a great victory on the winds, he could expand his numbers with the tens of thousands of Latinos in the Salt Lake Valley, giving him a true army. This morning, Francisco would spread the word among all Latinos: gather in Rose Park for food and shelter.

He awoke early. Prison hours forced early sleep and early rising. It had actually become his preference and, as a side benefit, he had gotten to watch his first sunrise in three years. The men who had been with him in prison were waking up, too, walking out into the yards of their host homes.

"Crudo, come here," Francisco ordered the first man he saw.

The man jogged across the street. "*Buenos dias, Jefe.* Tell me."

"Get all the lieutenants here in fifteen minutes."

Crudo's eyes widened. "Okay, *Jefe*, I'll wake them." He took off at a run.

• • •

It had all the makings of a historic morning. The lieutenants were in fine spirits, many of them warming their hands with hot coffee or *maisena*, compliments of their host families. The early morning air had just begun to chill enough to see their breath, and a thick head of steam came off the hot drinks. Just as they began their meeting, the sun peeked over Mount Olympus on the Wasatch Front.

"*Hermanos*, today we take back this land." Francisco looked at each of them. They smiled like kids on Christmas morning.

"The gringos' world is broken and they're like puppies without their mothers. Now is our time to take it from them. All of it. And we will give it to our mamas and our sisters. All their wealth and their homes will soon will be ours."

The men all nodded. In truth, most of them preferred money and drugs to visions of social justice, but it sounded like they were going to get both.

"First," Francisco said, "we need to call the Latinos in this valley to join us. Any man who wants food, water and a chance to better his family should go to the county fairgrounds on North Temple Street. Bring guns, ammunition and all the food they can carry. That will be our base of operations. It has plenty of room and the river is close for water and washing."

"Bastardo," Francisco turned to one of his older lieutenants, "you're in charge of the fairgrounds. We need to turn the river water into drinking water, and we need to settle all the families that come. Send me fighting men. We're hitting the Avenues today or tomorrow."

"*Si, Jefe.*" Bastardo nodded. The men shifted back and forth, their eagerness rising with the mention of raiding.

"Kermit, I want you to gather all the teenagers, and send them out as messengers to the Latino neighborhoods. Let them know we have food, water, and that Latinos are gathering at the fairgrounds. Don't mention fighting to the people. Most of them will need time to get used to the idea."

Kermit nodded.

"Digger, you'll be in charge of sending men to help us in the Avenues." Francisco pulled a map out of his back pocket and stepped over to a picnic bench. He opened the map and rotated it. The men gathered around, curious and excited.

"The fairgrounds are here." Francisco poked the map. "We'll be moving up Fourth Street, then turning north onto Seventh East." He drew a line on the map. "From there, we'll head up I Street and start jacking the Avenues, one block at a time. We'll run the gringos off and take everything we want. For now, leave the electronics. No TVs or stereos. We want food, booze, guns, ammunition, money, cigarettes… anything we can eat, drink or trade.

"Digger, you need to keep some men along this route to make sure we don't lose our road back to the fairgrounds. We need to be able to move men and supplies back and forth. It's only about two miles. Grab anyone you need from the reinforcements to keep these streets under our control. Position men with guns every block, right?"

"Sure. No problem, Francisco."

"Mad Dog, I want you to organize men to load the stuff we capture in pickups and bring it back to the fairgrounds. If we start handing out food and supplies to the families at the fairgrounds, we'll have thousands here within a day. Word will spread. You understand?"

"How do I decide who to give supplies?" Mad Dog looked confused.

"It doesn't matter, *hermano*. Give them to anyone who's Latino. You'll be just like Santa Claus—an ugly brown Santa Claus."

The guys laughed. Mad Dog was indeed ugly.

"The rest of you lead the home invasions. Start with your crew and, when more Latinos arrive in the Avenues, put them to work. *¿Comprenden?* Meet back here in an hour with as many men as you can. Go."

The lieutenants turned and headed out to find men. They weren't clear on the plan, but they all knew how to fight, and they knew they would figure it out along the way. The chaotic tempo of violence was nothing new to them.

• • •

Ross Homestead
Oakwood, Utah

Jeff watched morning light work its way across the valley. In a bit, it would peek over the hill and the day would start in earnest. He had that feeling of the calm before the storm. It would be a long day but, for now, he enjoyed his coffee and the view—orange-tinted oaks and maples, rolling up and over the hillsides and dropping into the muted valley, backlit by the dawn.

There were deer out everywhere, nipping at the mountainside fields of grass and wild alfalfa. The Homestead managed their perimeter security, and the deer were pouring into the safe zone created by the defensive line, an unintended but welcome game preserve.

Jeff didn't know a lot about wild game. He had spent his adult life chasing prey of the two-legged variety. Even though he was a native son of Utah, he had never gone hunting with his dad or brothers. Since he graduated high school, he had been deployed overseas or training somewhere during hunting season. Maybe now that he had retired from all that crap, he could get around to hunting.

Jeff smiled, noticing how even his mind hadn't adjusted to the new world. There might never again be a state-regulated deer hunt and here he was, thinking about the annual hunting trip with his brothers.

If Jeff could see the deer, so could the neighbors. Sure as hell, they would start trespassing, hoping to shoot some meat. It would be impossible to tell the difference between a neighbor and an invader. Both would be wearing camo and carrying scoped rifles. He would need to nail down a Standard Operating Procedure (SOP) to hopefully avoid shooting the locals.

Jeff's job was to keep the Homestead from being overrun, and that meant keeping strangers out of the Homestead and away from seeing their supplies. He couldn't allow anyone to even look at the Homestead grounds. If Jeff wanted to attack this place, he would recon it, nail down the security patterns, and hit it when it was most vulnerable.

Step one of defense, and perhaps the most important step, was to keep anyone from conducting a proper recon. That meant shooting people before they got a look/see. If the weak-willed jack-offs back at camp didn't like that, too bad. Jeff didn't want to kill anyone who didn't need killing, but that desire ran a distant second to fulfilling the mission and protecting his men and his family.

For now, the threat level hadn't risen to shoot-at-first-contact because Jeff hadn't seen anything to make him believe they were facing organized opposition. They had seen and deflected dozens of hungry wanderers. Almost every one of those wanderers had been carrying a gun. But they had responded like one would expect—like starving idiots heading to the hills. But if *he* were going to recon this place and take it down, that's just how he would make himself appear, like a lost soul wandering onto private property.

The SOP he would implement today would order a single warning shot to give trespassers one last chance to turn around. It would require more men, since they would need one position to provide the warning shot, while another position would be preparing to kill the intruder. It would be dangerous to have a warning shot come from the primary position, forfeiting surprise and putting that man at risk.

Adding more duty slots meant adding troop fatigue, and adding fatigue meant degraded readiness. Morale would dip, and that mattered quite a bit, especially when almost all of his men were civilians, and half of them were crippled by culture shock as it was.

Jeff toyed with the idea of using megaphones to give verbal warnings, but he didn't think they had enough megaphones to cover the perimeter. Plus a verbal warning would take several seconds, and that would give an enemy shooter time to dial in the location of the megaphone. He would be putting his guys at too much risk.

He could use non-combatants as the megaphone operators. But, if just one woman or kid got shot through the head while blabbing on a megaphone, the civilians back at the Homestead would lose their ever-loving minds. He might well lose a third of his civilian gunmen to the psychological trauma of a dead woman or kid. He couldn't rely on any level of discipline or mental toughness. These civilians were fragile, whether he liked it or not. A lot of them had trained to shoot fairly well, but that didn't mean a damned thing when it came to facing the foul realities of killing.

The best option would be a single warning shot. That was still bad, since a good enemy sniper could use that information to locate the shooter. Most of the perimeter was comprised of steep hills and canyons. That would work to their advantage, making the sound of a rifle bounce around like a racquetball.

On second thought, they could set up dummy locations around the perimeter: fake bunkers with shiny stuff, maybe make a dummy that resembled a dude's head. Perhaps they could sucker a shot from anyone meaning harm to his defenders. Decoys might be a good option.

The sun broke the hilltop, and that meant time for philosophizing had come to an end. Jeff would now have to talk to other human beings, not his favorite kind of work.

In fact, Winslow was walking up the drive, beelining toward him.

Jeff reminded himself of his priorities today. Get the security guys briefed. Assault the three targets down in the valley. Hospital. Pharmacy. Refinery.

Assaults… the word made Jeff smile. He could use a little adrenaline today, and he was pretty sure nobody would get shot rolling up on a hospital and a refinery. Easy stuff. He would get to put the wood to some targets, and it would be for their own good. What could be better than that?

Easy day.

• • •

Oakwood, Utah
Canyon Hospital

Jeff took a last look at the little hospital through his binos. It was the same as the recon report from yesterday: one rent-a-cop standing at the entrance to the emergency room. The guy must not have a family, Jeff guessed. He looked like he was in his twenties and soft around the middle. Typical single guy. The guard carried a sidearm, but Jeff was pretty sure he could win him over with his sparkling personality.

They were ahead of schedule. Turned out, the building Jeff had designated as the Objective Rally Point—where they rallied to assault the hospital—was also a pharmacy. Taking that pharmacy had been about as hard as asking your mom to dance.

An old gal, the former manager, had been there on duty, but she wanted to go home real bad and she was more than happy to turn the place over to anyone willing to take it. Amazingly, nobody had screwed with the drugs in the back. All the meds were right where they were supposed to be, with plenty of narcotics in neat little slots on a big rack.

Jeff checked in with the other elements of his assault team and gave the go command on the hospital. He didn't have to belabor the process with his lead guys; Evan and Alec were already moving their teams into flanking positions. He could count on them like a morning dump.

Jeff, his rifle slung around his back, walked straight up to the rent-a-cop in front of the emergency room. "Hey, buddy."

His two wingmen, both guys from the Homestead, fanned out, drifting behind cover but keeping their hands off their bang-sticks.

"Stop right there!" The security guard held out his hand and placed his other hand on his handgun.

"Whoa, brother." Jeff put both his hands out front, using the universal sign for *whoa*.

What the security guard didn't know was that Jeff had practiced quick draw and shooting from this very position about ten thousand times. Jeff didn't doubt he could drop the security guard before the guy's gun cleared his holster.

"Stop right there!" the security guard repeated.

"Here's the deal, bro. We're here to help. We'd like to join your security detail." Jeff figured it was only a small lie. "We want to help protect the hospital from looters. You good with that?"

The security guard kept his hand on his gun, his eyes darting about. "Wha... What do you want?" he stammered.

"Take your hand away from your gun and we'll talk this through. We want to help secure the hospital. I'm National Guard and so are my buddies." Another small lie. "We're from the 19th Special Forces Group and we're here to help." That one was a whopper. Only he and Evan could claim any connection to the 19th Group, and they definitely weren't here on orders.

"Okay. Do you have some ID?" The kid really wanted to believe him.

"Sure. I'm going to reach into my pocket, so don't shoot me, okay?" Jeff had no concerns about the guy shooting him. Out of the corner of his eye, Jeff could see Evan off to his right, leaning over the hood of a car with his M4. He would drop the security guard if he so much as itched his arm.

Jeff reached into a pocket on his chest rig and slowly pulled out his National Guard ID. Jeff reached out to hand it over, and the guard went to take it. With a flash of movement, Jeff had the guy's gun arm twisted behind his back. The guard's eyes went wide and he grunted with the sudden change of circumstances. One moment he had been in control of the situation and the next moment he was helpless.

"All right, pal. Now we've got that out of the way and we're good buddies, how about you take me to the boss?" Jeff used his free arm to reach around and pull the guard's firearm out of the holster. Jeff handed it off to one of his wingmen. He kept the guard's arm cranked behind his back for good measure, but he let up a little on the pressure. They would probably be on the same team with the security guard in a few minutes, so no point in damaging the guy's ego any more than he must.

The guard led Jeff and his two men inside and through the hospital while Evan and Alec covered the outside of the building. After a couple of turns down the inside corridors, Jeff came around a corner to find a disheveled doctor behind a nurse's desk in the emergency room, hiding from them. Somehow, the doctor had known they were coming.

"What is going on here?" the doctor shouted, seeing three guys in military clothes manhandling his security guard.

"Good morning, Doc." Jeff reached out his right hand, a big smile on his face, still pinning the guard's arm. "We're here to help."

"Yeah, then why are you holding my guard like you're his mean big brother?" the doctor barked.

"Sorry about that. We're just becoming friends and we still have a couple of things to work out." Jeff released the arm and pushed the guard toward one of his guys with a flick of his eyes that said *cover this guy*.

"How're you going to help us?" the doctor asked, unconvinced.

"Today, maybe tomorrow, this hospital is going to be overrun with druggies. Your mall ninja here isn't going to be able to stop more than one or two of those fellas coming for free OxyContin. Right?"

"Yeah, we've already been robbed twice." The doctor managed to look even more haggard when he said it. "We don't have much in the way of drugs here. If that's what you want, you're barking up the wrong tree."

"No, sir, we're not looking for drugs. We'd like to keep this place from being burned to the ground. We're Special Forces formerly attached to the 19th Group at Tooele." Jeff figured it would be a good time to dial back on the fiction, especially if he wanted long-term cooperation. The doctor was an asset he hoped to retain. "Here's my ID from the Army."

Jeff reached across the desk and handed the ID to the doctor. "We're not on orders, but we're looking to do some good deeds and we figured we'd help protect your hospital."

"Okay. Then what do you want?" The doctor sat down hard in the nurse's chair and rubbed his eyes, handing back the ID with his free hand.

"I just want to leave some guys here to help Mr. Security Guard," Jeff told him. "That's it. Can everyone get behind that plan?"

"Yeah, I guess we can give that a try. So long as you promise to leave if we ask you to leave."

Jeff said nothing and the doctor took it as agreement. He stood and shook hands with Jeff. "I'm Doctor Lewis and this is Steve." He motioned toward the security guard. "You should know we called the police when we saw you out front."

"Oh, your cell's working? Did the police answer?" Jeff asked.

"Well, we called a cop we know down the street. We had his cell number. He's on his way."

Like clockwork, Jeff's radio squawked. "Jeff, Evan. Over."

"Go ahead," Jeff spoke into the radio hanging from his shoulder strap.

"We've got us a boy in blue out here, and we're pointing guns at each other."

"Roger. I'm coming out. We made friends inside. It's all good. Don't shoot anyone."

"Copy."

Jeff motioned for his guys to stay with Steve, and he headed out the ER doors with Doctor Lewis.

The cop hunched behind his car, trying to cover fifteen soldiers at once with his Glock.

"Hold up, boys," Jeff shouted as he came through the door, placing the doctor between him and the cop.

"Doctor Lewis, you okay?" the cop shouted.

"I'm good, Officer," Doctor Lewis said. "These men are from the National Guard and they're here to help us protect the hospital."

"Is that right? Then why aren't they driving a Hummer, and why are they pointing their rifles at me?"

"I can explain," Jeff chimed in. "Officer, we're not under orders. We came here on our own to help out. We'd like to keep the hospital intact for everyone's benefit. That make sense to you?"

"Yep," the cop agreed, "that makes sense if you're not full of shit. From what I can see, you're robbing this hospital."

Jeff laughed. *Damn cops. No trust.*

"Does it really matter? This isn't a situation where your skeptical nature is going to buy you anything good. Am I right?"

The cop laughed, stood up straight and holstered his gun.

"You got a point there. So what's the scam?" He walked over to Jeff, ignoring the rifles pointed at him.

Brave enough guy, Jeff thought.

"Officer Jacobs," Jeff read the guy's name tag, "why are you in uniform? Ain't you heard? The police 401K has gone down the tubes."

Jacobs laughed. "I'm not on duty. I don't think anyone's on duty. I live down the street, and I told Doc Lewis to call me if any more druggies came by. I figure that wearing a uniform makes it slightly less likely that someone will shoot me. You guys apparently operate on the same theory."

"Yeah, something like that." Jeff had ordered all his men to wear multi-cam BDUs. They had tons of camo at the Homestead, and it made them seem more official and more lethal. Uniforms, patches, and even helmets, as useless as they might be, added an air of "don't fuck with me." That kind of thing, Jeff reasoned, went a long way in the new Wild West.

"Okay, boys, am I supposed to just go on home?" Jacobs asked.

"How about this?" Jeff had an idea. "How about you stay on the job—help us keep this hospital all nice and pretty?"

"And what do I get outta that? My 401K is in rough shape, as you pointed out."

"How about we feed your family and protect them behind a secure perimeter? How's that for a deal?"

The cop thought about it for a second. "I'm not sure how you'd do that, but that's the kind of deal that sells itself."

Jeff stepped forward and offered his hand. "We got us a deal. This is Josh and he's going to take a ride with you and show you and your family up to our little piece of heaven on that hill over there. How's that sound?" Jeff pointed to one of his trainees and then up the hill in the direction of the Homestead.

Jacobs shook Jeff's hand. "Okay then. Sounds like a deal."

Jeff turned and walked over to Evan.

"See? I can make friends and influence people. When are you guys going to start believing in me?"

"Not only is it the Apocalypse," Evan countered, "but we're seeing bona fide miracles. You're making people *like* you instead of just stomping on them. It's truly the Second Coming of the Lord Almighty. Next thing you know, lions and lambs will be lying down together, making sweet love."

The rest of the morning, Jeff's team rolled up another pharmacy and checked out two others. The big chain pharmacies were totally looted out, but they did manage to score a small mom-and-pop pharmacy that was being guarded by a shotgun-toting owner. Jeff turned on the charm and won the old guy over. No shots fired.

At each location, Jeff left an NCO—non-commissioned officer, basically the highest ranking enlisted guy—and a small contingent of men. He would need to send down supplies and relief troops daily from the Homestead.

His ham radio nerd up at the Homestead had hooked them up with three ham base stations, even though their little hand-held ham radios seemed to work well between town and the Homestead. The only thing that nagged at Jeff was the lack of communications security. Pretty much anyone who stumbled onto their frequency could listen in and figure out what they were doing. He had instituted a list of codes with his guys. But, if an enemy listened long enough, they would figure it out.

For their last stop, Jeff's team selected the smallest and closest of six refineries to "liberate." They had made that choice based on intel; the Homestead had a member who used to work at that refinery, and he knew how the plant functioned.

It wasn't as though the Homestead planned on refining its own gas, at least not for a long time. But the refinery maintained tens of thousands of gallons of fuel of several types in a dozen huge tanks. Until the gas went bad, they could use it or sell it. And, if they survived long enough to rebuild society, having an intact refinery would be a huge step ahead for everyone.

All that was gravy as far as Jeff was concerned. His primary goal was to keep the Special Operations boys busy. If they weren't given meaningful work, they would start breaking stuff around the house. Might as well get them doing something useful. Preserving infrastructure and assaulting targets fit the bill. Plus, Jeff suspected that gas and medicine would become the new money when things settled down. Being rich in consumables during the Zombie Apocalypse couldn't hurt.

As they reconnoitered the refinery, Jeff didn't like what he saw. Security around the facility showed organization, with three armed guards covering sensible fields of fire. The security forces were undermanned, but it looked like Jeff might have to get in a shooting fight in order to take the plant.

A choice had to be made: either assault the refinery or talk the guards into giving it up. He would sacrifice surprise by talking to the security guards, but there was a lot of upside to trying to talk them down. For one thing, he would avoid any risk of casualties or damage to the refinery. One stray bullet could cause a leak that he didn't know how to fix. Capturing a refinery with a hundred holes in it sort of defeated the purpose.

His team deployed in a rough perimeter, and Jeff marched straight up to the refinery gate.

Nothing happened. Jeff pounded on the gate, and, still nothing happened. Evan reported by radio that the guards had tightened their defensive positions, presumably because they knew there was an armed guy in military camo hollering at their gate. Two of the security guys were positioned on top of storage tanks and another was covering the gate with his rifle.

Jeff found some cover behind a guard shack, and he went through his options. He could still assault the plant. They could probably shoot all the defenders without losing anyone, but that would open up Pandora's Box of Combat—meaning: you never knew what you'd get.

Play stupid games, win stupid prizes, Jeff reminded himself.

He could sneak in and light a fire up against one of the storage tanks, forcing the security guards' hand. But that defeated the purpose of the assault in the first place, especially if the fire spread to other tanks.

Jeff routinely geeked out over military history, especially feudal warfare. It occurred to him this situation penciled out like a modern-day siege. Why not form a cordon around the facility and wait? The guards probably didn't have much water. They were probably getting water from the irrigation ditch to the west of the plant. His guys could deny them their water source without any risk at all.

That plan seemed to accomplish both of Jeff's objectives: keeping the SOF guys busy and protecting the refinery. If hungry pyromaniacs came around to light the refinery on fire, Jeff's guys would shoot them. Even though he had hoped for the thrill of victory today, bottling up the refinery accomplished everything he needed.

"Evan. Jeff. Over."

"Go ahead."

"How about we just let these guys sit for a few days? They've got to get thirsty sometime. Over."

Evan radioed back, ignoring radio protocol. "Oh, Great Lord Clovenhoof, we shall besiege the castle at your command… You're the tactician. Sounds good to me. Over."

"Copy. I'm coming back. Over."

Jeff trotted out from behind cover and ran across the field to Evan.

"I've got another idea," Jeff huffed, just a touch winded.

"Oh, boy." Evan started laughing. When Jeff got creative, life got complicated. Evan knew this from many years of adventure with Jeff.

Jeff steeled himself for a hard sell. "The Homestead could spare you and probably ten of these guys. I think Ross is working on adding a bunch of neighborhood guys to perimeter defense, and I can train those guys up in a few days. I think we have a little time. Do you want to go on a fun run?"

"Sign me up, brother. What could possibly go wrong?"

Jeff smiled. "This is just a thought, so don't shoot it down right away. Why don't you guys borrow a few toys from the Army Depot?"

Evan looked away, smiling. "Fucking thug. It's always gotta be wild and crazy with you. Do you have a couple dozen main battle tanks I don't know about? How're we going to take stuff from the Army Depot? They're actual troops, not dipshits like these guys." Evan waved back at the refinery.

"Hear me out." Jeff held up his hands defensively. "I was just out at the depot and that place was leaking guys like a wool condom. There's no way they can cover down on all those ammo bunkers; there's like two hundred of them. And, as you know, they've got good stuff. Not just .223, but belt-feds, high explosives. Dude, if the world keeps going downhill, ammo and guns will be the same as money. I don't know about you, but I like money."

Evan thought about it for a moment. "Sure. Fuck it. Let's go rob the Army Depot. Sounds like good times. Who do you want me to take?"

Twenty minutes later, Evan and ten guys marched west, looking for cars to steal.

• • •

Federal Heights,
Salt Lake City, Utah

Carl Redmund invited Jimmy hunting. Jimmy said yes, but ran through a long list of misgivings in his mind. This wasn't a world where a man should agree to something because he wanted to avoid conflict, but that's exactly what Jimmy had done.

Back in the old world—just one week ago, he reminded himself—Jimmy used to hold Carl Redmund in awe. Redmund had been a football player at the University of Utah and he had undoubtedly had sex with scores of women and had, literally, been the big swinging dick on campus.

That was twenty years ago and, even though Jimmy hadn't even gone to the University of Utah, it still factored into his thinking. Redmund had little to add in a relationship with Jimmy. After a few hunting forays to the cemetery, where Jimmy had brought back half-a-dozen deer, he had been crowned *The Hunter* on his street. He didn't know if it was self-delusion or self-discovery, but Jimmy now thought of himself that way now, too. Based on results, he was the apex provider in his neighborhood. Bottom line: he had fed a lot of people over the last few days, including Redmund and even the bishop.

Deer had disappeared from the cemetery and Jimmy hadn't been able to figure out how to dry deer meat, so they would need more deer in the next couple of days. From what he had seen, hunting up Tellers Canyon was a serious challenge. The mountain crawled with hunters and survivalists, almost all of them armed. Working around the competition and finding deer would be tricky.

Jimmy didn't honestly want to hunt with Redmund. From his new point of view, on this side of the Apocalypse, Jimmy could see Redmund was a blowhard. Despite Redmund's massive build, he fell drastically short in cardio fitness. But the social pressure was more than Jimmy could handle. He would go with Redmund, but Jimmy would insist on running the hunt.

It turned out to be a non-issue. By the time they had hiked four miles up the bottom of Tellers Canyon, Redmund was breathing like a blown pony. Jimmy was no picture of cardio fitness either, but he had been dropping Redmund on the climb, having to wait for him every quarter mile. The football player didn't have the wind to argue about anything, so Jimmy stayed a bit out in front, the default expeditionary leader.

They reached a tiny stream spilling into the canyon bottom over a moss-covered waterfall. Jimmy decided they had climbed far enough to get above most of the other starving hunters, and he turned up the tributary without consulting Redmund.

Redmund followed as they began the more serious climb. The stream cut through a deep gorge, and the woods around it filled in thick, like a thatched barricade meant to hold out man, but allowing deer to pass. The steep climb became twice as hard as the men ducked and wove between trees, deadfall and thick gooseberry. They crossed the stream back and forth, working around cutback embankments and impassable brambles. After half a mile, Jimmy began the even steeper climb out of the stream bed.

Their rifles snagged on branches every few steps, and several times they crawled on hands and knees through grown-over passages in the scrub oak. The back of Jimmy's neck filled with sharp chunks of bark and dead sticks, which then dropped down the back of his shirt into the waistband of his underwear like malignant thorns searching for a home. The frustration of the climb nearly overwhelmed Jimmy and he swore under his breath, hating the hunt, hating the mountain, and hating fat-butt Carl Redmund.

Why had he agreed to this?

After forty-five minutes of torture, Jimmy emerged onto the ridge. Thankfully, the trees and scrub opened up. The summer heat prevented anything from growing more than two feet tall out on the sun-baked, gravelly side of the mountain. Jimmy got his bearings while Redmund struggled up behind him.

As Jimmy had hoped, the number of hunters this high was far less than in the lower canyon. He saw about thirty guys, but that was on both sides of the canyon and mostly below them. They had maybe five guys within a mile to worry about. Jimmy watched them from afar and hated them like he had never hated other men in his life. He remembered something his brother always said on opening day of deer hunt. "The only guy I despise more than an anti-hunter is *another* hunter across the canyon from me on opening morning."

Yeah. No kidding, Jimmy thought. I can't even stand the guy I'm with.

As soon as Redmund caught up, Jimmy took off again, not really caring if the big man caught his breath or not. Jimmy hadn't seen any deer yet and he wanted to get even higher, even farther away from the other hunters, before the "golden hour." The last hour before dark always produced the best hunting—maybe twenty times as good as midday. After the climb, Jimmy was hell-bent on hunting to the bitter end of the day, even if that meant carrying an animal home seven miles in the dark. He knew it would be miserable, but at least it would be downhill and at least he would have meat for his family.

After ten more stops to wait for Fat Boy, Jimmy sat on a rock and took another look around. The light still hung too high in the sky for golden hour, so Jimmy didn't sweat the fact that he saw no deer. For the tenth time that day, he kicked himself for not borrowing binoculars. He would have loved to use this time waiting to scan the tree line for animals.

He could look for deer through his rifle scope, but holding the rifle up for any period of time exhausted his arms. His arms would start shaking. With the rifle shaking, he couldn't see a thing.

Redmund caught up. This time Jimmy waited for him to catch his breath. Jimmy needed to form a plan of attack for the evening hunt. They were near the top of the main ridge and it would place them above deer coming out at sunset. That was a good thing. So long as they stayed off the ridge, the deer would have a hard time seeing them, since the deer would be looking into the setting sun. The wind was another problem, since it blew downhill.

How were you supposed to hunt with the sun at your back if the wind's also at your back? Jimmy wondered.

The old hunting saying went: "Hunt with the sun at your back and the wind in your face." But what if the wind goes wherever it wants and the sun sets wherever it sets? How were you supposed to control that? If you had to pick one, which one should it be, wind or sun?

It didn't really matter, since Jimmy wasn't about to hike any more than he must. The wind and the sun could blow and shine whichever direction, and Jimmy wasn't going to walk a single extra step. He was too dog-tired.

His stomach had been growling for the last three hours. His legs throbbed. His thirst had reached epic proportions. His mind felt muddy. Jimmy dreamed about stuffing his face with a bunch of venison cooked at the site of a deer kill, assuming they could pull it off.

It looked like they would need one more big push to make it to the top. Jimmy set off without talking to Carl, and they climbed straight toward the pinnacle, their hands pushing on their knees with each step, both of them struggling. Across the trail, a piece of barbed wire blocked their way. Without a second thought, Jimmy lifted the wire up for Fat Boy, grateful for the brief respite. A sign jangled to the wire, something about private property and hunting, not that it mattered to Jimmy.

Redmund could barely climb under the wire and Jimmy's irritation flared. He couldn't be expected to lift the wire over the huge man. Finally, Redmund made it under and snagged his rifle barrel, jamming the barbed wire into Jimmy's hand. Jimmy's irritation went stratospheric, and he would have exploded with rage if he wasn't so completely exhausted.

"Whump!" A spray of rock dust erupted from a boulder ten yards from the two men.

"Booooom." A shot rang out, the sound delayed.

Jimmy's first thought was that someone had shot a deer and his mind raced, but his thoughts came out jumbled, lost in his heavy breathing.

He searched, glancing back and forth across the hillsides, looking for a deer—maybe a wounded animal or something running from other hunters.

Then he saw it—something not quite right on the ridge above them. A tiny glint of light. Probably a reflection off something man-made. Jimmy's curiosity kicked in and he shucked the rifle off his shoulder sling for a better look.

• • •

Winslow commanded this section of the perimeter—the high ridge—which made a lot of sense since he was a former Marine Designated Marksman.

Jeff had assigned a dozen men to this sector, running two overworked shifts of six men twenty-four hours a day. Jeff promised more guys within a few days, so Winslow and his shooters were making a good show of it, hanging on and staying frosty.

These combat conditions were even more fucked-up than Iraq. Shooting evil men, like the fundamentalist dickheads in Iraq, dragged a man's soul through the mud. Shooting American citizens, hungry and maybe a little stupid, would seriously fuck him up. It wasn't a responsibility Winslow was eager to shoulder.

Here, the enemy combatants were regular Americans. Under his ROEs, if the guys turned around at the wire—then they were harmless hunters. If they came through the wire into the Homestead, the lookouts were supposed to shoot to kill. Winslow preferred clear orders. It wasn't a responsibility he wanted for himself, who to shoot and who not to shoot.

He'd been watching two fat guys working their way up his ridge for the last two hours. They looked like they were headed straight into the Homestead "area of control."

Jeff had made it crystal clear: no person was to cross the line by more than ten meters. After that, the risk for the Homestead was too great. Any intruders who reached the ridge would disappear almost immediately into the forest. The forest continued, uninterrupted, for two miles right down to the Homestead lawn. In a nutshell, anyone entering the forest could be shooting at women and kids within twenty minutes, and there would be nothing they could do to stop them once they got under cover of forest. Also, anyone cresting the ridge could see directly into the Homestead. They could recon the Homestead positions, track their shift changes, observe their defensive strength, and ultimately mount a well-informed attack.

The rules were clear, and Marines didn't screw with the rules. When a person crossed the wire and ignored the signs, they would get one warning shot. After that, it was lights out.

The secondary position to the left of Winslow luckily could see these knuckleheads, so they would be able to place a solid warning shot. The shooter over there, Crandall, was a great aim for a civilian, and Winslow trusted he would make the six-hundred-fifty-yard shot, no problem.

Winslow's spotter, Eric, was still learning, and he sat back in their dug-in spider hole.

"Eric, come forward and spot for me. These guys are crossing the line," Winslow ordered. Shooting at two guys meant the second guy would be moving fast after the shot. If Winslow was forced to shoot, his rifle would buck and there would be a split second when he would lose sight of the targets. If the second guy bolted, Winslow would need to know where he had gone.

Eric slid up to the spotting scope on the ledge.

"The guys are two ridges over, right at the boundary line."

Eric panned the spotting scope toward the setting sun.

"Boooom…Whump!" Crandall made his warning shot and busted a boulder right below the guys.

That should make them think twice.

But the two guys just stood there like idiots. Eric panned the spotting scope a bit more.

Winslow saw one of the men look straight at them, as if startled. The man unslung his rifle.

"*NO, NO, NO,*" Winslow shouted in his mind.

• • •

Jimmy levered the 30-06 up to his shoulder to get a better look at the glint through his scope. Through the magnified glass, he saw a puff of dust from the same spot as the glint.

Then Jimmy had his last thought, actually more of a feeling.

"*…mistake…*"

Something slammed into his chest, like when he had been kicked by a goat as a child. He dropped to his knees and rolled over backward, tumbling head over heels.

Sky, ground, sky, ground, sky, ground and then a tangle of trees.

Jimmy gazed at the beautifully random tangle of tree branches and sky. The pain in his legs and his bumps and bruises drifted away on a gentle wind.

He exhaled, but the exhale went deep, so impossibly deep that he couldn't bring the breath back.

The last thing he saw in this world was Olivia. The light of his life, in her Disney Princess pajamas on Christmas morning. Then darkness.

• • •

Winslow wanted to scream. He wanted to yell at the dead man and call him a STUPID MOTHER FUCKER. But the Marine in him held back.

Winslow tracked the second man in his rifle optic, his emotions barely held in check.

The other man—a huge man—ran like a rabbit in the easiest direction possible—straight downhill. When the guy hit the barbed wire, he ran through it, flipped ass over teakettle, jumped up, lost his rifle and charged blindly down the hill.

Winslow gave thanks that he wouldn't have to kill this man, too. He was running away from the boundary now, no longer a threat.

When the big man bounded clear of the threat zone, Winslow put his rifle on safety, grabbed his jacket, buried his face into the wadded fabric and screamed at the top of his lungs.

"MOTHERFUCKER, MOTHERFUCKER, MOTHERFUCKER, MOTHERFUCKER!"

Winslow looked up at his spotter, who was staring back in disbelief.

"We need to displace. Now," Winslow barked. He grabbed his kit and his rifle and slid out the back of the sniper hide. His spotter followed.

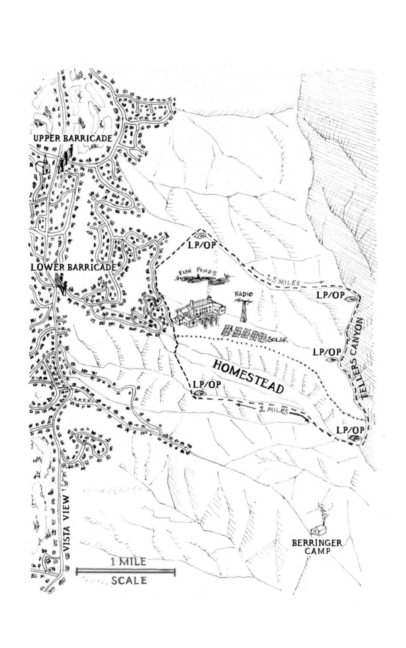

UPPER BARRICADE

LOWER BARRICADE

LP/OP

Fish Ponds

RADIO

SOLAR

1.5 MILES

LP/OP

TELLERS CANYON

LP/OP

HOMESTEAD

LP/OP

2 MILES

LP/OP

VISTA VIEW

BERRINGER CAMP

1 MILE
SCALE

10

"ANOTHER CALL FROM MY FAVORITE hottie on comms with the 5th Fleet in the Mediterranean Sea. Seems our admiralty has decided nobody gives a shit anymore about the Middle East and the entire task force is sailing home. Just in time to sweep up the ashes of America. Brilliant call, y'all…

"Also, I heard from a Drinking Bro holed up in the Blue Ridge Mountains of Tennessee… He just fought off a bunch of bandidos with his wife and father-in-law. Stay frosty, lads…"

Ross Homestead
Oakwood, Utah

Jeff sipped his third coffee of the morning, mostly in an effort to drive back his fatigue. Coffee had always been the booby prize for a sleepless night. Get crap sleep—enjoy a half-gallon of coffee the next morning. Except, as always in life, the easy solution was a junk solution. Coffee might keep his eyes open, but it sure as hell didn't improve his attitude.

This morning, Jeff felt like strangling someone.

He had returned late last night from the refinery and it had taken forever to get to sleep.

When his family originally arrived at the Homestead, Jeff had taken a couple of racks in the barracks as their temporary home. There wasn't time for him to fool around with tents and the area called the bunkhouse had been the simplest option.

Jeff didn't mind all the bodies and the snoring in the bunkhouse. He'd had plenty of that in the military. Jeff did, however, mind that his kids couldn't sleep with seventy people around making inexplicable noises. The kids fussed with him and Tara constantly throughout the night. He would lose it pretty soon if he didn't get some real sleep.

"Good morning." Jason walked around the colonnade in front of the office, greeting Jeff. Jason had his own coffee.

"Morning. Hey, before the day kicks off, could I ask a favor?" Jeff wanted to get this sleep thing fixed before the day got hairy.

"Sure."

"Can Tara and I get a room in the big house? I'm going to murder someone if I don't get some sleep, and the kids aren't sleeping for a damn in the bunkhouse."

"Yeah," Jason replied. "I'll ask Jenna to figure it out. No problem. Everyone appreciates you guys, despite the complaints from the peaceniks. Without you... dude, I wouldn't be sleeping at all."

"Okay. Thanks."

"How did it go with the hospital and refinery yesterday?"

"We got it all buttoned up. We're holding the hospital and two pharmacies. We don't quite own the refinery, but we'll get it soon. It's safe for now."

"Wow," Jason glanced back at Jeff with raised eyebrows, "you did all that without going to war with the town?" Jason's unspoken question was clear: *did you have to kill anyone?*

"No. We didn't shoot anyone. Actually, I added a few members to your—our—shindig here. One cop, one doctor, a security guard and a couple of pharmacists, and their families."

"Okay." Jason looked to the sunrise, making mental calculations. "That should work. Can someone on your team get me more info about the families? I already met the cop yesterday. Jacobs, right? Seems like a good addition. I need to keep my mind around our numbers." Again, the subtext: *you can add people, but there's a limit to how many we can feed.*

"Yeah. The cop will fit right in. Talk to Alec. He should be rotating back in this afternoon from the hospital. He'll get you the details on the additions."

Jordan walked around the office wing and waved at Jason and Jeff. There was an OHV parked in the round-about and Jordan liked to keep the grounds tidy and the vehicles parked where they belonged.

Jordan jumped in the OHV and gunned it around the corner, probably waking people in the bunkhouse.

Jeff went back to talking about the assaults the previous day, filling Jason in on the chain of events. He hadn't quite gotten to the part about sending Evan and ten guys out to the Army Depot when a commotion erupted behind the bunkhouse. Someone shouted and animated voices began cranking up, like an old forty-five record picking up speed.

Jordan came roaring back around in the OHV and jerked to a stop beside Jeff and Jason.

"Did you know there's a body back here?" Jordan said in a loud voice, pointing to a tarp in the back of the OHV. In fairness, Jordan couldn't speak in anything *but* a loud voice. He had clearly jumped into drama mode, so now he was virtually shouting.

A crowd of Homestead people poured out of the bunkhouse, heading for Jeff, Jason and the dead man in the OHV. A chill went down Jeff's spine, a realization that he had missed a step and now he would pay the piper. Jeff had meant to talk to his security forces about what to do with a deceased intruder. He had known they would kill someone soon enough, based on how often they were turning intruders at the wire, and it had occurred to Jeff that he would need to cover this eventuality and issue orders. But it had fallen through the cracks, lost in the shuffle of the hundred other things he had to do.

"That's trouble," Jason stated the obvious as the crowd surrounded the OHV.

Alena, the nurse, yanked back the tarp and sprang into action, checking the body's pulse. Apparently, the body had cooled sufficiently to make the verdict certain. It was a dead body and everyone was staring into the man's open, glazed eyes.

"What the hell is this?" Alena pointed at the body, consumed with fury. She shot daggers at Jeff and Jason.

"I don't know," Jeff replied matter-of-factly. He set his coffee down on the rail and walked over to the truck bed of the OHV. The dead man was curled up, probably so he would fit in the cargo area. It wasn't anyone Jeff knew, and the man had a bullet wound in his chest. To Jeff, it looked like a .308 rifle hole.

"Sorry. Sorry, guys." Winslow jogged up from the bunkhouse. "I screwed up. I couldn't find you when I came in last night from duty, and there was no one to tell about this." He pointed at the body.

Jeff stared at him blankly. Jason watched the crowd.

"I had to shoot him. It was me. He pointed his rifle at me and he was over the boundary. We did a warning shot. Well, Crandall did a warning shot and this guy wouldn't stop. I didn't have to shoot the other guy…" Winslow rambled. He had probably awakened from a dead sleep, remembering that he had left a body in the driveway.

"Stop talking," Jeff interrupted him. "Don't say another word."

In Jeff's mind, there were two kinds of people. Brothers, and all the rest. Winslow was a "brother." Pretty much everyone else standing there, except possibly Jason, fell into the category "the rest."

It was possible that Winslow had serious legal troubles. On the other hand, legal troubles weren't what they used to be. Maybe a man could kill someone in the mountains without legal repercussions now. This wasn't Iraq, but it might be pretty close. Jeff's mind swam with the repercussions of the killing, and he had to admit he simply did not know.

In any case, it sounded like Winslow had followed orders perfectly. Jeff needed time to think about it. He had known this moment was coming, but planning for something and experiencing it were two very different things. A surprise dead body in the back of an OHV would not have been his preferred outcome. He would have much preferred that Winslow bury the body somewhere on the hill or dump it over the boundary fence. But Jeff only had himself to blame. He hadn't gotten out ahead of this issue and he knew better.

Alena pointed her finger in his face. "You are responsible for this, mister shoot-first-ask-questions-later. This innocent man—LOOK AT HIM—he was probably just searching for food for his family, and your MEN gunned him down. LOOK AT HIM! This is no criminal. This is no ATTACKER. You killed him! All of you. Both of you!!" She glared back and forth at Jeff and Jason.

Jeff didn't know what to say, and mostly he didn't care. He looked at Jason, who was staring down the driveway.

Men from the neighborhood were arriving to start combat training on the Great Lawn. Bishop Decker had put the word out that men with guns would receive basic military training at the Homestead today. A number of the neighbors broke away from the group and drifted up toward the crowd, curious about what was happening.

Jason jumped into action to prevent a political calamity. "Jordan, please take that… man… down to the infirmary immediately. Cover him up. Do it now. Everyone else, would you please join us in the office?"

Jordan pulled the tarp over the body, fired up the OHV and nudged through the crowd. As the people filed into the office, the men from the neighborhood gradually headed back toward the Great Lawn. There was some intermingling of people—Homestead and neighborhood. Undoubtedly, a few words of gossip were exchanged.

• • •

"People, I know this is serious, but we need to talk about it in an orderly fashion." Jason packed the group into the office and everyone talked at once.

"Rules of order, folks. One person at a time."

"I'm concerned, really concerned about this." It was Jason's brother, Donald Ross. "The lights have been out for what? Eight days? We're already killing people. I just want to know; did this have to happen? Was this necessary?"

The room burst into a melee of conversation. Jeff could see the strain on Jason's face. If it had been anyone but his brother, a member of the steering committee, this would have been easier.

Jeff had observed this already about Jason and the Ross family. Every one of them had big opinions. Regardless of the effect on other people, they would jump into analysis and crank up a passionate position, certain they were right. That was probably why Jeff and Jason got along at all. They came from the same bolt of cloth—the same kind of family. Jason had largely learned to cloak his opinionated streak through decades of business politicking. But he still had the heart of a crusader and, given the chance, he'd glom onto big opinions just like the rest of his clan.

Another one of Jason's brothers, Walt Ross, shouted everyone down. "Guys, someone died. That's about as serious as it gets. Let's hear Jason and Jeff out. Why did this guy have to die?"

Jason jumped into the gap. "We'll never know. I'm sorry. We could get Winslow in here, grill him, then grill Jeff—Jeff wasn't even on the property when the shooting took place—and we *still* wouldn't know if this was necessary."

Frankly, Jeff had no idea where Jason was going with this. He didn't seem to be helping much.

"This is murder and we're all complicit," Alena shouted. "I can see no reason to kill people to keep them away from our stuff. Do we know we couldn't have just asked this man to leave? Did you see his face? He's not the kind of man to come in here and shoot our kids for food. I'd rather die than live like this. My family is leaving!"

The crowd roiled—some agreeing with Alena, some disagreeing and others shouting that she should go ahead and leave.

Jason broke in. "Folks, can I ask one thing of you? Please wait. Wait a day or two. Your families' lives depend on making the right decision. Waiting a day or two before you go out those gates won't hurt anyone. If things get better in town, you'll be better off waiting. If things get worse in town, you may decide that shooting intruders to protect your children is necessary. It's possible, right? Those fires down there," Jason motioned toward the valley, "they're not campfires. The big ones are savage violence. People are dying down there. Wait a day. Wait two days. And God help us if it keeps getting worse."

With that, Jason moved toward the door and opened it, signaling the end of the meeting. Jeff had the feeling that more talk wasn't going to lead to more understanding, and he agreed with Jason that the meeting should end.

Personally, Jeff would rather let all the loudmouths leave. He had no idea why Jason cared if they stayed or went; the plea to stay made no sense. The Homestead didn't need those people, and more food meant better odds of survival for those who remained.

But he had his own job to do, so he'd let Jason handle the politics… for now.

• • •

Jeff sat down in a chair after everyone filed out of the office. Jason turned to him.

"Jeff, do you have time to meet with Bishop Decker? He should be here any minute."

Jeff looked out the windows and saw four men walking up the driveway, greeting folks as they approached.

"Were you expecting four guys?" Jeff asked.

"It's the Bishop, his two counselors, and someone I've never met before. I'm not sure how to feel about that," Jason said.

The four men walked up to the office wing and stamped off their feet before coming inside.

"Bishop, gentlemen, good morning." Jason shook their hands. "This is Jeff Kirkham. He's our head of security." Jeff didn't know why Jason invented that title, but he probably had a reason. They had never discussed a title. Everyone knew him as the committee guy over defense. "Head of Security" was a new twist, probably something for the Mormon leaders' benefit.

Bishop Decker stepped forward. "Good morning. This is my first counselor, Brother Ingram, and my second counselor, Brother Todd. This is Brother Masterson. He's the executive secretary from the Cherry Harvest Ward below us on the hill, and he's on the county emergency committee. I hope you don't mind that I brought everyone along for our morning meeting."

"Of course not. Come on in," Jason said. All the men shook hands, and Jason showed them into the conference room.

"Did men show up from the ward for training today?" Bishop Decker asked, even though he already knew the answer.

In Jeff's mind, this was a bad start—Decker highlighting that he had done them a favor. Now, the bishop would ask for something in return. Jeff couldn't think of a single thing he wanted to give in exchange for the privilege of helping the neighborhood protect their families. Apparently, the bishopric was still under the impression they had a negotiating position. Correcting that mistaken assumption meant conflict, and conflict could cost lives.

"Yep, your ward men are down on the lawn training right now," Jason answered.

"Excellent. We spoke with the stake president last night, and we'd like to cooperate with your group as much as possible." Bishop Decker's eyes flicked to Masterson.

"Great," Jason answered.

It seemed obvious to Jeff that there was a "but" in there somewhere.

Masterson spoke up. "The stake president had a couple of requests, and we think they're good ones."

Jeff gave it fifty-fifty odds that the stake president hadn't come up with the requests Masterson was about to make. The moment Masterson spoke, Jeff knew he was the man in charge. Bishop or not, Decker didn't have the horsepower to keep this man in check. Masterson controlled the conversation.

To his credit, Jason said nothing, waiting Masterson out.

Masterson continued. "If we're going to combine with your defense, we think we should also combine supplies—food, water, equipment. We can share supplies and pull through this together until FEMA and the Church get here with relief."

Jeff couldn't read Jason's body language. Poker-faced, Jason stared back at Masterson, waiting. Nobody had ever requested combining supplies before. This was a new wrinkle.

"If the ward's providing the bulk of the men for security, we feel like Bishop Decker should be in command," Masterson stated firmly. "It's important for the Mormon men to know they're being led by someone who holds the mantle of authority." Masterson looked at Jason and Jeff with dramatized gravitas.

As far as Jeff was concerned, the meeting was over. If Jason agreed to any version of this plan, Jeff and his men would find a plan of their own. To some degree, Jeff believed in this process—in this slow wheels of diplomacy. He knew war intimately enough to know that almost any alternative could be better. But sometimes there existed such a serious experience gap between men that they would never cross that gap. Not only were these four Brethren entirely ignorant about military command, but they had a pie-in-the-sky understanding of what was happening in the world. In Jeff's experience, men who didn't know what they didn't know were the most dangerous kind.

Neither the Church nor FEMA was coming to save them and recovery would, in all likelihood, take years or even decades. That stuff burning down in the valley—and burning in Los Angeles, Denver, Chicago, and St. Louis—that was America's *means of production.* Without a modern means of production, America would hit medieval reality like a runaway train. There would be no turning back. The sudden loss of the cushy, American lifestyle had already sent Americans raging into the streets, and they were burning it all down. Recovery would be a long way off.

Masterson's fantasy might well get everyone killed. No matter what anyone said, and no matter how everyone smiled at one another across this conference table, Jeff would not let his family be murdered, raped and spit-roasted by barbarians. He would kill everyone in this room before he would let that happen.

Jason smiled, still giving nothing away. "Okay, gentlemen. I'll need some time to talk to my steering committee and consider what you're proposing. Is there anything else you need right now? Anything more we can do for the neighborhood?"

Bishop Decker answered, "Nope. We're good for now. Shall we get back together tomorrow? Same time?"

"That'd be perfect." Jason stood and showed the men to the door. He tossed a glance at Jeff, indicating he should stay.

Handshakes went around, and the men made their way out the office door and into the mid-morning sun, smiling vacantly.

As soon as the door closed, Jeff lit into Jason, "If you agree to any of that bullshit, I'm out."

Jason turned to Jeff, now with anger in his own eyes. "I'm not agreeing to anything."

"Why didn't you tell them 'no,' then?" Jeff fired back.

"Because I want a day to think it through. I want to talk to you about it, and I want to hash out options. I may want to talk to a few of the Mormon people in our group. Waiting until tomorrow to respond to Masterson costs us nothing. If I had spoken up now, I would've spoken from anger, and that's hard to fix. We don't have time to mend fences, so I'd rather not tear through fences in the first place."

That, at least, made sense to Jeff. His confidence in Jason's ability bumped up a small notch.

Jason sat down and turned to Jeff. "What did you see happen in that meeting?"

Jeff ticked off his observations on his thick fingers. "Bishop Decker isn't running the show. Dickhead number four controls the group because he's the only one willing to throw his weight around. We could probably work with the bishopric, but Masterson won't rest until he's in control of everybody and everything. We're trying to help them and they're responding by horse-trading with us. The big problem: they're too inexperienced to know just how fucked they are, and that bullshit artist Masterson is going to drag the learning curve out, probably until everyone gets dead."

Jason thought about it for a minute. "Going back to your analogy of the convenience store buried in volcanic ash... do you think Masterson falls in the category of a 'selfish strong man?'"

"I don't care where he falls. He's going to get us all killed. Problem is, that kind of guy never stops. He'll never step back. We have our own problems right now. We can't afford to be fighting enemies on multiple fronts."

"Solutions?"

"We can have him shot." Jeff got the obvious suggestion out of the way.

"Do you have suggestions that don't include shooting anyone?"

Jeff thought about it. "Screw those guys. Let's not use neighborhood men at all. Let's recruit from the men camping in the tent city outside the barricade on Vista View Boulevard. We could select guys to train and give them food for their families in exchange for serving in our militia. Those new guys could be our first line of defense. Why rely on the locals if we can recruit hand-picked men?"

Jason raised an eyebrow. "That's definitely an option. My preference would be to draw from the neighborhood and feed the neighborhood since it ensures cooperation and it removes the need to guard the Homestead against our own neighbors. But I don't see how we can get around Brother Masterson at the moment. I'm not going to agree to share resources, and I'm definitely not going to share military command with neighbors who know nothing about security."

Jeff wondered if Jason knew that same thing about himself. So far, Jason hadn't interfered with security decisions, but would that hold? Most smart guys, in Jeff's experience, assumed they are smart about *everything*. Jason—not having been in combat—didn't know a damn thing about running a war. He worried that Jason might labor under the impression that being a "gun guy" before the collapse qualified him to have a military opinion.

Switching back to the question of recruiting men from the barricade, Jason rubbed his chin. "Where would we get the food to pay recruits? I don't want to feed them our freeze-dried or fresh-grown food. We need good food here to keep up morale."

"You smell that?" Jeff asked.

"Yeah." Jason glanced up. "What is it?"

"The ladies figured out how to bake bread *en masse*. Somebody figured out how to grow yeast off the grape skins. Now they're baking bread by the dozens of loaves per hour. We have four stoves and we could get them turning out loaves for trade. Baking bread only costs us wheat and a little yeast, plus ramping up production of bread will keep some of the loudmouths around here busy."

"Hmmm." Still rubbing his chin stubble, Jason's thoughts turned to diplomacy. "We could feed the hungry, do some good *and* increase our security at the same time. The wheat could come out of the reserve we set aside for feeding the neighborhood. Baking bread for the hungry would definitely give our people something to do besides worrying about Homestead politics."

"You justify it however you need to. I don't care about making the sensitive souls around here feel better about life." Jeff found all of this distasteful. He preferred to keep it simple. If folks were too stupid to deal with the threats facing the Homestead, they should leave.

"Fair enough." Jason seemed to read Jeff's thoughts, and he didn't bother pitching him on doing the right thing. "Do you want to handle the selection process down at the Vista View barricade?"

"Yep." Of course Jeff wanted to control the process. He didn't want to have to train any more prima donnas. He had already dealt with Homestead and neighborhood guys, and many of them were more trouble than they were worth. A lot of them were totally lost, still unable to get their minds around the fact that they had been thrust back into the eighteen hundreds. Jeff would rather work with men who would be fighting to feed their families and who Jeff could fire when they failed to perform.

Training and leading neighborhood volunteers was like going to war with the cast of Glee. Most of these guys were still up to their eyeballs in emotion.

"You don't have any chain-link fence and razor wire stashed around here, do you?" Jeff asked.

Jason nodded, obviously proud of himself. "That I do. It's in the Conex boxes by the pond. I also have razor wire gloves and all the connectors and hardware. Do you need me to show you where?"

"No, I'll figure it out." Jeff got up to leave. "This neighborhood thing… this is where *you* need to produce. This diplomacy is on *you*. This is where wars are usually won or lost and, if you can't figure out solutions with the neighborhood, you're going to need to consider alternatives, maybe violent alternatives."

"I'm sure it won't come to that." Jason slapped Jeff on the back and walked him out of the conference room.

• • •

Jeff left the office and Jason sat down hard. He leaned back in his chair and asked himself again, Is it really worth all this?

210

In the stripped-down mathematics of survival, Masterson added up to more of a threat than any fifty guys trespassing across the Homestead boundary. Masterson had to be removed as a factor or his lust for power would get people hurt. The Homestead needed the neighborhood as a buffer against incursion, plus the extra manpower from the ward would significantly increase their defense. If looters began flooding the neighborhood, it would be better for everyone to mount a coordinated effort. Masterson was slowing that process down, and they might not have time to work through his game. People in town were getting hungrier by the moment.

Masterson must have known in advance that there wasn't a chance the Homestead would dump all their resources into the neighborhood collective. He must have known that sticking point would kill their chances of working together. Jason concluded that Masterson had come up this morning intent on poisoning the well, keeping the Homestead and the church apart.

If Jason was reading this correctly, Masterson would pay any price to remain in control of the local church leadership. If the Homestead disagreed with his plan, then Masterson would control hundreds, even thousands, of the local faithful. And the stake had way more men than the Homestead.

Of course, not all men were created equal on the field of battle, not by a long shot. One man like Jeff or his SOF guys equaled fifty regular gun guys. And one guy trained and commanded by a man like Jeff, even if that trainee was a civilian, would equal twenty untrained men. Homestead forces could wipe out a larger army, for sure, especially after Jeff added mercenaries from the refugee camp down below the barricade.

But Masterson had no way of knowing that and he might precipitate an armed conflict with the Homestead based on faulty confidence, and the resulting rift between the Homestead and the Mormon Church would be irreparable. The Mormon Church had a deep history with armed conflicts against "Gentiles" and they had a long, long memory.

Jason suspected, long term, the Mormon Church would rise up and take the reins of power in this region. The Homestead must preserve a good relationship with the LDS Church, no matter what. The Church was the one large organization with any hope of holding things together. It might not matter so much right away, since the Mormon Church was still pining for government help. But later, when the Mormon Church took matters into its own hands, being friends with the Mormons would become a survival imperative.

Jason got up from his chair and went looking for his dad. He might need his dad's help to avoid the biggest mistake of his life.

He found his old man tinkering with the water turbines, trying to pull electrical power from the Homestead's water loop. A spring almost a mile up the canyon supplied the loop, and it accumulated tons of water pressure on its way down the hill. Burke wanted to turn some of that pressure into electricity.

Burke Ross couldn't help but tinker, even if it meant needlessly complicating a project. The water turbines were the kind of thing that would keep him up at night, fantasizing about all the "slick" gizmos he could put to use.

"Yo, Dad. You get that done yet? You know it's the Apocalypse already, right? Time's up."

"Yeah, yeah, yeah."

Jason always needled his dad about being slow. For decades they'd worked together doing metal fabrication projects. Their predispositions were set. Their opinions about each other were well-established, their banter well-worn and comfortable.

"Can I bug you for a minute?" Jason wanted to talk about something other than Homestead gadgetry. He needed a Mormon thinker.

Burke Ross spent his adult life in the LDS faith, serving in nearly every position in the church. Burke believed Mormon theology through and through. He also knew from personal experience that, even in the "true church," things could go wrong. When it came to loggerheads with the predominant religion, or even the neighborhood, Jason turned to his dad for perspective.

"Okay." Burke turned up his hearing aids.

Jason retold the conversation with the bishopric and Masterson, leaving nothing out.

Burke waded in. "I know Masterson. He's an asshole."

Mormon or not, Burke had been a metal worker most of his life. He barely hesitated when it came to swearing. "Masterson's the kind of guy who uses priesthood authority unrighteously whenever it suits him."

"Jeff Kirkham's going to recruit new militia from town. He doesn't have the patience to deal with Mormon politics or the neighborhood."

Burke thought about that for a second. "Bad idea. You should do whatever you can to keep Bishop Decker and the stake president cooperating with the Homestead. We should be working together, not competing."

"I agree. So what should we do?"

Burke leaned over with a grunt and a tipsy lurch, trying to reach his tools without bending his stove-up knees. Jason helped him pick up the tools, returning them to the tool bucket.

"Let's go for a walk. Better yet, can we take one of your OHVs?"

"Sure." Jason headed back to the house, looking for an available OHV.

After a couple of stops around the neighborhood, Burke Ross figured out where the stake president lived.

Jason looked about nervously as he and his dad passed through the Homestead barricade, eyeballing the crowd of hungry people who had gathered just outside the gate. Jason had grabbed his gun belt and an AR-15, sliding the rifle into the scabbard of the OHV. When they passed through the concrete barricades, Jason reached around and pulled the rifle across his lap. The barricade, and the park next door, were packed with squatters. For no apparent reason, hundreds of people were camped at the entryway of the neighborhood below the Homestead. Even the rumor of food, apparently, drew a crowd.

"You might want to leave that gun in the OHV when we knock on the stake president's door." Burke glanced at the assault rifle suspiciously. Jason's dad didn't mind guns, but he wasn't a big fan of the military temperament that had overtaken the Homestead. He'd done his time in the military, but he didn't have much use for guns in his golden years.

A few minutes later, they knocked on the stake president's door, and his rotund wife answered as though nothing had changed in the last week.

Burke led out. "Good morning, Sister Beckstead. We're hoping to chat with President Beckstead. Is now a good time?"

"Good morning. I think he's in the garden. Come on in."

She led them through the house. Jason noticed white buckets of food storage cracked open on the kitchen counter. A hand-powered grain grinder stood next to an electric grain grinder, but only the hand-powered grinder had wheat dust around its base.

Sister Beckstead caught him looking at her kitchen mess. "I'm baking fresh bread. If you'd come an hour later, I could've offered you a slice."

That made Jason curious, "How're you baking bread with no electricity?"

"Oh, Randall fixed the oven to run off natural gas. The gas still works. I'm not sure what I'm going to do if it goes out. Oh, well, the Church will fix things by the time that happens, right?"

Jason nodded unconvincingly.

Out back, President Beckstead, wearing a gigantic straw hat, knelt beside a row of cauliflower. He looked up and grinned.

"Gentlemen, forgive the sombrero. Looks like the gardening I've been doing all these years is finally paying off."

"Indeed, President," Jason spoke first; he was an unrepentant gardening geek himself. "My name's Jason Ross and this is my dad, Burke."

"I know who you are, young man." President Beckstead stood and extended his hand. "You own that beautiful place up the hill. I've heard you have one heck of a garden."

Jason loved to talk gardening. "I do try."

"Brother Ross Senior…" The stake president shook Burke's hand. "What can I do for you this morning?"

"President, we're hoping to help the neighborhood pull through this mess." Burke cut right to the chase.

Beckstead nodded. "Right now, Church headquarters isn't providing any food assistance to our stake. They have wards and stakes in worse shape than us in the poorer areas of town, and those members come first. We're on our own for now. I'm frankly concerned. A lot of our members didn't prepare very well, and I'm seeing that none of us is totally prepared, not even Sister Beckstead and myself. I'm not sure if my wife can even bake bread once we lose gas to the stove. Without our stove, what will we do with all the wheat? That's most of our food storage."

"Have you asked the wards to pool their food?" Burke drilled down, hoping to poke holes in Masterson's story.

"No, I've left decisions like that to the bishops. So far, I don't think any of my wards have pooled food. Some homes are more prepared than others, and it's definitely not fair to force them to take food from their families and give it to families who failed to heed the prophets. But, if a ward decides to share, that's between them and their bishop."

"I see." Burke paused, not sure how to approach the question of guns. In the old world, a week ago, talking about protecting a neighborhood with guns would've been unseemly. But today? "President, have you thought much about defense?"

The stake president's expression fell. "Yes. Yes, I have. Guns aren't something the Brethren have spoken on, but we've already had a number of break-ins in the stake. We had a family held at gunpoint for an hour not three streets over. Luckily, nobody was hurt. But the family lost everything—all their valuables and their food storage.

Some wards are posting guards now, but many of the streets in and out of the stake have no protection now that the police aren't taking calls."

"We'd love to help, President," Burke said. "We have Special Forces soldiers at Jason's place, coordinating defense and training security guys. They know exactly what to do and how to train the men to protect the neighborhood. We have plenty of military firearms and ammunition."

The stake president nodded, wise enough not to commit to a solution, especially considering that Jason Ross was, in all practical respects, not a church member. His dad was a member in good standing, but President Beckstead knew Jason had fallen away, and that gave him pause.

Burke continued. "But there's a hiccup. Our bishopric asked today for us to give them command of all security, both their men and ours. As you can imagine, we're reluctant to do that. It'd be crazy to remove experienced Special Forces soldiers from command and replace them with church leaders who have no combat experience. Did you ask them to do that?"

President Beckstead's expression subtly changed now that he seemed to understand the purpose of this visit. The Ross's were asking him to run interference with Bishop Decker's bishopric. If he was like most Church leaders, President Beckstead would be slow to contradict one of his bishops, no matter how good Burke Ross's solution sounded.

"Brother Masterson mentioned they might request that of you when they visited a couple of days ago."

President Beckstead wasn't just a church leader. He had worked in business for decades. He was obviously beginning to see that he had been used by Masterson to gain leverage, but Beckstead wasn't going to contradict another anointed church leader.

"That seems like a reasonable request, at least to discuss. However, I wasn't aware you had professional military with your group. That might change things."

Burke pressed his advantage. "We have four Green Berets, three Navy SEALs and numerous Marines in charge of our forces. Would you consider authorizing those men to train, arm and lead all security forces in your stake?"

Beckstead waffled. "I think it's a good idea. But, Brother Ross, you know how this works. Bishops aren't called by me. They're called by the Lord. As stake president, I don't direct the bishops. I support them. The final answer on this question rests with Bishop Decker."

Beckstead was overstating the independence of the bishops. Both Burke and Jason knew it. President Beckstead could direct Bishop Decker in this matter. But President Beckstead had already exposed Masterson's exaggeration—the stake president hadn't requested pooling of resources, nor had he requested that Bishop Decker command security forces. Masterson had lied.

Neighborhood violence would increase, given enough time. President Beckstead would eventually ask the Homestead to take over neighborhood security, but one or two families would have to die first. Even considering that reality, pushing the discussion at that moment would galvanize the stake president's position and further delay a resolution. Jason ended the meeting on a positive note. "Very well, President, we needed some direction from you. Thank you for the time away from your garden. If you need anything, have your ham operator reach out. He knows our frequencies." Father and son reached over to shake President Beckstead's hand.

When they climbed back in the OHV, Jason grabbed his rifle and slipped it beside his seat.

Burke said, "That could've gone better."

Jason's first impulse was to disagree. "Even if President Beckstead gave us clear approval to handle defense, we'd still have to deal with Masterson. He's not the kind of guy to go down without a fight. In any case, your church can't move any faster than it's moving, Dad."

"It's your church, too," Burke said. Burke never missed a chance to point out that Jason was still Mormon, at least by baptism.

Jason smiled. "I'm not sure my church would be so slow to see the writing on the wall." He thought about it for a second and recanted. "That's probably not true. After all, my Christian church never even talked about being prepared for a disaster. At least *your* church preached preparedness."

"Ah, ha!" Burke seized upon the opportunity to be right. "So you admit the Mormon Church accurately prophesied this collapse?"

"Yes. I suppose it did. So did Benjamin Franklin. And Rand Paul. And Ayn Rand. I'm pretty sure none of those folks were conversing with God. Hey, I'd be singing hallelujahs with your church if we could get the stake president to move things along." Jason cocked his thumb at the president's house.

"Yeah," Burke agreed. "Something terrible is going to have to happen before these guys take this seriously, I'm afraid."

Between the rumble of the OHV and his hearing aids, Burke wasn't going to hear anything anyway so they drove home in silence.

• • •

Josh Myler commanded Quick Reaction Force Three, or QRF Three, as the guys called it. He hadn't been a veteran. As a close friend of Jeff Kirkham, he'd had a lot of firearms training and, with the collapse, he had received a crash course in small unit command. With Jeff's SOF guys running around the valley on missions, Josh had been tapped to lead one of the three elite teams of gunmen. Somewhere along the line, Josh heard that Emily Ross could shoot, and he wanted her for QRF Three. Emily had grown up in a family of shooters: her dad, a lifelong gun fanatic; her brother, a United States Marine; and all of her uncles were avid hunters. Emily killed her first deer—with a two-hundred-yard shot at nine years old.

In one of her favorite pictures of herself, sixteen-year-old Emily posed with an AR-15, mugging for the camera in one of the canyon bottom gun ranges at the Homestead. She smiled her million-dollar grin with a triple rivulet of blood running down her face. She had shot a steel target in the trees, and she had been hit in the head with a chunk of copper jacket. Emily finished shooting the rest of the course before heading to the ER for stitches. The doctor found the chunk of copper jacket under the skin of her scalp, and she'd kept it in her jewelry box ever since.

No panty-waist high school boy could hope to match her when it came to shooting. Emily smoked them all on the rifle and the handgun range, and that's how she liked it.

Emily Ross, screwing up millions of years of gender bias.

She supposed her medical training had something to do with it, but getting on a QRF unit in the Homestead definitely said something about her shooting skill. Almost everyone on the three QRF teams had trained extensively before the stock market took a dump. They were the gun guys but, more important, everyone on the QRF units previously trained on dynamic shooting, land warfare tactics, and all of them had maintained their personal fitness.

Emily hadn't done as much combat shooting as any of the guys on QRF Three, but she had been a distance runner and cyclist since the age of twelve. Also, the unit needed a corpsman—someone to treat battle trauma until they could get wounded back to the Homestead infirmary. Emily's medical training, gun training and fitness made her the obvious choice, the weaker sex or not.

The Homestead had almost overdone it with doctors and nurses, making Emily one of the lesser-qualified medical professionals. They had three surgeons and one ER doc, plus a gaggle of seasoned nurses.

Emily would have rather been doing surgery, but a QRF slot was nothing to sneeze at. She would get top-notch combat training from the Special Forces guys, a few of whom were single and definitely hot.

And she would no longer have to spend six hours a day in a dirt hole, endlessly scanning the hillside. Being on the QRF meant being off guard duty. Membership definitely had its privileges. The QRF guys spent their days on the Homestead grounds, training and alert for a call. She would have to wear military kit all day and some nights, including a battle belt with a gun holster, bump helmet, chest rig with magazines, and a rifle. But Emily could live with that. Being on QRF meant you were a rock star in this new world. Being a female on the QRF meant you were a rock star among rock stars.

Some slice of her female brain lit up with the black guns, racy camo and macho coolness of it all. The handful of single guys around the Homestead thought of her as the ultimate bad-ass chick: gorgeous, smart and combat-ready.

She could live with that. It held back the ennui that might overtake her if she thought too much about the horror just a couple of miles down in the valley. Columns of smoke, snaking up from the city below, haunted the bucolic fiction of the Homestead, where the aroma of baking bread intermingled with the titter of playing children. Like a phantom lurking just out of reach, she knew that the malignancy among the fires could gobble up this refuge. It was never far from Emily's mind that the poor masses weren't strangers. They were people. They had been her friends.

• • •

Jacquelyn heard the commotion that morning but couldn't bring herself to look at the dead body in the OHV. She and Tom had talked about the death that would accompany a social collapse and they had known it would come to this.

The first dead body had arrived at the Homestead, and she had chosen not to look at it. Based on what she had heard about the shooting, she assumed the dead man had a family and children. His only sin was to be desperate and careless. Even so, her own children came first, and that meant she would refuse to take the journey of conscience. She would refuse to dwell on the morality of killing a man to protect herself and her family.

Screw it all, she thought, intentionally throwing off the version of herself that had taught New Age consciousness classes, counseled people on spiritual health, and lived life by a modern ethic.

She remembered all her fancy New Age beliefs about a universe that could be trusted to deliver on positive mental attitude. She found those beliefs irrelevant in a world where her child's chest could be pierced by a bullet at any moment.

She dedicated her adult life to higher thinking and now, with her children filling her whole heart, she abandoned those beliefs wholesale. Like rejecting the idea of buying an expensive car because the family budget couldn't bear it, Jacquelyn left behind the carefully laid philosophies of a hundred self-help books and countless hours of soul-searching. She believed in just four things now: her husband and her three children. *One. Two. Three. Four.*

The rest were luxuries she could no longer afford. It wasn't that she had become a woman without principles. Quite the contrary, her principles were now embodied in four human beings.

Jacquelyn's mind wandered as she hung Tom's camo pants on the clothesline. The forest outside the kitchen and wash area was festooned with a massive amount of drying clothing, with yards and yards of parachute cord strung between the trees. Homestead residents had finally run out of clean clothing, and had at last resorted to washing their clothes by hand in the large, tin wash basins, complete with old-fashioned washing boards.

It had come like the ultimate surrender to the Apocalypse—finally washing clothes by hand. The women admitted to themselves that no help was coming. In the strange calculus of large groups, the women had given in to that truth all at the same time. That first wash day meant they were in this for the long haul. It also meant that an enormous number of garments needed to be air-dried at the same time.

How're we going to dry our clothes in the winter? Jacquelyn wondered.

Between the forest of trees and the forest of hanging clothes, she saw Alena hanging her own family's clothing, more denim than camo. Jacquelyn debated approaching her. Both women had emerged as natural Homestead leaders, even though Alena was actually on the

221

committee and Jacquelyn was not. Jacquelyn hung her last pair of pants and walked over to Alena.

"You doing okay?" Jacquelyn touched Alena's arm lightly, startling the nurse out of her reverie.

"I guess I'm all right," Alena answered. "I'm just so angry about the killing of that poor man."

Jacquelyn hesitated. "Yeah. Who would've thought a month ago we'd be responsible for something so terrible?"

"We don't need to kill people," Alena exclaimed, her voice climbing an octave.

Still touching her arm, Jacquelyn stepped up to the conflict. "I wanted to make sure you knew where I stand on that… seeing as we're a couple of the 'power ladies' around here." They both laughed.

"I support Kirkham and the military guys in doing what they have to do to protect our families," Jacquelyn said without ambiguity.

Alena's face screwed a little tighter, rising to the disagreement.

Jacquelyn's hand left Alena's arm and she continued before Alena could interject. "I understand your position on this. I truly do. But I'm going to stand firm on any choice that makes my kids safer, even if that means we do things that are hard to understand. Alena, please consider the possibility that the world has changed very quickly. If we don't change with it, I'm afraid our families won't survive. It's nothing personal, but I'm going to stand with the gun guys whenever this comes up. I choose my kids over anything else."

Alena looked at Jacquelyn, not sure how to answer. After a second, she asked, "Even if that means killing innocent people?"

Jacquelyn nodded. "Yes, innocent people are going to die. I'd rather the innocent people be people other than my children. I can't afford the same kind of principles I could a week ago."

Alena nodded. "I disagree, but thank you for talking to me directly. I'm not saying you're wrong. I'm saying that we stand a better chance if we do what's right."

Jacquelyn reached out and pulled Alena in for a hug. It started awkwardly, but melted into a sincere embrace. Alena's body shuddered as she stifled a sob. Jacquelyn held her until she stilled.

They drew apart and Alena wiped her nose.

"Sisters, no matter what, right?" Jacquelyn asked.

Alena looked up, a little embarrassed. "Sisters, for sure."

They both went back to hanging their laundry, a slightly uncomfortable silence between them.

• • •

The Avenues
Salt Lake City, Utah

In 1860, the Mormon settlers in the Salt Lake Valley laid out a neighborhood proximate to downtown, but far enough away that small merchants could afford to build. The Avenues were originally without water, shoehorned between the Mormon temple, the state capitol building and the University of Utah. Over time, the "Avs" evolved from being low-income merchant housing to the preferred neighborhood of Mormon prophets and politicians. The neighborhood would ultimately become one of the premium locations for up-and-comers, as well as old money of Salt Lake City.

Just nine days after two nuclear attacks and the crash of the American stock market, residents poured out of the Avenues, fleeing death and destruction, almost all of them barefoot. Gunshots crackled every minute or two, and fires crept from "A" Street steadily toward Virginia Street.

The Los Latigos gang had ballooned to somewhere around a thousand men by the time they went to war in the Avenues. It had been a stroke of genius to send hand-delivered messages to all Latino communities. Only a tiny percentage of Latinos came, but a tiny percentage of three-hundred-thousand Latinos added up to an army.

Few of the Latino men had guns when they arrived in the Avenues, walking in small groups down the corridor Francisco mapped with his lieutenants that morning. For the most part, only gangsters carried guns and they weren't ideal for house-to-house fighting.

But every second or third house in the Avenues had its own stock of rifles and handguns. After raiding just a few blocks, the Latigos gang accumulated more guns and ammunition than they would ever need.

Francisco joined the first raids to show his men he hadn't lost his edge. They burst through the front doors, usually unlocked, and moved room to room. When they found residents, they herded them into the family room and pointed their guns at the kids. After that, the adults would tell them anything: where to find guns, ammunition, drugs and alcohol. It was a piece of cake—the easiest score Francisco had ever made.

It amazed Francisco how reluctant the white people were to shoot back. A lot of the gringos had guns when the gangsters entered their homes. But most white people wouldn't pull the trigger. His men were ready to pull the trigger in the first instant of confrontation, and it lead to many unnecessarily dead whites, though that didn't matter to Francisco. The evicted white people were likely to starve in a week or two anyway.

Killing the residents proved disgustingly easy. It wasn't until an hour or two later, after the area had experienced extended gunfire, that some residents began to shoot from their windows as the gang approached. Rather than execute the white people in their living rooms, Francisco ordered that all residents be permitted to walk away, so long as they went shoeless. He had made the decision on a whim, but it turned out to be another stroke of genius. Somehow, sending white people away shoeless lit a fire in the hearts of his Latino fighters.

He didn't want to wax too dramatic, but this was a glorious day to be a Mexican, and watching the shoeless exodus of white people, abandoning their haciendas, made the perfect picture of social justice. Generations from now, children would read about this day in their history books. As his men fought their way through one of the richest neighborhoods in Salt Lake City, they took up the chant: "¡*Vive Villa!*" Whenever he heard it, Francisco felt the pull of fate. He was the right man at the right time.

His lieutenants marshaled their forces, moving the conquest steadily eastward through the wealthy neighborhood. They had experienced only a few casualties, three men shot by homeowners. A Latigos victory seemed assured.

Francisco ordered the finest homes to be left untouched so that the mothers of his fighters could enjoy them, furnished and pre-supplied. Francisco sent a runner back to the Salt Lake County Fairgrounds and ordered Bastardo, his man coordinating the fairgrounds, to send families of his lieutenants to the staging area at the LDS Hospital on "C" Street. He could see no reason not to move families into the haciendas they had already taken, making the most of any food and supplies left behind.

A couple of hours later, two school buses arrived carrying Latino families. His men had cleared almost ten blocks from North Temple to the top of the Avenues and east all the way to "K" Street. The Latino families could barely hear gunfire as they came down off the bus and were led away by his men, a few at a time.

One of the most impressive homes, an old-time mansion, had been set aside for Francisco's mama. She climbed off the bus, holding the handrail as she took the last step down.

"Mama, come see. I've found a new home for you." Francisco held out his arm.

She took his arm, apprehensive. "But I was comfortable in our home in Rose Park. You didn't need to get me a new one. And where's my food? I have a good stock of *frijoles* and rice set aside back at our home."

"Si, Mama. I know. The boys are bringing your clothes and your *frijoles*. They'll be here shortly. Come see your new home." He led her away from the bus drop-off.

They walked a block and a half to a three-story home owned by one of the old Mormon prophets of years gone by.

"Oh, Francisco, it is so beautiful. I don't need a home like this, but it is pretty to look at."

He didn't argue; he just walked her through the gates and into the rose gardens.

"*Dios mio,* the roses," she shouted in glee. "How can these gardens be so lovely?"

Francisco grinned. The whole revolution drew down to this moment—his mama enjoying a beautiful rose garden, no doubt every rose bush planted and pruned by Hispanic men. His mama deserved this home and this garden as much or more than any human being alive.

She had suffered through Francisco's many incarcerations and through the death of his father. She had taken tireless care of her children and her own mother. Thousands of meals. Thousands of hours doing laundry and washing dishes.

Wasn't this justice? His sweet mama enjoying her sunset years in this rose garden?

"But, Pancho, where is the family who lives here?" she asked as they walked through the stained glass front door. Pictures of happy white people lined both walls of the entryway.

"Mama, they've traded houses with us. They're ready to live in a smaller house now." It was a small lie, but essentially true.

A cloud passed over her face, distrust of her oldest son lingered on her brow, but she moved deeper into the house, oohing and ahhing at the delicate craftsmanship of the small mansion.

• • •

"Señor Francisco." One of the young messengers approached him cautiously. "Crudo is asking for you to come up to "K" Street. He needs your orders on something he's found."

Francisco knew better than to ask what. Crudo had always been his most reliable lieutenant and he would never call him forward without good reason.

A pickup truck appeared, sent by Crudo. Francisco grabbed the lever-action rifle and a bandolier of bullets he had found that morning and climbed into the passenger seat.

The truck turned uphill and carried them to the top of the Avenues to an otherwise uninteresting home. Crudo met Francisco in the front yard.

"Pancho, I thought this might be worth your time. It's around back. The family's inside the house." Crudo led Francisco through a small gate in the side yard around back to a tiny garage that opened onto a narrow alley behind the house. The garage looked well-kept but, strangely, it bristled with antennas and solar panels, like someone's private, cobbled-together cell tower.

"*¿Que cosas?*" Francisco wondered out loud. "What the hell is this?"

They stepped through the small door into a room packed with gadgetry. An old white man sat on a stool, with a Latino guard standing over him. The man's face was twisted into a look of fierce defiance, his eyes boring into Francisco with hatred.

Francisco almost laughed. The man had to be eighty years old.

"You go ahead and kill me. I'm ready to meet the Lord and the Prophet Joseph. Get it over with."

Francisco couldn't help himself; he had to laugh. "*Señor,*" Francisco used a title of deference, "we're not going to kill you. If we wanted to kill someone, we'd kill your family."

The old man's face came undone, like it had been held by a drawstring in back and someone suddenly cut the cord. "Don't you touch my family!"

"*Señor*," Francisco began again with feigned gentleness, "I will personally protect your family. But I need something from you."

"What?" the old man sneered.

"I need you to tell me about this." Francisco motioned to the equipment. "What does it do?"

The man began slowly, but picked up speed as he explained. He couldn't help his enthusiasm when it came to the shelves of gadgetry, even when discussing it with a mortal enemy.

Francisco understood only half of what the old man said, but he didn't want to interrupt. The value of the find was becoming increasingly apparent as the man blathered on about his roomful of toys.

Francisco interrupted with a question. "So, are you saying this equipment can talk to people anywhere in Salt Lake, and then listen to people anywhere in the United States?"

The old man went off again, talking about weather conditions, line of sight, repeaters and a bunch of other jargon that didn't mean anything to Francisco. The gist of it was, yes, the equipment could communicate with Francisco's men all over the valley, as well as listen in on events across the globe. But they would need more handheld radios in addition to the four little radios lined up on charging stations on the old man's desk.

Crudo and Francisco stepped into the backyard to talk in private.

"Send a team to look for any other homes with these antennas." Francisco pointed to the rooftop array. "And carefully bring every piece of equipment you find back here." He wished they had known about this earlier. Francisco could have ordered his men to detain anyone with radio equipment. For now, he would have to count on this one old man to run the equipment. By the look of him, he might die any minute.

"Pick three of the boys—the smartest ones. Have them sit with the old man and learn everything they can. Oh, and if you find another radio like this, don't send the family away. We'll need leverage."

"Okay, *Jefe*," Crudo said, heading back around to the front of the house.

• • •

Ross Homestead
Oakwood, Utah

Jeff startled awake with ice-cold feet against his legs. His middle son, Erik, had climbed into bed between Jeff and Tara, taking Jeff's body heat like a birthright. From her stirring, Jeff could tell the boy had awakened Tara, too.

With one hand, Jeff lifted Erik and pulled him onto his pillow. He pressed one of Erik's cold feet between his meaty hands, slowly warming the six-year-old. When one foot reached body temperature, Jeff switched and massaged Erik's other foot as well. After a few minutes, the boy's feet weren't so shockingly cold. His hands on Jeff's chest were chilly, too, so Jeff warmed them one at a time as well.

"What're you doing?" Tara asked, perplexed by the movement in the dark.

"I'm warming up his hands and feet. He's freezing."

"The other boys must've stolen the covers," she guessed.

"He has piano player hands," Jeff mused.

Like a lightning strike building in the clouds, the atmosphere between Jeff and Tara turned ominous, even in the pitch dark. Voltage crackled inexplicably from her to him.

"There is more than one way to be a man, Jeff," she said with deadly seriousness, flat-toned and pregnant with enmity.

In the shorthand of a couple who had been married more than fifteen years, volumes were spoken in that sentence, the import slowly descending on Jeff. It occurred to him that he had stomped on a mother's love for her child and a daughter's love for her father all in one sentence.

He has piano player hands…

229

Jeff had been holding Erik's cold hands and warming his son's long, slender fingers—a genetic curiosity, considering Jeff's own stumpy, cigar-shaped fingers. Erik's hands had skipped a generation, getting their form from Tara's father.

Tara's father had spent his adult life as a piano salesman, tinkling the ivory keys for Utah housewives who might like a piano for their home. He had been a concert pianist at one point, then a music teacher, but money had lured him from music to sales. He had provided for his family, as many men had throughout history, by giving up his dreams in exchange for a steady paycheck. His hands, long and lithe, had served him well in his chosen profession.

The questionable masculinity of a piano salesman, in contrast to his warrior son-in-law, set the stage for conflict. Tara's father and Jeff had drawn battle lines within a year of the marriage. Conscripts had been recruited from the family. A cold war had settled between them. "Piano player hands" was anything but an innocent comment and the implications of the statement reverberated between Tara and Jeff in the dark of their bed.

"Why are you mad? I didn't mean anything by that," Jeff argued.

"You meant everything by that," Tara hissed.

Jeff couldn't deny it. He had taken a cheap shot, banked off his son, aimed at his father-in-law—a man who had refused to admit that Jeff was the better man to protect their family. Right now, the old man was hiding in his cabin, maybe dead. The thought made Jeff feel disgusted with himself, but he couldn't figure out why.

"And you're doing it here, Jeff. You're alienating these people, too."

Jeff couldn't help himself. "I didn't alienate your father. He's the one who chose that cabin over his own survival."

"Goddamn you, Jeff Kirkham," Tara swore, keeping her voice low to avoid waking Erik. "You sent my dad away years ago when you made it clear you thought of him as less of a man. You sent him and my mother to that cabin long before the collapse. You make people feel like fools. You're doing it here, too. A lot of people don't like you, Jeff. A lot of people feel like you're running rough-shod over them. A lot of people, especially the women, think you're taking too much control."

"Why do you care? You didn't want to come here anyway," Jeff whispered.

"*Don't you do that.* Don't play CIA mind games with *me*. We agreed to come here and now you need to make this work."

Jeff didn't think he was playing CIA mind games but apparently Tara did. So he chose his next words carefully. "I don't know how to make these civilians happy. If I do my job, strangers die. If I don't do my job, we die."

The words hung in the air. Then Tara replied, "That may be so. We may need to fight to survive. But, for a smart guy, you almost always reduce things down to just two options… you do that a lot."

Jeff heard her roll over, her signal that the conversation was over.

Erik stirred in his sleep and Jeff pulled his son closer. Jeff could sense the searing truth of what Tara had said, like a cloud of ozone hanging over their bed. At the same time, he had absolutely no idea what to do with the information.

11

"JT TAYLOR, HERE, BRINGING YOU news of a world gone mad. It's two a.m. in the morning and I have no idea how so many of you are doing this thing sober. What's wrong with you people?

"Just heard from Kelley Barracks in Stuttgart, Germany. They're barricaded in and taking fire from Muslim forces. I still don't understand where Muslim forces came from. Where'd they get the guns? Inquiring minds want to know.

In case you were wondering, it looks as though the United States Army has decided to let me keep my Humvee and my trailer. Thank you gents. You only tried to blow me up twice, so I guess we're friends now.

I'm hearing from two ham operators out of 19th Group in Salt Lake City, Utah. Get this: the Mormon Church is calling anyone and everyone to come join their army and defend their big-ass temple. Sounds like 19th Group Special Forces—or what's left of them—might send some boys to whack a bunch of gangbangers..."

The Avenues
Salt Lake City, Utah

Crudo handed Francisco a pair of binoculars. The lenses kept collecting tiny droplets of water from the early morning dew. Francisco used his shirttail to wipe the moisture away. They had slipped into the back of a house on Virginia Street to observe an enemy army. Overnight, the Los Latigos advance in the Avenues met serious resistance, and Francisco had no idea who they were.

The two gangsters belly-crawled up to the window and peered through the slit between the curtains and the windowsill. Snipers hiding in the houses across Virginia Street had already killed a dozen of his men this morning. Even taking a look posed a risk.

At a glance, Francisco could see twenty or thirty men, which meant there were probably a hundred fifty men dug in. His men could overrun that many men and absorb acceptable losses.

The opposing force was spread up and down the entire length of Virginia Street, hiding behind vehicles, tucked behind hedges, and peeking out from windows. They weren't in uniform, though he could see men in military camouflage, police uniforms and even hunting camo.

Two things concerned him. For one thing, the opposing force had made a coordinated stand. It wasn't dumb luck that they held Virginia Street. Somebody in command had made that decision, and the men involved had enough discipline to hold the line. A fighting force taking orders from someone would be ten times as threatening as a gang of men with guns.

The second thing he noticed sent a chill down his spine. Barely visible down 3rd Avenue was an armored vehicle, one of the kind employed by police. The vehicle itself didn't concern Francisco so much. He had faced such vehicles before, and they were nothing more than transportation. The men inside eventually had to come out and fight.

What concerned him flapped in the breeze over the vehicle—a blue, square flag. He took his time inspecting the flag: blue square with a yellow figure in the center, blowing a long trumpet.

Whenever asked, Francisco would call himself Catholic, though he had never taken much interest in religion. But he lived in Utah long enough to recognize the emblem on the flag. It was the same gold angel blowing a horn that Mormons placed on top of their temples.

The Mormon Church had fielded its own army, and that army had come together in a matter of two days to block his army. The only force stronger than pride, so far as Francisco knew, was faith. If the Mormon Church requested fighting men from the surrounding neighborhoods, and if the church provided coordination, the thousand men of Los Latigos could be chewed up and spit out by day's end.

Men fighting for faith and for the protection of their families would be ferocious opponents. The days of mowing through white people, at least in the Avenues, had come to an end.

As he thought through the implications, Francisco pictured the map of the Avenues they had laid out on the picnic bench in Rose Park two days ago. To their east, they had come against this line of Mormon fighters and, so far, any attempt to cross Virginia Street had been met with instant death.

To their north, the mountains rose above them, blocking attack or retreat. One exception might be Tellers Canyon, with its road curving deep into the mountains. That road might become a trail up and over the ridge, but only for men on foot. He didn't think there was a road going over that ridge.

To their south, downtown Salt Lake City opened before them with twenty or more wide streets that would be difficult for an enemy to blockade unless they had thousands of men. Even so, the streets of downtown didn't offer him much in the way of pillage. The downtown area had degraded over the years into a series of old tenements, and the forage opportunities wouldn't be worth the risk.

To the west, they faced the Mormon temple, along with the church's corporate offices and meeting centers. He guessed the Mormons had fortified their temple and only afterward had sent men to stop his eastward advance. Having a strong force to his rear made Francisco uneasy. His mama, as well as the families of his men, had settled in homes that would be the first to fall if the Mormons pushed his west flank from their temple.

Profound disappointment washed over Francisco. All this progress, all this promise, and it would amount to nothing. There was only one reasonable course: retreat. That meant removing his mama and the families they had already given homes. Leaving them in place put everyone at risk. This Mormon army would only grow in strength if he continued this push, and then everything would be lost.

He had captured an enormous store of food, guns and prescription drugs. They could retreat to the fairgrounds and claim victory. They could feed their people for weeks and attract more fighters with drugs and supplies.

"We retreat," Francisco finally said out loud.

"*Sí.* I agree." Crudo had reached the same conclusion.

"*¡Pinche madre!*" Francisco swore.

"Before we go, I need to tell you about something from last night."

"Okay, let's get out of here first."

The men crawled out of the room and went out the back door, climbing over the fence to get clear of the battlefront.

As they walked away from Virginia Street, Crudo reported. "Last night, the old man with the radio picked up some gringos talking. He thought they were chatting back and forth at the top of Tellers Canyon, maybe above Oakwood. Francisco, I slept at the radio garage last night and listened to some of their radio talk. It sounded like they were organized, well-supplied."

Francisco had a lot to think about. He would extract his men from the Avenues. After that... he didn't know yet. Momentum was important, especially while the gringos reacted slowly to his attacks. He needed to make the most of this opportunity.

But he couldn't commit a large force in one direction without understanding the risks and the rewards. He needed to know what he would be facing. He didn't want to lead Los Latigos into another dead end.

He should have known the Mormon Church would respond so quickly to protect its temple. It hadn't crossed his mind while planning his attack on the Avenues, and the slip-up frightened Francisco. He had started to believe that fate guaranteed their success. That thought first came to him when the prison fell, and the feeling had grown stronger since. Trusting fate wasn't a plan. It was superstition.

No more fate, he reminded himself. They would either succeed or fail based on his decisions, his intelligence. He needed to *think*.

"Send ten men up that canyon with radios. Have them take a look and radio back what they see. I want to know what's happening up in the haciendas there above Oakwood. Send them right now. They are to *look only*, not fight."

"*Sí, Jefe.*" Crudo started to walk away.

"Hold up." Francisco held up his hand. "Make sure every piece of that old man's equipment makes it back to the fairgrounds with us, *comprende?*"

"*Sí, Jefe.*"

• • •

Ross Homestead
Oakwood, Utah

One of Jason's business mentors was fond of saying, "You can be right or you can get what you want. Pick one."

As he watched the bishopric walk up the driveway, Jason ached to be right. He wanted to crush Masterson. The man had lied, and he

236

had done it for control, no matter who got hurt in the process. Worse yet, Masterson had been too stupid to know how destructive it would be for him to get his way. And, by the time he figured it out, there would be scores of dead.

Masterson had twisted the words of the stake president in an attempt to gain control of the resources of the Homestead. Jason could embarrass Masterson with that information, make him look like a liar in front of the bishop. Even as his blood boiled, Jason knew he wouldn't do that, at least not directly.

You can be right or you can get what you want.

Too many lives depended on Jason for him to indulge his need to crush Masterson in front of the bishopric. In any case, the bishop already knew Masterson had twisted the stake president's words. Soft-pedaling Masterson might increase Jason's credibility with the bishop and his counselors. Downplaying Masterson's lie would build bridges instead of burn them.

But Jason hated the game. It exacted a stiff price. Verbal smash-mouth was more his natural groove and, God knew, Masterson had it coming.

"Good morning, brothers." *Go big or go home.* Jason smiled to himself, despising every minute of his duplicity. Jeff joined them, exchanged handshakes, then slumping down in his chair like a bag of bowling balls.

Masterson took control of the meeting right out of the gate. "Have you considered President Beckstead's request that we come together as a neighborhood?"

Jason swallowed hard.

"I can't help feeling this is a huge decision, and I'm not getting any clear answer through prayer." It was an outright lie on Jason's part. He hadn't prayed about Masterson's plan. Jason had prayed about how to approach this meeting, but there was never a moment when he had actually considered putting Masterson in charge. He had put enough stupid questions before God to know that God didn't like playing "Magic Eight Ball" when common sense could do the job.

But bringing up prayer would resonate with the men of the bishopric. The Mormon faith promoted reliance on personal revelation, and going to God for a decision, or indecision, would be seen as a valid response. Appealing to prayer would put a full stop to Masterson's drive for an immediate decision.

Jason continued. "One of our other committee members and I sought counsel from President Beckstead yesterday." Masterson's eyes widened. He hadn't anticipated they would close the loop with Beckstead, and the flush on his face belied his fear of being caught putting words in his stake president's mouth. It would certainly affect future callings of leadership if President Beckstead felt Masterson had abused his priesthood authority.

Jason said, "President Beckstead counseled making a prayerful decision about our group and the ward, especially since the Lord blessed us with professional military leadership." As the words left his mouth, Jason knew this was both a masterful piece of diplomatic gerrymandering and a load of horse shit.

In one swoop, he had distanced Masterson from the decision-making process, and made it clear the stake president knew about their Green Beret trainers. Jason had been working on that one sentence in his mind for almost twenty-four hours. It was critical that he not make Masterson's rookie mistake of attributing orders to the stake president that he hadn't given.

Masterson looked like he could barely control his anger. The men of the bishopric received the response as entirely appropriate. They had undoubtedly been a little uncomfortable with Masterson's overreach the day before, knowing he had exaggerated. They were more than happy to let Jason push back on the aggressive man's agenda.

Jason made no mention of pooling resources, kicking that issue down the road for now. He figured, if he delayed a decision long enough, it often decided itself.

"Bishop," Jason turned to Bishop Decker, "would you let us know if the neighborhood decides to pool their food?"

"Ah, yes. I will do that. We're not sure what to do right now."

Excellent, Jason thought. He's admitting the ward isn't pooling food.

It tore the guts out of Masterson's plan. The bishop hadn't yet decided that sharing was the right thing to do. The truth was now in the open and understood by all: Masterson's plan had been a ham-handed attempt to get his mitts on the Homestead's resources.

Communism actually had historic roots in the Mormon Church. During a fifty-year period in the eighteen hundreds, the Church practiced the "Law of Consecration." All members pledged everything to the Church while bishops redistributed property as needed. Like so many other collectives in history, the Law of Consecration eventually collapsed under the weight of selfishness. But buried in deep doctrine ran a vein of prophetic utterances calling for outright collectivism.

In a confusing contrast, all the twentieth century prophets had defended the virtues of American constitutionalism and capitalism. Most Mormons voted straight red, Republicans to the core. Liberalism ran almost synonymous with falling away from the Mormon Church. Despite the fact that the Law of Consecration could have been authored by Karl Marx, modern Mormons were also capitalists to the core.

Any suggestion that a ward pool resources would be met with powerful opposition from some members who had their own food storage. Many members would resent anything smacking of mandatory socialism, but hunger was a powerful motivator. The need to feed their families might drive many others to reconsider the Law of Consecration.

In this red letter moment in the history of the Church, during the Apocalypse that just might herald the second coming of Jesus, just about every Mormon ward would be split; people who had food

239

storage and people who didn't. Both groups would have differing viewpoints on the path of righteousness.

But Masterson wasn't carrying water for Mormon theology. He wanted power, and his gambit to control the neighborhood, for the time being, had been blunted.

Jeff saw this as an opportunity to push the envelope. "Gentlemen, I'd like to propose that we move the barricades down to the foot of the mountain so we can protect more homes and give ourselves more room in case of a large-scale attack."

Bishop Decker looked dubious. "Surely it won't come to that. Who would attack us?"

"I don't know," Jeff admitted. "But, if I did know, it'd be too late."

Jason jumped in, wary of Jeff's diplomatic skills but eager to achieve the same goal. "If we move the barricades down to the bottom of the hill, we can blockade fewer roads and get a better result. The mountain would do most of our defensive work for us. Would you be offended if we moved the barricades?"

"No, we wouldn't be offended," Bishop Decker said.

"As I mentioned in our first meeting," Jason said, "we need more men from the neighborhood. Right now, we're offering bread to men camping outside the barricade to train them for our defense forces."

That was news to the bishopric. Masterson stared intently across the table, struggling to get his mind around the new information. By seeking men elsewhere, Jason and Jeff were executing an end run around the ward. The Homestead would get their men one way or another, and it vastly reduced Masterson's bargaining position.

"I'd rather train neighborhood men, and maybe give bread to the folks in the neighborhood who have no food storage," Jason said. "That is, I'd rather do it if you're comfortable with our veterans controlling all defensive efforts."

Masterson interrupted, eager to play his final chip in the big game. "Before we talk about ward members fighting for your army, we're very concerned about reports that your men shot and killed someone yesterday."

"Yes," Bishop Decker snapped back to life. "Did we hear that correctly?"

There's Masterson's counterattack, Jason thought. To be expected.

"Sadly, we were forced to shoot a man on the east boundary. He crossed our fence, ignored a warning shot, and then pointed his rifle at one of our men. The man who shot him is a professional soldier. I'm certain he had just cause."

The bishopric men looked uncomfortable.

"How do we know it was justified? That seems very extreme," Brother Ingram spoke for the first time.

"I know what you mean. These are tough times. A shooting was inevitable. People attempt to trespass on our land many times a day. Almost everyone turns around after a warning shot. This man didn't. And he aimed at our men with a long rifle." Jason did his best to explain, but it wasn't helping.

"One question," Bishop Decker held up his hand. "Was the man you shot a member?"

In thinking through this meeting beforehand, Jason would have preferred to avoid this question above all others.

"How would we know?" Jeff asked, already knowing the answer.

"Was he wearing garments?" Masterson asked. Faithful Mormons almost always wore sacred undergarments, morning, noon and night. If the man wore garments, it would be proof-positive that he was an temple-attending member of the Church.

Jason couldn't do anything but forge ahead. "Yes, I believe he was wearing garments."

Masterson stood up abruptly and the bishopric followed suit.

"Gentlemen, this is a problem," Masterson gloated. "We may need some time to pray about this and talk more with the stake president. Maybe we should call Church headquarters."

As the men filed out, Masterson made sure he was last out the door. He turned back and quietly took at parting shot at Jason and Jeff.

"You aren't the only ones around here with guns, you know."

• • •

"That man is a threat to everyone," Jeff fumed, pointing a thick finger at the door.

"This is my 'ten acres.' Let me handle it," Jason argued.

Jeff held up his hands, "So we're not counting on the ward for anything, right? No men from them. Right?"

"I think all we can expect for now is more hand-wringing," Jason agreed. "Those guys are going to delay until it's too late. Move the barricades down the hill and keep recruiting from outsiders."

"Started yesterday." Jeff wasn't a man to wait for anyone's say-so.

• • •

Jeff stood on a bluff overlooking the main road, Vista View Boulevard, from the backyard of one of the McMansions. The owners had disappeared, probably staying with family or "bugging out" somewhere. He saw that more and more these days.

Jeff considered this road the greatest likelihood of attack. It was one of three major roads climbing to the neighborhood around the Homestead. If you drew a line from the population centers of Salt Lake City directly to the Homestead, this road fell exactly on that line.

There were six other streets that reached up to the Homestead, but those streets would force an attacker to fight through a mile or more of neighborhood—burning time and ammunition. Jeff ordered his men to set up permanent barricades on all six connecting streets, and he had three QRFs ready to pounce if anyone tried to advance up those residential streets. He could focus his main effort on Vista View Boulevard.

Nine times out of ten, a soldier could count on people traveling established paths. Men felt somehow safer, more in control, when using the clearest and easiest route. Human psychology betrayed a man in numerous ways. The United States trained Jeff, over decades, to exploit them all.

Capitalizing on lines of natural drift was *Ambush 101*, in the *Encyclopedia of American Ass Kicking*. From the bluff where he stood, Jeff could rake an attacking force with fire. He would have to design blocking positions and counter-flanking positions on the road itself. The more he looked at it, the happier he felt. This road served up strong advantages. He would have to sucker an attacking force into committing itself here if at all possible. Even then, no experienced military commander would fall for it.

Jeff knew to prepare for the most obvious attack first. Later today, he would figure out how he would assault this area if *he* were the enemy, and then he would concoct defensive plans against those assaults as well.

Jeff climbed back aboard his OHV and drove down to the lower barricade at the bottom of the hill. He had ordered a tent erected and a dry erase board set up.

"Will Trade Bread for Work as Security Guard."

"Looking for: former military, trained in firearms, tradesmen (wood, metal work, mechanical)."

One of his men, an old Marine named Carl, interviewed potential soldiers from the tent city that had sprung up below the barricade. A line of men stretched over a hundred yards, waiting to be interviewed.

Jeff popped into the back of the tent. Carl was in the middle of an interview. The old Marine sat facing a moderately fat man, balding, wearing dirty khaki pants and a filthy polo shirt.

"Where did you receive your firearms training?" Carl sighed, apparently having the same conversation for the umpteenth time that day.

The man pulled at his collar. "I've been a lifelong hunter and my brother-in-law is a highway patrolman. He took me out shooting many times."

"Okay," Carl said. "Please clear and safe this." He handed the man a beat-up Glock handgun.

Sweat sprung from the man's brow. He took the Glock from Carl, looked at it from a variety of angles, sweeping himself, Carl and Jeff with the barrel. He pressed the magazine release and dropped the mag into his lap. With his free hand, he picked up the mag.

"It's empty and safe." The man looked at Carl and Jeff with obvious hope.

"Thank you for waiting in line. I'm sorry. You're not what we're looking for." Carl looked down at the clipboard in front of him, abandoning the man's eyes.

"I can learn. I can learn anything real fast. I managed people at the largest call center in the state. I was a senior director. Give me a chance," he pleaded.

"I'm sorry. Please respect my decision." Carl looked up and shouted, "Next man, please."

Another man, younger than the first, but equally as unlikely, stepped into the tent.

"Hold up," Jeff interrupted. "Can you give us a minute?"

The next interviewee stepped back outside and the bald man stood up, defeated. He handed Carl the empty Glock.

"My family has nothing to eat. You've got to give me a chance. My kids are hungry." The man switched from begging to anger in a split second. "I'm not asking you. I'm telling you. Give me some bread for my family."

Jeff and Carl looked at the man, and then at each other. Unless the man had a bomb under his polo shirt, he wasn't a physical threat to either of them.

"Stop," Jeff warned. "Just leave before you earn yourself a broken arm."

The man's shoulders slumped. He turned and walked out of the tent.

"Jesus," Jeff swore, turning back to Carl.

"It's been like that all day." Carl looked down at his clipboard. "I've only found six guys out of maybe two hundred who could fight their way out of a Ziploc bag."

"Why are you asking for woodworkers, metal workers and mechanics?" Jeff pointed at the dry erase board outside.

"I added that because I've talked to guys all morning and only found one guy who could clear and safe that gun without looking like a goddamned Girl Scout. Hell, at this point, I'd take a Girl Scout. I added the wood and metalwork thing because I figured I could at least train someone who worked with their hands. All I've been getting are cubicle monkeys and human resource managers with expertise in the Equal Opportunity Employment Act." Carl had to look down at his clipboard for that one. "So far, most of the guys I've had in here who are worth a damn don't speak English."

Jeff thought about that for a second. "Most of the guys I've trained over my career didn't speak English. I suppose I would need to speak Spanish, right?"

"*Si*, Boss."

"*No hablo Español*," Jeff said, still thinking. "Okay, let's change your board. Get rid of 'trained in firearms' and add 'farm work, welder, auto body, and mechanical maintenance.' Getting rid of the firearms thing should cut down on creampuffs who think they're outdoorsmen. Maybe add 'law enforcement,' too. I'll send someone else down so two of you can interview at the same time."

Jeff's radio crackled. "Crandall to Jeff, over."

Jeff had his own assigned frequency. The hand-held radios pinged off the repeater at the Homestead so he could talk to his crew anywhere on the hill with perfect fidelity.

"Jeff, over."

"Something odd's going on here on the ridge. It looks like a deliberate push. Six to twelve men, and they're ignoring our warning shots. Over."

"On my way. Follow the ROEs. Shoot them if they go over the line. Jeff out."

Jeff trotted to his OHV and raced up the hill.

• • •

"See how they're taking cover. They keep moving, even though we've shot at them eight or ten times. I think we've hit two of them. Still, they keep coming." Crandall pointed toward a clump of cover underneath the canopy of maples.

Jeff kept the binoculars glued to a spot where he had seen two men drop down behind a log and some bushes.

"Give me all their locations," Jeff ordered.

"I think there are three where you're looking behind that log. Two more are up that same canyon just a bit. One guy is in the bottom of that canyon behind a rock, and three or four more are on the side of the canyon we can't see from here."

"Okay," Jeff said. "And where are your men?"

Crandall thought about that for a second. "Several of them have fired and moved, so I don't know their exact locations. I have two in a hide above us on the ridge, and two more displaced down canyon to get a better shot at the guys we're looking at right now. They should be popping over that ridge soon."

Jeff ducked down into the sniper hide and keyed his radio. "Homestead. Send QRF One to Ridgeline Tango. We're under attack. Please confirm."

The radio came to life. "Homestead, confirming. Send QRF One to Ridgeline Tango. Position is active. Over."

"Roger. Jeff out." Jeff turned back to Crandall. "Crandall, call the team moving to the flank. I'm going to maneuver opposite their sector of fire down that other canyon and I don't want them to shoot

246

me. Okay? Can you make sure of that? It looks like none of the bad guys are wearing camo. It shouldn't be hard to tell us apart."

Everyone on duty for the Homestead wore multi-cam camouflage. Wearing a uniform, Jeff figured, would make folks fear them more and screw with them less. For whatever reason, Jason Ross had stocked up on old, used multi-cam before the stock market crash.

"Right. The trespassers are all wearing street clothes. They look like street thugs to me," Crandall said. "What're you going to do?"

Jeff grabbed his rifle, a Robinson Arms XCR-M .308 with a Trijicon ACOG scope. If he had to pick any rifle for this particular shoot-em-up, he would take this exact one. The big .308 bullet pulverized virtually anything other than vehicular armor, far superior in performance to the pencil-thin .223 bullet most guys used. While fighting overseas with the military issue M4 rifle, Jeff lost respect for the diminutive .223. Far too often, a branch would tap the bullet off its path and, even with a solid hit, targets often failed to realize they had been shot. With the burly .308 rifle round, targets not only knew they had been hit, but they knew better than to stand up again. More importantly, Jeff could pierce wood, trees, rock and even some concrete. For post-Apocalypse survival work, Jeff had no idea why so many guys choose the AR-15 rifle and its .223 round.

"I'm going to slide around the ridge and get a flank on these guys. Are you positive they're all in this canyon?" Jeff asked.

"Sure as can be… But I can't see into the next canyon."

"Okay. Make sure our boys don't shoot me."

Crandall made the call and confirmed that Jeff would be on a ridge opposite his teams and to double-check their targets.

"Take it easy. And if it's easy, take it twice." Jeff waved and slid out of the sniper hide, double-timing it behind the ridge, making ground in leaps and bounds between clumps of maple trees. As soon as he was about half a mile from the hide, he slowed down. While everyone *thought* the entire opposing force was contained in the canyon, nobody could see down into the next canyon. Jeff would have to clear that one himself.

Jeff pulled his binos out of his chest rig and visually picked apart the mountainside for his next leapfrog. Since it faced the summer sun, most of the foliage was stumpy and thin, so Jeff would probably see someone hiding on the slope. It was possible someone might be hiding in the canopy in the bottom of the canyon.

Unlikely, he thought, but not impossible.

Even though he was pushing fifty, Jeff hadn't let his cardio go downhill. Sure, he packed a bit of a beer belly, but he got away with it in a t-shirt because of his ape-sized upper body. Jeff ran the occasional endurance race along the Wasatch Front and he always did pretty well. If he paced himself, he could run all over this mountain. Very few men could do the same at any age.

Cashing in on his cardio, Jeff took the long route. He dropped down into the canyon bottom one over from the intruders and trotted along, rifle at the high-ready. If someone was waiting for him down in this dark mess, he would be running into an ambush. Still, when you flanked, you rolled the dice. You couldn't flank all the way to the moon and back. You had to take your chances at some point.

As he guessed, nobody lay in ambush in this canyon. Setting a counter-flank so far from the enemy force would have required near-professional levels of military discipline, and there wasn't anything about these guys that implied military discipline. Jeff worked his way half a mile down the canyon without a snag.

He stopped to catch his breath. He figured he was parallel to the bad guys. Ideally, he could scale this hillside and be above them, their flank exposed to his Robinson .308. The other team of snipers should be on the ridge directly across from him. Crandall and the third team would serve as a blocking force. If everything worked as planned, they would have the dirtbags in a pocket, surrounded, with all the high ground owned by Jeff's men.

Jeff tried to remember, had anything like this ever gone exactly as planned? He could remember a few times... a few times out of a couple of hundred. He took a last drag from his camelback and sprinted up the sunward slope, knowing he had jack-shit for cover until he reached the top. Everything was going great until about three-quarters of the way up the slope.

"Thwack!" Something slapped the ground twenty feet to his right. "Bam, bam, bam, bam." Somebody was shooting, dumping a mag on him.

Jeff's legs pumped like a motorcycle engine, pounding up the hillside. He closed on the trees on the ridge, taking what seemed like an eternity to get there. Along the way, his adrenaline-drenched brain went into tactical mode. It wouldn't make any sense to stop and return fire, especially since Jeff would have to find the shooter first and since the shooter, apparently, knew exactly where to find *him*. The shooting wasn't coming from a rifle, thank God. The numb-nut shooter was trying to hit Jeff with a handgun from a long ways away. Still, Jeff didn't want to get shot, even with a handgun.

Finally, Jeff made it to the ridge and dove into a thicket of oak brush. The guy must have changed mags because he started shooting again. None of the fire seemed effective; Jeff couldn't even tell for sure what the guy was trying to hit.

"Booooom." A single rifle shot rang out, but it came from the next canyon, probably his own team. The handgun fire ceased.

Jeff keyed his mic. "Report."

"Crandall here. Our team on the far ridge thinks they downed the guy shooting at you."

"Copy. Jeff out."

Low-crawling through the oak brush, Jeff popped up with a hundred new scratches and a brand-new position. He scanned all possible shooting lanes and saw nothing.

Finally, after searching for a full minute, he spied a leg sticking straight up in the air, snagged on an oak limb. The enemy shooter must have been on the same ridge as Jeff. More likely than not, the dude had been dragging ass, unable to keep up with his buddies.

With his binos, Jeff checked to make sure the guy was truly out of the fight. All he could see was a blunt-nosed Nike shoe and black socks. The pants leg had slipped down, almost out of sight in the brush. Definitely not a hunter. More likely a gangbanger.

"This is Jeff. Report in, all teams."

"This is Crandall. All enemy in approximately the same positions as before."

"This is Wali. I'm on the ridge across from Jeff. Just killed that gangster with the pistol. I've got four guys in the bottom and one on the north-facing slope. Maybe two. All tangos are within our boundary now."

"This is Ron. I'm not seeing anything else."

"Jeff. Copy. All teams: begin firing on all targets of opportunity. Unless they fly a white flag or run outside the boundary, keep up fire."

Almost immediately, the big rifle across from him boomed and the team reported another hit.

Jeff worked his way along the ridge, looking for a window that would give him a shot at the intruders. He stopped every ten feet and scanned through the tangle of trees with his binoculars, trying to pick out targets. With the last shot from his men, he noticed bad guys scurrying about. Firing straight through the trees, Jeff hammered their positions with the .308.

"This is Crandall. I've got two targets down and out on the south-facing hillside at the canyon bottom, over."

Jeff slid up and down the ridge, firing on even the slightest suggestion of a hoodie or baseball cap. Gun fire popped now and then as his men chipped away at the enemy force.

A short while later, the QRF showed up and joined the shooting. Jeff deployed them down both sides of the canyon. Over the course of two hours, fire slowed. Jeff counted nine reported hits plus the hand gunner who had tried to shoot him earlier, making a total of ten bad guys dead or wounded. Now came the part he hated most: digging supposedly dead enemies out of their holes.

While they had counted their hits, that didn't mean targets hadn't been overlooked or were wounded but still fighting. Men didn't fall down and vanish when shot. They did all kinds of unpredictable shit, and Jeff could hear at least two men moaning down in the forest. Walking around like Roman conquerors would get one of his men shot.

Jeff had a strong suspicion this fight had been a deliberate probe. He couldn't let bad guys walk away with any information, or their next fight might not be so easy. Jeff picked his way down the ridge, scanning through the trees for new targets. He found a man lying still, some hundred fifty yards away, probably dead. He put two more rounds in him. Jeff found a gap in the forest a quarter mile below the battlefield. He would post up here to see if someone tried to slip out the backdoor.

"Everyone. This is Jeff. I have the canyon bottled up below. Wali, stay on overwatch. Ron, maintain the defensive perimeter. Look for other threats. Crandall, split the QRF and send the teams down the canyon, staying high on the side walls so they have high ground. Shoot anything that looks like a tango, dead or alive. Copy?"

The teams checked in. After ten minutes or so, Jeff could see one of his QRF guys—the one across from his ridge—moving down the side of the canyon.

"QRF, go slower," Jeff radioed.

The QRFs had been pulled from his best men—former military or men with a lot of firearms training. Jeff had trained and selected most of them himself. The idea was to assign trained hunters to handle the defensive perimeter, like long shooters or expert hunters who could glass an area properly. Then they would fill out those ranks with new trainees.

But, if a battle touched off, Jeff could call in one or more of his three QRFs. These were his most fit and experienced troops, and he felt confident they would clean house against all but the most dedicated military opponents. The QRF guys clearing the forest were doing a hard job and taking considerable risk, but they were also the guys most likely to survive hard-core fighting.

Another hour on the mountain ticked by with periodic shots from his men. When the QRF reached Jeff's position, they turned around and ran a grid pattern back up, policing up all the dead bodies and their equipment. There were ten enemy, and they were definitely Hispanic street punks.

Given the steep slope, it would take them all night to carry the dead men back up to the ridge where the OHVs could haul the bodies out. Dusk sat on the horizon. Carrying ten bodies up the hill would draw down their defenses for an unacceptably long time.

Jeff gathered the QRF. "We're not taking any of these assholes out of here. They're not worth the haul. Drag them down to the barbed wire and lean them up against fence posts. Maybe that'll send other intruders a message. Gather any equipment and round up all weapons and ammo. Get going. I want to be out of here before dark."

As gruesome as it was, Jeff would rather leave the dead bodies. If he took them down to the Homestead for a proper burial, it would ignite another shit storm. Half of these dead guys had crapped themselves, and the other half were so full of holes they looked and smelled like road kill.

The good folks down at the Homestead had probably already heard about the battle, but *knowing* about something and *seeing* something were two very different experiences, and Jeff didn't need to borrow trouble.

"Jeff," one of the guys from the QRF ran up to him holding a radio, "this came off that dead guy over there." He pointed back over his shoulder.

Jeff looked closely at the hand-held radio. It looked almost exactly like the radios he and his men carried. He didn't know much about ham radio, but he could tell the difference between a ham radio and the kind of radio you buy at Walmart. This radio definitely wasn't of the Walmart variety.

"Son of a bitch," Jeff swore. "This is not good news."

• • •

Highway 80 (West)
Rawlins, Wyoming

Chad lay in a sand trap in the dark of night, dreaming about golf. Since leaving the SEALs, he had toyed with the idea of spending the rest of his days in pastel polo shirts, with an extra thirty pounds around his middle, driving a golf cart, puttering away at golf.

He looked back at the Rawlins town barricade, a hundred yards from the golf course. As usual, his mind wandered.

He had done the hard-core thing in the Navy and, frankly, he had had his fill. He got the t-shirt and got out. If he never felt cold, wet or uncomfortable again in his life, that would be just fine with him. But then the collapse came and screwed up his plans of sucking off the tit of civilization, playing endless rounds of golf.

After an hour of recon, he had reached the same conclusion he'd reached four other times at four other roadblocks: this was another dumb roadblock with the same ole rednecks. Robbing this roadblock would be like taking candy from a baby. Again.

He and Pacheco were on a roll. They had become a regular Bonnie and Clyde, except Pacheco was a baby-faced Honduran instead of a cigar-smoking hot chick. Chad figured he could easily pass for a handsome Clyde Barrow.

In the last forty-eight hours, they'd heisted four roadblocks and amassed a small fortune in post-Apocalyptic trade goods. He and Pacheco had been able to back-door every barricade, taking the guards by surprise and stealing back everything the roadblock had stolen from other travelers.

Only once had they discovered a roadblock with a rifle overwatch near the town of Saratoga. In that case, they had ambushed the overwatch guy first, tied him up, then knocked over the barricade. It had proved even easier to take a roadblock with overwatch because the guards had been particularly over-confident.

253

This roadblock beside the golf course didn't have any high ground for miles, so Chad set Pacheco up in the sand trap, which had the advantage of being comfortable, and Chad had learned never to underestimate comfort when it came to warfighting.

With a sigh, Chad got out of the sand and jogged away from Pacheco, making a big dogleg to get far behind the roadblock before approaching. He didn't want to give away Pacheco's position. After running the mile loop, he walked straight up the highway behind the guards.

"Gentlemen," Chad said, getting bored with his whole coup de grâce routine.

"Who's that?" The three young men behind the barricade jumped up like someone had stepped on their tails. They jerked around, pointing their rifles at Chad's chest.

"Go easy, boys. I've got a buddy out yonder and he's got an itchy trigger finger. Damned kid can shoot the dick off a gopher." Chad treated them to his most dazzling smile. He'd left the NVGs in the car this time. Boredom made him sloppy.

Truth was, they had accumulated more stuff than they could carry in both cars. He would rather do some horse trading with these guys than rob them. Rawlins was a bigger town compared to the one-horse barricades they had been robbing.

"What're you doing sneaking up on us?" one of the boys asked in a drawl. Then the boy suddenly decided they had the advantage. "Give me your guns."

Again, Chad hit them with the smile. "How many?"

"How many what?" the other boy asked.

"How many of my guns do you want?"

The Wyoming boys looked at each other, confused.

"How many you got?"

Chad thought about it. "I've got a truckload of guns, plus booze, plus freeze-dried food, plus drugs, plus beer, plus weed, plus a really nice bear rug. What're you guys trading?"

"Trading?"

"Yeah." Chad knew he wasn't dealing with the sharpest knives in the drawer. And, in fairness, he had blindsided them. For whatever reason, the dumbest guards got the night shift.

"Gentlemen, you're not taking anything from me by force because I don't have anything on me and because my sniper buddy will shoot you if you try. Instead, how about I make you a great deal on some supplies?"

The young men looked at one another, then sidled closer together so they could confer in private.

"You say you got weed?" one guy asked Chad.

"Yessir." Chad clapped. "We dealing here or what?"

The guys conferred for another moment. "Tell you what," the apparent leader stepped forward, "we'll go get the mayor, and you can make a deal with him. For going and getting him, give us some of that weed."

Chad wasn't sure he was following. "You want me to give you some weed for going to get the mayor?"

"Yeah. It's real late. He's gonna be pissed."

Chad laughed out loud. "Okay, boys. I'll give you one ounce of high-grade Wyoming marijuana for bringing the mayor here right now."

One of the guys whispered something to the spokesperson, apparently a reminder. The spokesman nodded.

"And you can't tell the mayor about the weed."

Chad doubled over laughing. When he got himself under control, he agreed. "Okay, mum's the word about the *Mary Jane*. Go get the mayor."

One of the guys took off toward town on a dirt bike. Chad fished a radio out of his pocket. They had picked up a couple of FRS radios from the last roadblock robbery.

"Pacheco. You still alive?"

"*Sí*, Chad."

"Hang tight. They're getting the mayor to negotiate. Please don't shoot the mayor, okay?"

"*Sí*, Chad."
I might just adopt that boy.

• • •

They had apparently awakened the mayor from a dead sleep, based on the fantail at the back of his head. Even so, he seemed downright jovial.

"Sir!" the mayor climbed down from his giant pickup truck and thrust his hand out to Chad. "I'm Mayor Spears."

Chad shook his hand, noting how small men always seemed to have the biggest trucks. As a man of "moderate stature" himself, Chad made a mental note never to buy a big truck, no matter how strong the urge. Too predictable.

In the age of firearms and coach airline seating, being a large man offered few advantages. Chad would rather be "moderately sized" and overly badass. At least that's what he told anyone who brought it up.

Chad was pleased he was about two inches taller than the mayor.

"These boys tell me you have a sniper out yonder, and you're both military boys who want to trade?"

"Yessir, though I didn't tell them we were military." Chad liked to hold back information whenever possible.

"So are you military or not?" It seemed important to the mayor.

"Okay. So what if I'm a Navy SEAL, let's say?" Chad had no idea where this was going.

"Well, son, if you are a Navy SEAL, I have a proposition for you."

More curious than anything, Chad decided to proceed. "I am a SEAL and my buddies out there are under my command." Chad lied about the number of men and lied with the implication that they might be SEALs, too.

"Fantastic." The mayor rubbed his hands together. "I'd like to offer you a job."

Chad waited. Usually, people had a hard time believing he was a SEAL, because a person so rarely met a true Navy SEAL. The mayor seemed excited to believe him, which should have set off alarm bells.

After an awkward silence, the mayor went ahead. "Our Walmart distribution center—the one that belongs to us—was overtaken by bandits. We think they're bandits. Well, they might be Rock Springs police and some bandits. Maybe they're truck drivers."

The mayor was rambling. Chad got the idea, though. They had no idea what was going on with the Walmart distribution center other than someone else was there, presumably with guns.

The mayor gathered his thoughts for a second. "We need someone to get it back for us."

"What's in it for me?" Chad asked.

"What do you need?"

"I need a lift to Salt Lake City." Chad had no idea how a podunk town would give him a lift to Salt Lake City, but he might as well negotiate big.

"Perfect!" The mayor slapped his hands together. "It's a deal. You get our distribution center back, and we'll fly you to Salt Lake City."

Chad thought about it for a second. *Fly* to Salt Lake? That hadn't occurred to him.

"Four passengers, plus gear?" Chad raised an eyebrow.

"No problem, son. We've got a municipal airport, planes, pilots and plenty of gas." The mayor thrust out his hand to shake on it.

Chad knew how these kinds of deals worked; they grew hair. If he agreed to this, it was going to get weird, guaranteed.

"Why do you want to take control of the distribution center?"

The mayor answered with certainty, his hand hanging in the air. "We have people who'll die without the medication in that warehouse. Rock Springs has the regional hospital and the folks there refuse to share medicine. The next best source is Walmart, but our local Walmart is running out of pills for our old folks and kids."

Chad's B.S. meter was going redline, but he really liked the idea of a flight to Salt Lake City. He was bored with jacking roadblocks, and eventually he or Pacheco would end up killing one of the young idiots guarding them. That would definitely suck the fun out of the whole enterprise.

Assaulting a Walmart distribution center fit his modus operandi perfectly: pull crazy shit that makes for a great story later.

Chad returned the mayor's handshake. "Okay, I'll do it. I'm going to need twenty guys, including these three." He motioned to the barricade guards.

"Done."

With that handshake, Chad became the ranking military authority of Rawlins, Wyoming.

• • •

The Walmart distribution center sat almost smack dab between Rawlins and Rock Springs, making the mayor's claim of ownership a bit cloudy. Chad supposed the real claim of ownership went to the town of Wamsutter, if the town had been anything more than a few dozen rusted-out, double-wide trailers. The sparkling new distribution center stood just off the Wamsutter freeway exit.

Other than the Middle East, Chad had never seen a land so desolate. This part of Wyoming gave the desert a bad name. Were it not for the oil and natural gas being pumped out of the ground, Wamsutter's primary export might be sand.

As the sun came up, Chad started making sense of the mayor's rambling. He used the pre-dawn darkness to crawl to the top of a small rise in the barren, rolling hills where he could look down on the distribution center with his father-in-law's crappy binoculars.

Chad had taken one of the barricade boys with him, sending Pacheco back to get Audrey and his little girl. The mayor had agreed to put them up in the Holiday Inn while Chad figured out the assault.

Scattered around the outside of the distribution center, Chad counted thirty semis, five cop cars, fifteen passenger vehicles and at least five hundred semi-trailers. Without a doubt, the place contained

258

a lot of interesting bling. In the zombie Apocalypse, this would be known as a "high value target."

Chad regretted his request of twenty men. He had spoken too soon. He might need a couple of hundred just to cover the size of the place. It was huge. Shaped like a fat letter "L," the distribution center had almost a million square feet under roof. And who knew what the inside actually looked like? Essentially, Chad thought, it would be like assaulting a small town, except with a roof over the entire thing.

He didn't spot any defensive positions. He'd only seen one man step through the doors, probably a trucker, to get some fresh air and smoke a cigarette. The trucker hadn't been armed.

Chad tried to imagine what they were doing inside. There had to be at least five law enforcement guys from Rock Springs in there, since there were five cruisers outside. He thought there was maybe one guy per semi and one guy per passenger vehicle. That added up to about sixty men; maybe eight or ten of those might be women. He didn't want to make too much of his guess but, based on the smoker not having a rifle, they might not have enough guns to arm all sixty men.

It was a wild guess, Chad reminded himself. Rock Springs, no doubt, had plenty of guns, and they might have packed one of those cop cars with rifles to arm everyone inside. Based on the level of defense, it looked like a light presence, as though Rock Springs was claiming *dibsies* on the place, but not much more.

Chad turned to the boy from Rawlins lying next to him in the dirt. "Have you guys hit this place yet?"

"Nope. Mayor Spears had words with the mayor of Rock Springs over it, but that's all."

"Hang out right here and don't shoot." Chad told the boy. "I'm going inside to check things out."

• • •

As Chad worked his way down to the massive parking lot, he thought about the distribution center from a defensive point of view. It would be nearly impossible to cover all the ways into the building. There had to be two hundred outside doors, not counting the big roll-up cargo bays.

If it had been Chad, he would have put early warning pickets on the roof. That would have made it a lot harder for him to get inside to recon the place.

But a defensive perimeter was tougher to maintain than people thought. After about ninety minutes of guard duty, most men became combat-ineffective. Maybe the ADHD generation was to blame, but one couldn't expect a military trained guard to remain combat-effective past an hour and a half. Without two men on guard at each post, there would be no way to ensure one guy wasn't sleeping. With civilian guards, it would be even harder.

Maybe the cops had already tried to maintain a perimeter and they had given up. More likely, they had pulled back to some central location in the warehouse and were sitting around playing cards, not expecting an armed incursion.

Even at low levels of readiness, sixty armed men weren't going down without a fight. Chad would have to come up with something clever.

Armed with an M4 they had purloined, Chad peeked in one of the doors. A steel door, way out on the end of the fat "L," had been left unlocked. The industrial door didn't actually have a manual lock. It appeared to lock automatically by magnetic solenoid. Since the grid power was out, the doors must have defaulted to locking open. Chad couldn't imagine why. Maybe Walmart's legal department was more worried about not locking people inside in an emergency than they were worried about locking thieves out.

Chad slipped inside, closing the door softly. Inside, everything was dead dark, and it took a minute for his eyes to adjust.

As he began to make out shapes, nothing made sense. He had expected to find big racks stacked with pallets, like a Costco on steroids. Instead, all he saw was level after level of rolling conveyor belt, winding through the warehouse like ribbon pasta, intersecting here and there with junctions under robot arms as tall as backhoes. The place smelled like putrid fruit mixed with rotting meat.

The layout reminded Chad of illustrations of the "Cities of Tomorrow" that he saw in his Grandpa's old Popular Science magazines, as though some ambitious city planner had stacked a dozen miniature gleaming California freeways on top of one another in mid-air.

The more he saw, the more he deduced that he had walked into an ultra-modern sorting and shipping facility. Many of the boxes were open, filled with fruit, rotting seafood and Saran-wrapped meat and vegetables. Apparently, the robotic arms would grab boxes and add them to pallets. Then, robotic pallet jacks would run the pallets out to semi-trailers at the bay doors.

All of the bay doors were closed, though, and it looked like the place had halted instantly when the power went out. There was no way this much machinery could run off generators.

It wasn't clear to Chad how to walk through the jumble of conveyors, so he stuck to the outside wall. At least staying to the outside, he would only have a one-hundred-eighty-degree threat area. If he walked through the middle of the jumbled processing floor, he would have to pay attention to a three-hundred-sixty-degree area with hundreds of blind spots.

Chad stalked down the entire arm of the "L" without seeing or hearing a soul. By the time he reached the bottom corner, he figured it out; this arm of the building was dedicated to shipping and receiving perishables. After more than a week without power, it was obvious why nobody guarded the area; it smelled like the south end of a northbound hog.

As he turned the corner on the other arm of the building, Chad heard voices. This other half of the distribution center made a little more sense. Like the other arm, there were tracks, trolleys and robots going every which way. But here, the place was packed with three-story racks holding pallets and boxes.

The nasty smell began to abate, so Chad figured this for the dry storage area. All these boxes probably held canned food, cereals and other dry goods. After ten days playing Road Warrior, the warehouse looked like post-Apocalyptic Fort Knox. Anyone holding the distribution center would be rich like Rockefeller. If Chad didn't have friends waiting for him in Salt Lake, he might consider holding onto this place for himself.

Based on the voices—laughing and joking—Chad could tell the inhabitants weren't on high alert. He thought about it for a second. Based on the parking lot, he guessed that people would be cycling in and out from Rock Springs, doing guard duty, then heading home. Maybe the truckers were camping here full time, but the citizens and police officers would likely rotate between the town and the distribution center. If he was right about that, a stranger in their midst might not raise an alarm.

Chad noticed a Carharts coat hanging on one of the robot arms. He slung his rifle around to his back and cinched down his two-point sling, pulling the rifle tight against his lower back. With the bulky coat, he might get away with concealing both his rifle and his handgun.

The trick, Chad had learned, was the walk. If you convinced yourself that you belonged there, everyone else would be convinced, too. Chad strode across the lanes of racking at a casual gait, looking straight ahead. Right away, he noticed someone at the far end of a row and gave him an insouciant wave. The stranger waved back.

Chad made a full loop around the outer ring of the dry goods warehouse. Five people noticed him and none thought anything of it. When he returned to his starting place, he shucked the jacket and hung it exactly where it had been. With his recon complete, he headed back into the nasty-smelling section and worked his way back to the door where he'd entered.

What he had seen didn't surprise him—human nature on display. Laziness always defeated vigilance and, once a person settled into a routine, it was hard for him to imagine anything interrupting it.

Chad chuckled to himself when he realized that was precisely what had happened to America. The country hadn't experienced an economic collapse in living memory. Almost everyone who had seen the Great Depression had died. Consequently, the rest of the country assumed it couldn't possibly happen because things in their lives had always been okay.

To take the distribution center with a minimum of bloodshed, Chad would exploit that same trick of human psychology. He would take advantage of people's tendency to ignore threats they had never personally seen.

Now outside and heading back the way he'd come, Chad jogged clear of the distribution center, using the natural hills and draws to get back to his cowboy companion without being seen.

"How'd it go?" the boy asked Chad.

"Good. Do you guys have a country western band in Rawlins?"

• • •

Ross Homestead
Oakwood, Utah

"I'm telling you right now, that's NEVER going to happen." Alena and Robert stood facing each other, a hundred yards into the forest, arguing.

Robert stared at her for a minute, gathering himself. "Honey. I love you, but this is something I've got to do."

Alena didn't consider herself argumentative. Powerful, yes. Opinionated, probably. But, in the last week since the world started going crazy, she had raised her voice an awful lot. She didn't like being that woman, but now wasn't the time to back down.

"There's plenty that needs to be done around here. You don't need to become one of those gun-toting idiots." Alena dropped her voice at that last part, not wanting to offend anyone who might be passing by. Almost every one of the men here carried a firearm. Some carried several.

"Alena, it's not about guns. It's about protecting my family and doing my part. I'm not going to do it your way this time, so you need to get okay with that. I start training tomorrow."

"The hell you are. You do that and I'll leave you." Her eyes brimmed over with tears.

Robert smiled.

"Why are you laughing?" she demanded.

"I'm sorry, sweetheart, I'm sorry. It's just… look at the world. Nobody's leaving anybody right now. We're in this together for the duration, whether we like it or not."

Alena tried another tact. "You're not going to become a henchman for that Kirkham person. Just look at his eyes! He's borderline evil. They killed more men today; did you hear? And they were probably all Hispanic. We're NOT that kind of people, Robert. We stand for justice in the world, not gunning people down because they're different than us or because they're hungry. That's not us, Robert!"

"Believe me, sweetheart, I've had those same thoughts. But, when it comes down to it, no matter what you or anyone else says, I'm a father and a husband. I have a duty."

"To hell with your duty!" Alena screamed. "You could die! You don't know anything about guns."

"That doesn't matter. And I know more about guns than you think. I'm in the Army, for gosh sakes, Alena. This is something I have to do. Look at me." She gathered herself, sensing defeat. "I won't die. Okay?"

She leaned into him, sobbing.

"Don't die. Please. Don't die."

264

"Honey, it's just guard duty. Just a precaution. Everyone needs to do their part. I'll be careful."

12

"THIS IS JT TAYLOR. ALCOHOLIC of the Apocalypse... Drinkin' Bro and Lover Divine... broadcasting from a SINGCARS Humvee, telling the story they don't want told, the reality of the shit sandwich we once called America.

"I haven't heard from our Drinking Bros stationed in Europe, which could just be because of the clouds today.... we're praying for our armed forces inside of Europe, where ISIS is somehow on a bizarre winning streak. If you're wondering WTF, then join the club.

"I just got a call from North Dakota. Sounds like the Air Force base there just closed up shop. The commander poured a bunch of concrete down his missile silos and sent everyone home. Sounds like they ran out of MREs.

"My trailer's getting low on drinking water—thanks to the boys in Scottsdale for the re-supply of Leadslingers Whiskey. Guess I could just switch to whiskey in my Cheerios. So I'm roving around Northern

Arizona. If there are any Drinkin' Bros out this way who are still down to party hearty, ring me back on the 49 meter band, 6000kHz, right on the nose..."

Salt Lake County Fairgrounds
Salt Lake City, Utah

The last two days had been a horror show for Gabriel. All of the bravado, all of the Mexican patriotism, all of the glory of running people out of their homes... all of it smacked of nefarious bullshit to him.

The only thing Gabriel hated more than hypocrisy was disloyalty, and he wasn't about to be disloyal to Francisco, so he kept his mouth shut.

Somewhere in the back of his mind, a voice told him he had suffered trauma with the murder of his *abuelita* and the homeless man, and his thoughts couldn't be trusted.

He kept reliving the moment when he had put the rifle to the homeless man's chest and shot him, leaving dirty starbursts on the man's shirt. He kept seeing those starbursts with a black hole in the middle. No blood, just a black hole.

How strange, not to trust his own mind. Gabriel knew his brain could be affected by things outside his control, even chemicals produced by his own body. Without a doubt, his sister turned into a hag once a month, and hormones definitely accounted for that. Could the same be said of Gabriel? Could trauma warp his mind, leading him down mental paths that weren't entirely sane?

But if he couldn't trust his own mind, what could he trust?

For now, he would keep his head down. He would do what his brother asked and he wouldn't draw attention to himself.

They had returned to Rose Park, to the fairgrounds where thousands of Latinos had gathered, called by his brother's gang to unite for a grand Hispanic cause. Gabriel wondered, especially after their defeat and narrow escape from the Avenues, how could so many people believe in this insanity? How could anyone think getting behind a gang like Los Latigos would result in a righteous outcome? Gabriel knew enough about government to know there wasn't an ounce of legitimacy in what his brother and his gang of criminals were attempting.

"Gabe. *Ven acá,*" Francisco called him up to the front of the recreational vehicle.

As soon as they had returned from the Avenues, Francisco and his men had "borrowed" many of the RVs in the KOA next door to the fairgrounds. Of course, Francisco and his family got the best—two forty-five-foot luxury motor coaches with automated lighting, satellite TV, automated curtains and a whisper-quiet generator. The RVs were far nicer than their home in Rose Park. Their mama complained about them being "too fancy" for her.

Francisco spread his Salt Lake roadmap on the marble dining table attached to the wall of the RV. His top lieutenants, Crudo and Kermit, leaned over the map, listening intently.

"I want you to hear this too, *hermano,*" Francisco said.

Gabriel joined the men over the map.

"Let's look at our options," Francisco said. "Option One: we can stay here at the fairgrounds." Crudo nodded his head, obviously favoring Option One.

"The problem with staying here," Francisco continued, "is that we will run out of stuff. We'll be raiding for food in our own neighborhoods. We might be able to take down the Mormon food storehouse over on 800 South, but I don't think we're ready to go up against the Mormon army again. Let's not hit the Mormons until we're ready."

The defeat at the Avenues and yanking their families out of those homes had been embarrassing enough, Gabe thought to himself.

"We need someplace rich, but easy. We can hit the mansions at the south end of the valley, but that's a long way to travel. A lot can happen in ten miles and our supply lines would be strung out. We'd have to move everyone down south, maybe down by the prison.

"Or, we could hit Olympus Cove, here." Francisco pointed to the map, since his guys wouldn't know where "The Cove" was; it was another white enclave. "But attacking there will stretch us thin, too, and we'd be moving past the Mormon troops we ran into yesterday."

"Or we can go north. There are a lot of rich neighborhoods here, here and here." Francisco poked several locations against the mountain on the map. "These are neighborhoods full of little mansions. That might work for us because, with our backs against the mountains, the Mormons could only hit us from one direction. To chase us, they'd have to leave their temple and come after us."

"Pancho," Crudo interrupted, "the men we sent up Tellers Canyon yesterday… they haven't returned." This was news to Francisco, and he raised his eyebrows, waiting for details.

"They radioed yesterday afternoon, saying they were fighting men with guns. But they never called back. Either they're stuck in the canyon or they got popped."

Francisco stopped to think. To Gabriel, it sounded like heading into those mountain neighborhoods could be trouble. Still, he said nothing.

"Tellers Canyon is too far from these wealthy homes for these neighborhoods to have played a part in whatever happened to our men." Francisco pointed at Oakwood on the map, not knowing that he'd placed his finger exactly on top of the Homestead. "And look, we have a direct route." He sketched a line down the frontage road of the freeway and Valley Vista Drive as it climbed up the hill.

Gabriel finally spoke up. "Can I scout that area first? Before we do anything?"

Francisco smiled and put his arm around his brother's shoulders, shaking him playfully. "Good idea, *hermanito.*"

• • •

The freeways reminded Gabriel of cholesterol, like the cars had passed through smaller and smaller gaps until the freeway was completely blocked. There were long stretches of wide-open road, and then the freeway suddenly clogged wall to wall with cars.

Most of the city streets weren't jammed with cars, though. Gasoline had disappeared quickly, with no way to refill gas tanks. Almost nobody drove. The effect was more like a ghost town than a traffic jam. Driving through town became eerie, with people staring warily from roadside camps or peeking from behind closed curtains.

Francisco insisted that Gabriel take at least two of his foot soldiers. The more men who accompanied him, Gabriel figured, the more conspicuous he would appear. His plan was to drive around the Oakwood neighborhoods and get an idea of the defenses, then return to the fairgrounds. With three Latino guys, they would look suspicious, especially in a car.

His plan changed as soon as Gabriel saw a military-style barricade exactly where Francisco wanted to make entry into the Oakwood neighborhood. Gabriel drove straight past the barricade. He turned up a residential street, looking for a way into the neighborhood. Every street led him invariably up the hill and into another barricade.

Gabriel started getting nervous. All the barricades were manned, and all the men had radios. Eventually a guard would report their car and they would be pegged as suspicious. After turning around four times, Gabriel decided to head back to the biggest barricade off the frontage road, Valley Vista Boulevard. Neither of Francisco's soldiers objected. Apparently, they were serving as body guards, not supervisors.

Stopping several blocks back, Gabriel and the two men walked to the roadblock. There wouldn't be much risk of being noticed, since a tent city surrounded the barricade. People lived in their cars, in tents and on the pavement by the hundreds. Gabriel got the impression they were waiting for handouts, waiting for work, or maybe just waiting for someone to let them inside.

Gabriel asked his brother's foot soldiers to back off, and he made his way to the front of the tent city. The refugee tents radiated out from a big army tent. Uniformed men in camouflage stood behind the barricade and in gun emplacements overlooking the road. A large sign hung on the side of the tent offering work for tradesmen. A line had formed, presumably to apply for work. Gabriel stepped into the line.

Looking around, he reached two conclusions. First, the families on the hill had organized. They were armed and coordinated beyond anything he had seen since the power went out, even better than the Mormon army. It seemed very possible the group was aligned with the army, though Gabriel saw no military vehicles.

Second, the neighborhood had resources. If they were hiring men from outside, that meant they had food and money to spare. Gabriel scanned the little mansions lined on the main road, dotting the mountainside. For some reason, these rich people had prepared a defense against people exactly like his brother and his gang.

Gabriel considered the tent city, full of suffering families of every race and social standing. If his brother attacked this place, these families would pay a price in blood.

Gabriel reminded himself of his duty to his family. He turned back to the barricade and the defenses, taking careful note of the number of men and where they were positioned. He would try to convince his brother to abandon his attack, but Francisco couldn't usually be swayed once he set his foot to a plan.

When Gabriel felt like he had seen enough, he stepped out of line and headed back to the car. His guards fell in behind him. They passed a pet store and a funeral home, and four men drifted out from behind the funeral home in their wake.

Gabriel noticed the men immediately because he had been wary of being followed by the guards at the barricade. These men were not part of the rich peoples' army. They were clearly gangsters like Gabriel and his bodyguards.

Gabriel insisted when they left the fairgrounds that they wear no gang colors. His brother's men had done the best they could, wearing brown and black work shirts. But one wore a baseball cap with an

Arizona Cardinals' logo, and the other guy stuffed a red handkerchief in his back pocket.

Regular citizens wore whatever colors they wanted without much consideration. But a gangbanger paid close attention to the colors he wore. Any other gangbanger would notice; neither of Gabriel's men wore even a shred of blue. Brown, black and white were "neutral" colors, indicating nothing about gang affiliation. The red handkerchief in the back pocket and the Cardinals cap were dead giveaways.

In Salt Lake City, the gang colors weren't really necessary. A gangbanger would automatically know; Gabriel and his men were Hispanic. The four men following them were Pacific Islanders, probably Tongan or Samoan. With few exceptions, Latinos affiliated with "Bloods" and Polynesians affiliated with "Crips." The bangers that followed them now wore blue and that meant serious trouble. A few feet in front of them, two more bangers stepped out from behind a dumpster.

"Hey, *ese*," one of the men said ominously. "What're you doing up here?"

Gabriel's guards reached for their knives, but didn't pull them. They knew pulling knives or guns at this point would be a death sentence. Even in the old world, this confrontation stood a good chance of ending in blood. Today, with the cops all but dead, Gabriel and his companions would be very lucky to survive a fight with these "Polys."

"Step back here, *ese*," the lead Polynesian gangbanger herded the three Hispanics back behind an equipment rental office. Gabriel had a knife in his back pocket, but fighting their way out of this wasn't going to happen. Six on three, especially when the Polys had the initiative, wasn't going to end well for the Latinos. For one thing, the Polys each had at least fifty pounds body weight on the three Mexicans.

Latinos fought with numbers, guns and exceptional brutality. Being ambushed, unprepared, didn't play to their strengths. And Gabriel wasn't a gangbanger, anyway.

Gabriel calculated that his best chance of survival was to play this with confidence. Fear meant death. "My brother wants to talk to you."

"Oh, yeah, brown boy? Who's your brother?" The last word sounded like "braddah."

"Francisco Peña." The Polynesians stared blankly. They didn't recognize the name. "El Barbero. The Barber." The nickname definitely rang a bell with the Polys.

"So when we kill you, we kill the brother of The Barber?" The head Poly smiled.

"You're not going to kill anyone. You're going to tell your bosses' boss that Francisco Peña sent me to reach out for a meet-up. Los Latigos rolled up the Avenues yesterday—the entire neighborhood—and we have drugs, guns and booze to trade."

"Trade for what?"

"My brother needs men. He's got a big job coming up."

The Polynesian made a distasteful face. "What kinda job would a Blue take from a Red?"

"The kind of job a foot soldier like you wouldn't understand. You deliver the message. My brother will be at Warm Springs Park, neutral territory, at one o'clock tomorrow."

"And I'm supposed to let you walk away?"

"See you tomorrow." Gabriel nudged between two of the Polynesians, careful not to telegraph any aggression. Polynesians were the most easy-going race on the planet, right up until the moment they went full barbarian.

Gabriel's guards followed suit, turning out their hands as they passed.

"Your brother better be there tomorrow," the Poly shouted, "or next time I see you, your brains will be on the sidewalk, *ese*."

• • •

Masterson Home
Oakwood, Utah

"Are they going to give you anything today?" Tim Masterson's wife Melinda begged for the third time that afternoon.

"I told you already," he fired back, "I've been asked by the bishop to train the men as defense because of my military background. Once I get that going, I can ask the bishopric to take up a collection and compensate me for my time and expertise."

Melinda wiped her hands on her apron nervously and spoke. "The Bogens gave me a few cups of wheat and some dried milk this morning. I soaked the wheat in milk and the kids are eating, but they're complaining a lot. We're all real hungry, Tim,"

"Don't you think I know that? What more would you have me do? What do you think nagging is going to accomplish?"

"You always tell me that you're the head of the house and that I should listen to you. I'm just letting you know that the children and I are hungry. All I'm doing is reporting back to you as you asked. I'm trying to be a good wife. I know these are hard times for you right now." Melinda reached out and rubbed her husband's shoulder.

He shook her off. "If you want to do something, go ask some of the neighbors outside our ward for help. Don't let the ward members know we're out of food. We can't project weakness. I need to be seen as strong right now. Do you understand?"

Melinda nodded her head.

"Now, if you could, please leave me alone," Tim said, turning back to his desk, leaving his wife standing behind him, "I have to prepare for the training exercise this afternoon. I need some peace and quiet." Melinda faded back through his office door.

Tim focused on the book on his desk, the "Combat Leader's Field Guide." The graphics with combat formations made some sense to him, but the text in the book made no sense at all. The intricacies of

274

military planning might as well have been Chinese. Even though Tim Masterson failed to understand the checklists and procedures, the book gave him plenty of what he *really* needed: military jargon.

When it came to training the men of the neighborhood, he knew he would need to inspire confidence. It was more important to inspire confidence than to possess skill. If a leader had bullet-proof confidence in himself, the men would get onboard. Once everyone had gotten behind a strong leader, anything was possible, even if that leader had little experience. A clear and confident plan was always better than no plan at all.

Tim Masterson reasoned he probably had more military experience than any of the Mormon men in the neighborhood. He had been an Eagle Scout, like most Mormon boys, but he had also spent several months in the ROTC in high school. While he hadn't made it to boot camp—he had chosen to go on a Mormon mission instead—he had experienced numerous training days at the Army ROTC camp above the university.

How much more complicated could training be than that? And more to the point, as long as he kept the veterans from the compound away from "his" men, nobody would know the difference. Tim Masterson was the most military-experienced Mormon in the neighborhood as far as he knew. Virtually all the other Mormon men had gone on missions when they were at the age when they would otherwise have been serving in the military.

While he searched the field guide for tidbits of military knowledge, Tim's mind wandered, thinking about his father, long since passed. Tim's dad had been a closet alcoholic and a physically violent man, no doubt owing to the nightmare he had endured as an infantryman in the Viet Nam War.

Without anyone in the Church ever finding out, Tim had been punched in the face by his father dozens of times. It was a dubious honor, but Tim felt like the beatings had given him strength. It set him apart from softer men. While the men of the ward dithered and debated, Tim saw himself as a man of action, a man suited for this season of hardship. Even though he hated the very memory of his father, he knew that the man had passed down a legacy of toughness to Tim.

His dad built the home Tim lived in now with his own two hands, a hold-over in the neighborhood from before luxury homes. When Tim's dad built the house, they'd had two hundred acres perched high above the valley. His father planted peach and apple orchards, raised chickens and even kept a few cows. Over the years, Tim had been forced to sell off all but the single acre of his dad's land around their home in order to raise money for business ventures, none of which had been successful.

In his youth, his father forced Tim to work like a slave, claiming to teach him a strong work ethic. The indentured servitude had the opposite effect. Since his father's early death, Tim had avoided work at all costs. He had become adept at projecting confidence and insinuating himself into positions of authority such as city planning commissions, church callings, and his current position as part of the county emergency committee. Tim had chewed his father's inheritance down to almost nothing, but everyone else in the area considered him one of the wealthy, old boy's network, and he hung onto that advantage with deft machination.

His efforts to craft his reputation in the neighborhood would now catapult him forward into leadership and control and ensure his family's survival. He had been born for this moment, and he had every intention of seizing neighborhood leadership.

Like his despised father, Tim would carry a gun into battle. Unlike his father, Tim would lead instead of follow. He pictured his father looking down from heaven, seeing his son take command like his father never had in Viet Nam.

Tim smiled at the knowledge that seeing him lead men in battle would make his old man turn in his grave. His father had frequently railed on Tim about being a boy without talent or ambition—a complete disappointment. Now, with everything turning his way, Tim would finally prove to the dead alcoholic what a fool he had been.

276

• • •

Ross Homestead
Oakwood, Utah

Like a tick dug in deep, the private security guards still held the refinery. It felt like unfinished business to Jeff, but he knew better than to risk lives to tidy this up. The stalemate at the refinery nagged at him, and he decided to take a quick field trip to see if he could break the logjam.

Jeff and Josh Myler grabbed a Chevy Suburban and drove outside the barricades. Jeff rode shotgun with his Robinson .308 poking out the window.

Everything in town appeared to be looted out. Just eleven days after the fall of the stock market, people had resorted to pulling up the hardwood lanes at the bowling alley for firewood. Jeff watched as a father-and-son team carried a long bundle of maple out the double glass doors of the Excelsior Bowl.

Fires burned everywhere, big and small, most of them in front yards where folks consumed any wood they could find—furniture, fencing, molding, even plastic and tires. It had taken a little more than a week to burn through everything that could be considered firewood. Now people were tearing up anything the slightest bit flammable. More than once on the four-mile drive, Jeff saw men attempting to ignite trees they had just cut down in their yards, green wood that only smoldered and smoked.

The first thing to run out in the Apocalypse was firewood, something Jeff had never considered. The trees in the valley were too green to burn, and the trees in the mountains were too far away to collect. Heading to the mountains for firewood consumed more calories than anyone could afford. People were collecting and chopping firewood much of their day. America hadn't seriously utilized wood as fuel for generations, so the realities of how much work firewood actually required shocked everyone and, because of

America's tidy landscaping, there had been precious little firewood to be found within walking distance of urban and suburban homes.

Dirty water required a LOT of fire to boil. Open fires consumed an enormous amount of wood, with only a small transfer of heat energy. Very few people had the knowledge or equipment to burn wood with any level of efficiency. Dry firewood had run out in a matter of days, burned wastefully on open campfires.

Now people were sick and dying right before Jeff's eyes from an inability to boil water. One case of *pool shock*—easily-available chlorine tablets—could have saved whole neighborhoods, reducing the need for wood. Chlorine had been dirt cheap back in the days when factories turned out chemicals and drugs for next to nothing. Today, with Home Depot and Right Aid in shambles, those miracle chemicals might as well have been sitting on the moon.

When Jeff looked down from the Homestead at the Valley, he imagined the fires he could see were cooking fires. This turned out to be untrue. Most of the tendrils of smoke Jeff had seen came from boiling water.

They passed a number of canals carrying water from the Wasatch Mountains to the Great Salt Lake. People gravitated to those canals, schlepping water in buckets, pots and milk jugs. Half of everyone on the streets looked to Jeff like they were traveling to and from water.

Little more than swamp water, the canals could ease the discomfort of thirst, but they brought the scourge of diarrhea. Jeff watched as one woman took an emergency squat on the dirt bank beside the canal. Jeff fretted about his men at the refinery drinking downstream from this pathogenic nightmare.

In a field tucked between a row of bungalows, another woman harvested weeds with a kitchen knife, probably to feed her family. Down another street, Jeff did a double take when he saw a guy chasing a dog, trying to kill it with a roofing hammer.

When they had almost reached the refinery, Jeff spotted a man walking across the wetlands carrying a dead crow by the feet, its wings flopping open like some sort of inverted firebird.

278

I wonder what crow tastes like. Jeff shook his head.

More than anything, Jeff was amazed at how listless people had become; they shuffled about like zombies. Almost everyone in the valley had dropped from three thousand calories a day to less than one thousand calories a day, and many of them blew those calories out of their bodies a few minutes later, from one end or the other.

The view from the Homestead lulled Jeff into thinking that people down in the valley were hanging in there, perhaps roughing it. From ground level, he could see they hovered on the brink of death, as though one good flu could wipe out the entire town.

As they approached the refinery, Jeff shook off what he had witnessed. No matter how haunting, the valley couldn't become his concern. The townspeople might as well be living in Africa. There was nothing he could do about their situation, so why torture himself worrying about them?

Jeff spotted his campsite a couple hundred yards from the fence of the refinery, and he directed Josh toward it. Six men had been rotating in and out of guard duty, keeping the refinery bottled up and denying the guards access to ground water. Jeff rolled out of the Suburban and shook hands with the off-duty fighters hanging out at camp. Somewhere in the folds of the swampy wetlands surrounding the refinery, the rest of his garrison stood guard.

"They getting thirsty in there yet?" Jeff couldn't believe the security guards hadn't reached out to make a deal. It had been three days since his team surrounded the refinery.

"Nope. Not a peep. Nobody has stepped so much as a pinkie toe outside those gates."

"Unbelievable." Jeff shaded his eyes and gazed at the buildings, tanks and smokestacks of the refinery. Someone handed him a pair of binoculars. Jeff could see one guard behind some kind of sandbag bunker on top of one of the big fuel storage tanks, watching him back.

"Okay." Jeff handed back the binos. "Radio your men and let them know I'm going in."

"Roger." One of the guys jumped on his radio and made the call.

Jeff reached in the SUV and grabbed the pair of bolt cutters he'd brought with him. He left his handgun and rifle on the front seat of the Suburban and walked to the gate.

"Hello! I'm coming in." Without waiting for a reply, Jeff cut the chain on the gate, stepped inside and walked down the middle of the refinery.

"Don't shoot. I'm unarmed. I just want to talk."

As he sauntered into the jumble of pipes and valves at the heart of the facility, a man burst out of an office trailer, whipping his assault rifle toward Jeff. The man looked like he had been taking an afternoon nap.

"Stop!" the guy yelled. Jeff didn't have to be told twice. He already had his hands in the air.

"I just want to talk," Jeff repeated.

"How'd you get in?"

"I cut your chain. Sorry, I'll buy you a new one." Jeff smiled.

Afternoon Napper held his sights on Jeff, waiting. Soon, another man came around the corner, his rifle pointing at Jeff, too.

"What the hell are you doing in here?" one of the men demanded.

Jeff turned slowly. "I came in for a parlay. How about it?"

Nap-hair guy held his rifle on Jeff while the other guy walked closer. The new arrival slung his rifle and pulled a big zip tie from a pocket in his vest. Both guys wore chest-rigs with six or seven rifle magazines, plus mags for the handguns on their waists. These security guards looked ready for World War III. Of the five refineries in Davis County, Jeff had inadvertently selected the one guarded by the Mall Ninjas from Hell.

Jeff could have pulled some Taekwondo on the guard as he approached with the cuffs, but even if he shot both men with their own guns, which was something he thought he could pull off, he would still have to deal with the shooter on top of the fuel storage tank.

Jeff let the guy cuff him, making sure his hands were in front, where Jeff could quickly snap the zip tie if necessary. Once the security guard had him trussed up, he steered Jeff into the trailer office along with Afternoon Napper.

Jeff couldn't believe his eyes. The place was packed with Mountain House, ammo cases and three big barrels of water. The office trailer looked like it had once been the security office of the refinery. Now it looked and smelled like an Apocalypse apartment for three single men.

"What's all this?" Jeff couldn't help but ask.

"What do you want, coming in here uninvited?" the older of the two asked, ignoring Jeff's question.

"I want to talk about joining forces. What's your name?" Jeff reached out his cuffed hands to shake hands.

The older guy, probably in his mid-fifties, made no move to return the handshake. "My name's None-of-your-business. Why would we want to join up with anyone? We're doing just fine."

Jeff could see a security uniform shirt draped over the chair in the corner. The embroidered name on it said, "Morgan." Jeff walked across the room and sat down in the chair.

"Are you Mister Morgan?" Neither guy responded.

"Okay, Mister Morgan. I'm with the guys camped outside." Jeff motioned with his head in the direction of his outpost. "We're here to make sure this refinery doesn't get burned down by the criminal element. We'd like a little gas for our trouble once things settle down."

"Does it look to you like this place is getting taken over by the criminal element?" the old guy sneered.

"Nope, looks like you're doing a fine job. In fact, we'd like to work with you. We can help you with food, information, good company, showers… we even have a few single ladies around our place." Afternoon Napper's head snapped around at the mention of single ladies.

We might have something to offer them after all, Jeff thought. The old guy stood up and the smell of unwashed man wafted over Jeff.

"We're doing just fine. Screw off." The old guy grabbed Jeff's cuffed hands, levered him out of his chair and marched him down the steps from the trailer office and out to the chain link gate where he unceremoniously gave Jeff the boot in the ass.

"If you come back, we'll shoot you," he said as a parting shot.

Jeff walked back to the campsite, not happy about returning in cuffs, but unwilling to risk cutting his wrists to break free.

"That go well, boss?" one of his guys asked while the others chuckled.

"All part of the plan," Jeff lied. "Cut me out of these things."

One of the guys had his Leatherman out and he cut the zip ties with the dikes.

"You wouldn't believe what they've got in there. It's like they set that place up for Armageddon. I'll bet they have six months of food and water in that damned office trailer. They must've made some kind of prepper pact and supplied the hell out of that refinery right before the world fell apart. There's no other staff in the facility—just the three security guys. This is their Alamo."

"What are our orders, then?"

Jeff scratched his bald head. "Just keep on doing what you're doing. Bottle them up and help defend the place from marauders. I'll think of something."

Jeff figured he would just leave the bolt cutters at the gate. They weren't worth going back for and getting shot. He climbed into the Suburban, grabbed his rifle and said his goodbyes.

• • •

Two miles above the refinery, on the mountainside just below the Homestead, Emily Ross sat on a park bench watching women talk and children play. Several hours at a time, Emily could forget that everyone she knew, outside of her dad's compound on the hill, probably lived in terror, if they weren't dead already.

But what could she do about it? Absolutely nothing. There was nothing she could do but pray for them. She didn't know what to pray for. More food? Government relief? Protection from violence? It would be best not to think about it, especially since it made her feel guilty. Perversely, she loved the Homestead lifestyle, especially since the failure of civilization. Perhaps owing to the ever-present risk of dying, living inside the walls of the Homestead felt *alive*.

As part of QRF Three, she no longer pulled guard duty. Emily spent most of the day training with her team. When they weren't running react-to-contact drills, they trained on radio protocols. When they weren't training on radio protocols, they were shooting on the dynamic target range. When they weren't shooting on the dynamic target range, they were practicing bounding drills.

QRF shooters burned at least five hundred rounds of ammo per week. Emily couldn't figure out how they could afford the ammo. To support this training tempo, her dad would have had to stockpile a million or more rounds before the collapse. Who would ever have thought that much ammunition would be necessary?

Besides training, Emily spent her day helping in the infirmary, working in the cook shed, tending animals, picking fruit, and canning. Working with her hands, surrounded by family, making food and handling survival needs—something about this life felt profoundly right to her.

Contrary to popular belief, throughout six million years of human development, women had provided most of the calories to the human race. Men had occasionally brought home a shank of woolly mammoth or a dead rabbit. Anthropologically, though, humankind had survived on the labor of females. Most of the calories fueling the rise of man came from collecting roots, nuts and seeds, with men nowhere in sight.

A man's role, across eons, had been to fight and die on the battlefield, securing peace that would last until the next batch of men was old enough to fight and die on the battlefield. Men were designed to solve a problem created by men. That, and they were nice to look at, Emily admitted.

Just two weeks back, Emily would have argued that the cycle of warfare had ended—that new, modern gender roles would last forever, setting the stage for a peaceful, utopian future. But everything had gone primitive literally within a matter of days. Women were back in the kitchen, producing the bulk of calories and men were back on the battlefield, fighting and dying. She would never have believed it possible for the foundation of society to transform so quickly.

But not everything had reverted to the bad, old days of gender inequality. She'd been tapped to fight in one of the elite units of the Homestead.

I guess that's progress, she thought.

The other women liked her, even the anti-gun ladies. Regardless of how they felt about guns, the women enjoyed seeing one of their own matching the ability of the men. Emily wasn't the only woman who carried a gun—many carried sidearms—but she was the only woman on a QRF.

Even more than working in the infirmary, Emily loved to bake bread. At any given moment, two massive cooking operations were underway at the Homestead: cooking the next meal and baking bread.

As the closest thing to money these days, fresh-baked bread had become currency between the Homestead and the world. Whenever any salvage was needed from the valley, they'd slap the notice on a dry erase board at the tent city below the barricades, list a value of the item in loaves of bread, and pretty soon somebody would show up with that item. Mattresses, water filters, grass seed, Romex wire. Anything that hadn't been eaten or burned down in the valley could be had for a few loaves of bread. Jeff Kirkham paid new recruits in fresh loaves, feeding their families in exchange for providing security. Every day, the four Pioneer Princess wood-burning stoves of the Homestead pumped out loaf after loaf of bread, feeding scores of families. The Homestead forest contained hundreds of cords of dried wood, since it was located far up the mountain, nested in the oak and maple forests. The stoves could run for years on the dried wood provided by Mother Nature within a short walk of the cook stoves. A troop of ladies and children went out every day with chainsaws and axes and brought back a half-cord of wood, feeding the roaring maws of the Pioneer Princesses.

Emily's favorite job was kneading the dough. Her forearms burned after kneading for fifteen minutes, but it was good work, honest work. She could picture the yeast bubbling inside the dough, bulking up the loaves, filling them with an earthy aroma. Maybe none of that mystique mattered to the families surviving on this bread; maybe calories were calories to them. But Emily liked to think it mattered. Maybe she was doing something to alleviate suffering after all.

Down the hill, near the bottom of Vista View Boulevard, a small park had been set aside for the families of the "hired guns." That had been the unfortunate name given to the defense force hired by Jeff Kirkham. A work crew had thrown together the shanty town in Vista Park, complete with a fresh water tank.

Burke Ross, Emily's granddad, had located and bought six surplus FEMA-made, solar-powered poop processing plants. Somehow, these big fiberglass vats took a bit of solar power, tons of poo, and turned it all into fertilizer soup. The shanty town had been loaned two of the solar poop processing plants.

The fifty families in the shanty town had mashed all the grass around their tents into a muddy hard pack but, otherwise, the tent town was clean and disease-free. They even had a garden going behind the poo-processing plant, watered by the "compost tea" coming out the back of the poop pods. Emily wasn't sure she would eat that lettuce, but her grandpa assured her the compost tea was "clean as a whistle."

Around the shanty town, Emily watched the children play in the playground and the women laugh around the park benches, cobbling together whatever they could for a meal in addition to their daily bread.

Life goes on, she realized. People love and laugh and make stew out of weeds.

At least here, behind a wall of guns, people had a chance at a life worth living. Maybe someday, if they all did their jobs and kept hope alive, the pall of doom would roll back across the valley and people would live without fear once again.

• • •

"A month ago, I'd never feed my kids this carbohydrate crap," Jacquelyn complained to Jenna Ross as they ladled soup and handed out bread to the long line.

Protein and fats were scarce during the collapse, even with the Homestead's outstanding food storage. Feeding two hundred members, and another hundred and fifty families in the shanty town, required a remarkable amount of food. Even at an average of fifteen hundred calories a day per person, that meant half-a-million calories *per day*.

One pound of wheat flour came in at about fifteen hundred calories, which meant that wheat carbohydrates went further than anything else, consuming four hundred pounds of wheat per day. At that rate, they would run out of wheat within a year.

All food isn't necessarily *good* food, Jacquelyn and Jenna knew. Carbohydrates provided bulk calories, but they were arguably the worst kind of calories, giving energy but little else. Fresh fruits and vegetables, eggs, dairy and lean meats would be critical for long-term survival. Carbs wouldn't do much more than keep people from starving.

Carbs were mostly what they had. It was the Gordian Knot of food storage. Carbs kept well. Proteins and fat went bad fast. Wheat, rice, sugar and other carbohydrates would keep in an oxygen-free bucket for thirty years or more. Vegetable oils wouldn't keep past a

286

year, with virgin olive oil lasting just two years. Animal fats went bad within a week or less. Fresh fruits and veggies, even in cold storage, would struggle to keep over a winter.

The Homestead had freeze-dried food, too—where proteins and fats could be better preserved—but freeze-dried food for two hundred people would have cost millions, and it would have had to be rotated out every thirty years, same as dried food.

The realities of growing fresh food presented a vexing set of problems. The Homestead had seven glass greenhouses, two three-thousand-square-foot grow houses, and kept over a hundred livestock: dozens of chickens, four fish ponds and a hundred rabbits. Even so, those resources required careful shepherding—not killing any animals required for future breeding. And the greenhouses needed two months to spin up production, assuming perfect fortune from the gods of agriculture. Even at full tilt, the livestock and grow operations of the Homestead could produce only about a quarter of the caloric needs of the group, which left them eating mostly dried carbohydrates.

Any way they sliced it, the people of the Homestead would experience a seventy-five percent reduction in fats and proteins from their pre-collapse diets. Compared to early American Indians, that would still be a big step up in the quality of the menu. Compared to pre-collapse society, it was a woefully unappetizing proposition.

Just ten days after the collapse of the stock market, folks at the Homestead were already sick to death of the food. Flavorful food had vanished like a hooker after church. Without meat, butter, cheese, cream, and fresh vegetables, the cooks could only do so much with salt and spices to make the food interesting.

Fresh meat required waiting for breed stock to get breeding. Dairy required waiting for the female goats and cows to give birth. Fresh vegetables required waiting for the greenhouses to kick in. Ramp-up time would take as long as six months, especially to get dairy running. It required breeding cows, dropping calves, and then continuing to milk them to maintain lactation. Since Homestead farmers didn't have time to milk dozens of cows prior to the sudden collapse, most of the cows were dry when the shit hit the fan.

The Homestead food crew had to rack their brains to come up with acceptable food options. Every day they burned deeper into their store of freeze-dried and every day they listened to good-natured complaints from the folks in the food line. It would be a losing battle until the greenhouses kicked in and the animals got knocked up and, even then, they would eventually run out of wheat.

• • •

"You're doing a crappy job with the politics around here," Jeff complained to Jason Ross as evening descended on the Homestead.

The two leaders of the Homestead stood on the colonnade looking over the neighborhood. From where they stood, they could see Tim Masterson on his front lawn, a quarter mile down the hill, leading fifteen men in combat drills. To Jeff, it looked like blind porcupines having sex.

Jason took a sip of tea. "Yes, indeed. I'm about ready to give myself a negative performance review. In my defense, my job description did not include managing megalomaniac neighborhood control freaks."

"I wasn't even talking about that Masterson dipshit. I meant you're doing a crappy job with the *Love and Light* crowd here." Jeff pointed down at the courtyard, bustling with people. All fifteen acres of the Homestead grounds were packed with survivors going about the business of the Apocalypse.

"Why? What's happened now?" Jason prayed he already knew all the bad news.

"By my estimation," Jeff told him, "the anti-war group here is about a third of your two hundred people, and that includes about a third of our men-in-arms. A good chunk of the men of this group can't be counted on to carry out orders because they're of two minds about shooting trespassers under *any* rules of engagement."

288

Jeff took a breath, then continued. "The wives resist the idea that their husbands should be pulled away to train, patrol and work guard duty. Half of the people here are depressed as hell. Another bunch are experiencing culture shock that's nearly debilitating. A growing number are mildly sick, slightly injured or are otherwise hampered by little things that might have been a big deal to an office worker back in the old world, like a pulled muscle, a cough or achy knees. A bunch of your guys are being crybabies and are hanging back with the womenfolk."

Jason thought about it for a second. "Basically, you're saying that our men are wussies."

"Yeah," Jeff replied, "but being a wussy these days has consequences."

"Okay. I'm on it. Do you have any good news? I could use some good news right now."

"All I've got are good news/bad news combos. We still haven't taken the refinery, but it hasn't burned down yet. We're getting the Homestead guys up to speed on firearms training, but I'm not sure we can count on them in a fight. We recruited eighty guys from the barricade, and we're training them. Their families have been moved to the shanty town just above the barricades. That's costing us eighty loaves of bread per day, plus we're burning about a thousand rounds of ammo per guy we train—and that's with us being miserly with the ammo. It's not anywhere close to the best training I've conducted. Even so, we're burning through our .223 and 9mm stockpile fast. We still hold the hospital and the two pharmacies, but that pulls about fifteen of the Homestead troops off the line every day. So we have eighty recruits, sixty Homesteaders and just about every one of the neighborhood men is now training with Dewey Dumbass down there on his lawn." Jeff pointed at Masterson's house.

"Here's my biggest worry." Jeff handed Jason a hand-held radio.

"Is this one of our radios?" Jason asked.

"Nope, we pulled it off a dead Hispanic kid in that gunfight yesterday on top of the mountain."

"This is a ham radio," Jason said, considering the implications.

"I believe we are being probed."

Jason's face fell. "I think I know, but please tell me what that means."

"That means someone is thinking about making a move on us. You don't use radios unless you're communicating. You don't communicate unless you're coordinating. You don't coordinate unless you're thinking. Whoever is on the other end of this radio is thinking. They're thinking about us, and they're not thinking about inviting us to a neighborhood picnic."

"God help us. This soon?" Jason set his tea down on the limestone railing.

"We killed every last one of those guys from their recon patrol, so maybe they got the idea we're a hard target. Maybe they'll look for greener pastures elsewhere."

"It's ironic," Jason mused. "You killing those Hispanic kids…"

"Soldiers," Jeff interrupted, "those guys were soldiers."

"Okay. Killing those *soldiers* triggered even more drama among our people. Our members are now even more convinced that taking up arms is wrong. Every time you shoot an aggressor, we get weaker. How are we supposed to win this fight if we get weaker every time we defend ourselves?"

"Sounds like a political problem to me." Jeff turned to Jason. "And it's a more serious problem than this radio." Jeff took the radio back.

The door from the office burst open and Alena rushed onto the colonnade. "Jeff Kirkham, come now! Fast!"

Before anyone could ask, the nurse turned and ran back through the office with Jeff and Jason in tow. The three rushed down the stairs and through the door of the garage-turned-infirmary. A small knot of doctors, one working a blood pressure cuff, stood over a gurney. Tara Kirkham was there, too, looking scared.

Jeff pushed his way into the group and his eyes fell on Leif, his youngest son. The boy laid on the gurney, flushed and breathing rapidly. Jeff could see nothing wrong—no open wounds.

"What's going on?" he demanded.

Doctor Larsen replied curtly, busy working to save the boy's life. "Jeff, your son has been bitten by a rattlesnake. I'm going to need you to step back now."

"The FUCK I'm going to step back," Jeff bellowed as he allowed the doctor to nudge him aside. Doctor Larsen moved around the gurney to take the boy's pulse.

"Get him away," Doc Larsen ordered Tara Kirkham.

Jeff's wife, holding herself together, put her hands on Jeff's shoulders and steered him away from the nurses and doctors, guiding him to the camp chairs set up on the far side of the garage. "Jeff, you need to calm down."

"What the FUCK happened to our boy?" Jeff shouted again, startling the nurses.

"Leif was helping with firewood, and a baby rattlesnake was hiding in the wood pile. The doctors are doing their jobs, and we just need to stay out of their way."

"Ross!" Doctor Larsen shouted over the din.

Jason turned.

"Do we have antivenin in your stocks?"

Jason shook his head slowly, regret in his eyes.

Doctor Larsen talked while he worked on the boy. "I didn't think so. It's not something they keep in a pharmacy or that they'll have in that hospital. Antivenin is perishable and it used to get shipped in from the university when the locals needed it. We'll just have to make do."

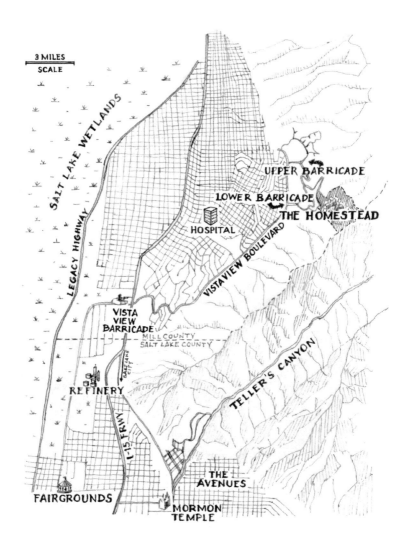

3 MILES
SCALE

SALT LAKE WETLANDS

UPPER BARRICADE

LOWER BARRICADE

THE HOMESTEAD

LEGACY HIGHWAY

HOSPITAL

VISTAVIEW BOULEVARD

VISTA VIEW BARRICADE

MILL COUNTY
SALT LAKE COUNTY

SALT LAKE CITY

REFINERY

TELLER'S CANYON

I-15 FRWY

THE AVENUES

FAIRGROUNDS

MORMON TEMPLE

13

"...HERE'S SOME SLIGHTLY GOOD NEWS from this ass pellet of a world: our joint base in Lakenheath, Great Britain called in to say that they're doing okay. England closed its borders, suppressed a huge riot in London—killing over fifteen hundred rioters. Now they're not letting any U.S. military stationed there to leave base. Not that anyone really wants to be in the United States. So England's doing better than most. Maybe they can throw a little of that good fortune our way. Hopefully, they're not still pissed over that Boston Tea Party thang...

"Got a call last night from Tyndall Air Force Base in Panama City, Florida. Check this out. The rain flooded their sewer system and a pump failed. Without civilian contractors, the toilets backed up into a literal shit-storm. The brass moved their HQ to another building, which caused rumors that they'd abandoned the base. So then everyone abandoned the base. So Tyndall Air Force Base was literally taken out by shit. Literally.

"And, if the FCC is listening—which I doubt—I'm sorry about fucking up your frequency allocations and saying so many bad words.

I'm very, very sorry. In my defense, you government bastards did let the world burn…"

Salt Lake County Fairgrounds
Salt Lake City, Utah

Francisco hadn't waited for his brother to finish his reconnaissance to prepare for the attack on the rich Oakwood neighborhood. Gabriel hoped he could talk his brother out of attacking, but the whole thing felt like a train that had already left the station.

At the morning meeting of lieutenants, Francisco jumped right into ordering the attack without waiting to hear Gabriel's report. Francisco was excited about the "tanks" they were building out of bulldozers and front-end loaders.

Francisco passed around pictures on his iPhone of heavy equipment with steel plates welded over the body and cockpit, protecting the driver and forming protective shooting boxes with firing slits. Gabriel begrudgingly admitted to himself that the low-tech tanks had been a great idea.

"We should be able to blast through roadblocks, walls and even homes," Francisco said. "And we're loading up hundreds of Molotov cocktails for burning those people out." Gabriel grimaced at the thought of homes and the tent city burning with families and children trapped inside.

Gabriel didn't hold out much hope, but he had to try to slow this down. "*Hermano*, can I give my report now? I've seen their defenses," Gabriel reminded Francisco.

"Sure, *hermanito*. Go ahead. What did you see? Certainly they're not ready for our tanks, right?" The lieutenants all laughed at the joke, savoring the idea of another easy victory.

Gabriel laughed along with the gangbangers. "First, I may have screwed up. Please forgive me, Francisco, but I told the Tongan Crips that you'd meet with them today on neutral ground." Gabriel left out the part about the meeting being a gambit to save his own life.

Francisco didn't look mad. He seemed to be considering the idea. "Why would we want to meet with the Crips?"

"I thought you might want to trade some of the drugs and guns from the Avenues for more soldiers."

Francisco's eyebrows jumped. It triggered an idea. "We could use the Polys as shock troops. They won't be reliable, but they hit hard. I don't know what the trade would be, but it could work. It'd be like the German mercenaries George Washington used in the Continental Army." That meant nothing to anyone at the meeting except maybe Francisco. He never missed a chance to mention military history, proud of the few books he'd read in prison.

It wasn't entirely unusual for Norteños to work with Crips. Los Latigos were Bloods—but they weren't committed to the Bloods versus Crips gang war in Los Angeles. That was an African-American thing. Mexicans and Polys were a bit more flexible on the matter, especially in Utah. Making a deal with the Crips could be dangerous, but they had done it several times in the past, mostly in prison.

"I'll talk to them," Francisco decided. "When and where?"

"Warm Springs Park at 1:00 p.m."

"Good. Now, tell me about the Oakwood mansion neighborhood."

He told them first about the neighborhood's military organization—their uniforms, helmets, assault rifles, defensive barricades, and bunkers. Some of the lieutenants looked uneasy at the mention of military equipment. Francisco asked a few questions and came to his own conclusion.

"So they're not actual military…"

"I don't know, but they're well organized. They're ready for an attack. I saw men with hand grenades on their vests, and all of them were wearing body armor." Gabriel had no idea if they were real hand grenades or not, but it made an impression.

296

"How many, *hermanito*?" Francisco asked the question Gabriel had been avoiding.

"Maybe fifty men at the barricade at the bottom of the hill," Gabriel exaggerated. He had only counted thirty-five on guard, and that was with women, many of whom probably didn't belong to the defensive force.

"*Good!*" Francisco smacked the park bench they had been standing around. "Fifty men should be no problem! We have fifteen hundred men, and that doesn't count the Crips, and it doesn't count the tanks."

Gabriel's heart sank. He hadn't known the army had grown so much. In his mind, Gabriel conceded to the inevitable.

"How do we attack?" Gabriel asked.

"With fifteen hundred soldiers? Simple." Francisco smiled. "Frontal assault."

• • •

Walmart Distribution Center
Wamsutter, Wyoming

As the rising sun washed the sky over the Uinta Mountains, painting it gray, Chad did a final review of his team.

On the rooftop of the Walmart distribution center, he had placed the forty men he'd requested from the mayor. They tiptoed around the roof in socks. It was the only way Chad could guarantee they wouldn't make too much noise. The rooftop guys carried a variety of rifles, mostly scoped hunting rifles.

Pacheco took his normal position—on overwatch with a radio—monitoring the interstate for unexpected guests from Rock Springs.

On the ground, in the parking lot with Chad, another ten men took up positions around the front doors where the people in the distribution center seemed to come and go most frequently. Chad and his team waited out of sight, behind the closest rank of semi-trailers.

Last, Chad positioned the *Medicine Bow River Band,* a country band out of Rawlins, behind the farthest row of semi-trailers, completely hidden from view. Chad didn't know much about country western music, but he knew this wasn't a great band, but they would do for the job at hand.

With everyone in place, Chad gave the "go" command.

The band began playing, *You Should Be Here,* which had been a chart-topping country hit when the power went out. The music wafted over the parking lot, amped by the generator-driven speakers they had set up facing the distribution center.

The band played for several minutes with no response from the people in the building. Chad began to worry. The band was the lynchpin of his scheme. *The Medicine Bow River Band* didn't have much of a discography of modern country; Chad was pretty sure they had only six or seven songs before they would have to start repeating.

As of yet, the cops and truckers inside the distribution center had grown more complacent and more convinced they were safe with each passing day, based on Chad's observation. Chad had this one opportunity to take them down without bloodshed. Otherwise, the Rock Springs contingent would be dug inside, with food and water for the next hundred years.

As the first song of the band's set ended, Chad went to chew on his nails, then noticed he was wearing Mechanix gloves. The band moved on to *Nobody to Blame,* Number Eighteen on the Country Western Chart when the stock market dropped a deuce.

One of the steel doors cracked open, and people started pouring into the parking lot from the distribution center, drawn to the music. Chad guessed the first thing they would think when they heard music coming from the parking lot at 5:00 a.m., was that the radio had come on in one of the semis. People were inherently hopeful, and Chad figured they would never guess it was a live band playing for them in dawn's early hours. They would naturally conclude that a radio had magically switched on in the parking lot with civilization somehow restored.

298

As Chad watched folks rubbing their eyes and cocking their ears, he laughed. Little lambs, drawn to hope.

More and more people wandered out, hitching up their drawers and smoothing over their flyaway hair. Chad tried to get a head count. He came in at about forty-five people, and just a few had grabbed their guns on their way to check out the music.

Chad clicked the second "go" signal on his radio, and his men on the roof quietly moved to the edge, peering down over the parking lot.

Chad stepped out from behind a semi-trailer. "Put your guns down, right now." The distribution center people jumped as Chad and the rest of Chad's crew appeared, rifles leveled at their guts.

"I got people on the roof. Put 'em down NOW."

The stunned crowd, almost in unison, gaped at Chad, then turned to look at the roof. Dozens of rifle barrels pointed down at them. Sleepy, confused, and clearly caught off guard, everyone with a gun complied.

"Now, move around to the side of the building. Now. MOVE!" Chad pointed to his right. Men from Chad's team ran up and herded the people around the corner of the building.

Just then, the doors opened again and another small group wandered out to check on the music. This group saw their friends being herded off, but they were still too confused to know what was happening. As soon as the door clicked shut, Chad ordered them to put down their guns as well. That added five more to the number of captives. By Chad's best estimate, that totaled about fifty prisoners. The band played two more songs and nobody else came out.

"Cut the music. Tell the band to pack up and head back to Rawlins," Chad said over the radio.

The plan had worked better than he had hoped, but he figured there might still be at least ten men inside the distribution center. Chad called over the radio and ordered everyone to begin phase two of his plan.

His men re-deployed, with all but six of the rooftop gunners climbing down the ladders they had brought from Rawlins. Everyone else covered the doors in case someone came out shooting. A school bus drove into the parking lot and swung around to collect the fifty prisoners. They would drop them off near Rock Springs later that morning.

Another team hopped into four of the semi-trucks and drove them out of the parking lot and toward the westbound on-ramp, setting a roadblock to prevent Rock Springs from counter-attacking. It took almost half an hour to get everyone set for phase two and, since nobody new had come out of the distribution center, Chad assumed that whoever remained inside knew they were under attack and had set a defensive position, ready for bear.

• • •

Chad pictured the tactical situation inside the distribution center. The walls of the warehouse did nothing to protect the defenders, since there were hundreds of doors opening to the outside. Defenders couldn't cover even half of those doors. The warehouse walls rendered them blind to what was going on outside.

If Chad had been the one trapped inside, he would have constructed an interior fortress, a place where he could take cover and fight. Based on his reconnoiter, Chad would probably build his fortress against the logistics office in the center of the dry goods area.

Chad made entry with thirty of his men, mostly guys with assault rifles. They entered on the far end of the perishables arm, which smelled even worse than before. Meeting no resistance in the perishables area, Chad split his group into two teams, and each moved along the outside walls, heading toward the dry goods section. Chad had given his men strict instructions not to fire until Chad fired or until fired upon. He still held out hope for a peaceful resolution.

As he and his men fanned out around the dry goods area of the warehouse, Chad stole a couple of looks at the office. Exactly as he had predicted, the remaining defenders had set up a fortress made of cardboard boxes. Based on the labels, Chad assumed they were boxes of canned goods, perhaps the best ballistic protection available inside the distribution center.

Once his team had fully deployed, completely surrounding the makeshift fort, Chad hollered out, "We have you surrounded. We don't want anyone to die. All the rest of your men are in our custody. Why don't you come out with your hands up, and we'll give you a ride home?"

After a second or two, a gravelly voice responded. "Screw you, you bunch of thieves. I am the duly-elected sheriff of Sweetwater County, Wyoming. You're not taking our town's food. It rightfully belongs to *us*. We were here first, and we have permission from the town of Wamsutter to hold and distribute this food. We're not giving it to anyone without a fight."

Chad shook his head. His shitty deal with the Rawlins mayor grew more hair every second.

"Sir, I understand what you're saying. I surely do. But I have almost a hundred armed men from Carbon County inside this building who claim this food as theirs." Chad thought that lying about their numbers was justified given that it might save lives.

"I'm not from around here," Chad continued, "so I really don't give a shit about what belongs to who. But it looks to me like we've already taken this warehouse. Our men are bringing the semis around right now to empty this place. These Carbon County boys won't give back this food. So there's only one question remaining: are you and your friends going to die in here? Because, either way, the food is gone."

"Come and take it from us. Without this food, people will die in Sweetwater. It might as well be us that dies here right now."

Chad considered his options. Winning this gunfight would be easy; the outcome was a foregone conclusion. The canned food around the sheriff and his men would stop the first few bullets but, as his men smashed and drained the cans, bullets would start sailing through and bouncing around inside their fortress like bees in a Wonder Bread bag. Everyone inside would die.

As Chad thought through the tactical situation, a rifle boomed. Chad didn't know who shot first—his guys or the sheriff's guys.

Then all hell broke loose. Like so many gunfights he had seen before, Chad watched as his men emptied their guns and all their mags into the fortress of Del Monte green beans. Give a man a stack of bullets and half a reason to use them, and that man will burn through those bullets before having two thoughts.

Eventually, the gunfire died off. Chad felt the foreboding that accompanied the end of a shooting match. Winning a gunfight was like having sex with a hooker. It seemed pretty damned exciting in the doing, but the come-down dragged a man's soul through the mud.

While his men hooted and hollered their victory, Chad approached the stack of boxes. Green bean juice mixed ominously with other, darker fluids. He stepped through a breach in the boxes, rifle at the ready, his adrenaline pumping.

The scene inside didn't surprise him. He had seen it before—six men and one woman posed in the contortions of violent death. Some lay sprawled. One perched precariously on his knees, his head slumped low on his chest. All of them had been shot dozens of times. One or more of them had defecated in the throes of death. One young man's belly had split open, his entrails mixing with the bile and blood of his friends on the floor.

Chad felt the old familiar rage rising, like a tide of acid in his belly. Once again, he had done battle at the behest of old men, men with enough testosterone to want to kill something but not enough testosterone to do it themselves.

Only part of his anger pointed at the politicians of the world. The larger part focused anger on *himself*. Once again he had allowed his talents to be manipulated by men whose only virtue was an ability to trick people into voting for them.

As soon as he confirmed that all the defenders were dead, Chad walked out of the building, cleared his rifle and handgun, and walked across the parking lot to the Chevy Blazer he and Pacheco had stolen from the first roadblock. He left no instructions with the men of Rawlins. His job was done and the dickweeds who had hired him could figure out the rest.

"Pacheco, Chad. Over."

"Go ahead, Chad."

"Walk out to the freeway. I'm coming to pick you up."

"Okay, Chad."

● ● ●

Ross Homestead
Oakwood, Utah

Jason and Jeff stood once again on the colonnade, waiting for their daily meeting with the bishopric. The bishop was late.

"How's your boy?" Jason asked, already knowing the answer.

"He's resting. His temperature is running hot and he's breathing shallow. They don't know if he'll pull through without antivenin. It's been a long time since any of the doctors have seen a snakebite that wasn't treated with antivenin."

Jeff gave the update but the truth was that he hadn't been to see his son this morning. Visiting his son in the infirmary rattled Jeff so badly that he wasn't sure if he could visit his boy daily and remain operational. Nobody else at the Homestead could do Jeff's job. Nobody else could guarantee the safety of all the families. Jeff felt guilty as hell for not going to see Leif, but he had to put the mission first.

There wasn't anything more for Jason to say. "Have you noticed the chill this morning?"

Jeff thought about it for a second and did his best to stop churning through worry about his son.

"Is the winter going to help us or hurt us?" Jeff asked Jason.

303

Taking it as permission to change the subject, Jason replied, "We're not planting anything right now, not even in the greenhouses. The winter will take a lot of lives down in the city unless the government or the Church comes in with some big shipment of grain. We should be okay up here; we have around fifteen thousand pounds of grain and another ten thousand pounds of dried food. But the people down there... the winter will definitely hurt them. And that may become a serious problem for us up here."

"Yesterday, I drove through the valley," Jeff said. "It's gotten bad fast. People are sick from drinking surface water and they're about out of firewood. Everyone I saw looked like they had diarrhea."

Jason exhaled. "I can't afford to worry about the people in the city. If they're already sick, and if the wood's already gone, almost everyone down there is going to die in the next two months. God help them."

Jeff turned the subject to defense. "We need to survive until the people down there are no longer a threat. We could be attacked at any moment. Starvation turns good men into vicious animals. At least some of the people in that valley are starting to look at their guns and ammunition and ask themselves, 'how can I turn this into food?' We are an obvious answer to that question."

Jason looked at his wristwatch. He had started wearing a watch as soon as cell service died, since his phone had become just one more weight in his pocket. The Homestead could produce about forty thousand kilowatts per hour with its solar arrays, even in October, so keeping their phones charged wasn't an issue, but a manual wristwatch was a better solution now that phones were obsolete. "I don't think the bishopric is going to show. Yesterday, one of the neighbors told me that families are starting to go hungry in the neighborhood. The bishop might be working out a way to keep them fed. I also heard that they're planting gardens in some of the yards."

"How's that supposed to work?" Jeff looked up. "Will stuff grow this late in the fall?"

"It's not going to work at all. By the time they have starts, it'll freeze and kill them, even in cold frames. Plus the photo period is going to go down each day over the next two months. Any planting now is futile, at least without grow lamps."

Jeff looked at his own watch. "I need to get to work. Today we're setting up a second layer of roadblocks and concertina wire on the streets in the neighborhood."

"Thank you. I know you'd rather be with your son right now. Let me know if there's anything I can do."

"There's nothing you can do unless you can go back in time and stock antivenin."

Jason's face fell. Not wanting to leave things on a sour note, Jeff gathered himself to leave. "I need to focus on things we can control. Right now, the best thing I can do is to keep this camp from being overrun by zombies."

Jason turned to Jeff, apparently at a loss for what to say next. "That's got to be hard."

"The only easy day was yesterday," Jeff replied, a shallow attempt to escape the conversation. He took his mug and walked away with a nod.

• • •

People were lining up at the Homestead's water spigot two streets below the Homestead.

At least we're able to get our neighbors clean water. I wonder if they appreciate it. Jason watched a group of men doing marching drills on Masterson's yard. He didn't know much about military training, but he doubted the value of what he was seeing.

Jason turned and watched as one of the Homestead Pinzgauer trucks rumbled up a dirt road on the mountain, taking a group of replacement guards to change shifts. Luckily he had purchased a small snowcat right before the collapse. They would be able to shuttle troops up to guard duty during the winter, too. Walking all the way up the mountain would burn calories they didn't have to spare.

Jason looked out at the Salt Lake Valley. He couldn't see the entire valley from his point of view, but he could see enough to get a mental picture of the millions of people drinking filthy water, running out of food, and burning the last of their firewood.

Jason could barely imagine their suffering. He felt a great disturbance coming from the thousands of tiny fires burning in yards, parks and streets. He wanted to connect to their suffering, to give them full regard. But another sensation took precedence, blotting out the tragedy before his eyes.

Those people in the valley felt like a mortal threat—a hungry, crazed, burgeoning cyst that could explode any day, dragging his family into horror. The dying people had become objects to him despite all his Christian ideals. The sullen waves of menace radiating off the dead and dying nibbled at Jason's commitment to humanity, chewing it down to a fundamental terror: that he might watch his children die in the weeks to come.

Something drew Jason's eye to Tim Masterson, standing on his front lawn giving orders. Jason's fear focused on the man, drawing that fear into a red-hot point of rage. One petty, egomaniacal man became the incarnation of the evil that hunted Jason's children.

The entire clusterfuck of an Apocalypse could be placed at the feet of people like Masterson—men with shallow, selfish myopia; men who ignored the lifeblood of a nation in order to advance their dingy ambitions. Politicians, bureaucrats, the power-hungry, the greedy, the self-absorbed; America had become a nation of narcissists and now millions of children would suffer terror, pain and then death.

As he weighed the cost of the nation America had become, Jason didn't even feel a ghost of his old drive to be a better man. Instead, his heart did a hard one-eighty from morality, turning toward another, more ancient emotion.

Rage.

• • •

"Jeff, hold on." Teddy ran up to Jeff with a square piece of material about the size of a phone book. The square had been shot to hell. "Check it out, dude. Armor for the OHVs. We've got door armor and it'll stop a rifle round."

The interruption irritated Jeff. He had been worrying about his son. He stared at the weird, black chunk of material and struggled to catch up with what the hippie guy was saying.

"What is it?" Jeff took the black panel and turned it over in his hands.

"It's armor. For the OHVs," Teddy repeated.

"It's not going to work." Jeff said, still trying to grasp what it was he was holding in his hands. He had tried a million materials as experimental armor back in Afghanistan for his Afghani troops, and the only thing that worked to stop bullets was heavy AR500 steel.

Teddy shook his head with a crooked smile, knowing Jeff was wrong. "When I woke up this morning, I thought maybe I'd get the chance to show you something new. I think we did it."

Jeff examined the panel again closely. Teddy had bonded several layers of fiberglass, making a thick back plate. Then, he had glued a bunch of glass marbles to the face and slathered black truck liner paint over it, sticking the marbles to the fiberglass. Rifle rounds had hit the test plate and marbles were blown away in two-inch circles. True to Teddy's claim, the rifle rounds hadn't penetrated the fiberglass. Jeff looked at the back and couldn't find any exit holes.

"Where'd you get this idea?" Jeff asked, astonished. How could this young longhair invent effective armor out of marbles and truck liner when multi-million-dollar defense contractors had failed to accomplish the same thing?

"I dunno," Teddy shrugged. "I thought it might be cool if we had some bullet-proofing for the OHVs. Maybe save some lives. Your QRF dudes could get to battle a lot faster with armored OHVs. The marble thing... I started thinking about what we had around the

Homestead in big quantities. The marbles came from Jason's daughter's wedding two years ago. He bought a zillion marbles to fill up glass lanterns and never threw them away. We probably have three hundred pounds of marbles. And we have at least three gallons of bed liner. I had the fiberglass fabric set aside for a pond liner we were going to make, but then decided to buy a rubberized liner instead. Bro, I think I can armor all the OHVs in the next couple of days: it would just be the doors and a little front shielding, but it'd be something."

Jeff handed the panel back to Teddy. "Very cool. Do it." Teddy took the panel back and smiled. "Right on."

Jeff walked toward the ham shack by the bunkhouse. He wanted to check on his buddy Evan again. Since the day Evan left for the National Guard Armory, he had only checked in twice. The last time was four days ago. Jeff knew Evan's team had made it to the Army Depot in Tooele, but he had no idea what had happened since. Ham radio could be finicky, and it was possible that the ham repeater up on Oquirrh Mountain had run out of battery and died. The repeater stood between the Army Depot and the Homestead. If the battery backup on the repeater had crapped out, Evan's comm link would be dead, too.

Before he reached the ham shack, Alena cornered him. Jeff's blood turned to ice, anticipating bad news about his son.

"Jeff, can you hold on a second?"

"Sure, Alena. Is everything okay?" Jeff asked, frigidity in his voice.

"Leif is the same. He's resting and he's got a fever. Can I please talk to you about something else?" Jeff nodded, his neck muscles going slack. "Robert is hell-bent on serving in your army."

It required a moment for Jeff to understand what she was saying. His body had steeled itself to get news that his son was dead. He took a big breath and regathered himself like a spilled bag of leaves.

Jeff did his best to answer her. "Robert wants to do his part to protect his family. Any man would do the same." He was beginning to see where she was going, and part of him wanted to scream at her.

Why aren't you in the infirmary taking care of my son! Stop being such a controlling bitch and do your fucking job!

Alena went on, oblivious to Jeff's internal struggle. "Robert knows nothing about guns and he's going to get himself killed."

Jeff's eyes narrowed. "Robert's a grown man and he's an Army specialist. He knows what he's getting into. We'll train him as quickly as we can. That's all I can promise you." Jeff went to walk way, but Alena pressed the issue.

"That won't be good enough. I know my husband, and he's not cut out for this kind of thing. Can you give him clerical duty or messenger duty or something like that?"

"I could do that, Alena, and he'd know you interfered. If he asks me, I won't lie to him. I realize you think I'm some kind of mindless soldier, but men who serve… we have an agreement to treat one another *like men*. I'd never insult him by treating him differently than any other man, unless he can't physically do the job. Does that make sense?"

Alena didn't want it to make sense. "No. It doesn't make sense." She started to tear up. "I can't raise a family without Robert and, by putting him out there to fight, you're putting our children at risk. Please don't do this to us."

Jeff softened and actually felt a little sympathy for the woman. He could see her for what she was: a strong woman fighting to survive in a strange and dangerous world. The strategies she had used to navigate her past life—hard charging and strong words—they weren't getting her what they once had. This wasn't a world she could control with her practiced tongue and iron will. The dangers in this world would have to be met with a more physical response.

"Here's what I'll promise you," Jeff held up his hands, conceding as much as he could. "I'll train him myself, and I'll do my best to give him duty that's suited to his ability. That's all I can promise."

Jeff didn't wait for a reply, assuming she would keep mounting new arguments until she got her way, and Jeff knew that wasn't going to happen. Today, he didn't have that kind of patience. If he kept arguing with her, he knew he would get angry—really angry. Given his state of mind, he wasn't sure he could control that kind of anger. He turned, heading toward the ham shack, before she could speak again.

• • •

Warm Springs Park
Salt Lake City, Utah

There was something ludicrous about two tattooed criminals sitting together on a picnic bench. Watching from a distance, Gabriel thought it was an honest illustration of thug life. For all their violence and posturing, the two gangster captains sitting on the bench were just two confused little boys at a park—his brother Francisco and Aleki Tapu'o, the captain of the Tongan Crips.

The two gang leaders did their best to look tough, each man straddling his picnic seat with one arm on the table, sitting on opposite sides, glaring at one another.

"Why should I trust a Mexican?" Aleki challenged Francisco, raising his chin. The Tongan was a massive man, his arms easily the size of Gabriel's legs, with tribal tattoos covering his biceps, back and legs.

Francisco refused to answer. "This is just business. Either you want to make some money or you don't."

The Tongan smirked. "That's the problem with you greasers. You don't understand family."

With that chilling comment, Gabriel knew they had misjudged the meeting. Gabriel had called the meeting as a way to save his own skin, but the Pacific Islanders had used it to set a trap.

Gabriel looked around, his anxiety spiking. In the distance, as he had feared, men filtered into the park from every direction; all Pacific Islanders. Many of them didn't look like gangbangers; some of the men were in their fifties.

Aleki continued to talk, not glancing at the men he knew were moving in to surround the meeting. "When your man Digger here ass-raped my wife's cousin in Oxbow Jail last year, MY family didn't get a chance to have a funeral. Our little cousin hung himself in his cell from shame. We thought maybe we could have the funeral right here, today, *hermano*. Maybe we'd have a little potluck dinner, Island-style. Maybe we'd roast a pig in a pit. Problem is, with all the shit going down, we couldn't find a pig. We figured maybe it'd be just as good to roast a Mexican. I've never eaten a burned-alive Mexican before."

With over a hundred Tongans converging on the park, Gabriel saw no way out of the trap. Francisco ignored the threat and the hundred hulking men slowly surrounding him. "You're saying Digger here raped a Poly boy in jail?... Come here, Digger."

Digger walked over to Francisco, the fear of imminent death dancing in his eyes. In a flash, Francisco whipped his straight razor out of his back pocket and waved it past Digger's throat. For a moment, nothing happened. Then Digger coughed. A gout of blood exploded from a straight, dark line that appeared across his throat. Digger's hands flew to his neck, but his head tipped back unnaturally, as though all the muscles and tendons had sprung loose at once. His hands caught his now-floppy head, returning it to its proper place. Blood cascaded down the front of his shirt. His eyes looked down at his chest, he crumpled to his knees, fell over sideways and died.

Aleki held up his hand and the men surrounding them paused.

"It's a good start." Aleki looked down at Digger's corpse and spit on his still-warm face.

Francisco continued as though nothing had happened, as though there weren't a hundred men standing around them ready to tear them limb from limb. He wiped his straight razor on the inside of his shirt, taking his time, folded it carefully and slipped it into his back pocket. "We can give you half a semi-load of dried and canned food if you lend us a hundred fighting men two days from today."

The big Polynesian thought about the offer, mulling over his options. He had clearly planned on ambushing the Latinos and killing them. The possibility of food seemed to give him pause.

"Give us a full semi-load of food, give each one of my men a gun and ammunition, and add two hundred bottles of booze to the deal. Then, maybe I'll consider not killing you right now." Aleki negotiated from a position of strength.

"Fuck you," Francisco countered, glossing over the threat. "I'll give your men guns and ammunition, half a semi-load of food, and one hundred bottles of hard liquor. That's my final offer."

Aleki considered the deal, curling his lip. "Who'd we be fighting?"

"Do you really care?" Francisco challenged, knowing the Polys were a warrior clan and they would relish any chance to do battle.

"Not really," Aleki chuckled. "I might want to know if we were going to fight the army or police or something."

"We'll be fighting white people—rich white people. Stupid people. Can you handle that?"

Aleki waved away the question. "Okay. Half a semi of food, guns for all hundred of my men and a hundred and *fifty* bottles of booze." He stood up from the bench.

"Okay. Let's do it." The men shook hands, reaching across the bloodless body of Digger.

14

"...KELLEY BARRACKS IN STUTTGART, GERMANY is still holding out. They killed a bunch of ISIS fighters trying to rush the base gate. But they're running out of food now, so keep them in your prayers if you're into that.

"Here's a weird story: Jennifer Watts, a Drinkin' Bro-ette off of Galveston, Texas radioed in from a flotilla of boats all tied together in the Gulf of Mexico. They can't make landfall because of the gangs out of Houston, so they're just drifting around, eating whatever fish they can catch. A cargo ship carrying produce out of Brazil called in yesterday and I think I've got it on a rendezvous course with the flotilla. I'm like the Tinder of hungry people now, using ham radio to hook up grub to girls and girls to grub.

"Strange days. This is not what I thought I'd be doing when I grew up..."

Ross Homestead
Oakwood, Utah

Jeff awoke from a dark dream to knocking at his door. He grappled with a maelstrom of emotion as the nightmare faded. It was one of those dreams that felt like a portent, heavy with apprehension and malignancy, a harbinger of ill fate.

In the nightmare, Jeff had been fighting a Norse battle with a shortsword in his hand. He was losing, surrounded by death, but still slashing and hacking his way through the enemy. He felt the deceptively painless sensation of razor-sharp cuts, draining him. Life slipped away with each slice. His consciousness ebbed. His family drifted farther and farther away. He grew slower, less able to parry the blades of the enemy. His feet mired in sludge. His arms hung heavy.

The knocking finally dragged him free from the nightmare. Rarely did anyone wake up earlier than Jeff. He and Tara had moved into a guest suite in the big house. They were finally getting some uninterrupted sleep.

Jeff grabbed a t-shirt from his cluttered nightstand and answered the door in his underwear. It was Walter Ross, another committee member. "Something's up. There's an emergency meeting in the office."

"Hold on a moment." Jeff closed the door, leaving Walter standing in the foyer. With a big gulp of air, Jeff realized he had been holding his breath, fearing bad news about his son. He figured the emergency meeting would wait for him to brush his teeth, so he made short work of it. He grabbed sweats, running socks and running shoes and headed out the door barefoot.

As soon as he exited the suite, closing the door softly so as not to wake Tara or the kids, Walter filled him in. "Tim Masterson is dead. Someone shot him in front of his house last night. Do you know anything about that?" Walter looked crosswise at Jeff as they walked down the gallery, heading for the office wing.

Obviously, Jeff would be the prime suspect. Killing Masterson made sense. Jeff probably should have killed him, but he hadn't. "I didn't kill him," Jeff answered.

"Well, the assumption is that one of our men killed him. So the next question is, did you order it?"

"No, I did not."

"Be prepared to answer those questions again…" Walter opened the office wing door and showed Jeff in. About three-quarters of the committee were already there, milling around, agitated.

"Let's get started. Everyone please find a seat," Jason Ross started the meeting. "Tim Masterson from the Cherry Harvest Ward is dead, shot in front of his house last night, apparently from a long-range rifle shot. I'm guessing the neighborhood suspects we had something to do with it."

"Well, did we?" Burke Ross interrupted.

Everyone looked at Jeff. "I didn't kill him, and I didn't order him killed."

The faces in the room showed one of two reactions—either relief or doubt. Because of Jeff's background with clandestine government activities, almost everyone believed Jeff played games with information, that he wasn't to be trusted. The group saw him as something of a spook, and it showed in their expressions.

"I'm only going to say this one more time. I didn't kill Masterson nor did I order it or even suggest it. I probably should have killed him because that asshole was well on his way to compromising our safety. But I didn't." The room sat in silence for a long minute.

"Well," Jason broke the silence, "does anyone have anything they want to add to that?"

Nobody spoke. The relief in the room was palpable. Even if Jeff was lying, the murder wouldn't be on their collective conscience. They could deny involvement.

"This is going to make it hard with the Elk Ridge Ward and the stake president," Burke Ross spoke up. "They're already dragging their feet about working with us. This will throw them into even more confusion. With all the guns on the mountain right now and in the streets, there's no way they can pin this on us. But they will suspect us, and that'll make them slow to cooperate."

Jeff shook his head. "Right now they're worth less than tits on a hog. Almost all their guys who we had been training left to train with Masterson. We're not losing anything we haven't already lost. We're working around the problem as we speak.

"We've got bigger issues than those bozos," Jeff continued. "Half of our own men are falling apart. I've got men pretending to be sick and staying in bed all day. I've got other men moping around barely doing their jobs. I have one guy who didn't show up for drill yesterday because his dog got something in its eye. Yesterday, we were running react-to-contact drills in the forest, and we found Brad Townsend's seventeen-year-old kid with his pistol in his mouth getting ready to blow his brains out. I've never had to deal with men suffering from a case of *Blue Mondays* like this before. Can somebody please fix this before I have to start shooting people for dereliction of duty?"

"They're depressed," Walter Ross interjected. "It's a horrible world."

"Of course they're depressed," Jeff fired back, "but I'm about fifty percent convinced that we're being probed by a serious enemy force. If even one guy on perimeter duty misses someone sneaking across the line because he's butt-hurt over God ordering up the Apocalypse, we're all going to die."

"What makes you think we're being probed?" Walter Ross asked.

"That group of Hispanics we killed the other day. They had a couple of radios on them. And they weren't using them to listen to AM 440 Mexican Radio." The implication settled heavy on the group.

Jeff went on. "Morale is a serious issue. People have lost wars throughout history because men got in a funk. I'll teach our men to defend this place, but you guys…" Jeff pointed his finger at everyone in the room, and his finger came to rest on Jason Ross, "you guys need to fix this problem. I need men who'll do exactly what they're told, no matter if their dog has something in its eye or not."

Walter Ross spoke up first, "We'll get on it."

If anyone disagreed with Jeff, they weren't saying it. The committee launched into solution mode. There were nine members plus spouses. Every committee member had an area of responsibility, but many of those areas, such as livestock, gardening or stored food, were non-critical at the moment. Right now, it would be all hands on deck. Whatever qualms the members had about Jeff's warmongering were put aside for the time being, at least in the committee.

Rich Orton, the livestock guy, waded in. "I think we need to break out some booze. I know we're hanging onto it for trade, but burned-out guys are probably more dangerous than drunk guys."

"No way," Jeff said. "Alcohol ain't going to help."

"Hear me out," Rich fired back at Jeff. "The guys are worse off than you know. They're talking a bunch of shit behind your back. They're near their breaking point. Training, patrol and perimeter duty are exacting more of a toll than you know. You're about to lose them. I'm hearing a lot of guys saying crap like, 'I'd rather die than live like this.'"

"Fucking civilians…" Jeff was getting angrier by the second.

"We can fix this," Rich recovered the conversation. "Just let me handle it. We'll get them *a little* drunk tonight. We'll play some music. We'll eat some meat… I'll kill a goat today and we'll roast it up. We're almost ready to supply hot water to the outdoor showers. Let's bust out some shampoo and maybe even hand out some condoms. Nobody's doing bam-bam in the ham. Did you know that? Everyone's so jacked in the head, it's like we're living in a labor camp some days. We need to remind everyone what we're fighting for, that life's worth the stretch."

"So, Jeff," Jason interjected, "are these guys—the ones who're dragging ass—are they going to come around? Are they going to pull it together eventually?"

"Most of them will, yes, if we aren't killed first."

The meeting ended soon thereafter. Jeff doubled back to Jason's office. When he poked his head in the door, Jason was staring out the French doors, looking over the neighborhood.

"Jason," Jeff interrupted. "Seriously. Between you and me, I didn't have Masterson smoked."

"I believe you," Jason said.

"So did *you* order him shot?" Jeff asked the question and cocked his head. As unlikely as it seemed, he had to ask.

Jason looked straight in Jeff's eyes. "No." The pause lingered.

"Okay, then." Jeff said, "I guess we can chalk it up to the gods of Olympus smiling upon us. I'm heading to check on Leif."

Jason turned back to the window.

• • •

Holiday Inn
Rawlins, Wyoming

Chad held Samantha's little hand so she wouldn't trip down the rough-scrabble stairs of the Holiday Inn. It felt like holding on to the last bit of *clean and pure* in this jacked-up world. Chad knew he could live with this dirty feeling he was packing around inside. He had done it before. It hadn't been the first pile of human bodies he'd seen.

Now that he had successfully raided the distribution center, his family supposedly had an airplane ride to Salt Lake. The price for four plane tickets had been seven human lives.

The deal he'd made with the devil had put Chad very close to making good on his promise to his father-in-law: to get Audrey and Sam to safety. For all he knew, Audrey's dad, Robert, moldered somewhere in Omaha, dead and discarded by the onward slog of the vicious.

Ain't that just like life: do something noble and get repaid with a shit sandwich. Well, at least Chad wasn't buried in a shallow grave in the sand of Wyoming like those seven folks from the Walmart. At least he had won the contest, like always.

His little group looked like a family—Chad, Audrey and Samantha. To keep matters simple and civil, they had left it at that. Nobody needed to know that Audrey had divorced him.

The town of Rawlins served daily breakfast in the town square around the Carbon County Courthouse. Chad guessed the population of Rawlins fell just under ten thousand. Rock Springs numbered two-and-a-half times that, which might actually make it harder for Rock Springs to regroup and counter-attack. Once a city hit a certain number of souls, maintaining organization and civil order became impossible, the big town unable to feed everyone and maintain the peace. Say what you want about Mayor Spears, he had kept this town in one piece. By the look of things at the community breakfast, the town had marshaled resources and pulled together. If Chad had parachuted into the scene, he would have thought it was a town holiday.

His family needed to eat breakfast, otherwise Chad would have avoided the townspeople altogether. Picturing a bunch of people slapping him on the back for the Walmart massacre sent chills down his spine.

He needed to firm up plans with the mayor for his flight out. Hopefully, Mayor Spears hadn't sold him a load of crap. That would be the height of stupidity, considering what he had hired Chad to do. Only a fool double-crossed a mercenary. Chad saw the mayor across the lawn and made a beeline for him. Along the way, he awkwardly took in a dozen back slaps and *hoo-rahs*. It made Chad want to climb out of his skin.

"The man of the hour." Mayor Spears met Chad half-way across the lawn and shook his hand.

"Thank you," Chad said. "I wish it'd gone down better than it did."

"We won, didn't we?"

"That depends on whether you wanted to start a war with Rock Springs. I'm afraid you've got one now."

The mayor raised his red Solo cup of orange juice. "That is exactly what I wanted to talk to you about. We need someone like you to help us defend our town and our food supply."

Chad exhaled loudly. This was what he had dreaded. If Rawlins had been willing to screw Rock Springs, they could be willing to screw Chad Wade. "Mr. Mayor, are you able to fly us to Salt Lake City?"

"Of course. Of course we're *able*. But I wanted you to take a day or two to think about my offer. You stay here and run the defense of our town—military training, building fortifications, and helping us keep the Walmart warehouse. In exchange, your family will be well-fed and protected. It's a win-win deal."

"Okay," Chad replied after thinking for a moment, "I'll consider it. But I want to know you're dealing in good faith. I'd like to see the plane and meet the pilot."

"Certainly." The mayor thrust out his hand. "You can't blame us for falling in love with you and your little family."

Chad accepted the handshake. Just touching the mayor's hand felt like consenting to a communicable disease. Damned politicians. It was always a mind-fuck with those guys.

• • •

Salt Lake County Fairgrounds
Salt Lake City, Utah

Francisco stared out the window of his luxury motorhome. A Latino woman, probably Mexican, carried two buckets of brown water from the Jordan River. A little boy followed, stopping occasionally to squat down to look at rocks or bugs, then scampering to catch up.

This could be a scene from Ciudad Juarez in the early eighteen hundreds. We have regressed more than a hundred years in two weeks, Francisco thought, watching the woman.

The history of the moment weighed on him. This land, which he had begun to think of as "Northern Mexico," would be defined by great men who rode a wave of power to justice.

Francisco didn't think of his father very often. His papa had died before Francisco became a man—taken by an industrial accident at the recycling center where he worked. When Francisco became a great man—a great revolutionary—his father would be proud.

Again, it felt like the Fates touched the chords of his mind. The import of this moment resonated in his soul. Francisco had been placed here, with an army at his command, like Francisco Pancho Villa. He knew he possessed the vision and the intellect to accomplish something historical. The decisions he made now would make history, perhaps for all time.

Someone knocked, the RV door rattling.

"Come in."

Bastardo, the lieutenant he had placed over the fairgrounds, entered the RV with another man behind him. "*Buenos dias, Jefe.* This is Alberto Romero. He's a maintenance manager for the Jordan Valley Water Company."

The men shook hands, an interesting exchange because, two weeks ago, a respected man like Romero probably wouldn't have been caught dead with a felon like Francisco.

"Señor Romero brought me some ideas about what we can do to improve the conditions for our people. We have some problems that are causing people to leave."

"What kind of problems?" Francisco grew impatient. How could minor problems with the camp compete with planning the upcoming offensive against Oakwood? But Francisco respected Bastardo's opinion, and he owed him consideration.

Alberto Romero answered, "The Jordan River collects almost all the surface pollutants from the Salt Lake Valley. People here are

321

drinking the raw sewage of everyone defecating near every stream, river and canal in all of Salt Lake. Almost everyone drinking water out of the Jordan River is sick here, no matter how much we filter or boil it, because the water is heavily polluted. We would have to fully distill it to make it close to safe, and distillation requires an enormous amount of fuel and effort."

Bastardo chimed in because he could see Francisco becoming frustrated with the bad news.

"Francisco, we're also running out of wood to boil water or cook food. We've torn down every wood building on the fairgrounds and all the homes around us. I've done an inventory of our food and we have about two weeks' supply of food. We're feeding about three thousand people right now. So far, the *caca* still goes down the toilets, but I don't know how long the toilets will keep working. Mister Romero says the sewage will soon start to back up and overflow."

Romero, used to being the expert, continued with the thought without allowing Francisco to comment. "The sewage is already backing up in parts of the city, and that's partially why the Jordan River's more polluted than normal."

"So what do you suggest?" Francisco interrupted. He wanted solutions, not problems.

"I recommend you abandon this camp," Romero said.

"*Hijo de puta*," Francisco swore. "Where would we go?"

Bastardo could see his boss losing patience, so he took over the conversation. "We could move closer to the mountains. We could get away from the city, maybe a rural town near a stream where we can get clean water, where we can grow food in the spring. We have the laborers: farmers, mechanics, builders. If the world keeps going this way, we can grow food and trade it with the city. Soon, food will be the only money that matters. We can control the food, Francisco. The Latinos are the only people in the valley who still know how to work with their hands."

Francisco and Bastardo's friendship went way back, all the way back to when they were snot-nosed teenagers stealing bikes downtown. He and Bastardo were *O.G.*, *Original Gangsters.* Two of the first Norteños in Salt Lake City, they had founded Los Latigos together. He owed Bastardo, but this conversation was trying Francisco's patience. He had a war to win.

"Where would we go?" Francisco asked again.

Alberto Romero opened a map from his back pocket. "We've picked three possible towns. Each one is close to Salt Lake City. Each one has a year-round stream. And each one has grain silos that should be full this time of year."

Bastardo took over, sponsoring the idea, even though he knew it was a hard sell. "Francisco, the town of Malad is just an hour north of here. We can join the town and control the I-15 Freeway, maybe even charge a toll for anyone driving through. Or south of here, we can go to the town of Nephi. It has a stream coming out of this mountain, here." Bastardo ran his finger down the canyon that supplied ground water to Nephi.

"Or we can join the town of Tremonton," said Romero. "It's closer to Salt Lake and grows maize—corn for cattle. All of these places are clean, and we could easily move in and offer a deal to the townspeople: work with us and we'll provide security and labor."

"Think about it, Francisco. We could have an entire town for Latinos, a place where we make food for the whole region, from Salt Lake City all the way down to Saint George. The only people in this city who know how to work nowadays are *Latinos. Work* is our weapon. We could own everything. We could trade food for land, food for buildings, food for houses. And food will never be worth more than it will be worth over the next year. The white people will trade everything they own for a little maize or wheat in the coming weeks. We would become rich and it would be *honest* money."

His words were pregnant with an unspoken truth between them. But Bastardo couldn't say it with a stranger in the room. *At our age, shouldn't we be living honestly?*

"Give me the chance to talk to these towns, Francisco. Let me see if they'll work with us. Every one of these towns is being overrun with people fleeing from Salt Lake. We can protect the towns from being flooded by starving people. Los Latigos can handle security—man their roadblocks. We can bring them the medicine we've captured. We can provide labor for the fieldwork come spring. I just need two days to talk to them and strike deals. Two days, Francisco."

Bastardo looked up from the map, praying Francisco would see reason. He knew Francisco planned to attack another neighborhood soon. If they were ever going to retire from the thug life, this would be the time.

Francisco stared at the map. "Thank you, amigo." Francisco clapped Bastardo on the shoulder. "You've given me something beautiful to think about. It's quite a dream. Please send in Crudo." With that, Francisco ended the meeting.

Bastardo and Romero climbed down from the RV and closed the door. A few minutes later, Crudo knocked.

"Come in."

"*Sí, Jefe.*" Crudo stepped inside and walked over to the table.

"We attack Oakwood tomorrow at first light. Every man fights."

• • •

Ross Homestead
Oakwood, Utah

In the middle of the night, gunfire crackled across the Great Lawn of the Homestead. Jeff and his teams had been fighting this battle for thirty minutes, and they still didn't have a clear picture of the enemy. As was usually the case with a night battle, nobody could find their ass with both hands. Being shot by your own side became a bigger risk than being shot by the enemy.

Jeff guessed that a small group—maybe just ten or fifteen men—had penetrated the upper perimeter in an attempt to sneak in and rob the Homestead. The bullets now thudding into Homestead buildings probably came from a thrown-together group of armed, hungry men,

324

most likely not the gangbangers. Most of the Homestead buildings were made of stone, and all of the tent-people had retreated into the bunkhouse. As long as the property didn't get overrun, their families would be safe.

Because of the dark and because of their limited training, Jeff didn't dare send more than one QRF into the forest after the attackers. If two QRFs went, they could cut each other to ribbons.

Earlier in the gun battle, one of his perimeter defense guards had shot one of the QRF guys accidentally—the first Homestead casualty—and it didn't look like the QRF guy was going to pull through. Jeff sent all the perimeter defense men to their duty stations to keep them from wandering around and to prevent further blue-on-blue shootings. Except for the QRF, the Homestead perimeter defenders didn't have enough training to fight in the dark.

The best way to kill the invaders without shooting one another would be the surgical application of night vision, thermal vision and excruciatingly careful gunfire. Every one of the QRF fighters wore an infrared sticky badge on the back of his bump helmet. At a quick glance, with night vision, the Homestead fighters could see the badge and refrain from ventilating one of their own.

QRF One ran the fight in the forest. One Homestead fighter had been wounded by the intruders, and another guy was in surgery, shot by the Homestead's own guys. Based on the radio chatter, Jeff surmised that the squad leader of QRF One, Tim, was moving his guys carefully across the forest and down the canyon, herding the intruders in front of them toward the Great Lawn.

Even though it pushed gunfire toward their families, the plan made sense. QRF Two and Three, both at full strength, had set up a U-shaped picket around the Great Lawn. With open fields of fire, the blocking force would shred anyone stepping onto the lawn. The fight blazed dangerously close to the home, but it was the only sure way to contain and eliminate every intruder.

Winslow had a team of snipers set up on the ridge facing the forest, and they were carefully picking through targets with their thermal scopes as targets appeared between the trees. The first blue-on-blue shooting scared everyone straight, and the process of identifying targets slowed to a crawl. Everything had to be done with great care to avoid another needless death.

Tim's QRF One all wore NVGs, but that wasn't the end-all-be-all solution to winning a night fight in the forest. Yes, the team could see in the dark, but picking through a dark forest with NVGs was like trying to find *Where's Waldo* while someone kicked you repeatedly in the balls. The forest looked like black-and-white scrambled eggs through NVGs. Half of the QRF guys carried big infrared floodlights to light up each chunk of the forest, one section at a time. Only the NVGs could see the floodlights.

The QRF had IR lasers mounted to the fronts of their rifles and handguns, allowing them to sight and shoot without shouldering their weapons. The IR lasers helped identify friendly forces; the QRFs could tell one another from the bad guys from the sweeps of the IR lasers back and forth. This kept the QRFs in a line. Also, every QRF fighter without an IR floodlight had a thermal monocular, scanning the forest every ten paces.

It was the Easter egg hunt from hell, every step methodically executed, and every pull of the trigger checked and doubled-checked before letting rounds fly.

"This is Winslow, Sniper One. Everyone stop and point your IR lasers straight up. I need you to copy that. Point your IR lasers straight up."

"Copy. QRF One pointing lasers straight up."

"This is Winslow. We think we have a bad guy in front of you fifty meters, but I need to confirm that it's not one of you. QRF One: wave your lasers, please."

"Copy. Waving our lasers."

"The target is fifty meters in front of the sixth guy from the bottom of the canyon. Sixth man, please wave your laser."

"Copy. Standby." Three minutes passed.

"This is Winslow. That's the fifth guy up the line I'm seeing wave his laser. I need the *sixth* man from the bottom to wave his laser."

"Copy. Sixth man waving his laser."

"This is Winslow. Okay. I'm seeing the sixth man. Repeat. Target is fifty yards in front of you. Can you see him with your thermal?"

"This is QRF team lead. No, we cannot see the target."

"This is Winslow. I'm going to shoot. Please confirm."

"This is QRF team lead. All team accounted for and online. You are weapons-free to shoot target."

"This is Winslow. Shooting."

All night long, the snipers and QRF teams worked through the intruders, making every step a deliberate action and adding to their exhaustion and bone-numbing stress with each shot.

After four hours, QRF One finally approached the Great Lawn. They had killed eight intruders, two deer and a porcupine. Luckily, they hadn't shot any more friendlies.

Jeff reminded himself just how right he had been. They should have burned the forest down.

"Jeff, Tim calling, over."

"This is Jeff. Go ahead, Tim."

"QRF One is two-zero-zero yards from the Great Lawn. Estimate five Tangos between you and us. We have approximately eight Tangos down so far. Over."

"Copy that. Do NOT get any closer to the Great Lawn than one-five-zero yards. Jeff out."

The pace of fire picked up over the next twenty minutes, with the last remnants of the intruders fighting desperately, sandwiched between two forces. The QRFs methodically annihilated them like rats driven by fire from a cornfield. Every time a stranger squirted out onto the Great Lawn, pushed by QRF One, they were cut down by the blockers.

After another hour of painstaking night fighting, all gunfire ceased. The men of QRF One combed every inch of forest again with their thermal monoculars, IR floodlights and NVGs, finding only dead and wounded.

The Homestead med staff rushed into the gap as soon as the battle slowed, pulling men out of the tangles of Snowberry bushes and Oregon Grape, hauling the still-living to the infirmary.

Once Jeff felt confident they had eliminated all the enemy, he turned his attention to his wounded. By his count, his men had taken two casualties; one of them a "blue-on-blue," friendly-fire incident and he had already died in surgery.

Jeff had seen the medical staff carrying a number of bodies and that worried him. He hopped into his OHV and headed to the infirmary.

Doctors and nurses rushed about like ants, patching men up and preparing others for surgery. Right away, Jeff knew he had a problem. Most of the men on gurneys in the doctors' and nurses' care were enemy combatants.

He had tried to raise this issue ahead of time, of providing medical care to the enemy, but he had never reached an agreement with the medical staff or the Homestead committee.

"Ladies and gentlemen," Jeff shouted over top of the chaos, "I respect and honor your commitment to treating the wounded. But we will NOT be keeping enemy combatants here, nor will we be providing them medical aid."

The doctors and nurses howled in protest, but Jeff brooked no discussion. He couldn't allow enemy eyes inside the Homestead wire, observing their resources, noting their defensive strength and consuming their precious medical supplies. Every moment these wounded men remained here, the risk increased that they would contribute information to the next attack.

Jeff scooped up a man from a gurney, shot in the gut, and threw him over his shoulder. An IV line popped out of his arm and the attending nurse shrieked in anger. Jeff walked to his OHV, and dumped the moaning man into the truck bed.

Jeff ignored the raging protests from the nurses and doctors. He scooped up another man, this man shot several times, and sat him beside his comrade.

The medical staff went crazy. Some of them tried to physically block Jeff from their patients. Jeff brushed them aside, men and women both. Other nurses and doctors worked even faster on their patients, trying to give whatever aid they could before Jeff came, like a pugnacious Grim Reaper.

Jeff loaded four enemy combatants unceremoniously into the back of his OHV and ordered the commander of QRF Two to stand guard, not allowing anyone but Homestead troops to receive medical aid.

Leaving screaming nurses and bellowing doctors in his dust, Jeff roared up the mountain to the upper perimeter at the top of the ridge, some two miles behind the Homestead, intent on laying the dying men beside other dead trespassers.

"Don't leave me here to die," one man pleaded as Jeff lifted him out of the back of the OHV.

"Why wouldn't I? You tried to kill my family." Jeff sat the man back down in the small bed of the OHV, half on top of the man's friend, who looked like he might have died on the trip up the mountain.

"You tried to kill my family first," the dying man croaked.

"How so?"

"You poisoned our water. We found the rotting porcupine you buried in our stream. That was our bug-out location. We had nowhere else to go. You made our kids sick. One little girl in our camp, she died because of the bad water. You attacked us first. We didn't see it coming and that camp was the only way we were going to survive this thing. So we fought back. But don't leave me here to die, please."

"Humph." Jeff neither confirmed nor denied poisoning the stream. He hadn't thought about the porcupine since he had put it in the Beringers' water supply two weeks ago. Had he caused this attack? He didn't like that idea at all.

"You're from the Beringers?" Jeff drilled down, hoping he wasn't.

"Dick Beringer." The gut-shot man reached out a blood-and-gut-soaked hand to Jeff. Out of reflex, Jeff shook the dying man's hand.

"I can't take you back to your camp," Jeff blurted out his bottom line. His fault or not, he couldn't endanger his family and the rest of the families by allowing this man to return to his camp.

"Then can you stay with me while I die?"

Jeff sagged in his own skin like the air had gone out of him. He rolled his neck and gathered the man in his arms. Jeff propped him against the wheel of the OHV and lowered himself down to sit beside the Beringer man.

Jeff had sat beside many dying men. With the battle over, he had always felt begrudging respect for any man who fought for a cause, no matter how mistaken their philosophies. Given the circumstances this night, it was an easy choice to see this man as a fellow sword-bearer off to Valhalla.

"Talk to me," Dick Beringer pleaded.

"What do you want me to talk about?" Jeff asked.

"It doesn't matter. Tell me about yourself."

Jeff babbled about his military career, starting from his early days in the army, serving in Asia and making his way to his many deployments in the Middle East. Jeff talked for ten minutes, looking into the night, before turning back to Dick Beringer. While he had talked, the man had passed.

Jeff wiped his face, only then realizing that his hand smelled like guts. He sat next to the corpse of Dick Beringer for another fifteen minutes, taking in the smell of death, mingled with the scent of autumn. He needed a little time just to sit. It had been a very bad night.

After there was nothing else to think, Jeff got up and carried the dead men, one by one, over to the fence posts marking the boundary of the Homestead. He leaned one dead man against each post, a warning to others who might trespass.

• • •

It was almost dawn, and Jacquelyn sat on a plastic chair in the
infirmary, her hands hanging between her legs, staring at Tom's body.
Like a lawn mower that refused to start, she couldn't get her mind up
to speed to accept this latest piece of information.

Her husband was dead. He had been shot by one of the
Homestead's own men. Nobody would tell her who.

It was information, like numbers in a column on a massive
spreadsheet that she couldn't begin to understand. It didn't help that
she hadn't slept and it was six in the morning.

The kids were asleep in the bunkhouse. How was she going to tell
them their father was dead? She needed someone to give her the
words because she wasn't coming up with anything.

Kids, your daddy's gone to heaven…

She and Tom hadn't made religion a priority. Talking about
heaven wouldn't mean anything to the kids.

Kids, your daddy died last night protecting us…

What would happen when they found out he had been killed by
another Homestead man by accident?

Kids, I'm falling apart, and I'm not capable of being your mommy
anymore because your daddy is dead, and I don't have the faintest
clue what to do next…

Oh, my sweet lord. She could not, would not, make this worse
for them. But Tom's death would change them, and not for the
better. They would break, each in some fundamental way, and then
spend the rest of their lives trying to heal that wound. She had seen it
over and over again as a therapist. Less than an hour from now, her
kids would receive a shock they could not bear, and their sweet,
innocent minds would rip, and blackness would flow into the
wounds, forever darkening their lives.

Oh, God, why?

Her mind turned again to God, even though she didn't really believe in Him. So why did she keep thinking about Him as though He were gravity pulling her at every turn.

Oh, God, be with my children. Make the wounds such that they can heal. I know the wounds will be deep, but make them not so deep as to forever scar.

There she was again, praying to a God she didn't know existed.

Give me the words. Give me the heart. Carry me and hold them as I tell them their father is lying on a plastic table, lifeless forever.

And then she felt God around her like a blanket. Or maybe it was the universe. It was something. Whatever it was, she felt not-alone for a moment.

It will be okay.

From the bottom of her soul, she cried for her children. Then she cried for herself. Then she cried for this simple, honest man who only ever meant to be a good man.

It will be okay.

Oh, God, please *be real* and please make it okay.

Jacquelyn gathered herself and headed to the bunkhouse to see if her children were awake. Maybe they would still be asleep, and maybe she could spend a few minutes with them in bed, just smelling their hair.

If she could have that, she could make it through this day.

15

"GOOD EVENING, LADIES AND GENTLEMEN. A special shout out to any Drinkin' Bros out there still breathing. You don't know how lucky you are. I just breezed through Albuquerque and let's just say that it was never a beautiful town, but now it's as though God left a steaming turd on a parking lot. Some poor bastard on the street told me the cartels have started coming in at night, raping and burning just for fun. If you're planning on wintering in Albuquerque, I would reconsider travel.

"Halsey Field in San Diego, California called in. The entire Coronado isthmus has been locked down since the collapse. The naval base has a nuke ship supplying power and water. Sounds like a large armed force from Mexico — probably cartels — had been sweeping through San Diego looting until they ran into the SEALs and Navy boys holding down Coronado Island. Big mistake for the cartels. The Navy's planning an offensive to clear out San Diego soon. What is it the cartel says, 'plata or plomo?'" Give 'em nothing but lead, Navy boys, nothing but lead.

"On a personal note, I'm running low on water and, quite frankly, I can no longer pretend that my blow-up doll is a real person. If there are any Drinkin' Bros listening in who would like to invite slightly ripe-smelling radio show host to Sunday dinner, I would be greatly obliged..."

Holiday Inn
Rawlins, Wyoming

In the wee hours of the morning, long before daylight, Chad rousted his family. They had packed everything the night before.

Pacheco drove Audrey and Samantha in the Blazer, dropping Chad off on the corner of a residential street just outside downtown Rawlins.

The day before, Chad had been introduced to his pilot, gleaning enough information to figure out where he lived. The town owed Chad a flight to Salt Lake City, but Chad had become eighty percent convinced the mayor intended on dragging his feet, forcing Chad and his family to stay in Rawlins, forever prostituting themselves to the town's interests.

Chad pretended to consider the offer, quietly gathering the information necessary to take matters into his own hands.

The back door of the pilot's house had been left unlocked, a bad habit during the Apocalypse. But Rawlins had never been a town that required locked doors. Chad slipped quietly inside, wearing his NVGs and carrying his 1911 handgun.

After exploring a bit, he found the main bedroom and stepped to the foot of the bed. He carefully laid back a heavy quilted comforter and tapped the pilot's big toe with his handgun.

"Whaaaa...?" The pilot sat up, groggy.

"Hey, bro," Chad whispered. "I'm Chad. We met yesterday. Our flight's been pushed up. We're leaving now."

The pilot stared at the dark shape at the foot of his bed. "Why're you in my bedroom?"

"It's all good," Chad calmed him. "We need to get in the air. We have an early departure time."

"Okay, let me get my pants on." The pilot slid off his bed, groggy enough not to question anything. Amazingly, his wife kept snoring.

• • •

Ross Homestead
Oakwood, Utah

Dawn broke clean and crisp, fall now undeniably upon the Homestead. One of the doctors, Doc Eric, smoked a cigar, standing on the cobble drive outside the infirmary.

Jeff hadn't slept, spending the night cleaning up the night battle. The last thing he needed was for more wounded enemies to end up in the infirmary. He stayed up to make sure all the bodies had been policed up from the forest and deposited outside the mountain perimeter.

Doc Eric had acquainted himself with assault rifles and handguns long before the collapse. Few knew this, but Doc Eric scored as one of the best combat shooters in the Homestead. Even so, he would probably never pick up a gun in anger, his skills as a surgeon more urgently needed in the infirmary. Unlike the other four doctors who were part of the group, Eric carried his Glock 17 everywhere, including the infirmary and surgical bay.

Jeff walked up silently beside Doc Eric, testing the waters.

"You got yourself a passel of trouble this morning, big guy," Doc Eric said, taking a puff on his Swisher Sweet.

"I suppose you're right about that," Jeff said.

Doc guffawed. "On the positive side, your boy is hanging in there strong. He's still sleeping and feverish, but my money's on him making it."

Jeff nodded, thankful for the update.

"I couldn't let those wounded men stay here," Jeff launched into his explanation. "The longer we worked on them, the more we'd want to keep them here, and the more they'd find out about us. When we finally decided to send them away, they'd be a gaping wound in our security—a massive leak of information."

"Trust me," Doc Eric said, "I understand. Those men had to go, but that doesn't change anything. The med staff, and everyone who listens to the med staff, have convinced themselves that you're the new head of the Gestapo."

"I guess that makes me Adolf Hitler."

"No, I believe that would make you Hermann Göering."

• • •

More a lynch mob than a meeting, a group of concerned citizens of the Homestead gathered outside the infirmary. A night's sleep had done nothing to temper their anger.

As the crowd formed on the cobblestone drive outside the doors of the four-car, garage-cum-infirmary, an angry debate circulated around the mass of people, the tide leaning precariously toward revolt against Jeff Kirkham and, by extension, Jason Ross.

Alena Jameson did more than her fair share of the shouting. "If we allow this to continue, every one of us is complicit in murder. If we choose to live like this—like barbarians—then why is there any reason to live?"

Doctor Hodges followed. "I cannot, in good conscience, practice medicine like this. I've taken an oath. I could be stripped of my license for what happened last night."

"Who elected these men to run this place anyway?" another person shouted.

The mob raged on and, as it did, contrary voices arose.

Walter Ross shouted, "I'm no fan of killing. But I have to trust that our military people know what they're doing. I trust that what Jeff Kirkham did is an appropriate response to being attacked."

"They aren't behaving anything like military professionals," Alena hissed. "We don't stick enemy wounded on fence posts to die. When has America ever done that?"

Round and round the shouting went. The tides of fear and anger came and went, smashing against one another. Many feared the violence, worried it might turn against them. Others feared for their children's safety, willing to accept violence to protect them. Others channeled their despair—brought on by the collapse of society—and turned it against Jeff Kirkham.

Above the infirmary, standing back from the edge of the balcony so he couldn't be seen, Jeff listened. Then he did what he always did when faced with a threat: he acted.

Switching to the radio channel reserved for his commanders, Jeff called in all QRF squads. He ordered his men to surround the meeting, weapons ready.

As Jeff spoke into his radio, giving orders, he didn't notice Jason Ross silently stepping around the corner of the balcony. Jeff turned and regarded Ross, knowing he had been overheard ordering troops to take up arms against the people of the Homestead. Jeff and Jason looked one another in the eye for a long moment. Jason nodded and took another sip of his coffee.

It took five minutes for Jeff's armed men to file into the courtyard. Nobody appeared to notice. The argument had taken on a life of its own. Without restraint and leadership, the debate could go on for hours.

"Are your men ready?" Jason asked.

Jeff nodded.

"Good, then I'll go down and talk to the crowd. Agreed?"

"Agreed," Jeff replied.

Jason descended the stairs and walked into the middle of the mob. In a show of human pack hierarchy, Jason's bearing bought him free passage to the head of the conversation. Watching from above, Jeff smiled at the unspoken, primitive ways of the human mind. *The Alpha Wolf arrives.*

Strangely, Jason hadn't done anything to win the group's deference, except maybe being a successful businessman in a lifelong past. He couldn't claim to be a superior fighter, athlete or even a talented people person. But, in the post-Apocalyptic world, through the strange alchemy of human sociality, he was the natural choice for head of state.

One thing was certain: Jeff didn't want the job. Even with near-total control of the Homestead security force, Jeff wanted nothing to do with political affairs. And, without this mass of idiots down below, his men would have nothing to eat, nobody to farm for them and no one to patch them up when they were injured. As much as he hated politics, Jeff needed the Homestead. That meant he needed Ross, at least for the time being. But there were limits to his patience. He would not let the safety of his family be compromised, no matter how much he needed them.

The arguing subsided as Jason took center stage.

"How are you going to deal with these *barbarians* you have running things around here?" Alena launched into a new offensive.

Jason waited a moment. "I think we've heard enough to know where you stand, Alena. That goes for the medical staff as well. Now I'm going to tell you how it is. When I'm done, if you don't like it, you are welcome to leave. We'll even send you away with a few buckets of food."

"No, we won't," Jeff interrupted loudly from the balcony above. He wasn't willing to let that stand. Jason stared at Jeff for a moment with an inscrutable expression. A silent message passed between the men.

Let me handle this.

Okay, but only if you don't dick out on our survival.

Jason's face went red, his fury restrained beneath a thin veneer of practice. "Jeff's right. The disposition of food will be a decision made by the committee. But that will be my recommendation: that anyone who leaves will leave with a week's food," Jason partially corrected himself.

338

"Who's in charge here, anyway?" someone in the crowd shouted.

"When it comes to military decisions, and until the threat has passed, Jeff Kirkham's word is absolute. We cannot second-guess combat orders and expect to survive. I will not quibble with Jeff, and I sure as hell won't support you in quibbling with him." Jason pointed a finger at Alena and let it drift over the doctors and nurses, his hand beginning to shake.

"And what if he refuses to give up control?" Doctor Hodges interjected.

"If that means we've survived the threat of annihilation, then I'll be thrilled to deal with that problem when the time comes. I don't think you're aware of just how close we are to being wiped off the face of the earth. If we survive this next month, it'll be a miracle. We do not have *the luxury of ethics* today. If our children are to survive, we must *be* barbarians. I realize that we should've had this conversation before we invited you to join the Homestead, back in the old world, the world that's gone. But, right now, I offer no apologies and neither does Jeff. We will probably be forced to fight again—like barbarians—if our children are going to continue to live. Respectfully, Doctor, and Alena, fuck your ethics and fuck your license to practice medicine. I choose for my children to live."

The crowd gasped. They had expected assurances. They had expected compromise. They hadn't expected an ultimatum.

"You're welcome to leave right now with nothing but your personal belongings. If you want to argue for anything else, you'll have to stay until the committee has time to make a decision. If you're willing to sacrifice the lives of your children on the altar of your anger, then Godspeed. Leave right now. It gives me no joy to tell you this; you will die out there. But I pray you have the strength and wisdom to rein in your pride and shut your mouth. Stay and live, or leave and die. Those are your choices."

"I'm leaving, and I'm taking some of the food I worked for," someone shouted in the crowd. Jeff couldn't tell who had spoken.

Jason looked at Jeff on the balcony. "Jeff…"

Jeff shouted the order: "QRFs, stand by."

The seventy-five members of the three QRF squadrons, standing on the outer edges of the crowd, racked their slides and came to the low-ready, stepping back. Most of the crowd jumped, startled by the unexpected show of force.

Jason let the moment percolate, giving the crowd time to digest this new dynamic. Literally, they were now under the gun.

Wailing its woeful drone, the emergency alert began to sound from the ham shack on top of the hill.

Jason shouted above the noise. "Jeff, what's going on?"

"Stand by," Jeff shouted back.

Jeff spoke into his radio, calling the ham shack.

"Zach, this is Jeff. What's going on? Over."

"Jeff, the barricade on Vista View Boulevard is being attacked by a large force."

Jeff shouted to Jason, ignoring the crowd. "We're being attacked at the Vista View barricade by a large force. Time to go. Now!"

The crowd erupted in conversation and Jason shouted them down. "Either you fight now or you're gone. No conscientious objectors. If you want out, gather your kids and head out the gate. Otherwise, get your gun and run down to the barricade or to your duty station, double-time. This conversation is over."

Jason looked up and Jeff nodded agreement. Jason took off at a run, going for his rifle and gun belt.

People mulled about, confused.

"Move!" Jeff yelled at the top of his lungs. As far as Jeff could tell, every single person headed for their duty stations, willing to set aside their ethics for the time being.

• • •

The sawgrass on the hillsides had long since surrendered to the coming winter. The fall chill frosted the edges of the dried grass, making everything crisp and frozen until the touch of the dawning sun.

Everywhere a man stepped, the frost vanished, leaving boot-shaped trails behind the attackers as they crossed the park strips and vacant margins alongside Vista View Boulevard. There were hundreds and hundreds of boot paths snaking up toward the neighborhood of the Homestead.

Vista View Boulevard twisted up the hillside in a series of sweeping switchbacks. In the distant past, the area had been a gravel quarry, giving the neighborhood a terraced look, like a stack of sixty-foot-thick pancakes. Small mansions serrated the edges of each bluff, tracking with the turns of the boulevard and the cuts of the old gravel pit.

For some reason, Utahans didn't mind building luxury homes on busy streets, so most of the homes were wedged between the boulevard and a steep mountainside, providing spectacular views of the Great Salt Lake but little room for a yard.

Over the last two weeks, Jeff had invested considerable time envisioning an attack on the big barricade at the base of Vista View. Because of the steep hill into Oakwood Highlands, only a few roads made the climb, cutting across the slopes. This played to the Homestead's advantage, forcing attackers into a half-mile fatal funnel where Jeff's forces could control the high ground. His plan, however, didn't contemplate a tsunami of fifteen hundred armed gangbangers.

As Jeff raced his OHV around the last bend in the boulevard, his breath hitched in his throat. The first barricade, at the base of the hill, had already been overrun by hundreds, maybe thousands of men. A smattering of gunfire continued, but the battle for the gateway to Oakwood Highlands had already been lost.

Jeff had no idea how many of his men had died and how many had retreated to the second barricade, but he could see the enemy pouring over the top of his belt-fed machine gun overlooking the lower barricade. He had placed a lot of hope in that machine gun nest, figuring that no mob had the sack to walk into sustained machine gun fire.

This enemy obviously had the discipline and manpower to storm a Browning 1918 belt-fed machine gun. This was no mob; this was an army.

Jeff stared in wonder as four steel behemoths on wheels trundled up to the lower concrete barricades, shoving them aside like empty cardboard boxes. The machines looked like nothing he had ever seen in battle but, after watching their wheels crab around the discarded concrete walls, he realized that the enemy's battle plan centered around these four grotesquely armored front-end loaders—heavy equipment that had been welded up with metal plates and tasked for battle. Unless they defeated, or at least neutralized the armor, the Homestead had no chance.

Losing the neighborhood and the Homestead no longer seemed a theoretical possibility. It seemed very likely to Jeff. As a student of military history, he knew that an army with greater numbers usually won, and the army arrayed below him had the Homestead outnumbered at least ten to one.

Jeff couldn't think of a single historical battle where a force as small as the Homestead had defeated a force this large.

• • •

Directly above Jeff, Chad Wade looked down from a Cessna twin-engine airplane.

He struggled to make sense of what he saw. A surging mass of people pushed up Vista View Boulevard. At first, he thought it might be some kind of protest march, with hundreds of men filling the road from gutter to gutter. But then he noticed the armored vehicles and realized he had arrived at the exact moment of a large-scale attack on his Oakwood friends.

"Circle around," Chad ordered the pilot.

He watched impotently as more than a thousand men marched up the road toward his home.

"Goddamnit! Goddamnit!" Chad yelled in the small cockpit, pounding on the armrest of his seat. "Get us on the ground!"

The plane peeled away from its banking turn and headed toward Davis County Airport.

• • •

Francisco rode into battle on the armored platform of a front-end loader, shouting orders and shooting his AK periodically at nothing in particular. Having led gangs his entire adult life, he knew to keep things simple and brutal.

His plan was Stalinesque. Each of his Los Latigos men lead a troop of twenty Latino laborers. He had given his trusted gangbangers strict instructions to herd their men out in front of them, shooting any man who faltered or ran.

With time, perhaps he could have developed loyalty and discipline among the new recruits, but with time they would also lose the initiative, allowing the whites to organize. Francisco knew the lethal efficiency of whites who organized. He had no intention of subjecting himself to it ever again.

As planned, his army rolled up the frontage road along the freeway and slammed directly into the defenses Gabriel had described. The Latino army didn't regroup, didn't reset their order of battle. His lieutenants ran directly into the barricades. They crushed the few defenders at the bottom barricade and quickly brought forward their tanks.

From his position in the center of his army, Francisco heard the low roar of a machine gun. The thundering rumble drowned out the staccato pops of rifle and handgun fire, heralding death of a more voracious kind. Francisco grabbed a megaphone he had brought and screamed for anyone and everyone to assault the machine gun.

Several of his lieutenants massed their men behind the scant cover around the machine gun position. Men piled behind dirt berms, trees, trash cans, fences and an electrical junction box. By horrifying trial and error, the Latinos learned which cover would stop the heavy rounds of the machine gun and which wouldn't. Men behind trash cans, cars, fences or even medium-sized trees died, cut in half by the machine gun, the rounds punching through almost anything. Others, behind thick dirt berms or lying pancaked on the ground behind the rise of the earth, survived. The terrified men stacked up deep behind the little cover they could find.

The roar of the gun paused occasionally, changing the belt of ammunition or swapping out a red-hot barrel. In those lapses, the Latino men sprinted forward, coming closer to the gun position. With every bound, the men not only got closer, but they spread out further around the machine gun, forcing it to traverse back and forth at an ever-greater arc, giving brief windows where the men could shoot back at the machine gun operators. Eventually, Latinos occupied an almost three-hundred-sixty-degree circle around the gun emplacement. The last hundred yards to the machine gun were taken in a single, mad rush.

The belt-fed swung madly, scything men down like an invisible blade. Eventually, the hundred fifty-round belt ran dry, and the pause allowed men to overrun the gun emplacement. The machine gun operators died, fighting hand to hand against fear-crazed Mexican gardeners, short-order cooks, and factory workers.

Bodies lay in a gruesome fan about the machine gun, piled behind bits of cover. Well over a hundred men had died, but only a few of Francisco's Latigos gangbangers had been lost. Francisco sent in one of his lieutenants to figure out the gun's operation and press it into service for the next assault.

In Francisco's mind, the initial assault had gone off without a hitch. He had mostly lost only laborers—none of whom meant anything to him—and he had proven his battle strategy. They had taken the whites' most powerful weapon, and he had only lost two or three Latigos soldiers in the process. He could keep this up all day and, by his best guess, he had already destroyed the bulk of the defense force.

While Francisco didn't hesitate to spend men's lives on his private campaign of thievery and power, he had been unwilling to place Gabriel anywhere near the battle. So he invented a safer mission for Gabriel. Francisco sent his brother and six men to recon the flank of the enemy. His mother would be inconsolable if anything happened to Gabriel.

As soon as the heavy equipment cleared the lowest barricade, Francisco got on the megaphone and ordered his men to march up the boulevard, heading toward the string of little mansions.

After a couple of hundred yards, his army slowed. A massive barrage of gunfire descended on them from the homes above. Even from a quarter mile below, Francisco could see his men dropping at an alarming rate. Francisco's irritation rose. In his mind, he had already defeated the whites. Why did they insist on making this more difficult than necessary? Okay, then, he fumed, we'll make them pay. And, if they keep this up, we'll make them watch their women and children pay.

The gunfire from above proved too vicious even for his lieutenants and their hundreds of men. Panicked for cover, his men flung themselves over the downhill embankment, tumbling away from the fight. Some stopped their fall and climbed back into shooting positions; others rolled away from the fight, picking up speed. With few exceptions, when they came to rest at the bottom of the escarpment, the Latino conscripts gathered their wits and ran away.

"Shoot those cowards!" Francisco screamed into his megaphone, pointing at the handfuls of Latinos running back toward the city. Nobody could hear him except for the men hiding around the armored bulldozer where he stood. They turned their guns on the men running away, over six hundred yards down the hill, shooting half-heartedly in their direction.

Francisco watched as one of his gangbangers, wearing a red hoodie, walked fearlessly up and down on the sidewalk beside the road, executing Latino men too scared to fight. Then his man's head blew apart in a red mist, dropping him to the pavement.

"Bring up the tanks!" Francisco screamed. "Bring up the tanks now!"

• • •

Not for a second did Jeff consider surrendering. In this world, surrender meant certain death for his family and friends. This enemy would strip the Homestead bare, and they might even massacre everyone still standing. Without food, water and wood, agonizing starvation would be a certainty. For the Homestead, this battle would be fought to the last man.

The vast number of enemy wasn't something Jeff had anticipated, but he and his men had planned for this battle. The road leading up to the neighborhood gave them every tactical advantage so long as they executed with precision.

The lessons of the Roman battle of Cannae cut both ways. This enemy came to battle with elephant-like battle armor. But the lie of the land heavily favored Jeff Kirkham. With a steep slope on the downward side of the road, and an even steeper slope towering above, Jeff's QRFs could rain death upon the advancing army with precision shots and the advantage of high ground.

The Battle of Cannae was considered one of the greatest defeats in Roman history. A large Roman army came against the army of Carthage, led by Hannibal at the Aufidus River. The Romans numbered ninety thousand, and Hannibal's army numbered half that many. Hannibal carefully deployed specialized troops, such as his Numidian and Spanish cavalry and his expert rock slingers, to maximize their advantage. Then Hannibal blocked his flank with the river, concentrating the Romans in a tactical pocket where he could attack them on three sides.

346

The hillsides above and below Vista View Boulevard would block out most attempts to flank his forces, plus Jeff's shooters would fire from the homes above, hopefully stalling the enemy's advance and winnowing their numbers, forcing them to linger in front of each roadblock. Like Hannibal, Jeff bet everything on sucking the enemy into a pickle barrel where his small army could shoot at them from three sides.

Jeff ran forward to join his defenders at the second barricade. The approaching army couldn't see the second, third or fourth barricades from their position. They would be wading into a fight they didn't understand. Jeff prayed they hadn't reconnoitered beforehand.

The Homestead only had one belt-fed machine gun, and it had already been lost. But Jeff had arranged firing positions in the homes and backyards that towered over the boulevard. Every time the enemy slowed to clear a barricade, they would die by the scores. Then Jeff's troops could retreat farther up the road, harrowing the enemy yet again.

Each retreat of Jeff's defenders would force the enemy to pass through a gauntlet of highly accurate rifle fire. Every one of Jeff's men carried an assault rifle, battle rifle or scoped hunting rifle, and they had trained extensively for two weeks and, in some cases, they had trained for years.

The gangbanger army appeared to employ a random assortment of weapons—rifles, shotguns, .22-caliber rabbit guns, and even some assault rifles. Jeff didn't know it, but he faced the guns stolen from the Avenues, mostly handguns and hunting rifles.

As Jeff watched the Latino army surge up the road, he could see no coordination other than a general push forward. No apparent effort was made to expand the fighting front of the enemy. The entire front line seemed to be confined to the width of the boulevard and the park strip on the downhill side. Jeff hoped against hope that the enemy would continue as currently disposed, in a massive frontal assault.

The first phalanx of men marched up the road toward Jeff's barricade like a hoard of rats intent on overtaking the farm.

"Bring the fifties and the hunting rifles up *right now*." Jeff spoke into his radio, careful not to shout. "We need to kill that armor."

Jeff grabbed two of the men closest to him and laid out a strange, desperate plan.

• • •

Jason geared up in time to jump in with QRF Two in the back of the Pinzgauer truck. Eight guys sat wedged in the back of the little personnel carrier, racing down the mountain toward battle. Jason had put in a little time to train with QRF Two, but he hadn't been fully spun up with the team. Alec, the team commander, would be using him in a special unit with two other shooters.

Before the collapse, Jason had trained with his SOF buddies, but that didn't mean he knew the ropes in QRF Two. For one thing, he had missed too much training to be clear on their radio protocols, and he didn't know their react-to-contact procedure. So Alec wouldn't be using him in his main force.

As he raced into combat, Jason didn't feel prepared. His stomach was doing back-flips and he knew the only cure to those jitters was training, training and more training. The thing that bugged him most was his rifle. He had been busy managing the Homestead over the last two weeks, and he hadn't had a chance to put together his .308 battle belt and chest rig.

Jason was kitted out with his ultra-light AR-15 rifle, with the diminutive .223 round . The four-pound gun felt like a toy, legitimate killing power in a package that weighed the same as a plastic Nerf gun. He had built the gun before the collapse because he knew he could wear it on his back all day without setting it down. While it was incredibly convenient, it wasn't the rifle he wanted for battle. Besides shooting the underwhelming .223, his custom ultra-light was even more unreliable than a standard AR-15. The titanium bolt was better

348

suited to competition shooting. All Jason could do was pray the little rifle wouldn't let him down.

All his angst coalesced around the gun. He kept looking at it, cradled between his legs, and wished he were carrying one of his big SCAR Heavy .308 rifles. *A rifle is a rifle is a rifle,* he kept telling himself, but he couldn't help but obsess over the insufficiency of the ultra-light AR-15. The gun was a convenient place for his angst to land, and it was fogging his brain.

Jason shook his head like a dog trying to clear its anxiety. The Pinzgauer squeaked to a stop and everyone piled out the back.

• • •

The partial pincer strategy, borrowed from the Battle of Cannae, worked even better than Jeff anticipated. He watched through his ACOG scope as the enemy dropped like God himself smote them.

A man in a red hoodie walked among the Latinos huddled on the pavement, and began shooting them, presumably for cowardice. Jeff let out half a breath and put a .308 bullet through the man's skull. He fell to the ground as though his legs had turned to pudding.

Still they came. For every dozen men felled by his overwatch shooters, a hundred more appeared from below. After the third wave, the Latino assault died in the no man's land beneath the bluff. There, Jeff noticed a pattern.

"QRF One. This is Jeff. Over."

"Go ahead."

"Target anyone wearing red. They are command. Do you copy?"

"Copy that. Kill the bastards in red. Over."

Jeff dropped the radio back into the pouch on his chest rig and looked around the concrete barricade with one eye. More men appeared over the slope in the road, as if rising from hell itself, cloaked in the shimmer of early morning mirage.

As he worked back and forth with his .308, putting careful rounds into one head, then another, Jeff felt the deep rumble of something heavy, groaning through the pavement. The vibrations came up through his feet and reverberated in his gut: the sound of a machine coming to grind them under its wheels.

A new volley of desperate fire rained down as his men on top of the bluff reacted in a panic.

"Slow your fire, QRF One. Slow your fire," Jeff called over the radio, knowing his teams above had to be running low on ammunition.

"Jeff," the QRF commander spoke over the radio. "We're bingo ammo. I've called for resupply, but they're five minutes out."

Jeff answered on the radio, "I'll be dead in five minutes."

"Roger. Making it happen." Tim's anguish came through even over the tinny radio. Jeff pictured the battle from Tim's point of view. They had cover and high ground. They had been killing enemy as fast as they could pull the trigger without any substantial risk to themselves, until they ran out of ammo.

"Tim. This is Jeff. Consolidate ammo and wait for my command. Repeat. Hold fire. Consolidate ammo and wait for my command."

"Copy, Jeff. Awaiting your command."

Jeff did a quick inventory of his little team behind the barricade. As far as he could tell, he hadn't lost anyone, and he believed he was full-force. The battle had lulled, everyone waiting for the slow-moving heavy equipment to make its way into position.

The rumble down the road turned to thunder as two of the four armored vehicles appeared above the rise in the blacktop. Dozens of Latino men jumped up from the down-sloping side of the road and ran behind the pieces of heavy equipment, using them as cover to advance. Short on ammo and under orders to hold fire, Jeff's QRF above held.

Behind Jeff, the two men he'd sent away earlier crouched, cradling four bulging, thick-ply trash bags filled with lawnmower gas. Jeff waved two more men over, knowing he would shortly sentence them all to die.

"Each of you take one of these trash bags. You're going to sprint straight at those front-end loaders, and you're going to hit them on top with these trash bags. Do *not* throw early. Make sure you're right on them before you throw. This is the only way your families live. Do you understand?"

A shadow passed over each man as realization dawned; he would die in the next five minutes. One by one, they nodded, saying nothing.

"Wait for my order. Again: *do not throw early.* Do you understand?" Again, they nodded.

Jeff had sent men to die before. The calculus of battle demanded it. No matter the rising flood that threatened to choke his throat and drown his eyes, Jeff knew he mustn't feel—mustn't hesitate. He shoved that part of him deep down and turned his gaze to the battlefield, mostly to avoid looking at the dead men kneeling by his side.

As the trundling machines neared, Jeff made rough calculations. How close were the machines? When would his men have the greatest amount of cover?

In a last-minute panic, Jeff shuffled through his chest rig, pulling out magazines one after another, dropping them on the ground. Eventually, he found one with red-tipped ammo—incendiary tracer rounds for night fighting. He dropped the mag out of his Robinson, slammed the tracer mag home and racked the slide.

Almost too late, he looked up to see the armor bearing down on them. Jeff grabbed his radio.

"QRF One. Commence firing. Repeat. Commence firing."

"Roger." Three seconds later, the QRF on the bluff opened up on the men stacked behind the front-end loaders.

"Go."

The four men leapt up from behind Jeff's barricade and ran full-out. Rifle fire from the armored boxes behind the drivers' cages shifted toward the rushing men, dropping one of them within twenty paces.

Jeff's three remaining men ran directly in line with the cages where fire couldn't reach. QRF One on the bluff tore into the enemy crouched behind the armor, dropping a dozen men and forcing the rest to shift around to the downhill side of the front-end loaders.

Amazingly, three of Jeff's men made it within five yards and tossed their bags full of gasoline. One of the bags hooked on a magazine stuffed in the man's pocket, dousing the man with gas. He stood in the road with his hands furiously rubbing his eyes until he was gunned down.

The other two bags slapped against the front-end loaders, one each, exploding gasoline out of the mouth of the bags, drenching the roof, sides and tires. Both men turned and ran for cover. One of them took several rounds in the chest.

Jeff unleashed a hail of tracer rounds, shooting past and around his final man, who was running straight at Jeff and the barricade. The incendiary rounds touched off the gasoline and both armored vehicles burst into flames. The men hiding behind the armor leapt back from the burning machines, many more of them falling to the hail of bullets from the bluff. Others ran into the homes beside the road, seeking any cover they could find. Jeff's man reached the barricade and slipped into a flesh-grinding slide behind cover.

The tires of the armored vehicles began to burn briskly, licking up into the drivers' cockpits, where wires, plastic and fluids began burning as well. Both drivers and gunners burst from their metal boxes, attempting to shoot their way out of the death trap. Jeff's men riddled them with bullets and one man fell from the front-end loader directly on his head onto the pavement.

The battle lulled again as the surviving Latinos took cover in the homes, controlling houses on both sides of the boulevard now. The gangbanger army, burrowed into the McMansions on both sides of Vista View Boulevard, turned their attention to QRF One on top of the bluff. The Latinos with scoped hunting rifles found places within the homes where they could shoot from concealment—windows, door frames and fences—and they started firing carefully at the elevated shooting positions of QRF One. Tim lost two of his men to head shots before radioing Jeff.

"Jeff, this is Tim. Over."

"Go ahead."

"We're taking casualties from the road. I've lost two men in the last five minutes. They're shooting from those homes in front of you with big rifles. It's a pretty even fight and they have a lot more men than I do. What are your orders?"

Jeff could no longer force his enemies into the funnel of death up the boulevard. Now they would be fighting house to house, and Jeff knew his forces couldn't sustain a war of attrition.

The low rattle of the two remaining armored vehicles forced Jeff's hand. "All units. This is Jeff. Pull back to barricade three. Repeat. Pull back to barricade three. And, for the love of God, where's my fifty-caliber?"

"Jeff. This is Winslow. I'm moving into position over barricade three. ETA three minutes. I had to get the fifty from the top of the ridge. Almost in position."

"Do me a favor," Jeff radioed back. "Be a damned Marine and kill those two tanks, please."

"Roger that." Winslow signed off.

• • •

A thick column of inky smoke rose behind the screen of McMansions up the road and around the corner from Francisco. He tore at his hair, anxious to know what had happened around the bend. He had sent in his ultimate weapons—two of his four pieces of armor—and the black smoke worried him to distraction.

He tried to contact Crudo and his other lieutenants over their radios. He had more than five hundred men stacked half-way up the hill, infuriatingly inactive, waiting to advance. Francisco had no idea what was holding them up.

His forces had definitely taken ground. They had fought through the barricade at the bottom of the hill, but something had brought them to a halt half-way up the mountainside and Francisco couldn't see what it was. As if to punctuate his frustration, the sun peeked over the mountaintop and stabbed Francisco's eyes. The harsh sunlight blotted out the softness of the fall morning, as if to say the honeymoon was over for Francisco and his men. The Latino army would fight it out in full daylight, and to Francisco, the harsh sunlight felt like a message: the easy victory had eluded him again. Now he found himself in a serious fight.

How was he supposed to succeed without knowing what was happening? How could he lead his men in battle without any reliable way of commanding them?

Finally, the radio squawked "Francisco. This is Crudo. Both tanks are on fire. We're in the homes now and the gringos are retreating. Send more men. Most of my men up here are dead."

Francisco's eyes flared, and he tore at his hair with ferocity. He couldn't imagine how four hundred men could be "mostly dead." And how did the tanks catch on fire? He felt like he was suffocating from lack of information. How was he supposed to use the two remaining tanks if he didn't know how to keep them from catching fire?

"Crudo. How did they catch fire?"

Crudo answered, but the first half of what he said came through clipped. It sounded like, "trash bags and gasoline," which made no sense whatsoever.

"What?" Francisco pleaded into the radio. "How did they catch fire?"

Crudo replied, but his words were drowned out by the rumble of the two front-end loaders driving past him.

"¡Hijo de puta!" Francisco screamed at the radio. He came close to throwing it, but thought better of it at the last second.

Francisco grabbed his megaphone and screamed at the hundreds of men crouched in the middle of the boulevard. "Move up, *cabrones*! Move up!"

• • •

Alec had assigned Jesse and Victor to Jason's "special purpose" element. Since he had missed much of QRF Two's training, Jason couldn't be integrated into the main force of the team. Instead, Alec ordered Jason and his two friends to execute a wide flank, where they wouldn't need to coordinate so closely with the rest of the team. Jason's radio was tuned to Alec's command frequency rather than the team frequency. This would de-conflict any mistakes Jason might make on the radio.

Jesus, Jason thought, making radios work is a bitch.

QRF Two had been assigned to the southern flank of the blocking force. Jeff had taken a big risk, placing one-third of his best assaulters in a position to block the enemy from climbing straight up a mountainside. In all likelihood, no enemy would do that. The risk to the Homestead forces, if anyone *did* happen to climb straight up the mountain, would be astronomical. Even a small flanking force coming up the mountainside could cut Homestead QRF Two, and then Jeff's main force, to ribbons, firing on them from the side. Jeff couldn't risk a flank, so he had sent Alec's QRF to counter-flank, which meant some of his best shooters might end up sitting on the sidelines for the entire battle.

Alec had assigned Jason's three-man contingent to conduct an even deeper counter-flank by sending them farther to the south. More of a recon element, Jason, Jesse and their buddy Vic would sound the alarm if the enemy tried to come at them from the deep south. If QRF Two was an insurance policy, then Jason's team was an insurance policy on top of the insurance policy.

On one hand, it seemed like a waste of good shooters to Jason. He wanted to fight, and there was no doubt; he *was* a good shooter.

On the other hand, Jeff and Alec knew exactly what they were doing, so Jason didn't waste time worrying about it.

Jason's three-man team spread out on the lip of a precipitous drop in the mountain. They could see all the way to the bottom, but the dried grass looked deep, and the folds in the terrain could easily hide an enemy force. From where they sat, they could hear the battle raging on the boulevard five hundred yards to their north—thousands of rounds being fired in waves like pounding surf.

Jason tried to imagine why the gunfire wasn't sustained, and why it would crescendo then diminish, almost coming to a silence. Then the gunfire would rise again in a mysterious rhythm that sent chills down his spine. His friends were dying. His precious daughter fought for her life in the middle of that orchestra of death.

While his mind stressed over the battle just a quarter-mile away, Jason's eye caught slight movement below his position on the face of the drop-off. He snatched his binoculars from a pouch in his vest and zoomed in on the area. His blood chilled and his ears began to ring as he squinted through the binos at an undeniable shape: the top of a man's shaved head.

The fight was coming. Jason keyed his radio. "Alec. This is Jason. Over."

"Go ahead."

"I have an unknown number of enemy coming up the mountainside. Will advise."

"Copy," Alec replied. "Unknown enemy force approaching your position. Over." Alec clicked off, probably jumping to another radio frequency to let Jeff know about the imminent flank.

Jason didn't bother to radio Jesse and Vic. They were close enough to each other to whisper. "Jesse. Enemy below. Get ready. Pass it along to Vic."

Jesse's eyes went wide, and he reflexively checked the chamber of his assault rifle and peeked up and over the berm. He turned to Vic, whispering loudly. A moment later, all hell broke loose. Nearly a hundred men appeared from behind tall grass down the hill, leaping up from cover. But they didn't charge. Instead, they began a guttural shout in unison, stomping their feet, pounding their chests and shouting at Jason and his men.

"Oh, fuck," Jason muttered to himself. He knew exactly what this was. These hundred men, a football field away, downhill from his little defensive position, were either Tongans or Samoans. He peered through his binos and could see they were all shirtless in the frigid October morning air, most with elaborate tattoos. Some of them carried war clubs in addition to their guns.

The scene made no sense to the three gunmen at the top of the hill. How was it they were facing a vicious horde of shirtless Polynesians in the middle of Utah in the middle of the fall?

What sprung to mind was the battle of the Island of Lanai. Jason had hunted mouflon sheep on the island once, and the guide had showed him a deep canyon where the men of King Kamehameha fought straight up a grassy cliff to defeat the defenders of the island. The two cliffy mountainsides looked almost identical: Lanai and Oakwood, Utah. Kamehameha had crushed the defenders despite the steep climb.

The violent war cry was coming to an end and, Jason had to admit, it scared him shitless. With a final pound on the chest and a stomp, the islanders launched up the hillside with a roar. Jason and his buddies began firing, wildly at first, but then slowing into a rhythm. They had to make the most of the seconds it would take for the attackers to charge the hill.

Why didn't we just shoot them while they were doing their *Haka?* Jason wondered as he picked another target and squeezed off a three-round burst. The target went down and Jason moved on, methodically putting bullets into men.

Jason would shoot a man, knowing he had made a good shot, and the guy would keep coming anyway. As this happened over and over, Jason knew they were losing the battle. His damned AR-15 was punching pencil-sized holes in gorilla-sized men. As one might expect, the fast-and-tiny holes delivered by his rifle were failing to drop pumped-up Polynesians. Every target required three, six or ten rounds before the man would fall. At this rate, they would run out of rounds before stopping the assault.

Jason swapped his fourth mag when the first screaming man reached him. With a palm smack to the slide release, Jason ran the bolt into the battery, whipped the sight into position and snapped a shot into the man's forehead. The tattooed Tongan paused mid-step and arced over backward, rolling back down the hill.

Jason moved onto another target, a huge man closing on him, and began firing into his torso. After placing four quick rounds into his chest, Jason's AR-15 jammed. In a flash, he ran his malfunction drill—slap, rack, squeeze—but nothing happened. Trying to stay calm, Jason flipped the gun sideways and glanced into the ejection port. He saw a tangle of brass and dropped the useless rifle, going for his handgun.

The huge man was on him, bleeding from four holes, but still very much alive. Jason's Glock came up just as the man's battle club came down, crushing Jason's bump helmet and knocking him sideways into a rock. The combination of impact from the club and from the rock made Jason's world go wobbly. The last thing he saw before darkness descended was the AR-15 lying on the ground in front of his face.

• • •

Jeff had located the third barricade around a bend in the road. This next defensive section wasn't nearly as good as the first two. There were homes on both sides of the street and that would give the enemy the cover of McMansions on both sides, allowing them to suppress for one another. Still, the Latino army wouldn't be able to circle around behind them. The tiered levels of the gravel quarry continued to provide Jeff's men with a significant defensive advantage. The enemy couldn't flank. They had to come straight up the road. The boulevard continued to funnel the attackers into a fighting front less than forty yards across, allowing only a few dozen Latino guns to join the battle at a time.

Jeff moved QRF One up to the next road, allowing them to fire down from the homes over the section of road. The tactical situation wasn't as golden as the fatal funnel they'd had in front of the first two barricades, but it was still a decisive advantage.

QRF One redeployed and rearmed from ammo stores they had pre-positioned. They moved up one street and then into the backyards and back windows of the homes on the bluff above the road, giving them a similar elevation advantage to the one they'd had before.

"In position, Jeff," Tim called over the command frequency.

"Roger. Here comes the armor." The two front-end loaders turned up another switchback in the boulevard. Whoever commanded them had learned from the last two. Rather than letting the armor get in front of the troops, they held the tanks back and used them as shooting platforms and cover for the middle of the street. The gasoline-and-garbage bag trick wouldn't work twice. Anyone trying to make a run on the armored vehicles would be cut down before they could get half-way to the tanks. Jeff wished they had more fifty-caliber rifles. As it was, he would be betting everything on Winslow and his Barrett.

• • •

Emily Ross deployed to the battle with her unit, QRF Three. She didn't know for sure how many men she had just killed from the bluff, but it had been a lot. She could see the scope picture in her mind's eye, then the crack of the rifle. She had placed the crosshairs and pressed the trigger, and men had disappeared. She didn't know how many.

She moved like a ghost, in a listless state. Some part of her mind struggled to deal with the death she had dealt and with the last horrifying thirty minutes, when in any given instant a bullet might pass through her own head.

She had been drenched in adrenaline for almost an hour. She had always been good at compartmentalizing, but the battle overwhelmed her ability to control her emotions. Her fingers tingled, as though from lack of oxygen, and she couldn't feel her toes. Worse, she couldn't shake the urge to sob. Reloading her magazines required a massive amount of willpower, just to force her fingers to perform the simple function of snapping .223 rounds into the mouth of each mag.

Press, snap, slide. She willed her fingers to do their job.

"We're moving out," Josh shouted. "We're the blocking force on the west side of the street. We need to make sure nobody climbs the bluff. We gotta move. They could already be climbing up on us."

Emily finished her last mag and ran to catch up with her unit. She was supposed to be the corpsman in the group—providing medical care when needed—but all she had done so far was kill people. Considering the size of the enemy they faced, medical treatment was the least of their concerns. The Homestead fought against total extermination.

As the team fanned out and took up their blocking positions, Emily slipped into rearguard, the position she had been assigned in training. She set up her rifle in a second-story window in what was previously a child's bedroom, covering a sector that might expose her team to a flanking action through the long row of homes.

Ten minutes after she had settled in, she saw a glimmer of movement in a backyard three houses down. Her adrenaline rose again, making her dizzy. All the families in this neighborhood had evacuated an hour earlier. She had no immediate backup, and the movement she had seen could only be one thing: the enemy.

"Josh. This is Emily. We have movement behind us. Repeat. We're being flanked down the row of houses behind us to the north."

"Copy, Emily. I'm sending help. Hold them up until we arrive."

"Roger," Emily squeaked, her throat constricting.

From the child's room, there were many ways an attacker could get around her; she had tons of blind spots. She would have to head downstairs into the backyard or risk being surrounded.

Emily ran down the stairs and slowed once she hit the main floor. Gently sliding the glass door open, she slipped into the backyard, scanning with her M4 rifle at the ready.

The backyard offered an open shooting lane that ran the width of the property. In order to pass by, the gangbangers would have to cross the gap. Emily found cover behind an air conditioning unit, crouched and waited.

Moments later, the vinyl fence shuddered.

• • •

Gabriel and his team moved carefully from yard to yard. It had taken them almost an hour to circle around the battlefield and climb the bluff. Now they were moving toward what he believed was the enemy's rear. So far none of his men had fired a shot.

He came to a white vinyl fence, the fifth one they had crossed, and he climbed on top of a doghouse and took a quick peek. He saw nothing in the next yard, so he slung his rifle and vaulted the fence, landing in a crouch.

He pulled his rifle around to his grip and placed his finger on the trigger in readiness. Just then, a girl in camouflage leaned around a gray metal box, pointing her rifle at his chest.

He paused, cocking his head at the sight. The last thing Gabriel saw was her long blonde hair swinging around her shoulder.

• • •

Emily opened fire on the man, shooting holes in his chest, shoulder and gut. He slumped backward, sprawling on the lawn.

Instantly, bullets punched through the vinyl fence, the enemy team firing blindly into her yard. Emily balled up behind the air conditioner as bullets slammed into the stucco wall behind her, stinging her head and neck with chunks of rubble. Assault rifle fire erupted from the other side of the yard, and Emily heard her own team joining the fight.

"Emily, moving up," somebody shouted, probably Josh.

"Here," she shouted, leaning out from around the air conditioner and returning fire through the fence.

Three members of her team bounded up to her, fanned out around the house and pressed their attack. After trading fire and enveloping the enemy position, Josh moved to Emily and smacked her on the shoulder.

"Last man."

"Moving," Emily shouted and moved forward, now on auto-pilot, following her training and moving around the fence, working from cover to cover around the next house.

Within a few minutes, her team wiped out the flanking force. Bodies of young Hispanic men lay cast around the yards, pools and play sets of the luxury homes, caught up in a gunfight they were ill-prepared to win.

As soon as the rifle fire died down, Emily checked in over the radio and headed back to the man she had first shot.

She looked down and noticed his face. More a boy than a man, he couldn't have been older than eighteen. She had seen him raise his rifle, then he had paused. He could have easily shot her, but he hadn't.

His eyes were closed, his face in repose. She struggled to find the enemy in the boy before her. The sorrow of the day rose in her chest, and finally, a sob broke free. She croaked loudly and covered her mouth with her hand and began to weep deeply, uncontrollably.

Through the tears, she thought she saw his chest rise slightly. Emily wiped her eyes and studied him, the med student taking over.

Yes, he was still breathing. She grabbed his throat and felt for a pulse. His heart beat, surprisingly strong.

Emily scrambled for her med kit at the back of her battle belt and
tore open a package of hemostatic dressing, working furiously to
staunch the bleeding. She ran through his injuries as she carefully
applied dressings: shoulder, stomach and chest, carefully rolling him
to check the exit wounds in back.

The shoulder round had passed clear through, doing little
damage. The chest shot might have missed his lungs, passing in and
out of the left side at an angle. The stomach wound… it would be
impossible to tell without surgery. Most people initially survived a
shot to their gut, but few survived without a full surgical center. No
matter. She would do everything she could.

He *had* paused. She felt certain. *He had paused.*

• • •

This time, five hundred men came at Jeff all at once. They
swarmed like bees in and out of the homes alongside Vista View
Boulevard, keeping pace with the clattering armored construction
vehicles.

Jeff had no suicide bombers with gasoline this time. He couldn't
see a way out of this fight alive. His men could never beat the invaders
fighting inside the homes. Maybe the odds had been carved back to
seven to one after the morning's killing, but he hadn't trained his men
for close quarters battle. They would inevitably be overrun, especially
considering the armor.

As the Latinos fought their way forward, the pace of fire picked
up, reaching a constant roar.

Just one thing left to do, Jeff thought. Fight to the death.

He leaned out, lying on the asphalt alongside the barricade and
began firing, picking targets as they exposed themselves.

A thunderous boom shook the battlefield, followed by another.
One of the front-end loaders turned hard to the left and rumbled
across a lawn, crashing into the front of a home, the driver
presumably shredded by Winslow and his fifty-caliber Barrett.

The gangbanger army began throwing one Molotov cocktail after another into the homes occupied by Jeff's men. While the flames forced his men to retreat, they also had the unforeseen effect of blocking the attackers. With several homes on each side of the road fully ablaze, the Latinos couldn't use the homes for cover. They were forced to advance in the open, directly down the middle of the boulevard, back into a fatal funnel. The infernal heat of the burning homes narrowed their advance even further, forcing the gangbangers away from the front yards and the cover of the houses. The Latino advance ground to a halt as they pushed up the middle of the boulevard, with only one remaining front-end loader as cover.

Jeff stretched out to make a shot on a red bandana-wearing gangbanger hiding behind an abandoned truck. An incoming round punched Jeff through the arm, sliding under his body armor and spalling into his stomach cavity. He gasped, steadied himself, and made the shot, nearly removing the gangbanger's head.

Jeff inched back behind the barricade as a flurry of fire erupted from a house on his left. Half a dozen Latino men ran up behind a corner with handguns and shotguns peppering his barricade with rounds. With the hole in his side, Jeff didn't think he could get up and run. He would have to fight from the asphalt.

Jeff hammered at the group with his big rifle, pulverizing the corner of the house where the enemy stacked. Two bodies slumped to the ground. Another round smashed into Jeff's head, knocking him senseless and removing most of his ear.

As Jeff faded steadily toward unconsciousness, he heard the sound he had been dreading: the roar of a belt-fed machine gun opening up from Vista View Boulevard.

The gangbangers had finally figured out how to run the belt-fed, Jeff thought as he faded into unconsciousness.

• • •

Jason came to with a screeching headache. He had no idea how much time had passed. It felt like someone had switched off his internal computer—no dreams, no thoughts, and no sense of time.

Little by little, his current disposition returned to him. He had been in a gunfight. He was still alive. His rifle lay in front of him on the ground. He had a scorcher of a headache.

As reality came back, he heard shooting behind him and pulled himself together. When he sat up, his head roared in protest. He looked around and saw he was alone. Jesse lay dead and, as Jason stood, he could see Victor spread-eagled on the ground, his face smashed. The bodies of dozens of Polynesian warriors sprawled around the dry, grassy hillside.

Jason and his two dead friends had levied a horrible price on the Pacific Islanders. But the Islanders had won, and he could hear the battle continuing at the edge of the condo neighborhood behind him. The rest of the QRF must have engaged the Polynesians after Jason's team fell.

Jason scooped up his AR-15 and looked into the breach. He saw two pieces of brass, stacked on top of each other in the classic, "type-three," double-feed malfunction. Jason pawed at his battle belt and pulled out his Leatherman, whipping out the needle nose pliers. Within a minute, he had the weapon cleared. He removed the half-used mag, replaced it with a full one and looked around, taking stock of his situation.

He had been left for dead by the Polynesian advance. He saw the giant who had smashed his head lying dead twenty yards past Jason's foxhole; he had probably bled out from the bullets Jason had put into his eighteen-inch chest. Up against the houses, he saw a few Poly fighters duck into a backyard. Jason had been left behind them. In the parlance of tactics, he had their "back door."

Time for payback, motherfuckers, Jason fumed through the grinding pain of his concussion.

He crouched and steadied. One careful shot at a time, he put a round through the heads of each of the three enemies in the backyard of the condo, missing slightly with one round and hitting the man in the throat. All three were dead before they could find the source of the rifle fire.

The thought of his two dead friends rose with his fury, exacerbating by his migraine. Jason maneuvered laterally behind a row of condos, finding small groups of Tongan fighters and killing them without hesitation. Now that he had already "died" in battle, Jason fought like a machine, without fear and methodical to the point of soullessness.

He lost track of his kills after fifteen men. Then he went to work on the inside of the condos. His hearing had been utterly compromised after shooting all but two of his mags, but he could tell which of the condos held enemy from the sound of their shooting, firing undoubtedly at the rest of his QRF.

Jason paused his killing spree, becoming concerned that he had moved down range from his own QRF and the firestorm they were unleashing.

He keyed his radio and spoke. "Alec. This is Jason. I'm down range. I want to start fucking these guys up inside the condos. Shift fire up. I'm going into the first condo on the far west. Do you copy?"

"Holy fuck." Alec radioed back. "You're still alive? Okay. Hold where you are. We're shifting fire." Alec clicked off, presumably jumping on his team radio. Jason heard a pause in the incoming rifle fire as the QRF shifted their fire up and over the condo he was about to enter. The enemy would still be pinned inside.

"Jason. This is Alec. Fire shifted over the condo on the far west. Proceed."

Jason quietly crossed the little backyard, going around a winter-dead garden and slipping through the open sliding glass door. He could hear several Tongans shooting and shouting from the front room of the house. Jason stepped carefully through a small kitchen and came up behind four shirtless men, darting to and fro in the living room. All of their attention was focused on the bay window facing the street.

366

Like a first-person shooter video game, Jason executed the four men, blowing the contents of their heads onto the glass of the window. As the last of the four fell, Jason stomped on the huge man's back and emptied his mag into his head and shoulders.

"House clear. Moving to the next target. Please advise."

Alec radioed back as Jason slung his AR-15, drew his Glock and checked the breech. "Target two condos over to the east of you. We'll shift fire in thirty seconds."

"Copy that."

Jason went out the way he'd come in and crossed two backyards. He radioed again. "Alec. This is Jason. Moving on the condo."

He again slipped into the back of the house and murdered three more men at close range, this time with his handgun.

After repeating the process in two more condos, Jason ran out of ammunition.

"We'll mop up the rest. Find cover and stand by," Alec radioed.

Jason crouched behind a small rock wall, ran through all his mags, consolidating remaining rounds into one final Glock magazine. Once complete, he stared down at his handgun and waited.

A sob built up in his chest, a harvest of grief, terror, anger and horror at killing more men than he could count. His eyes swam with tears as he struggled to hold them back. An unstoppable moan choked his throat, and he heard a noise come out of his mouth unlike anything he had ever heard before.

A giant, pregnant tear rolled down his cheek, and he mashed it into his face, confused and angry with his lack of self-control. He swiped his wet face again with the back of his shooting glove for good measure and ground his emotions out, reminding himself that the battle still raged.

16

"...I HEARD FROM CAMP LAJEUNE again today. Some Jar Head Drinkin' Bros checked in to say they're hanging in there strong and sending out good vibrations to all the Drinkin' Bros and their families. One of the Marines in LaJeune wanted me to reach out to his sister in Tallahassee. Barbie Martise. If you get the message, Barbie, your brother would like to know if you're okay. Call me on 30 megahertz, VHF. Just a reminder to the boys cooped up in Camp LaJeune: 'it's not gay if you're underway.' Since you're actually part of the Navy, I'm sure you already knew that...

"Got a call from Drinkin' Bro Zach outside of Salt Lake City, Utah. His group of survival types just repulsed a huge attack from looters — hundreds dead. Zach says the looters welded up bulldozers and used them as tanks. I guess that's what passes for military high tech now, welded up bulldozers.

"It's official, folks: I'm running out of MREs. My trailer runneth dry. I still have plenty of booze, so I guess I can survive on that. If you're in the Montrose area of Colorado, hit me up on 30 megahertz. I'm looking

for a place to bring this party in for a landing. I could use a good, solid survival compound full of hot women. That's my Christmas wish..."

Ross Homestead
Oakwood, Utah

Jeff's eyes opened. Alena and Doctor Hodges hovered over him. His eyes closed in a long blink.

The doctor whined, "I'm not that kind of doctor. I do liposuction, for Christ's sake. This kind of trauma is not fixable without a surgical center and a specialist. This man is going to die."

Alena yammered back at the doctor in that peeved voice of hers. Everything came through slow and foggy for Jeff, like watching TV from under a sheet.

Jeff blinked again, longer this time. He cracked his eyes as he felt someone jostle him. Alena was messing awkwardly with his gun belt, working Jeff's handgun out of his holster. She got it out, and pointed it straight down at Jeff's chest, holding the gun like it was a wet cat.

Jeff closed his eyes and time did a backflip. When he opened his eyes again, it was still Alena and the doctor standing over him.

Jeff could see Alena at the fuzzy edge of his vision, pointing his Glock at the doctor's head.

"You've got a choice, *Doctor.* Either get your hands to work in this man's gut, or the next surgeon who comes in is going to be cleaning your brains off the wall. What's it going to be?"

Jeff chuckled, then passed out.

• • •

Jason and Burke Ross drove Bishop Decker and President Beckstead down Vista View Boulevard in a pair of Homestead OHVs. The wealthy neighborhood above the third barricade resembled Beirut, a burned-out war zone.

371

Homestead men were using Bobcat skid steers to remove bodies and haul the blackened, shot-up enemy armor away from the boulevard. Men dragged the machines to the bluff and pushed them off, tumbling ass over teakettle until they came to a skiwampus heap at the bottom. They looked like giant, dried-out insects flipped over on their backs.

At last count, more than four-hundred-fifty of the Latino gang had died, most of them working men forced to fight. Almost all of the hundred Tongans had died in the battle. Another hundred wounded Latinos clung to life in a makeshift infirmary jammed between the homes below barricade one. With Jeff in a coma, the Homestead doctors did as they pleased.

The Oakwood men dragged dead Latinos to a pit at the base of the bluff near the corpses of the burned-out front-end loaders.

The battle had forever settled the debate over force of arms for the Homestead. Everyone now agreed; in this new world, God doled out survival in a fickle deal of the cards. Vigilance, combined with dumb luck, decided the daily breath of them all. Never again would the people of the Homestead feel entitled to the next sunrise.

Every Homestead resident capable of carrying a weapon would now spend all day every day armed to Jeff's standard. Gone were the days of only "gun people" carrying firearms. With hundreds of firearms littering the battlefield, every man, woman and reasonably-aged child would be armed.

Rifle. Handgun. Six rifle magazines and three handgun magazines. All men on guard duty will wear Level Three armor, capable of stopping a rifle round and a PASGT Kevlar helmet.

Jason and Burke had taken a moment earlier that morning to plan this excursion with the neighborhood's Mormon leaders. Father and son drove the OHVs up to a row of bodies, every one of them in multi-cam uniform. Thirty-one Homestead fighters had died in the battle. Jason and Burke said nothing for a full minute as the bishop and stake president regarded the dead in silence.

Jason spoke first. "Sometimes standing by the wayside, taking no action, does no harm. Other times, people die."

Bishop Decker turned his hands face up. "I would do things differently if I could. We just needed time to understand how things had changed." Nobody from his ward had fought to defend their neighborhood. The bishop hadn't even known about the battle until the sky filled with black smoke.

President Beckstead spoke. "These men died to protect our families. This will never happen again without our help." Bishop Decker nodded in agreement and shame.

Jason and Burke had nothing else to say. The four men stood in silence for another five minutes, then climbed back in the OHV and returned to their homes.

● ● ●

"How's it hanging, buddy?" Evan stood over Jeff's bed in the infirmary. "You getting a little R&R?"

Jeff's eyes fluttered. He felt lucky to see the world again. "How was your vacation?"

"We had a great time out at the Tooele Army Depot. Yep, they arrested us and put us in the stockade for a bit. I guess that's what they do when you're snooping around the ammo bunkers looking to steal from the Army. Then they let us out 'cause they ran out of chow. We literally ate our way out of jail."

Jeff laughed. "We missed you here yesterday."

"You didn't miss us. Who do you think came galloping up those guys' tailpipe with armored vehicles and belt-fed machine guns? Back door action, baby. Your favorite kind."

"Explain." Jeff wanted to know what had happened more than he wanted to joke.

"When they let us out of jail, we raided the military museum. Dude, we found some old British armor—you know, those Ferrets from the first Desert War, and those puppies run on unleaded gas. So we stole a couple of them, stole a bunch of belt-feds from the museum, and then we went back and stole a shit-ton of ammo from the ammo bunkers. We were like the Dirty Dozen, bro."

"So the gangbangers didn't get our belt-fed?"

"They sure as hell were trying to get it running when we pulled up. But, you know, we started punching holes in folks and they started running every which way. Then we rolled up the road with our armor, racking, stacking and packing 'em like gangbanger cordwood. We saved your ass."

"I had everything under control," Jeff smiled.

"I noticed that. That's probably why you were taking a little nappy-nap in the middle of the street when I came up, right?"

Jeff laughed, sending lightning bolts of pain through his abdomen.

Nurse Alena walked into the room and shooed Evan out. "No more testosterone comedy hour. Go... How're you feeling this morning, Mr. Kirkham?" She turned to Jeff.

"Like I got shot."

"That's because you got shot. Three times. And you undoubtedly have some more surgeries in your future. It's going to take some work to clean up the mess in your upper G.I. tract."

"How's Leif doing?" Jeff could see his son, now sitting up on his gurney watching something on an iPad.

"He's bouncing back fast. You're one lucky man."

Jeff looked at her, noticing something off in her tone. "How's Robert?"

Alena busied herself checking Jeff's PICC line. "My husband... actually, he died in the battle." She looked away, struggling.

"Damnit. I'm so sorry, Alena. *I'm so sorry.*"

"It wasn't your fault. I don't blame you. He died the man he wanted to be. He protected his family." A tear spilled down her cheek.

"He protected all our families," Jeff added, then changed the subject, not sure how to navigate her grief. "Where's my handgun?"

Alena pointed to a plastic table on the side of the room. "I put all your equipment over there."

"Did I see you waving my gun around last night?"

"Oh, that." She looked away. "I sort of used it to motivate Doctor Hodges."

"Don't go picking up guns until you know how to use them. Get me out of here and I'll teach you." Jeff shifted in his bed, trying to get comfortable.

"I believe I used your gun just fine, Mr. Kirkham."

"I suppose you did," Jeff agreed as a wave of exhaustion pulled him back toward sleep.

• • •

Chad, Pacheco, Audrey and Samantha hadn't reached the Homestead until late in the afternoon—the battle long over. It had taken them hours to cross the perilous town on foot.

Chad sat in Jason's office, his feet up on the desk, sipping the dark French Roast coffee that he and Jason traditionally shared first thing in the morning.

Jason worked the French press, depressing the plunger and squeezing the tawny oil from the last of his coffee. His head still throbbed like a son of a bitch. "I guess we won't have this for much longer."

"How much coffee did you squirrel away? How long's it going to last?"

"That depends on whether or not we share it with anyone else." Jason smiled. "We're nearly out of the good stuff. One of the great tragedies of the Apocalypse: coffee doesn't keep. We'll need shipping from Central America to come back before we see fresh coffee again."

Considering the hundreds of dead bodies being laid to rest, joking about coffee seemed inappropriate, even between friends. "I can't believe you got in a shooting fight without me." Chad turned the conversation to the thing weighing on both their hearts. "How'd you do? Your first combat experience?"

"Hmm." Jason thought about how lucky he was to be alive, and he avoided Chad's question. "We could've used you. It was a close thing."

"When I flew overhead and saw the hordes coming up the road… I thought you guys would be ashes by the time we got here."

"That was a distinct possibility," Jason said somberly.

"But you didn't answer my question. How did you do in combat? It's a big deal. First blood. You know some things about yourself that you couldn't have learned any other way. I'm asking you straight up: how did you do?"

Jason didn't want to talk about it but, if he couldn't talk to Chad right now, he would probably never speak of it. And it was rare for Chad to be so direct and garrulous.

"I killed a lot of guys. I almost got killed. I got angry and lost my temper and probably killed a bunch of guys that didn't need to be killed. Then I had a hard time not falling to pieces. How's that sound?" Jason had exhausted his words on the subject.

Chad looked him in the eye. "That sounds about right. So you're not a pussy and you still have a soul. All the other stuff is par for the course. You won't forget about the killing any time soon. You will lose some sleep. Get used to it."

Jason sat in his chair, silent. He didn't know what to do with his hands.

The office door burst open and Tommy Stewart, Jason's brother-in-law, barged in. He must have been on guard duty because he wore full camo with armor plates and a Kevlar helmet. He and his family had arrived from Phoenix right behind the carnage left by the gangbangers. Tommy had wasted no time joining the corps of armed men protecting the neighborhood.

"Jason, there's someone at the barricade named Sal, and he's asking for you. He won't tell me, but he says he knows something about my brother Cameron."

Jason and Chad jumped up, snatching their coats and rifles from the silver coat hanger and headed out behind Tommy.

• • •

As soon as the OHVs rolled up to the barricade, Tommy jumped out, breech-checked his rifle, slung it, and made a beeline for a man wearing a California Angels cap.

"Jason, Chad. This is Sal."

Sal shook Jason's hand and then Chad's. He reached into a backpack and pulled out a plastic gun case. "I believe this is yours."

Jason recognized the Kimber .45 from his Las Vegas house. He popped the plastic case open and examined the handgun.

Jason looked up at Sal. "Where are Cameron, Anna and the kids? We haven't heard from them in more than a week."

Sal shifted his gaze down and to the right. It wasn't going to be good news. "I saw them get shot outside Fredonia, Arizona by a band of polygamists. You know—those crazy fanatics from the reality TV show? Anna and the kids were alive last I saw. I circled back around on foot, and I watched the polygamists drag them back to town— Colorado City, I think.

"Your brother Cameron… he looked dead to me when they pulled him out of the driver's seat. They were crucifying any man they found alive, so maybe it was a mercy he was dead."

Tommy looked like he might throw up. He turned away, staring off in the distance, hands on his hips.

"You sure?" Jason asked the man. The gun in Jason's hands confirmed the man's connection to Cameron and Anna without a doubt.

"I'm very sorry. Your brother seemed like a cool guy. He loaned me your gun and some ammo to help me make it to Idaho. I've got people up there. I had to use most of the ammo to get here. Sorry about that."

"No worries." Jason closed the gun case and handed it back to Sal. "Why don't you keep this?"

"Seriously? Thanks, man." Sal reverently put the gun back in his backpack, almost as though he were handling Cameron's remains. In a way, he was.

Jason shook Sal's hand. "Good travels, friend." Sal turned away and headed toward a big truck parked on the road outside the tent city.

Tommy came back around and stood beside Jason and Chad.

"We're going to go get them, right?" Tommy asked.

"Indeed we are," Jason answered.

• • •

Salt Lake County Fairgrounds
Salt Lake City, Utah

"Francisco, where is my Gabriel?" His mother hovered over him. Francisco sat at the dinette in the luxury RV. His mama refused to take a seat. His sister stood beside her. Both of them were thick around the middle and both struck an angry pose. Hands on the hips. Heads jutting forward.

Right now, Francisco despised this RV. The rope lighting, stone countertops and fancy woodwork condemned him as the leader he now knew he was, a cheap imitation of greatness.

So much had gone wrong. Yesterday he hadn't seen any way he could lose. He shook his head with the mystery of it. How could fifteen hundred men be defeated by forty? Maybe there had been more white people than forty but, even with ten times that many, how could they have defeated his army and his armored tanks? Almost the entire battle had taken place where he couldn't see, and the radio communication with his men had broken down almost as soon as the shooting started. Worst of all, he didn't have a clue where his brother was. He had been lucky to get out of Oakwood with his own skin.

Actual military tanks had suddenly appeared from behind him on the mountain. Where the *pinche madre* had *they* come from?

"Mama, I don't know where Gabriel went. I told him to stay out of the fight yesterday. He might be on his way back home right now," more a lie than wishful thinking and Francisco suspected his mother knew it.

"Pancho, I'm going home to Rose Park. Maybe Gabriel will return to me there. I don't want your big homes or your big talk anymore. I want my son."

Francisco noticed she had said "son" singular, not plural. And he had no illusion she meant his younger brother. She had just invited him out of her life.

After losing a fight, especially one so costly, Francisco would be lucky to survive the day. It wasn't the gangbanger way—to lose and then keep on as captain. One or more of his lieutenants would come for him. Maybe Crudo would be the one to slit his throat or shoot him in the back. Francisco wasn't sure Crudo had even returned alive from the battle.

He couldn't afford to grieve the loss of his brother or worry about his mother's disdain. Once again, his own survival would come first.

• • •

Ross Homestead
Oakwood, Utah

Jason smelled Doc Eric before he saw him coming up the steps to the office colonnade. Back in the days of his youth, when Jason had been an Eagle Scout, one of his Boy Scout advisors smoked the cherry-blend Swisher Sweet cigars and now they reminded Jason of the outdoors. Even though he could easily afford Cuban cigars, Jason had taken to smoking Swisher Sweets when fly fishing in the backcountry of Yellowstone.

Days were shorter now that October had overtaken the Oakwood hills. The Homestead was festooned in a red-and-yellow patchwork of changing oaks and maples, the trees steeling themselves for another winter. The last of the day's light faded as Jason watched one of the big oil refineries in the valley burning with flames so massive they could be mistaken for the doorway to Hades.

"That's one big-ass fire," Doc took another drag of his little cigar.

"You got another one of those, Doc?"

Doc Eric pulled out a pack and handed it over. Jason fished one out and leaned toward Doc, completing the ritual. Doc cupped his lighter around the end of the cigar while Jason pulled on it, igniting the tip and releasing the fruity aroma.

Doc had been single long enough to forget how to live with family. Even so, Doc Eric took good care of his friends.

"Your daughter's in need of some consideration," Doc Eric said gingerly.

"Why?" Jason's reverie broke with a jolt.

"For one thing, she's downstairs right now doing surgery on a man, alone."

The words made sense, but Jason couldn't grasp the meaning. "I'm not following you."

"Emily brought back an enemy combatant and snuck him into the surgical suite. She's up to her elbows in the dude's guts and nobody's around. I just went in to check on Jeff's kid and caught her operating… solo… she's just a med student. I have no idea how she figured out the anesthesia without killing the guy already. Kirkham made it clear: nobody but Homesteaders and the neighbors were to be treated in the infirmary. We aren't supposed to be providing medical care to enemy combatants. What do you want me to do?"

Jason thought about it for a second. "Give me the rest of your cigar and get down there and help her."

"I was hoping you'd say that."

Doc handed over his half-smoked Swisher Sweet and walked away. Jason carefully scraped the cinders off onto the ground and slipped the remainder of Doc's cigar into his pocket for later.

17

"...I CAUGHT A CALL FROM a Drinkin' Bro in Boston, Massachusetts. He's hiding out at the top of his dorm building at Boston University. He's surrounded by co-eds, but that's the only good news. Boston is completely ransacked and full of looters. Being trapped with a bunch of co-eds would've sounded like a porno flick to me before this. I'm guessing the fun goes out of that proposition in about what? Four days without a shower?

"Sounds like my Drinkin' Bro Zach outside of Salt Lake City, Utah is giving me the invite to join them there, so I'll be working my way north to join their group. I got plenty of ammo but I'm running low on food. I still haven't figured out if they'll let me into Utah without multiple wives, but I guess I'll find out soon enough..."

Ross Homestead
Oakwood, Utah

For whatever reason, the meeting reminded Jason of one of those historical military surrenders where one general hands another general his sword.

"Jason Ross, I'd like you to meet Don Tobler, head of security at the Maverick Oil Refinery."

The men shook hands.

"What can I do for you, Don?" Jason wanted a friendship, not a surrender.

"I'd like to turn my refinery over to you in exchange for a seventy percent cut of the profits. We're seventy; you're thirty."

Jason knew he was being worked. The refinery would have been overrun yesterday by the gangbanger army without the help of the Homestead Special Forces garrisoned there. Nearly a hundred Latinos had approached the refinery, which apparently had been a target of opportunity. Between the three security guards and Jeff's men, working together, they had fought off the attack.

The refinery guards wouldn't have been able to defend against fifteen gangbangers, much less fifteen hundred, without the help of the Homestead. The refinery would have burned just like the Chevron refinery had been burning for the last two days.

"I'm sorry, Don, but you're barking up the wrong tree. I'm not interested in being business partners with you and your two men." Jason pushed back. "I'd rather be family. So how about this: we protect the refinery *together*, we share our food and conviviality *together* and we benefit from the refinery *together*?"

Don thought about it for a long minute. He reached out his hand. "Family it is."

Jason gloated a bit to himself and wished Jeff had been there to see him finally take down the refinery. Jason would have loved to rub it in: *diplomacy can win wars too.*

• • •

Jacquelyn carried Tom's M&P 9mm handgun now. She had her own gun, but it was a compact—a smaller pistol designed for concealed carry or for women with smaller hands. She liked Tom's gun better. It was easier to hit targets with the longer barrel, and the bigger magazine meant more bullets in a fight. She pulled his holster off his belt the morning after he died and slipped it onto her own belt.

All the magazines had been empty except one. That meant Tom had been fighting when he died. Even though he had been killed by friendly fire, Tom had given his life to protect those he loved. Somehow, that made it a little better.

Tom would like being the guy who died with an empty gun. In fact, he would think that was perfect.

Jacquelyn smiled, remembering what a good man he had been.

The kids were hurting. They were hurting bad, but she had seen Kayla smiling a little this morning while she played with the other Homestead kids. Many of them had lost parents in the big battle too. Everyone had lost someone they cared about. That didn't make it better, but it made it easier. Everyone shared grief, and it showed up in a hundred ways.

Jacquelyn walked toward the cook shed with a bucket of dried milk. They were going to make brownies for dinner. Jason had stashed a bunch of freeze-dried brownie mix, and the cooks wanted to make something special tonight.

This afternoon, they had buried their dead up on the knoll overlooking the Homestead. The view of the Homestead and the valley below was stunning from there. Those who had died could look over their loved ones eternally, continuing to protect them. The rest of the memorial service would happen after dinner. It was time to move on and celebrate the victory they had bought with the lives of their dear ones.

Jenna Ross joined Jacquelyn and helped her with the bucket, each woman with one hand on the wire handle. "How're you doing, sister? Anything you need?"

"You don't happen to have an extra husband around you can spare? I'm a little short this month." They both chuckled.

"Who needs 'em?" Jenna shot back.

"Right now, I definitely need 'em." Jacquelyn smiled, her eyes welling up.

"Yeah… I guess I need mine, too," Jenna said. "Tom was a good egg… Well, sis, we're in this together for the long haul, come what may. You and your precious ones can count on us—all of us. We're family and it'll take hellfire to pull us apart. You get me? *Mi casa es su casa.* My food is your food. My man is your man."

Jacquelyn stopped walking and turned to Jenna. "Thank you. That means a lot. Right now, my biggest fear is that Tom left me to protect our kids alone. I was counting on him to stand between us and the mayhem." Jacquelyn looked toward the valley, the endless smoke rising from hundreds of fires.

"After what's happened, I don't think any of us thinks like that," Jenna said. "I don't think we'll be tearing the group apart with our big opinions or petty rivalries anymore. I think we're a family now. We all live or we all die. End of story."

The two women started walking again. "Well, thank God for that," Jacquelyn said.

"God?" Jenna smirked.

"Maybe," Jacquelyn said with a smile, knowing she had been caught with her emotions showing.

Jenna pointed at Jacquelyn's big handgun. "Do you know how to shoot that hog's leg?"

"Yes, ma'am, I surely do."

"Teach me how."

"Jason never taught you?" Jacquelyn asked.

"Maybe once upon a time, but I need to start from scratch. I always had too much going on. I suppose even us gals should know how to shoot a gun now."

"Especially us gals." Jacquelyn adjusted the M&P with her free hand.

Jenna quieted for a moment, obviously thinking about the possibility of living without her husband. "I just about lost my guy, too."

"I heard. How's he doing?"

"He got his bell rung pretty good. The headaches are going away little by little. I know it sounds bizarre, but I would trade a lifetime of Gucci handbags and Four Seasons vacations for this feeling. We're together in a way I've never known outside of my immediate family. We work together. We fight together. We love together—as a family, all two hundred of us."

"I know what you mean. We're part of something bigger..." Jacquelyn trailed off, knowing she was neck-deep in feelings she might never understand. "And every last one of those couple of hundred folks is hurting for a chocolate brownie."

EPILOGUE

[Collapse Plus Sixteen - Tuesday, Oct. 5th]

Ross Homestead
Oakwood, Utah

"YO, JEFF." EVAN SAUNTERED INTO the gun vault while Jeff cleaned his Robinson rifle

"You come to gloat some more?" Jeff looked up.

"Yeah, maybe later. I've got something to show you. I couldn't tell you about it with that nurse hanging over my shoulder. Dude, I found something even more valuable than armor and belt-fed machine guns on my way back from the Army Depot. Check it out."

Evan reached inside his coat and pulled out a small Ziploc baggie. Jeff expected China White or black tar heroin. Instead, the bottom of the baggy bulged with dull green kernels.

"Holy shit," Jeff's eyes bugged, "is that what I think it is?"

"Yessir. We're going to be the Cartel of the Collapse. We're *rich*, brother. I found a whole warehouse full of one hundred percent unroasted green Guatemalan coffee beans. I'm guessing we're sitting on ten thousand pounds."

"Did you secure the warehouse?"

"Of course I secured the warehouse. I left two operators babysitting the place. They're probably caffeinated as fuck right now. Here's the best part: there's an old-fashion roaster, too. The boys are cranking out our first batch of medium roast as we speak."

Jeff smiled bigger than he had smiled in weeks. "This stays between you and me, right? Can your operators keep their mouths shut?"

"I doubt it. Not while drinking coffee all day. They'll talk a blue streak. Fuck that. I told them they live at the warehouse now."

Jeff nodded. "Smart. When things calm down, we'll figure out pricing and distribution. People will trade their left nut for a bag of this shit." Jeff took the plastic bag and held it up to the light. "This is Mormon Country, so we gotta keep a lid on it."

"Roger that," Evan agreed.

"Have you come up with a name yet?"

Evan nodded with a conspiratorial grin. "Given the circumstances, I thought we'd call it *Black Rifle Coffee*."

• • •

Everyone else had gone to bed, and a small group of men formed up by the ham shack around a picnic bench. A fire burned in the nearby fire pit, and Jason busted out some of the cheap whiskey he had set aside for trade.

Everyone sitting around the bench and the fire, except for Jason, was a former Special Forces operator. For the first time since the collapse, Chad joined them. As the liquor flowed, they began telling stories. They were stories none of them liked to tell sober. Iraq, Afghanistan, the Philippines, Haiti—each place held stories so sacred and vicious that they could not be told in the light of day.

Eventually, Chad told about crossing Wyoming. They laughed about his misadventures raiding cowboy roadblocks. Eventually, he told about the massacre inside the Walmart distribution center. Everyone listened quietly. They all knew what the story meant; it was both a victory and an atrocity.

Stories of violence mingled with stories of humor. As the hours passed, they talked about friends who had died in the line of duty.

Jason had always been a listener during these meandering, drunken confessionals, an outsider who hadn't experienced combat but who was welcomed anyway because he brought the booze. Tonight, Jason belonged. But the last thing he wanted was to talk about the death he had dealt, even among these friends.

The conversation turned to hunting, and Chad bragged about a winter elk hunt with Jason, a couple of miles above the Homestead. They had killed two cow elk while trekking on snowshoes.

"Two dozen elk scattered every which way. It was my first big game hunt and my instinct was to lay suppressive fire… that didn't work out. Finally, I downed a nice cow. There's probably still some of that meat in the freezer, right, Jay?" Jason nodded. The solar panels had kicked on after the grid died, and the walk-in freezer was still good.

"After I killed my elk, Jay killed another elk at six-hundred-fifty yards out with his big .300 Remington Ultra. One shot through the pump house. We should send a hunting party up there. It's a little box canyon that's hard as hell to find. I bet it's full of elk that've been pushed there by the zombies. It's not far from your OP/LPs." Chad paused to refill his tumbler with whiskey.

"You made a six-hundred-fifty-yard kill shot on an elk?" Jeff asked Jason.

"Yeah. I've made plenty of shots like that. Why?"

Jeff took another sip of whiskey instead of answering. He looked Jason dead in the eyes and both men knew what the other was thinking.

AUTHOR'S NOTE

I dedicate my part in this novel and its upcoming sequels to the operators of the United States Special Operations Forces, or SOF. I've had the privilege of working with many of them in entrepreneurial businesses as they've cycled out of long military service to the United States of America.

Here's what I've learned: they are our best and brightest and they have borne an inordinate amount of the work of death for our armed forces. They have carried this burden so the rest of us can enjoy the fruits of American freedom and American foreign policy. None of them have taken their missions lightly and they paid, and continue to pay, a high price for their service. Our tiny population of American operators carries a brutal load and they do so voluntarily and with professionalism. We owe them a debt, one I pray we do not forget. As a father with sons in the military, I take my hat off to our operators and thank them and their families for the risks they endure so other servicemen and women stand farther behind the lines of conflict.

The SOF boys of ReadyMan and Black Rifle Coffee have spent the bulk of their adult lives in parts of the world where the Apocalypse already happened: Kurdistan, Ramadi, Haiti, the Kandahar Province… In those places, the locals wouldn't even know the Apocalypse had come. It would just be another day. Operators know the lines of drift taken by the human race when civility and technology vanish. They know the cadence of chaos and the stench of collapse. Perhaps nobody in our modern society knows better how lightly we retain the Rule of Law than they do.

Today, the SOF boys of ReadyMan live stateside, teaching American citizens the hardscrabble reality that lurks beneath the chrome of modern society. Between training American civilians and experiencing dozens of global war zones, most scenes in this novel are derived from personal experience. Even stateside, our SOF instructors have seen American gun owners and survivalists crumple, time and again, when faced with the mind-shattering specter of mayhem. We have a long way to go before we can honestly consider ourselves "prepared" for a true collapse and the ReadyMan vets, along with thousands of other SOF vets, would like to see people trained and hardened to the reality that might suddenly punch through this wonderland of comfort. Jeff Kirkham, among others, would love to meet, train and share perspective with the readers of this novel and every preparedness-minded American. Check out Jeff's hundreds of instructional videos and his dozens of life-saving inventions at Readyman.com. Even better, log in to ReadyMan's Plan2Survive for a computer app that will guide you through the process of improving your families' preparedness one step at a time.

We hope this novel scared the hell out of you the way it scared the hell out of us. Some disasters arrive with foreknowledge, telegraphing doom, begging us to prepare. Other disasters, especially in complex, fragile systems like ours, come out of left field and leave us wondering what happened.

Economists call these historical surprises "Black Swans"—events like World War I, the Great Depression, 9/11 and the Crash of 2008—and they only make sense looking back. Black Swan events sideswipe history with regularity. No reasonable person can pretend a Black Swan couldn't happen again. We will never be that smart.

In this post-modern epoch of the American Empire, we run the risk of being blissfully unprepared for the rise of chaos and a resurgence of Mother Nature. It is safe to say that none of us is as prepared as we would like to think.

—Jason Ross

AFTERWORD

I tracked Jeff Kirkham through both of his careers, including his move to federal law enforcement, his deployment to the global war on terror, his transfer over to the realm of intelligence and his continued real-world, down-range assignments for both the U.S Government and the U.S. Army. Driven by an extremely high intellect and exceptional patriotism, no better thinker, soldier, trainer, operator, or man, exists.

As a lifelong Special Forces soldier myself and as a 35-year police officer and current Chief of Police, I'm uniquely positioned to understand the precarious nature of our continued freedoms in the United States of America. From where I stand, this book is fiction, *but it is also real.* The events in it are not just plausible, they are probable. We are in challenging times and with so many potential trigger events, it would take only a few at once to kick us into the exact scenario described in this book. "Black swan" events do happen, and they have side-swiped America into chaos more than once: World War I, the Great Depression, the financial collapse of 2007–2008. Our technology has not inoculated us from this threat. If anything, technology may have made us more vulnerable.

Black Autumn is more documentary than a work of fiction. No civilization lasts forever. The mayhem described in this book will likely become real. It is only a matter of time and a couple of key, black swan events. If you consider sections of Chicago today, you will identify many of the same conditions, albeit on a smaller scale.

This book, I hope, will strike the same chord in you that it did in me. I hope we realize our vulnerabilities, our limitations, our level of survivability, and most importantly, I hope we gain a strong desire to prepare.

Your family and your community are counting on you to become a civilian operator or perhaps a peacekeeper, taking personal responsibility *now* for those you love during, potentially, very dark times ahead.

These days are coming, more possible than we allow ourselves to believe. But face them we must. Special Operators like Jeff Kirkham, Evan Hafer and myself, have seen these very things occur in places around the globe. As a law enforcement officer here in America, I promise you: *we are not immune to chaos.* We pray to the God we worship that this chaos will not overwhelm our communities, our families. But we also recognize the reality of that potential.

We prepare and sound the alarm so that you are forewarned. This book is your clarion call. Share it. Put yourself inside the story and judge your place in the outcome.

God Bless.

Col. Steven "Randy" Watt (ret.)
Former Commander, U.S. Army Special Forces 19th Group
Chief of Police, Ogden, Utah

ABOUT THE AUTHORS

JASON ROSS has been a hunter, fisherman, shooter, and preparedness aficionado since childhood and has spent tens of thousands of hours roughing it in the great American outdoors. He's an accomplished big game hunter, fly fisherman, an Ironman triathlete, SCUBA instructor, and frequent business mentor to U.S. military veterans. He retired from a career in entrepreneurialism at forty-one after founding and selling several successful business ventures. After being trained by his dad as a metal fabricator, machinist, and mechanic, Jason has dedicated twenty years to mastering preparedness tech such as gardening, composting, shooting, small squad tactics, solar power, and animal husbandry. Today, Jason splits his time between international humanitarian work, the homeless community, and his wife and seven children.

JEFF KIRKHAM served almost twenty-nine years as a Green Beret doing multiple classified operations for the U.S. government. He is the proverbial brains behind ReadyMan's survival tools and products and the inventor of the Rapid Application Tourniquet (RATS). Jeff has graduated from numerous training schools and accumulated over eight years "boots on

the ground" in combat zones, making him an expert in surviving in war-torn environments. He spent the majority of the last decade as a member of a counter terrorist unit, working in combat zones doing a wide variety of operations in support of the global war on terror. Jeff spends his time, tinkering, inventing, writing, and helping out his immigrant Afghan friends, who he fought side by side with for over a decade. His true passion is spending quality time with his wife and sons.

PLAN2BUGOUT

A FREE BUG OUT BAG BUILDER!

Build your own customer bug out plan for **FREE**, with Plan2BugOut. Build a Bug Out Bag completely custom to you and your environment, giving you a comprehensive checklist of everything you need to survive a disaster. Plan2BugOut even separates your preparedness plans into Automotive, Semi-Automotive, and On Foot, so you have gear with you no matter how you travel.

Get started for **FREE** at:
www.Plan2BugOut.com

PLAN2SURVIVE

THE ULTIMATE SURVIVAL ENGINE

Plan2Survive—your ultimate survival engine for disaster. P2S was built from the ground-up by veterans of outdoor survival. Over 1,176 skills, a comprehensive checklist of survival gear, and an online community of like-minded individuals all at your fingertips. Track your own survival ability and take it to a whole new level with P2S.

Get started at:
www.Plan2Survive.com

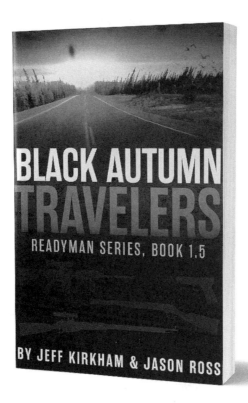

A Jaded special operations soldier, a self-doubting family man and a once-pampered teenager make their way from three corners of the country toward a survival compound in the state of Utah, but they must first pass through a land of chaos and death—a land that will no longer allow them to hide behind a post-modern artifice...

Get it at:

https://amzn.to/2SdjFfk

BLACK AUTUMN